DRAGONWING
Return of the Dragonriders
Book Two
by Raina Nightingale

AREAER NOVELS

Return of the Dragonriders
DragonBirth
DragonWing
DragonSword

Legend of the Singer
Children of the Dryads
Sorceress of the Dryads

Dragon-Mage
Heart of Fire
Scars of Fire
Healing of Fire*

Novellas and Standalones
The Gifts of Faeri
Kindred of the Sea
Gryphon's Escape
Promise of Fire

KAARATHLON NOVELS

EPOCH OF THE PROMISE: Dawn Unseen
EPOCH OF THE PROMISE: Vision's Light
EPOCH OF THE PROMISE: Wings of Healing
EPOCH OF THE PROMISE: Darkness Bright*

Other Novels

Kingdom of Light

*Not yet available

DRAGONWING
Written by Raina Nightingale

Paperback ISBN: 978-1-952176-01-2
Ebook ISBN: 978-1-952176-02-9

Cover art by MidnightRose.
Cover design by Raina Nightingale.
Maps by Raina Nightingale.
Interior Design by Raina Nightingale.
Illustration in chapter 32 by Raina Nightingale and Midnight Rose. All other illustrations by Raina Nightingale.

Published by Raina Nightingale
www.enthralledbylove.com

Author's Note

DragonWing is the second book in the Return of the Dragonriders trilogy, which I started when I was thirteen. If you read author's notes, you've probably already read the one for *DragonBirth*, and I need not repeat everything in there.

Mostly, I just want to say, I hope you enjoy *DragonWing*. In some ways, it might be the coziest of the three. When I first conceived this series, one of the things I wanted to do was write an epic fantasy that kept the closeness to everyday and mundane life that they sometimes start with. After all, you can't fight if you don't live.

And why should you fight unless you have something you love, something to fight for? Isn't that the more important thing to see?

That's even more relevant in a story like this, where the greatest enemy is one my protagonists must fight within their own souls. Other people might kill and torture them if they can, but their fundamental enemy isn't those people, but the nightmare, which is just as ready to consume them in fear and blind hatred as it is those who would harm them.

To fight an enemy like that, it's absolutely essentially to see what you're fighting for. You have to find whatever it is that you need, in order to confront the thing you fear, to face fear itself, and not be overcome.

As a result, this is a very cozy book, with cozy challenges spaced among sweet and quiet moments, as well as – to be perfectly honest – quite a few more actual fights than there are in *DragonBirth*. But it is also the story of that battle in Silmavalien and Noren's souls – one which they must fight within themselves, if they're to have even the chance at picking the right side when things start happening.

The dragons will fly again,
-Raina Nightingale

Table of Contents

Aelaza	1
Rest by the Pool	7
A Dragonrider's Nuisance	13
Hunting, At Least Trying	18
Saved by Slipping	23
Steep Descent	29
Continuing the Search	35
A Place Like Home	41
Sin of the Dragonriders	46
Caref	53
The Nightmare and the Bow	58
Minth Flies	62
The Demons Stir	69
Defeated	73
Nothing Left to Do	77
Light!	81
Lighter	85
About the Dragon-sword	89
Flight	93
Coroneth's Skills	97
A Matter of Horses	102
Decision	107
Command	111
Things to be Thankful For	116
Living on the Cliff-Ledge	122
Explanations, False and Unknown	128
Meeting Keya	132
Being Friends	137
Someone Else	142
Flying	147
Blue Eyes, Blue Wings	152
Best Attempts	157
Dying Away into Beauty	153
The Surface	168
Like Sisters	176
Winter on the Plains	182
A Request of Love	187
Return of the Shadow	191
Flying Through Storms	196
The Open Plains	291
Flaming Nightmares	206
A City in a Vision	211

Stealing Dragon Eggs   217
Elninya Cooks   224
Wings of the Mountains   228
Hopeless and Helpless   236
In the Shouting Winds   241
Island of the Volcano   246
Certainty of Death   251
The Clouds Open   255

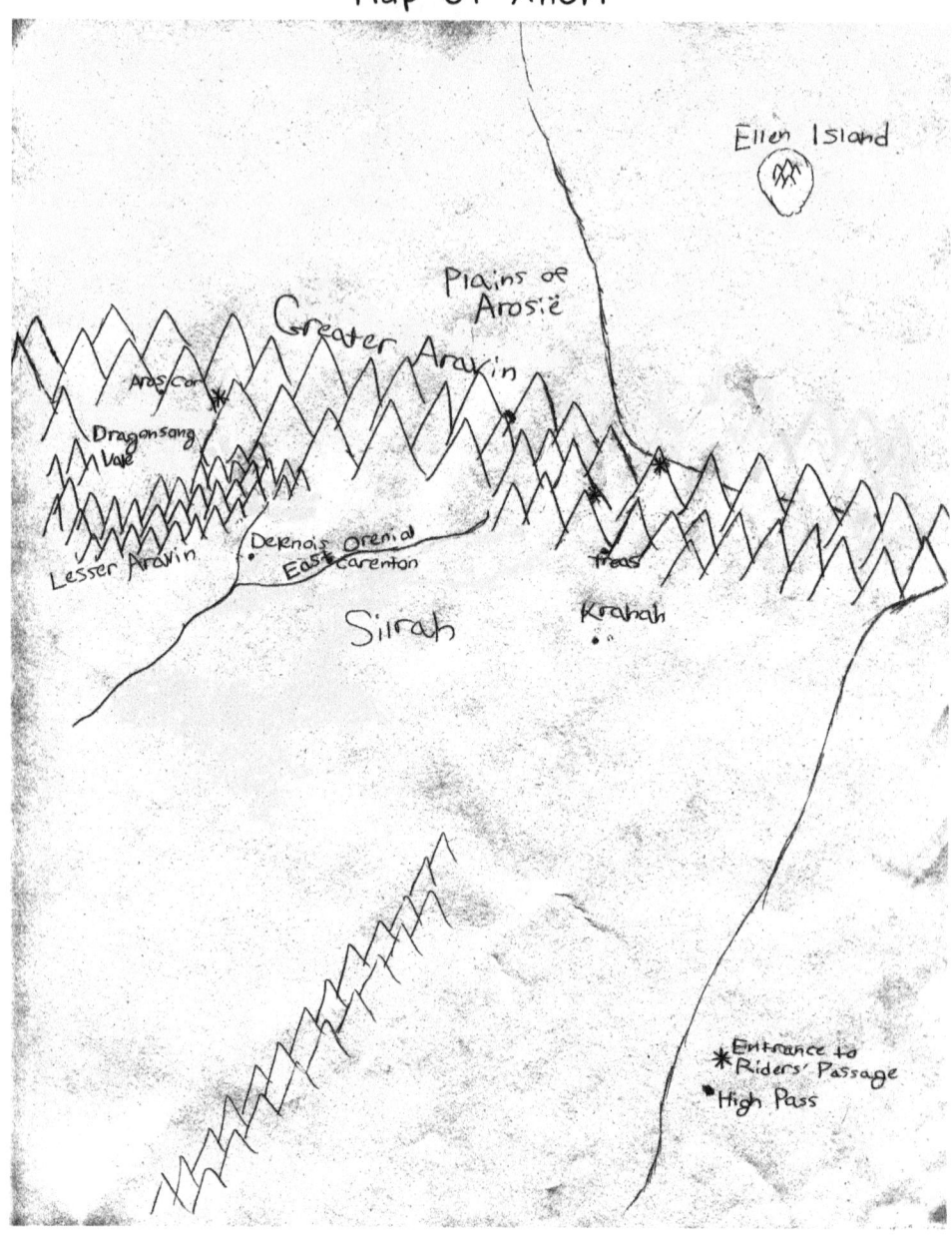

1

Aelaza

Silmavalien lay flat on her back, Minth's still-too-large tail a blur of white at the edge of her vision. Above them stood a woman. Her black hair, too dark and too shiny to be possible, was pulled over one shoulder and hung to her knees. Over her tall, slender form, covered with hard, taut muscles, she wore what appeared to be a sleeveless dress of black feathers that shone blue or green depending on the light, except it almost looked like the feathers were her own. Her hands, even more so her feet, were small, to scale the cliff so easily, and over one shoulder hung a quiver that carried a strange, beautiful bow, but only a few arrows.

But what captured Silmavalien's attention was her eyes: they did not glow like dragons' eyes, or if they did she could not tell in this lighting, but they were certainly not human. They looked like sapphires, complete with gemstone facets, gleaming out of her dark, dusky face.

Before Silmavalien could regain her composure, almost before she could draw breath, the woman asked, "Who are you?"

"I'm Silmavalien," she replied, rather dumbly.

"That doesn't tell me very much," said the woman, if a woman she was. Her voice was oddly like flowing or falling water. "I can see that you are a Dragonrider. What else?"

Something about her disconcerted Silmavalien. Between that, and everything she had been through, she could not think of anything to say. Finally, words slipped between her lips. "I don't know." As if that somehow restored her courage, she pushed the next words out as quickly as she could, based on the impulse of a sudden thought. "Are you an Ellen?"

The woman cocked her head slightly. "An Ellena. Yes, I suppose." This time she was silent for a moment. "Your dragon," she asked. "What is he doing? Sleeping?"

"He fainted when that awful Shadow showed up. His name is Minth."

"What have you been doing?" the Ellena asked.

"We took the Riders' Passage, and ran out of food. Now, we are thirsty as well." Somehow, the words were coming now, almost without effort, and almost without feeling, too.

"Well, there's no use in just standing here. Come on —"

Silmavalien got to her feet "– how are we going to get that dragon – Minth, I mean – back to wherever you left your things? *No.* You're in no condition to carry him. May I?" She asked, looking first at Minth, then at Silmavalien.

"Wait," said Silmavalien. She had felt Minth stir in his mind. His tail twitched. He was conscious. In the privacy of their minds she asked what he thought of the Ellena. Then she felt Minth touch the creature's thoughts, and the impression she gleaned through Minth was strange and alien, full of shapes she knew had meaning, yet had no meaning to her.

The Ellena stiffened at Minth's touch, and through Silmavalien heard her words. *"Do not do that again. Your general awareness of thoughts is enough – beyond what is given to me."*

Minth was indignant. His thoughts and emotions flowed forth in something like, *"Neither do you!"*

Pulling herself free from their argument, which seemed to have nothing to do with either fear or ill will on either side, she said to the Ellena, "You may."

As the strange creature stooped down to pick Minth up, he asked her name. Through him, Silmavalien understood her reply: she was Aelaza, and she had been born with the name as dragons are born with theirs.

"Would Minth be able to speak to a human like that, too?" Silmavalien asked as she limped behind the Ellena. "I know he couldn't when he was younger."

"No. Only Ellenari and a few Dragonriders can – Eli sindra!" Aelaza gasped. "So many dragons. Where are their riders?" She laid Minth down on the rock.

"They don't have any. I take care of them all, but I am only really bonded to Minth."

"Can you speak to all – each – of them?" asked Aelaza.

"Yes."

"You can probably speak to and hear all dragons."

"Thank you, Aelaza. You can g ..." Silmavalien trailed off, realizing the absurdity of it. Aelaza could go whenever she wanted, but Silmavalien still needed her help. And whatever she was ... Silmavalien's feelings were too confused about that, and Aelaza's reply cut off thoughts that could have gone nowhere anyways.

"Well, I won't. You are all far to close to the Fire Shadow's lair. Where was it you wanted to go? The pool?"

"... Yes." The pool was probably where that waterfall met the earth ... where she had been trying to go. "But how will we get past the chasm and the Fire Shadow?"

"You'll see. Get your stuff. The dragons will have to walk. I cannot carry nine of them. Follow me."

Silmavalien packed up the two blankets, pulled the bags over her shoulder, and followed Aelaza, the dragons trailing behind her. The Ellena's every step was springy, and she seemed to bounce as if she was not made to walk, but to bound up cliffs. Silmavalien suspected the pace she and the dragons could manage had to be exasperatingly slow to her.

Soon she brought them to a bridge of rock that spanned the twenty or so spans across the chasm. It hardly felt like a bridge as she crossed it, with sequoias growing between them and the edge, and ferns crushing under their feet.

When they reached the pool, Silmavalien collapsed on its banks, feeling like she could not get another step out of her legs if she had to. She gulped in great, heaving breaths, as if she had been running for miles, and took in the pool. A spray of water fell into its far end, near the cliffs, but where she lay it was still and shallow, and everywhere it was clear. A few paces from her, a small stream flowed out over some rocks.

It looked safe for the dragons to be around and drink from, even in their current state. The banks were so shallow there was no way they could fall in, still less be carried away. Veine seemed to sense Silmavalien's decision. She crawled to the pool, and when she flicked her tongue out to drink the sense of cold that flowed across their bond almost made Silmavalien's teeth chatter.

But Aelaza still stood there – like, like a stone, or a sunrise. Silmavalien shrugged out of her bags and got to her knees to mumble some sort of thanks. She'd have gotten to her feet, but she could not stand again just yet.

"Of course, it was nothing." Her tone was strange and inhuman, yet it was at once absolutely casual and sincere. " appreciate your gratitude. Please do not stray towards the Shadow's lair. It is still very near, and I might not be there to save you next time ... be careful!"

"Thank you," said Silmavalien again, "but was it really nothing to save us from the Shadow?"

Aelaza laughed, the sound like water running over stones. "When I saw the Shadow stir, and heard your cry, what *could* I do? I sprang sideways up the cliff, many times faster than I ever have before, but it was effortless. The Shadow did not fight me; I think it had something to do with your ring. I wanted to meet whoever it was that that Shadow found interesting enough to rise out of the abyss to destroy. Not everyone gets that response."

Silmavalien gaped open-mouthed as Aelaza described springing up the cliff, even though she had seen. But all that came out of her mouth was, "Ah. Goodbye."

"Siena norae," replied Aelaza, and Silmavalien gasped again as she sprang from where she stood a pair of tiny ledges in the precipice above. From there she continued, up and up, momentarily alighting on cracks of the rock too small to see. The wonder of it made Silmavalien's head spin. It was beautiful; awesome; glorious.

Like a rainbow or a sunset.

Then she tore her gaze away. She had to boil the water so she could drink it safely, and so the dragons could drink more without chilling themselves. Which meant she needed a fire. Which meant she needed wood. Which meant she had to get up and gather wood.

She somehow got herself to her feet, and felt the dragons urging encouragement – and wondering at her – as she stood and somehow fought back the dizziness and the weakness. She stumbled off, strictly following Aelaza's wander. She did not wander towards the Shadow's lair or the Riders' Passage farther than where she could still see the stream easily, but she did not cross the stream either. It was too cold, the footing too treacherous, and she was too weak.

A rabbit hopped across her path, and Silmavalien knelt where she stood beside a tree to string the bow. She gritted her teeth and struggled, a task that was once easy now nearly impossible, far harder than when Noren had first shown her how. Yet she managed it and looked up.

The rabbit was gone.

She did not unstring the bow, though. She was just collecting wood when she saw another rabbit browsing only a few paces away, seemingly ignoring her. She knocked an arrow and then tried to draw the bow. No matter how she strained, she could not do it. Finally, holding the bow flat under her arm instead of up, she managed to get it, but she had to try twice before she kept the arrow knocked.

Struggling to hold the bow, shaking and sweating, she raised it. Somehow, despite all the fuss, the rabbit had barely moved, as if it had not noticed even her grunts. Her arms shook violently, and she barely managed to release the string instead of letting it slip out of her fingers.

The arrow whizzed past the rabbit, and buried itself, almost up to the fletching, in the soft earth at the base of a young pine, not even close to the target.

The rabbit spooked and bolted.

Silmavalien struggled to her feet and pulled the arrow out of the ground, wondering why she was even trying. They might have gotten out of the passage, but they would have had to get out weeks ago to even have a chance. She could not hit a deer in this state, not even if it stood for her. There was no way she could take *anything* down.

She stood and walked back to the pool, dragging along what little wood she had already got. If they were all going to die, at least they would die together. And die they would, since with the best luck in the world she would not be able to get a bite for each of them.

The sun was already half way down the sky when she reached the pool, having walked even slower than she had to because she was so hopeless.

The day was near its end, and so were their lives, only just begun.

Then at the tingling urge of the dragons, Silmavalien finally raised her eyes and listened to what they had been trying to tell her for some minutes.

A freshly-killed deer was laying on the sand beside the pool, and the dragons were sharing rabbits. Silmavalien fell to her knees, as much from amazed relief as from weakness, and Minth looked up at her, his minty eyes bright with expectation and hope.

Only Aelaza could have provided that deer and those rabbits....

Or the Lord of the Light, by miracle.

2

Rest by the Pool

With new hope came a new realization of just how thirsty she was. But she was not going to risk getting sick from the water, not when she had the wood she needed right here. She got the fire going, and then got water from the pool in the boiling pot, every task harder than it had ever been before, but manageable.

Then she got out her knife to skin the deer, as much to keep her mind off her thirst as anything else. Somehow, setting the boiling water aside to cool and knowing she would be able to drink soon only made her thirst more tormenting, and it was all she could do to wait, and try to make sure she did not cut herself preparing the deer, since she could not keep her mind off her thirst.

Minth, his stomach now full enough for the moment, lay down next to her, and did his best to anchor her and distract her. He remembered for her how they had all their backs turned, doing or watching one thing or another. He had been about to fall asleep, and Daurth, Airrock, Wydth, and Songeth had already been fast asleep, when Tiela saw the food.

Her squeal of excitement had woken them all up, but he had felt sleepy the whole time, too lazy even to feel excited about this. He thought that was why she had not noticed.

Now, with his stomach full, he told her he felt even more sleepy. So tired.

"Then go to sleep," she told him under her breath. *It's good for you. Especially after a good meal. Even more, after a good meal after a long fast.*

But he wanted to be with her.

"That's okay." She spoke out loud this time. "You can be with me just as well if you sleep right there by the fire."

The quiet delight seeping all through Minth at her reassurance dampened for a moment everything else: exhaustion, pain, thirst. He closed his eyes, and she felt his breathing slow and his mind wrap itself in sleep beside her leg.

She could not endure the thought of trying to drink the water and finding it still too hot, and feared then her resolve really would break, so she waited a little longer than she thought she had to before testing the water. It was warm on her finger, not hot enough to burn but close to it, and she knew if she had not tried to wait extra long, it would have been far too hot. She tilted the pot and drank greedily, slowing down just enough not to burn her mouth on the hot water.

When she finally stopped, she had drank more than half of it, and she poured the rest of it into the skin and started more boiling. A few minutes later, she laid the first slabs of venison out to cook, some on a pan she had and some on a rock next to the rock. She sat by Minth, and cut more venison, between flipping the meat, which she had to every minute or two.

It was worth it. The venison on the rock was done first. Though unseasoned and unsalted, it seemed like the best thing she had ever tasted. She ate all the slabs, and started more, though she had only gotten a little wood and the fire was not going to last much longer.

She sat next to Minth, gently stroking his neck and head while she watched the meat. Even in his sleep, he leaned in her scratching when she got to where his wing came into his shoulder, but she had to get up almost immediately to tend to the venison. Besides, even that was making her arm sore.

Minth was gliding through an open space, huge, brilliant stars shining and twinkling all about him. Above him and below him, on either side, in front of him and behind him. Yet he was uneasy. Some fear, some withdrawn promise or joy, hung over him, like a darkness among the bright stars.

Then an abyss opened before him. A nothingness too deep for any light to pierce. A chasm in reality and light. A Shadow that blotted out the stars. Already, he was on the edge of it. He struggled to break free, to fly away, to flee, but suddenly his hunger and weakness returned. His strength utterly failed. Fear and terror overwhelmed him....

All at once, the nightmare crashed into her, nearly knocking her off her feet. The terror and pain she felt when Minth fainted, leaving her to face the Fire Shadow alone, leaving her to struggle to protect him ... all of that was there, mixed with his fear.

She was at his side in a moment, never mind whatever she had been doing. *Stay calm. Stay calm.* It would not help for her to feed the nightmare. She had done enough of that when he had been a hatchling ... he still was a hatchling. She knelt beside him, put her arms around him, whispered to him her reassurance, shared through their bond, real in a way nothing else could ever be. The frightful nightmare vanished, melting away before a dream of love and unity, friendship and joy, two souls that always needed each other out of love and held each other up. Of Silmavalien beside him, with him, in him. His dragon-mother.

A dream that only dragons can remember, but all beings know and crave.

Silmavalien kissed Minth, and quickly returned to the fire and her cooking. But she felt tired now as, at that moment, she could not remember ever feeling tired before. She put some venison in the water-pot next to the fire, hoping it would cook adequately from the left-over heat when the fire went out, then pulled out a bunch of blankets and threw them on the ground. Already her eyelids were threatening to close on her, but she half-carried, half-pushed Minth onto the blankets, then pulled the rest of the blankets over them both.

If the other dragons woke up cold, they could join them under the covers then.

S

When she woke in the morning, she knew immediately, from the feel of her body and something more indefinable, that she had slept for a long time. And that, as she'd expected, all the dragons were snuggled up under the covers now.

Hunger gnawed at her stomach, which gurgled as she sat up. She slipped out of under the covers and got a few slabs of venison, then sat on the blankets to eat and consider the day.

The sun was definitely up, but the whole feel of the world suggested it was earlier than that. All was in shadow, with only a few tiny glimmers of reddish light that she could see on the tops of the trees across the pool and the cliffs above. They looked less like rays of sunshine, and more like a few scattered reflections cast up water. She considered it, and decided she had slept for more than half a day and a night together, and Minth for somewhat longer.

Even as she watched them, the light patches grew and changed, though it would be a long time before they reached the ground. The dragons went on sleeping, barely stirring, and Silmavalien finished her venison and got her bow out, which she had forgotten to unstring last night. Hopefully, that had not hurt it too much. Sitting or kneeling a little ways from the dragons, she drew it again and again, steadfastly ignoring the pain in her arms. She had to get to the point where she could at least hunt rabbits and birds, and have a hope of hitting them. She could not, would not, expect or rely on gifts like last night's every day. Perhaps, if she could not provide for them, another would. But if she did not do everything she could to be able to take care of them, then they would starve.

After working on that until her arms burned and shook, even when she rested them, Silmavalien struggled to unstring the bow, before she pushed her strength past the point where even unstringing it would be impossible. Then she went out to collect more wood, weaving her way between the graceful ferns that glistened and dripped with the night's dew. The fragrance of the Cure of the Dusk when she trod it underfoot did something to steady her strength.

She knelt to pick up a few sticks, then looked up. A pine cone hung from a branch above her, and with a pang she realized she had lost the pine cone obtainer somewhere on the other side of the mountains. It would be nice to have now, even if she could never have brought it up the cliff, even if she was not sure she would have the strength to use it.

She knelt, staring at the pine cone for far longer than she needed to. It was … she would never be able to reach that high. If she were strong, she might be able to get her hands on it, but she doubted she would be able to pull it down. Maybe, if it were just ready to come.

She hefted a stick in her hands and stood. It was food. Delicious. The thought of it made her mouth water. She had to try. She raised the stick and swung it against the pine cone. After several tries, it fell, rolling along the ground, at the same time as she felt Minth wake. Hungry, but refreshed.

She went on, gathering as much wood as she could carry and limping under its weight. Minth told her when the other dragons woke, one by one, and they reached out to mentally caress her. Veine's touch was wordless, but it carried a deep reassurance that wrapped itself around her like wings, as if Veine were the dragon-mother.

As her stomach started grumbling again, Silmavalien made her way back to the pool. She could not wait to eat the pine nuts, but she was forced to go painfully slowly between her own weakness and the sticks, and she did want to put them down. Picking them again, and getting them to stick, would not be easy. But when she got back to the pool, she dropped the wood all at once, sticks clacking as they fell around her, and tore the pine cone open, despite the protests of her fingers, raw and cramped from the bow-string. Only when she had devoured the pine nuts did she looked around.

The dragons had clearly feasted on the deer, and somehow it seemed funny to her, while she re-kindled the fire and started more water boiling. She strung her bow, then tried to draw it again, and her arm twanged with pain, worse than it had in the morning, worse than it had picking up the wood or whacking down that pine cone. She unstring it with more pain and set it aside, then settled down to cutting more venison and cooking it, eating a bit now and again while she worked.

The dragons, those who were awake at any rate, often sat or lay next to her to watch her and give her support, but she struggled to pay much attention to any of them, even when it was Minth. Cooking the venison, and not slicing her hand open, took all the attention she had, and once she was done with cutting up the slabs, she was so tired, though she let Minth lay in her lap between flipping or changing the slabs, and sometimes she scratched his favorite spots while he hummed.

He did an amazingly good job reminding her to keep an eye on the venison so that it did not burn or cook too unevenly. He reminded her far more often than was really necessary, almost every heartbeat, but at this point she was wondering if she would remember at all, even if he was not there to distract her, without the reminders.

As the day crept on, she decided she would need another rock or two to cook on, if she wanted to get this deer done anytime soon, and got up to look for one. Minth had fallen asleep, but Songeth – who was awake at the moment and trying to remind her like Minth had, though he was not nearly as good at it – joined her, and together they found two that would do. Rather flat-topped, and not so heavy she could not move them. She shoved them into the flames to heat up, and then pushed them out with a heavy stick, groaning with the effort.

When she laid the venison slabs out to cook and sat back, slumping, Tiela and Coroneth nudged her, settling against her from either side. They loved her. She loved them. It meant so much to them, they sent. They wished they could help her ... They were glad. They wanted to comfort her.

She smiled wearily, and let herself emotionally lean into their embrace. It really did mean so much to *her.*

She changed the slabs again, then packed all the cooled ones into one of the bags, and ate again. She was not nearly done, yet she was already exhausted again. She sat down next to Minth, Tiela and

Coroneth now drowsing though they watched the flames and Tiela sometimes asked her when the last time she had checked on the venison was.

Then Minth woke up, happy and hungry, and after greeting her with something that was very much like good morning, he bounded as well as he could to the raw venison and tore into it. A smile stretched her face as she watched him, and his excitement woke her up a little. Then the other dragons started getting hungry and waking up, and that helped, too.

Finally, everything was eaten or cooked, and Silmavalien forced herself to draw the bow twice more before she crawled into the covers. He was not tired yet, but Minth offered to join her. With a tired smile, she reminded him it was not necessary. She would rather he play with his friends and give her happy dreams, then join her when he was ready.

3

Dragonrider's Nuisance

It was a couple hours after sunrise, and the realization that the partner of his heart – *Elninya* – was one of the persecuted dragons, whose existence he had till then doubted, still pounded in his heart. He understood now why the way Silmavalien regarded the 'gods' had changed in that last month or two. He had thought it was due to his own influence, but he suspected now it had nothing to do with him at all. She had discovered that the dragons, the declared enemies of the gods and of all good, were really creatures much like everyone else.

Alongside the pain of how she had scorned his trust, and the hurt just thinking about her brought, he felt anew his admiration for her. He had always known she was strong. He had not realized how strong. Her devotion had been real, he knew, not a lie like he was sure some people's devotion was. He could not imagine how it would disturb her, to have such strong beliefs shattered in such a way. She had handled herself amazingly, in the face of both the collapse of everything she believed, and the terrible, immediate danger she had found herself in.

His love was an imperfect, yet wonderful, person.

Now Noren rode towards the city of Delenois at a brisk trot, since he meant to cover the remaining several miles quickly. Elninya was hidden safely among his blankets in the thickest, darkest portion of the thicket, deep under the bramble where he doubted anyone would wander.

Several men stood guarding the gate, wearing the flag of Delenois – an elaborate rainbow on a yellow field – wrapped around their torsos, over good leather and steel armor. "What's yer name and where're ye from?" asked one, a bit roughly.

"I'm Noren," he replied. "I'm from Treas, which is in the foothills, east. Why?"

"This is a city an' its m'job ta' know who goes in an' out," the guard replied. His mustache waggled as he spoke, and Noren wondered what he had dyed it with to get that brilliant, strawberry red color. "Why're ye here, Noren?"

"To get supplies, like salt, for us. It's my first time doing this."

The other guard had meanwhile written in a sort of book. They waved Noren to go in, and he rode Evena through the gate, wondering what that had all been about. In a little village, it seemed totally reasonable to know who came in. But a city! Delenois was bigger than anything he had ever imagined, and he could see that without even riding into it. No one could know even half the people here, and if they were so comfortable living so close together with strangers, why did they need to know so much about him?

As he rode further into Delenois, it seemed even stranger. The city truly was filled with people. He was sure there were more people crowded around him on the wide cobblestone street than lived in Treas. He approached a lady in a lavender dress – the sort no one owned more than one, maybe two of, in Treas, but which people around here could afford not to even care for, judging by the fact this was not a festival occasion and several of the dresses were stained or pained – and asked where he could get salt and dried fruit.

"Salt would be the blue shop, two houses past the river, on your left. The dried fruit would be the Dorsons' on Lantern Street. That's seven houses from the First Rose of Spring Inn. You know, the big green building with the rose bud over the door post," she replied shortly.

"Thank you," said Noren. She was already moving away, and he felt he ought to do something more for her. "Oh – and your dress is very nice."

She looked back at him, with an expression which bewildered him. Was she pleased by the compliment and attention? What had he said wrong? He rode on, confused, looking for a 'Lantern Street' or the 'First Rose' inn. Surely the river could not be missed. But more important than the provisions he did not really need, at least not urgently, was the question of how he would get along with city people, whose customs were so different from his own. When a stranger did something for you they did not have to, you tried to offer something in return, even if it was very small, like a compliment ... but maybe if you lived around strangers all the time, then actions and words had different meanings.

The salt was very expensive, and he knew that he would have to use it sparingly. He asked the lady in the shop if she had heard of anyone named Silmavalien. She would probably do sewing and knitting, or something like that. He was told, No, why should she know, and what did he want? He replied that he was curious. He had heard of her, even met her, but he did not know where she lived. After that, he left, to look for the dried fruit seller.

He led Evena to the banks of the river, and held the reins while she drank. Then he wandered around the city, looking for the dried fruit shop on Lantern Street.

Soon he had spent most of his money, and he knew that he would have to make it somehow, if he wanted to have what he could not hunt. He wondered if selling deer-skins when he passed through a city would work. He continued to ask around for a lady named Silmavalien, who knitted and sewed, and lived on the edges of the city, but he changed his story for when he was asked why. Now he had met her and wanted to buy one of her scarfs, but had forgotten to ask where she lived.

And Silmavalien *would* make some nice scarfs, with beautiful designs, he was sure.

When the sun began to get low in the western sky, Noren rode out of the city. The guards at the gate stopped him briefly on his way out, as they did many others, making it take much longer than it needed to to get in and out of the city, even though no one was really meeting or talking to anyone else. He urged Evena into a comfortable canter once he had gotten out of the press, and as the wind flew in his face he decided he would have to ask someone about this strange custom of recording the people leaving and entering the city.

Once he reached the thicket, Noren picketed Evena where she could graze, and rushed to Elninya, urged by the hunger he had been feeling all the way from the city. She had stayed where he had left her, but she crawled out to him now, while he upended his bags for all the meat he had left, which he tossed to her before satisfying himself with dry bread.

Then he strung his bow and shot a squirrel, which he boiled to be Elninya's breakfast. There was no doubt in his mind that she would eat every bit of it. Then he snuggled with her in a few blankets under the brush, and contemplated the change that had come over his life.

In some subtle way – impossible to point to, invisible when attended to, but always there, hovering on the periphery of his awareness – everything had changed. Tastes, smells, sounds, colors, and even feels had all shifted in some indescribable way, or was everything just wider? Certainly, for his little Elninya, all was incomparable width and freedom. He glimpsed tattered pieces of thought and memory floating through the sky of her mind, and knew that she had spent innumerable ages cramped in the confines of that egg. Yet she always looked to the sky, and the impression and the yearning it aroused were in her mind and her heart.

Had he never really noticed the sky until now, still less understand or even consider what it meant? What it would be to be a bird or a dragon – a flying creature – was so far beyond him. Yet, through Elninya, he felt the desire, not only to know what it was like to fly but to actually fly, enter his heart and burn in his blood. It was a new thirst, one that might be satisfied by flight, but would never be quenched by anything else.

𝒩

Elninya woke Noren early in the morning so he could watch the dawn with her. After that, he shot a raven for her dinner and cooked it over a very small fire, while she devoured the squirrel from last night. He lingered in the shadows of the thicket with her for a few hours, then urged her back into its darkest, densest shrubs and went back into Delenois much later than he had yesterday. Somehow, he had a strong feeling that he did not want to meet the same guards twice, and he made sure it was different men standing at the gate before he approached. This time, he told them he was visiting an old friend, and then spent the day wandering the streets near the wall and the gates. Every so often he knocked on a door, and when it was answered – which was most of the time, as many of the homes had store-fronts – he told his story of being looking for a friend who had recently moved, named Silmavalien. But no one seemed to know of anyone who matched his description.

The world was shrouded in twilight when he returned to Elninya.

𝒩

The next morning, Noren shot a couple of quail, and while he watched them cook, he decided that it would be unwise to remain near Delenois any longer. It was more of a feeling than a decision, but it was one he meant to follow. He had no idea how strange his behavior was to others, or how long it would be before someone wandered what he was doing and why. If he was not a Dragonrider himself, he thought he could have risked the suspicion. But now he could not afford to draw attention to himself, lest he be investigated or questioned and give the truth away.

That was the one thing he hated about being what he now was, though he did not love Elninya any less for it. He abhorred having to hide, like a criminal. Elninya was worth it to him, and he would rather die with her than lose her, but he still hated the situation.

When the quail were done cooking, Noren gave one to Elninya, and put the other in a saddlebag for dinner. He packed most of his belongings around it, leaving only a few blankets out, while he explained his plans to Elninya. He could sense her distaste, but also her acceptance, and she willingly crawled into the other saddlebag and let him pack the blankets around her so she would be well-concealed. Then he bound the bag to Evena's saddle, with the tie a little loose to let her have more air. It was nearly noon when they finally got onto the road, heading away from Delenois.

They encountered a few travelers, and this time Noren noticed them more than he had on his way here, perhaps because of Elninya. She surprised him with her knowledge of every individual: those men were day-dreaming about selling their wares, and that man was concerned about thugs and Noren's quick-moving figure had aroused his fear, and that single woman was going to see the Oracle because she could have no children.

Elninya, Noren asked her, *can they hear you?*

No, they could not. She could only hear them think. She did not know them as she knew him, she only heard their thoughts as he could hear them speak.

As the sun prepared to descend in fire behind the world, Noren looked for a place for them to spend the night. He chose a grove of trees about half a mile off the road, and rode through the grasses to reach it, happy that it was a little farther from the road and seemed to be in an area not too often frequented or stopped in.

Tomorrow, he would spend the day hunting whatever kind of animals he could find in the savanna-lands between the Orenial Rivers. Two things concerned him: would the predators here be a danger to a dragon? These lands were still fairly civilized, but he was much more concerned about predators here than just outside the walls of Delenois. Those seemed like a place anything wild would avoid. And the other was that he was still close enough to civilization, he wondered how much he could find to hunt and, of less immediate importance, if their skins would be worth anything.

4
Hunting, At Least Trying

After breakfast, Silmavalien went out to hunt, or at least try. Even if she had the best of luck, she would not be able to hunt half of what they would need, and the venison was running out quickly. But she had to try.

She crossed the stream so she could range farther without getting too close to the Fire Shadow. Her legs were nearly numb from the cold water before she was through the stream, but she already felt like she was much stronger than she had been two days ago. She put her boots back on and strung her bow so she would not have to do that when she found prey.

Throughout the day, experiences flew back and forth between her and Minth. He ate, and slept, and played, and slept again. He woke for a third time, feeling so well that the feeling flowed over their bond and reinvigorated her. He played with the other dragons for a bit more, rolling on the ground with them, pawing with them, and chasing tails, his own or others, and sometimes Silmavalien thought he was not even sure whose tail he was pouncing on. His skin was in poor condition, and even their relatively gentle play broke it open often, and Silmavalien realized she would need to make oil for them.

After a while, Minth got bored of the game, as he was too often underneath the other dragons his size, and crawled away, mostly following the stream. She reminded him that he might be farther from the pool than he should be, but she did not press the issue. He kept on meandering, sometimes finding soft-barked trees to rub himself against, and then realized he was not sure which way was back. She remembered where the stream was for him, and after that it was obvious to him, too.

A few minutes later he was frolicking in the ferns near its banks, when he noticed a rabbit foraging a few paces off.

Hunt.

Silmavalien froze with him, as his instincts dominated their bond. She was with him, every motion of their muscles, every wordless thought and decision both of theirs, as he slowly and carefully got to his feet. Despite the immense effort and concentration it took, they lifted their bulky tail off the ground so it would not scrape and make noise, and then silently, gracefully, he crept away. Together, they obeyed an instinct and impulse older than either of them.

Minth circled around, taking it slowly so he would be fresh later, and Silmavalien wondered if he was part of her hunting like that. Then his instincts pulled them together again. They crept up on their prey, the tension in their muscles growing with every carefully silent step. It grew more and more unbearable, the need to release it overwhelming. They sprang forward with all the energy and strength in Minth's body, his tail propelling him almost as much as his four legs. They landed on the rabbit pinning it, uninjured, underneath them. It squealed and squirmed, but could not escape. With a sharp, jerky motion, like a bird pecking, they bit.

Silmavalien slipped out of the connection. She did not know any more about how to kill this way than Minth, and that guiding, wordless instinct that had pulled them both into itself was flopping, now. It let her go, and she distanced herself from Minth's messy attempt to kill it, even as she felt the echo of pain from the bites he received in the process.

But, when it was finished, she congratulated him heartily. He barely responded and immediately fell to devouring his kill.

She left him to eat and continued hunting, but she was not nearly so successful as he was. Many times she missed, scaring her prey off, and losing time finding the arrow. Fortunately, she always saw where it went, since she shot low and it often plunged into tree trunks. But when she returned in the mid-evening, all she had for hours of frustration and burning, trembling arms, was one rabbit.

She threw it across the stream, and got through the freezing, numbing water as quickly as she could. While she gathered more brush and wood for a fire, another of the dragons hunted a rabbit, though they did not seem to want to tell her who it was, and she let it be.

Once she got the fire going, Silmavalien examined Minth's bites. She rinsed his wounds with boiled wound, though it hurt and stung. He understood she was trying to help him though, and he held still, only whimpering slightly. He lay down close to the fire afterwards, while she looked through her bags for the healing herbs she had, cursing the fact she had not thought to keep an eye out for fresh ones while she hunted. She boiled some of them in water and then rinsed his wounds again, while others she simmered at a lower heat until they turned into a paste and spread over his wounds, then assured him they would probably hurt less tomorrow.

The next morning, after they ate, Silmavalien took them all down to the stream to a place where it was very shallow and wide, and easy to cross. Most of the dragons walked, but she carried Minth since getting cold would do his body any good fighting infection and healing. She also carried Daurth, because he was still very small. Then they followed back up to the pool, and Silmavalien left her bags there again, took her bow and left, with a reminder to Minth to stay warm and safe.

She thought she was both getting stronger already, as well as adjusting to the fact she was not very strong, since this time she managed to get three rabbits. The dragons only got one, despite the fact everyone tried, but she was glad no one got hurt again. She was also amazed that they were able to hunt at all. They were starved and weak, yet somehow they were doing better than they had a few months ago, the last time they had been healthy and got to practice.

Nonetheless, it was painfully obvious that they could not take care of themselves. That night they finished the last of the deer, and together they had only hunted enough for three of the dragons to eat well.

That night she sat by the embers of the fire, waiting for the herb-paste she was making to cool. Listening to the flowing, musical tinkle of the stream-spray falling into the pool, she wondered if there was anything she could do better. It was simply unendurable, not possible, to give up and fail now, after having come so far.

Finally, she remembered or realized that she should have put it before the Lord of Light and asked for his help long ago.

In the morning, she left to hunt and also hopefully find a stick she could make into another pine cone obtainer. She doubted she was strong enough to make a long one like she had had before, but even a little more reach would help her to get a lot more. Even though she could feel that Minth's wounds were healing well and no longer pained him, she could not escape the feeling that it was going to be a horrid day. Her attempt to hunt squirrels was a disaster. She hit the first one she tried, but the next time she missed and had to spend who-knew-how-long finding the arrow. Nonetheless, her hunting, as well as the dragons', was better this day than the last. Between them, they had a full six rabbits, which still was not enough to feed even the half of them well.

The dragons' hunger, as well as her own, gnawed at her stomach and made her grumpy. She ate only pine nuts from another cone she had got, and then tried to rein her unhappiness in check so it would not affect the dragons. Even after they had eaten the hunger gnawed at them, and it all reminded her horribly of their journey through the Riders' Passage, with food and water always rationed, and far too often not there at all.

S

Over the next few days and despite the fact they were always hungry, everyone was stronger every day than they had been the day before. The squabbles over what food there was, the fights when one of the dragons got a kill and devoured the whole thing before thinking to share it darkened everyone's moods, but the little dragons often made nearly efforts to fight back that urge and that hunger and share with their friends.

Tiela grew inexpressibly proud of her scales, which protected her from the teeth and claws of rabbits and squirrels, but she noticed every scratch and every speck of dust on her beautiful teal armor. She became obsessed with cleaning her scales and keeping herself as shiny as above, often washing herself meticulously in the pool and asking Silmavalien, or one of the other dragons, with help when there was a speck of dirt she could not get to. Silmavalien found it amusing, especially because her shape was still awkward and ugly, but she did not tell Tiela that. She just assured she would love her however she looked.

Tiela's antics did a great deal to distract her from her own unhappiness, and she sensed they helped some of the other dragons as well. Sometimes, she wondered if that was why Tiela took this obsession with shiny scales as far as she did.

Apart from being amused by Tiela, what Silmavalien enjoyed best was sitting on the edge of the pool and gazing up, up, up.

Up at the tall conifers, towering so high above her. Up at the precipices that pierced the sky, seeming to tower as far above the cedars as they towered above her. Up at the twisting spray of the waterfall that poured down its surface. There was something so awing and beautiful that it freed her soul from worry and concerns and unhappiness, about lying at the feet of something so much greater and higher than she could comprehend, and gazing up at its grandeur and loveliness. Both the desire and the awe of the skies and the high places was in her heart, as in that of every dragon.

Then, one morning as she gazed up at the immeasurable heights rising above her just as the early light of dawn kissed the rocks with its red light, Silmavalien thought about Aelaza's warning. The Shadow's lair was *really* not far.

Something like an intuition or foreboding formed itself in her mind, and she knew that, food or no food, it was time to fill their water-skins, and travel farther. If she could easily walk to its chasm, it might easily be able to reach her still. And, besides, the longer they dwelt here the harder it would be to hunt, and it was already getting harder to find pine cones she could reach.

Silmavalien packed up, and led the dragons along the stream, towards the edge of the lower precipice. She hoped to be able to get a better sense of where they should go with the view she would have there, able to see the cliffs above her, and find any streams that threaded their way down.

When she saw the light bright and clear beyond the trees, she told the dragons to stay back, away from the danger of the cliff edge if they stumbled, and stepped out into the open.

5
Saved By Slipping

For the most part, Noren had hunted large animals, mainly deer. However, he had some experience hunting small animals, especially when he had just been learning some of the hunter's skills as a small boy, and he quickly adjusted to hunting small animals again.

It did not take him long to get several rabbits, and while he was preparing them Elninya took an interesting in having one raw. He let her take it, and the taste of raw meat flashed across their bond as she tore into it. It was strange and interesting, and he understood why she loved it so much, though he declined her unspoken, hardly thought, invitation to try it with her.

The next day he saddled up Evena again and they continued as before. Since Elninya did not enjoy the way her bag bounced when Evena tried, he kept them to a brisk walk, and sometimes asked Evena for a gentle canter, while Elninya did not mind as much as the trot, though she did not enjoy it either. As he rode, he wondered how long it would be before she was too big to ride in the saddlebag and what he would do then. She was growing so quickly, and he was pretty certain that if that continued she would be too large well before she could fly, and at least well before she could fly well.

Dark clouds rose up out of the west behind them, and by mid-day they covered the whole of the sky. Ethereal blue lightning flashed above, and Noren saw a strike flash out of a far-off ridge that jutted out from the Aravin Mountains.

Then the rain began to fall in torrents, blurring the landscape with its silver curtains.

It was very pretty, but it was also very cold. Almost at once Noren was wet to the skin and shivering, though to his satisfaction Elninya was still as comfortable as she ever was while they rode. The saddlebag was keeping her dry, and with the blankets wrapped around she had hardly noticed the drop in temperature.

Evena seemed fine, too, her winter coat more than adequate to keep her warm in this kind of weather, so even though he was miserably cold, he was not in too much of a hurry to find a place to stop and try to get some shelter.

Suddenly, a man stepped out of a clump of trees beside the road and blocked it. A small knife gleamed in one hand, and the rain sparkled off a sort of sword in the other.

Noren wheeled Evena around, only to see another thug behind them, on the path. He thrust his arm into one of the saddlebags, pulling out his bow, along with two arrows. It took him only a moment to string the bow.

Meanwhile, one of the thugs declared, "Hand over yer horse, and ye can go free with yer clothes. Use that an' —"

In a flash, he held up his bow, knocking one arrow, and shot. The thugs screamed, as Noren's arrow pierced him. Others yelled and roared. Evena spun, and somehow Noren landed on his feet, with his next arrow knocked. A tiny, far away part of his mind remarked that he was acting with a speed and precision he never had before. Fire roared in his blood, he saw and heard and felt details he did not usually noticed, and he was faster, stronger. There was no fear: only the need, and the power, to act. And to protect Elninay, who lay frozen still and shivering with fear in the saddlebag.

A thug jumped for Evena, who spun in nervous circles. Effortlessly, Noren drew back the string and released the arrow. It buried itself in the backside of the thug, but he was already turning to face the others. He dropped the bow, useless now. The rest of his arrows were still in Evena's saddlebag. His hunting knife was no sword, but for now it must do.

A knife hurtled through the air, struck his elbow, hilt end first. He turned to face the thug he saw out of the corner of his eye, slipped on the mud, fell. A knife flew above him, where he had just been standing, and struck Evena's rump. She reared up, bolted down the path. Elninya screamed, and her terror bit in Noren's heart.

Then she fainted, leaving him alone. Alone as he had never been since he knew what it was to be 'together!' Alone as he had not been since she had hatched. Cold terror froze the fire in his blood into shards.

Two thugs ran at him from either side. He rolled away, knowing it was futile. No one could get up before one or the other reached him and plunged a knife into him. Confused emotions assailed him, one after the other, surrounding him in the blink of an eye. Horror and revulsion at the thought of a human body stabbed, run through, though he already shot two of them. Terror and horror of what it would feel like. Terror of death. Terror of dying. Regret that he had somehow not been, or lived, or died as he would have.

ELNINYA! How could he leave her alone, to die alone, as she now must?

The nearer thug slipped and fell. His knife plunged into the ground, narrowly missed Noren's thigh and pinned his pant-leg into the mud. He sat up and killed the man, but then the next man was upon. He closed his eyes, prepared to die.

Instead, a great weight suddenly pressed on his legs. His eyes flashed open, he smiled grimly, and killed again. Then he set about freeing himself.

Just as he got to his feet, all the little pains returned to him. He was shivering cold. His heart thumped wildly in his chest, his lungs ached as he gasped for air, and his elbow throbbed painfully. He hardly remembered when or how it had been hit.

A long line on his thigh stung, too. The knife had not quite missed him, though the wound was nothing and did not matter.

His bow. That was the first thing. He would never find it again if he abandoned it in the tall grass. And it would be ruined if he did not get it dry fast. He picked it up, tucked it under his body to shield it from getting any wetter as well he could, cleaned and sheathed his knife, and then went after Evena and Elninya.

The rain went on pouring, and he had to step carefully to avoid losing his footing in the slushy mud that the road had already become. It occurred to him he would walk faster in the soaking grass of the path, where the roots kept the dirt firmer. It did not matter that it was wet. He was already wet all through, even his boots drenched.

Thoughts about the damage to his bow vanished. Evena had gone farther than he had thought, and though he could follow her trail well enough, he needed to find her before someone else did. Before she ended up at someone's farm house with their horses. He cringed at the thought of that disaster. He looked to see if she might have circled back, or if he could even see her, and then his fear for Elninya brought back what he learned – what he suddenly realized he knew – about the thugs, the *men*, he had killed.

In the brief moments before she fainted, she had heard their thoughts and feelings, and somehow he had glimpsed them through her and remembered it, though he had not noticed at the time. He knew raiding travelers was the way they made their living. When they saw one of their comrades fall, they felt dismay, rage, and even sorrow, a sorrow that roused memories of a deeper, older sorrow they could never escape.

Yet all he knew of their lives was a vague shadow. Surely, they deserved their deaths, he told himself. They had ruined the livelihoods of countless others, and besides he had to defend himself.

Formless shadows of vaguer doubts entered Noren's mind, but he could not sort them out, and did not have time to think about things like this right now. He redoubled the intensity with which he looked for Elninya and Evena, and just then he felt the mind of her darling dragon stir.

He sent her as much comfort and reassurance as he could, fighting his own doubts and worries, and a few moments later he saw Evena grazing, a fair distance from the road. He left her trail and went straight through the grass towards her, and she greeted him with a soft nicker and let him catch her without any trouble. He did his best to quickly dry his bow and stuff it back in the saddlebag, and then climbed onto her again and they continued through the pouring rain.

They stopped in the first dense thicket Noren saw, a few miles past where the thugs had ambushed them, and a little farther off the road than the clump of trees they had used.

N

His throat was sore and lumpy.

Elninya's gentle touch brushed across his mind. It was morning! The rain was over, the sun was shining, she was glad he was awake, she loved him!

He smiled and returned the touch, then sat up and reached for his water-skin. Swallowing hurt, but he forced himself to drink anyways. There was no doubt about it now. He was sick with something, and he had slept far longer than he should have needed or wanted.

He still did not really feel like getting up, but he could feel Elninya's hunger, so he forced himself to eat some of the dried fruit he had bought in Delenois and then got up to hunt something for the both of them, since he would need to start hunting for himself too. He shot a few quail and two rabbits without leaving the thicket, and fed Elninya one of the quail, before building a small brush fire on the far edge of the thicket from the road to cook the rest of the food over.

The smell of the meat cooking ought to have been delicious and kept him eagerly awake, salivating with hunger, but instead he was just tired and miserable and struggled to keep awake and watch the fire. But he remembered to move where Evena was picketed so she could have fresh, long grass, before falling asleep again.

The next day, Noren lay dozing far longer, until the doubts and feelings roiling in his mind, tired as he was, forced him to get up and do something. He collected some straight sticks and started working on making them into arrow to occupy his hands so he could actually think, and Elninya lay down next to him. He could feel her attention on what he was doing, her quiet curiosity as she tried to watch and learn and understand, and he could sense her even stronger desire to somehow help him feel better, even just by being with him.

He could not get the rainy day's ambush and fight out of his mind, or the moment when he had slipped and falling had saved his life. Those moments played over in his mind over and over: he had slipped, fallen, lived, and then his ambushers had slipped, fallen, and died, he had killed them. The world had saved his life by tripping them, and killed them by tripping them.

What determined whether men lived or died? Why was death so feared? What did it mean to die?

In the stories, death was always followed by a life of bliss, or a life of torment, to which no end or deliverance could be foreseen, except in very rare situations. He had never truly believed the stories, but now he knew they had to be wrong in some major ways, and there was no reason to trust anything else about them. So what really happened when one died? He did not know. It had to be something, since existence could not become non-existence.

Either I am, or I am not, and I am. If I weren't, then 'I' wouldn't be.

That much was obvious.

Yet death was often felt as something fearful. That much he knew. It was what he had experienced. It was what those he had killed had experienced. And they were not alone in that. In the stories, the fear of death was something to be met and overcome.

Was death feared only because it was unknown? Because no one really knew, and even if they believed the stories deep down inside they knew they did not really know what death would bring to them. But why fear the unknown, unless there was something else one feared that might lurk in the unknown?

Unless something was not right in a big way.

Wrapped up in his personal experience of terror, had been the thought that he was not ready to die. So what did he mean by that? What would make him ready to die? The answer floated around him, clear but wordless. Some sort of satisfaction in his life. A completeness to who he was and what he had done and made of his life.

He was not quite sure what that would be. He was an accomplished hunter and a brave man, yet he feared death. He had not proved himself to Silmavalien as he wished to do. He had not been quite what he would wish to be. He had not always been as trustworthy as he wanted to be, and he feared both death and pain.

He could be content without perfection, but he did not think he could die in peace without it.

Again, his mind returned to how slipping and falling had saved his life.

6
Steep Descent

Once she had stepped out from the trees and the cliff's edge was only a few paces away, Silmavalien turned and surveyed the mountains above. She saw the waterfall that the pool they had been living up, and when she looked to both east and west, she saw the gleam of other waterfalls, but they were far, far away. She got down on her hands and knees, crawled to the edge of the cliff, and looked down.

Ten paces to her right the stream they were following poured itself over the edge. It tumbled down to the forested ledge far below in a twisting spray of rainbow sheens, through which she thought she saw a pool very much like the one above. She did not know how tall the cliff was, but if they could find a path down it, that might be the best thing to do.

She searched the precipice for the zig-zag strips of green she had seen before. One that looked solid and continuous threaded down the cliff not too far to the west – away from the Shadow's lair. She crawled back away from the edge and then led the dragons along the edge of the wood. There were rabbits everywhere in the lush grass that grew in the shallow earth on the ledge, past where the trees could grow and shade them, but she had to be very careful about shooting them, because if she missed her arrows could easily fly over the precipice where she would never find them again. She shot two rabbits, but she also lost two arrows, in the hour or so it took to reach the descending zig-zag strip she was looking for.

It was only less steep than the cliff itself, but it grew dense with trees and bushes, and boulders that jutted out of the ground everywhere. Silmavalien led the dragons down it, threading their way through the boulders and the thickets. In the places where the plants were less dense, she kept the dragons on the inside since they were much clumsier than she was, and that way if they slipped they would have to fall farther to go over the edge, and she would have more time to catch them. Sometimes, it was so steep she had to join the dragons in going on all fours for a while.

She kept her bow ready in all but the steepest places, but she made sure to always shoot in, so that the most likely way she would lose an arrow would be if it broke, and she tried to avoid shooting where there was a rock that could easily break the arrow too close, as well. She could not afford to lose too many arrows. But that meant that even though there seemed to be a lot of animal life on the strip, she only hunted a couple rabbits and one squirrel.

As they continued down, the strip varied more in width. Sometimes it was perilously thin, and Silmavalien struggled to keep her footing on the steep slope covered with thick pine needles, and struggled to keep her calm when she slid. Fortunately, the dragons did not seem as affected by either the slope or the slippery ground cover.

But then, sometime around noon or a little later, they reached a place where the strip broke off. The break was so narrow she had not been able to see it from above, and the strip continued just below, zig-zagged back in the other direction. A small precipice of huge boulders, resting one upon the other, connected the two. Upon consideration, it looked easier to climb than the cliff she had climbed to get out of the blizzard and into the Riders' Passage. Possibly enough easier that she would be able to manage even in her weakened state without too much trouble, and it was shorter, too.

In the end, it was even easier to clamber down than she had thought, and took only a minute or two. It was not that tall either, and

she could see she would be able to stand on a boulder near the bottom and reach up to take the dragons into her arms, then lower them down.

She called Minth to the edge, and though he was a little scared he stepped confidently into her upraised arms. She struggled to hold him in that awkward position, and knelt to lower him to the ground. Next, she called Wydth and Coroneth who were the heaviest to her, so she could do them while she was still fresh, and it was all she could do not to crumple under their weight, and put them down gently. Or gently enough not to hurt them, because her arms shook and it was not quite gentle.

But they did not mind, and proceeded to pounce and nip at each other as soon as they were both on the bottom together, before Minth scolded them for being careless, and she thanked him and turned her attention to reinforcing his warning. She called the next dragon to her, and lowered them in order of weight, little Daurth last since he was the lightest.

To Silmavalien's relief, the next stretch was the most gentle slope of the entire descent so far, gentle enough it could almost have been one of the forested ledges, except that it was still far too narrow. But getting the dragons down the small cliff had taken a while, and when she looked up and down the precipice, she realized they were not yet half-way down. There were no way they would get to the bottom tonight.

They were all getting hungry too, but Silmavalien urged them on. She was determined to get down the next day if possible, if only because they would run out of water. Her water-skin had done well enough when it was just herself and tiny Minth drinking from it, but there were so many more dragons now and they were all bigger. She expected everyone would be thirsty tonight, even after draining it dry.

Soon the sky became overcast, and a mass of clouds coming in from the west hid the sunset in dark glorious purples and reds. They stopped in the widest place Silmavalien could find and made camp, since it would be far too dangerous to continue in the dark. She started a small fire to cook a little meat for herself, but she gave most of it the dragons. Fortunately, they were not very thirsty after eating the raw, bloody meat.

They were all hungry in the morning, and the sky was all white, ripply cloud. Silmavalien had never seen the sea – except far, far below the cliffs, and then she could not really see it in detail – but it looked like what she imagined the sea might look like if it were white, and all the waves were frozen in motion.

They had only been on the move again for a little before a gentle, consistent drizzle started. Not long afterwards, Songeth stopped, and a moment later the other dragons also stopped, then took shelter behind rocks and big trees. Silmavalien knew what they heard, and now she heard it too: a whole herd of deer leaping down the strip! She strung her bow as quickly as she could, fumbling a little, but she was still ready in time.

Somehow, her shot was perfect. Her deer fell, and the rest of the silver-gray deer went leaping past and down, the buck with his beautiful horns in their midst. She felt again the sadness that she had to take their lives for her own and the dragons'. She felt the dragons' thoughts wrap around hers, and she did not understand it: somehow, they understood her sadness, and dismissed it, at the same time.

After that, they went much slower with her dragging the deer. But that was okay, since now they had plenty of food, and she knew the dragons would be okay getting most of their water from the raw meat, especially in this weather. The rain grew heavier throughout the day, and at this rate they would probably even be able to find a pool or a trickle of water, and she might even re-fill the water-skin.

But then the rain caused its own problems. First, the dragons got cold, and then the ground grew wet. Water streamed down the precipice and across the ground, and Silmavalien, and even the dragons, found it much harder to keep their footing. As they got colder they got hungrier, and as they got hungrier they got colder, and soon she was cold, even though she had to drag the deer.

Then, in one of the narrow places, she slipped, slid, found herself on the edge of the cliff, stopped only by the root of a tree. Her heart pounded in her chest as she crawled away from the edge, holding onto the deer.

It had been so close. And worst of all, there was nothing she could do to keep it from happening again. She had not been careless. Being more careful wasn't an option that could help.

Then, with a short of shock, she thought that she *should* have asked for the blessing of the Lord of Light, and thanked him for that amazing shot and the deer, and now for saving her from falling.

But she did not want. She did not want to admit her failure. She did not want to credit someone else for everything. Yet at the same time she wanted to. She went on without praying, fighting the two desires warring within her.

Suddenly she slid. The pine needles slipped out of under her feet, her feet slid over the smooth, wet rock. She fell, terror burning in her veins. This time, she would plunge to her death.

Somehow, she did not. She grasped the edge as it fell, but it pulled out of her hands. Then she found herself in a pocket of rock that faced back into the cliff. But she'd let go of the deer, and it had fallen to the bottom.

Minth's concern reached her. He was shivering with cold, but all he was thinking about was coming to her.

Stay away from the edge. I'm okay. Stay away from the edge, she told him, then knelt to make her prayer.

"O Lord of the Light, I have failed you. Please hear my plea. Please bless our lives and our efforts. Please protect us and do not let me die. Thank you for saving my life." She could not thank him for the lost deer. "Please, take care of us. Thank you for saving my life."

Silmavalien rose, and carefully climbed back onto the land. Then, she threw herself down in the midst of the dragons, and embraced Minth. "O dragons, dragons," she sobbed. "I have failed you, too. I am sorry."

They all tried to comfort her, many of them climbing on top of her and on top of each other as they climbed on top of her. Minth nuzzled her face as gently as he could. She thanked the dragons for their love, and then rose.

There was nothing for it but to go on.

Over the rest of the day, she only managed to shoot two rabbits and get five pine cones, and she worried that the little dragons would get sick. They were still far too thin, and she did not know how well they would manage the cold with so little food. They finally reached the foot of the cliff, just as it got quite dark. She split the rabbits and most of the pine nuts between the dragons, eating the remainder herself, and they huddled close in the driest place they could find, with the bear-skin over all of them.

S

In the morning, the rain had stopped. Everyone was hungry, but Silmavalien took them both to the stream, where the pool was inferior to the one above. It was muddier, less clear, especially in the shallows, and it was rockier. She told the dragons to be careful around it, since this pool would not be as nice to fall into, and then went hunting.

The dragons went hunting, too, and both she and the dragons shared their mutual excitement and encouragement over the others' success, and the dragons were much more successful now. They had learned to work together to sneak up and take down their prey, and it helped a lot. Her own hunting was poor that day, and she hardly did better than they did.

But, mostly, she was just happy for their success.

7

Continuing the Search

The morning sun dazzled his eyes, so Noren first noticed he was entering Carenton by the smell of the river. The wetness of the banks, the plants that grew in the water, and the general trees that favored the area gave the air a very different feel from the grass and weeds of the plains.

Carenton, Noren thought as he squinted into the sunlight, might be a much more attractive place for Silmavalien to go than Delenois. There was no wall around Carenton, nothing that could keep her and her dragon from leaving any time they chose, and he was sure she would find the city as uncomfortable as he did.

The only downside, Noren reflected, as he rode between the first houses, was that Carenton might still be small enough that everyone knew everyone else. She would get more attention there. It would be harder to avoid letting anyone get to know her without seeming suspicious.

But then again, Carenton was a lot bigger than Treas. He had not paid much attention to these things on his ride the other direction, when he had just been thinking about going to Delenois, finding out what the white oval was – or what the Oracle said it was, because he had never been certain the Oracle would not make something up – and then considered his options based on whatever he learned.

Now, he thought about how much like Treas Carenton seemed – at least compared to Delenois. It still wasn't a mountain village, and the homes were much closer together. A wave of longing for Treas came over him, and he wondered if he would ever seen it again.

Elninya stirred in her saddlebag and tried to send him a comforting thought. She could not understand how he could long for a place like that.

Still, he cautioned her gently, and she slipped back into sleep. This was not the road where he could put her on the far side of Evena from anyone he had to ride by. There were people walking between the houses, conducting business or going about their way. Carenton was more different than Treas than that first home-sick look had made him feel. It was a trading town, built on the river. It was not crowded, but it was full of more people, and people passing through, and more of the business of people's lives was conducted in the town and in working with the travelers, than out in the wilderness or the fields.

" – Zilmavi. She's certainly pretty, with that dark hair."

The sound of the name pulled Noren up straight. He halted Evena, who was eager to stop, and slipped off her side, pulling the reins over her head. – *But dark hair. Silmavalien's hair wasn't particularly dark* – He was already asking his question, as the chatting men and woman stopped and fell silent to look at him.

"Zilmavi?" The words escaped his mouth without thought. "How long has she been here?"

It wasn't Silmavalien's name, but if she wanted to have a name that blended in with the kinds of names people had here, outside of the mountains, it was one she might have chosen.

And these people might call her hair dark, Noren realized, actually looking at them … One of them even had hair that was almost yellow, and several more certainly had hair lighter than Silmavalien's or anyone else he had ever seen in Treas, except for that one bard whose name he had forgotten. He could not even remember what story he had told.

Was he about to find Silmavalien? So soon? Joy and delight crashed through him like lightning and wind and pouring rain in the year's first storm. He could not wait to see her voice!

Then anger rose, flaring like a fire. Hurt and resentment turned the storm dark, and a pit of conflicting emotions formed in his stomach. Excitement hardly to be borne. Resentment he could not deal with.

Not until now had he know either how much he wanted to find her, or that he did not even want to see her.

"Why?" the man asked. "Do you know her?"

"I think so," Noren replied, lost in his inner confusion.

"You think so?" someone asked, laughter in her voice. "Either, you know someone, or you don't."

"I know a young lady with a name like that, and dark hair."

"You know her, but you don't know where she lives?"

"She told me, but I just can't remember the name of the place." It was a lie, of course. "How long has she been living here?"

They all shrugged. "Since before we knew her. Who knows?"

"Thank you all, very much," Noren said. He got back on Evena, not wanting to leave Elninya in her saddlebag while he wasn't on her back, and rode away, at once disappointed and relieved. Yet through the crushing emotions, he noticed that several people gave him odd glances as he rode off and did not resume their conversation.

He knew he would have to learn how to ask his question in a way that seemed more normal to people. He could not afford to be suspicious, and he was not going to put off searching for Silmavalien until he figured out his feelings either. He would have to figure them out, together with her, after he found her, because right now his dream of finding her and marrying her at once had vanished. He did not know if they could marry at all. Or even if she wanted to.

At last, Noren found another group of people chatting, and stepped in, hoping that this time the way he asked his question would work better.

"Do any of you know a young woman who came to live around here in the past several months? She has dark hair and her name is Silmavalien."

Everyone stared at him as he spoke, and as soon as he finished, more than one person cried "No!"

He got back on Evena, wondering what they thought he was, and how he was going to find Silmavalien or verify she was not here without getting himself into bigger trouble first.

Elninya was awake the next time Noren tried to find a way to ask someone. Before he even finished his question he felt recoiling from something in the man's thoughts, and before the man could say, "No, I don't," Noren knew what it was. She had told him what she had understood, and though it was vague and cloudy, it was enough for him to get a sense of what it was.

They thought him a disgusting monster, asking these questions as a cover for a vile desire. But what about looking for a woman made him a monster?

These people knew traders! Surely they knew people who moved sometimes or – he did not remember the bards' stories that poorly! There were a dozen reasonable reasons a man might look for a woman. His was only one of them.

That thought formed another idea in his mind. He could say that Silmavalien was his sister, and she had left his village because she could not find any good men for her to marry there, but he wanted to pass by and see how she was. Was that something they would believe, assuming someone had not already passed the word around that he was a monster?

Especially when it was a lie he could not stand. Silmavalien was not his sister, and he could not think of her that way. Even if he could never marry her, he still could not think of her that way.

After a few more conversation, a man who seemed far more comfortable with him than the others assured him, "No, there's no Silmavalien here."

He was telling him the truth. He was not afraid he was a monster, Elninya assured him, and Noren thanked him and got back on Evena. Then, trying to make it sound like an afterthought, just as he was about to ride off, he asked, "Did she pass through?"

"Not that I'm aware of."

Noren acknowledged him and bid him farewell, then rode away, leaving Carenton behind. He stopped to refill his water-skins at the river, and a few miles later he came to the place where the main road turned southwards, towards Kranah, and the smaller, rougher road that led to Treas rose towards the foothills.

He turned onto the main road and then let his mind return to his mixed feelings about Silmavalien. He could feel Elninya in his mind, trying to help him know what he felt. He knew he still loved Silmavalien, and probably for the same reason he always had. Nothing about her, nothing she did, failed to impress him. Even her courage and wits, shown by her very betrayal and rejection of the trust he thought had, impressed him. Of all that she was and all that she did, only that rejection did not impress him.

And it hurt him to the core. He did not know if he would ever be able to move past it. But why did it hurt him so much more than he had thought at first, and why did it hurt him so much at all?

She did not hate him. She was just afraid. He thought. He hoped. Her letter proved it.

As the afternoon closed, Noren wondered how far what seemed like uninterrupted farmland went on. Would he be able to find a place where he and Elninya could hide for the night, or was it like this all the way to Kranah?

Finally, as it was getting dark, the fields grew a little more patchy. Noren found a small thicket in the middle of a field. He shot a squirrel and gave it to Elninya, and then they huddled together in every bit of clothing and blankets that he had. It felt cold enough to freeze, and he wished he could build a fire for warmth, but there were too many farmhouses around for him to dare risking the attention. Then, at first light, he and Elninya had a quick breakfast and got back on the road.

It was not safe to wait for day, when some farmer might come by before then, to tend to his fields or shoot a rabbit for his kitchen.

Noren soon began to worry that it was not going to work at all. The thickets and the patches of wild, untended land were not growing any larger or more frequent. Finally a little past noon, he found one that was bigger than most and had a few more trees and thickets. He picketed Evena and left Elninya there to go hunting. It still did not feel safe, but at least it was not inviting disaster.

He wondered for a moment, before he turned his back, if he should be keeping Elninya safe, not trying to find Silmavalien. But something in her own thoughts discouraged that thought. And Silmavalien and her dragon were probably in much greater danger.

N

Noren spent that afternoon and the next day hunting. It was hard to find much prey in this land, especially while making sure he did not attract attention, but at least he was able to build a fire to cook over, at a good distance from where he had left Elninya.

The next day they rode through another town much like Carenton, and Noren continued to search for Silmavalien, as if he were her brother. For some reason, that was less disturbing to most people, though some of them still gave him looks, and Elninya confirmed for him that several more feared he was a monster. But he did not find even a hint of Silmavalien, and somehow, even though he had known from the first that it was unlikely that she would be in any given town, and he found that disappointing. Even though he did not entirely want to find her, either.

For many days they went on like this, traveling one day and Noren hunting the next. He continued to be able to find fields to stay, though there were many more small towns, often at crossroads, and the road Noren was traveling continually grew a little larger, a little better maintained, and a little more traveled.

But nowhere could he find a trace of Silmavalien.

Often the travelers, always in groups of three or more with at least one weapon-bearing man, would ask Noren if he wanted to travel with them until their ways parted. Sometimes, he would fall in with the group for a while just to be polite, then urge Evena to a canter and ride far ahead. None of them rode horses, though some of them had pack donkeys, and Noren realized this might be why they spoke to him in an odd way, until something he said gave away that he lived in an obscure village. Then, they wondered why he was riding through the kingdom on horseback, and he had to be uncomfortably careful in how they answered him.

Until then, some of them thought he was someone "important" or related to "important" wealthier people, something like a prince. At least, that was what he got from the images Elninya showed him. He would not have known what they thought he was on his own, since they did not tell him, though he would have been puzzled at the way they spoke to him, as if they were almost afraid, or trying to gain his favor. But then, when he revealed his origins, they usually become either condescending, as if now it was they who were better and more important, or relaxed and friendly.

8

A Place Like Home

Silmavalien was not sure why she felt at once comfortable and uncomfortable, until she realized that it was just a feeling of strangeness. For so long – ever since she had fled Treas with Minth, that night before she was to marry Noren – she had traveled upwards, ever upwards, first to flee from discovery, but then so she could get over the mountains and find a place where she could live and be safe.

Now, she had done it. She had traveled *down* instead of up. She was there.

But life was still not like it had ever been before. It was not like it had been in Treas after Minth hatched when they had lived in constant fear, and it was certainly not like life had been in Treas before he hatched, even apart from the way that had changed her soul. She had no village now, and she did not take part in tasks with the other villagers.

Instead, she had nine dragons she took care of mostly by hunting, and she finally was starting to have time to spare from the constant struggle to survive and find the next meal. They were learning to hunt, and even if they were not that good at it at first, it made a real difference, so though she did not truly have time for leisure, she had time to play with them, and to make another pine cone collector, and to make new arrows.

It felt strange not only to have gone downwards instead of up, but not to be traveling at all, too. She did not exactly stay in one place, since she had taken to hunting deer as the best way to get enough meat for all the dragons, and that meant she would often have to go pretty far and spend several nights away from the dragons – something Minth did not like at all, though plenty of food and the time she spent with him afterwards always made up for that. But she was not traveling anymore, something that was really brought home when one day she got tired of crossing the cold stream, numbing her feet and stubbing her toes, and decided to spend a day laying rocks against the stream at a shallow place, so she could step from rock to rock without falling in.

A week or so after that, she left a deer at the camp for the other dragons to eat, and took Minth with her to explore. The others had grown a great deal, and Minth was now clearly the weakest of them, but he was far stronger than he had been in a long time, if ever, and

Silmavalien thought he would like having all the time with her to himself. The others, she knew, would be content with each other and the good food.

First, Silmavalien took him to a sequoia grace that they reached shortly before nightfall. They pushed their way through the youngest sequoias, short and somewhat bushy, and then straightened under the tall and slender spires of somewhat older trees, covered in fresh, brilliant green. It seemed to Silmavalien, or maybe to Minth, to be the color of life. The color of joy, peace, contentment. Relationship.

She led him through, on into the center of the grove where the mature sequoias stood, standing like blushing towers, their huge branches bearing scale-like foliage high above the earth. She stopped and looked up in awe that was as strong this evening as it had been the first time she had stopped here on her way back from a hunt, dragging a deer. These trees had given meaning in her mind to the mighty towers and citadels that some of the tales spoke up, and even if the stories were all wrong, the images this grove gave her were powerful and beautiful.

Minth chirped at her and she looked down. Then together they walked across the open space to the hugest tree in the very center, tall, majestic, and beautiful. Silmavalien placed her hand on the soft, rough bark. At Minth's suggestion she turned and looked up at the sky.

It had just been drizzling, but now a glowing apricot color spread across the silver gray as the sun set. Minth bade her watch and only listen, not even think, as the lights changed, and the apricot transformed into an enchanted purple hue.

When the purple faded to violet-gray and then darkness, Silmavalien spread out their blankets on the dry ground under the tree's huge primary branch, and they ate what they had left over from the morning.

S

After that, Silmavalien took Minth out on more adventures, just the two of them. Sometimes they went much farther out, especially as the dragons grew better at hunting for themselves and did not need Silmavalien to return to hunt for them. Together, she and Minth were able to discover things that were new to both of them.

One day they ran into a sort of very steep ridge that ran up to the cliff above. It was steep enough to be almost cliff-like, but looked like it would be fun to climb just because. Silmavalien smiled down at Minth, then clambered up onto the first boulder. She turned around and lay on her stomach to pull Minth up.

There was the small gap between the next rocks, but Minth wanted her to help him so he would be comfortable and not afraid of falling, even though it was really too small for him to fall into. So she stepped across, and then held onto him while he stepped across, and in this way they went on. Sometimes the steps were easier and sometimes they were harder, but altogether it was a fun challenge getting to the crest of the ridge together. There it smoothed out into an almost-plateau, full of grasses and thickly-leafed manzanita hedges.

It looked like a good, high place to see the land from. Silmavalien gathered several bundles of twigs and kindled them. It was a little different getting the manzanita to burn, and the fire that leapt up had a crisp, hot scent. She cooked a rabbit for herself over the flames and enjoyed the view while she ate it. She would have to cook over manzanita again, she decided, as it gave an interesting flavor to the meat.

Then they went back down, and found that it wasn't really any harder than getting up had been. For one thing, it was much easier for her to receive Minth from above her and put him down than to find a way to get him up.

S

The mild winter turned to spring, and sprawling blackberries leafed up and flowered, as did the grape vines that climbed up the trees to impossible heights. Silmavalien rejoiced when she found the first little strawberry, and the spring leaves and bulbs of other plants were a welcome addition to her meals.

The songbirds returned to the mountains. Once more Songeth sang with the winged and feathered singers, and Silmavalien knew no singing dragon would ever eat a bird of song. She delighted to her dragons squawk and sing, and the colors of the birds, the soft ones as much as the bright ones, brought joy to her eyes. She felt she had never enjoyed the world so much before, but it was an enjoyment tainted with regret. The fawns, and even the young rabbits and squirrels, meant as much to her as the songbirds, and she wished they did not have to eat them.

The dragons were learning to hunt better as they grew, but they also needed more food. It seemed to Silmavalien like they were able to get less of the food they needed, not more of it, as the months went on. The days spent wandering with Minth happened less and less, as she had to spend more of her time hunting. Before long, they had to move again so they could hunt more easily, and also so Silmavalien could continue to find enough food for fires. This time found a crack in the cliffs to settle by. Only a small rivulet of water flowed from it, so she did not have a pool anymore, something she thought she might regret once it was warm enough to bathe, unless she found a new one. But it was more than enough water for their needs.

As the months went by, Silmavalien could not wait for the dragons to learn to fly. Wydth and Coroneth were well bigger than she was, and their appetite was enormous. She had no doubt once they learned to fly, it would not be long before they could hunt the large prey they were meant to eat, like deer, much more easily. Besides, it just seemed right. They were still a little awkward looking and ugly, but every day they looked more and more like they were built for the open spaces of the sky. Those places would turn all the ways they were awkward and less than perfect into satisfying beauty, and she could feel the draw of the sky in their hearts.

The rains grew a little warmer with the summer, but it still drizzled as often as not, even pouring once every couple of weeks or so. The darker spring and summer storm-clouds often carried them a beautiful and eerie blue mist that seemed to glow. This side of the Aravin Mountains was turning out to be a very different climate than Silmavalien was used to, but though she found herself longing for more sunshine, and even the hot, dry days of the southern summers, the atmosphere of her life was calm and beauty and content, even when she had too much hunting to do.

The day came when the first of the blackberries began to ripen. Silmavalien gorged herself on them, and decided they tasted better than she could remember anything ever tasting before. She eyed the hopelessly underripe blueberries and grapes with impatience, and only the next day did she notice what her gorging had done to her clothes.

They were wearing out already, though she had not payed attention to that. She had torn the set she had been wearing even further on the thorns – dying them purple with the berry juice was not such a problem. But she could not replace her clothes, and even when she were careful when she could be, they were not going to last forever. Or even much longer, if she did not do anything about it.

The next time Silmavalien hunted a deer, she was careful with the deer skin, which she made into a tunic to wear over her upper clothes, to protect them better. Once it was ready, she carefully cut it to the shape she needed and use the point of her knife to poke holes down either side and lace it with yarn up to the deep V around her neck. She could not help trying to make it beautiful, despite the fact there was no one around to see her except the dragons, who she knew would not care about that sort of thing. Sometimes, she thought she would look as ugly to them as they had looked to her as hatchlings, if they had not thought of her as strong and graceful since they were born.

When it was ready, she decided the shiny, silky, silvery-gray color, dappled with whiter spots, suited her, and that it was probably the prettiest thing she owned. Prettier than the dresses that came up from the plains-kingdoms with the bards.

The next day, Airrock called her out to a boulder near where they were staying to watch. Clearly, Silmavalien sensed her intentions, and she sprang up and ran to the clearing below the boulder. The dragons who were not already there – Veine, Jareth, and Minth – ran alongside her, and knocked her down once or twice.

As soon as her dragon-mother was there to see, Airrock unfurled her wings and raised them high. Silmavalien watched her powerful hindlegs tense, and then she sprang. Her wings swept down, then folded in and rose again. Swept down. For a moment Airrock rose, then dipped.

Silmavalien felt her rapid, frantic struggle not to fall yet. She rose again, briefly, fighting with every inch of her vast wings, tail streaming tensed behind her. Then she swerved to meet the ground, panting.

Excitement soared through the dragons. They all started squawking and squeaking, as Airrock stood, heart racing as it had never raced before, even when she hunted. She took a few moments to catch her breath, then climbed back up the boulder and tried again, determined and not in the least discouraged.

Even such a short flight was a thrill, and she was going to do this.

9

Sin of the Dragonriders

Noren startled, and his arrow flew away. It arched high into the deepening blue vault of an evening sky, with a few stray misty or puffy clouds in it, missing his target entirely. Even his very first shot ever had not been that poor.

He shivered with the force of the cold fear that rushed through him. Somewhere in it he recognized Elninya, and tried to reassure her. Instead, he felt the source of her fear.

Even at the best of times her thoughts were not perfectly clear to him. Now, permeated with panic and fear, they were even more confusing.

Shadows. Black shadows. Shadow-men. Five men that were black shadows. In their hands flashed dark knives. In their minds lurked shadows of evil. Monsters of hate and bitterness, resentment for past wrongs. Self-pity and impenetrable lies. A dark sea of guilt.

He realized what it was he was seeing. He sprang up and wheeled in the direction of the thicket where he had left Elninya, sprinted towards it as fast as he could.

Pain in his side and gasping for breath, Noren plunged under the trees. He heard scuffing, while twigs broke in his breathless rush.

In the twilight under the trees a man in dark clothing lifted the blanket that lay over Elninya. Startled, he cried, "Singo! Mack! It's a dragon!"

Noren yelled inarticulately, a sound of panic.

Elninya rose up, screaming and hissing, every one of her sharp carnivore teeth bared. Noren knocked an arrow, raised his bow, and released.

The man who had lifted the blanket from over Elninya howled, fell writhing.

In an instant Noren had another arrow knocked. His eyes sought another thief. Elninya crouched, her eyes flaming red, her teeth bared, hissing, one paw raised to strike, her tail twitching. Her whole body trembled with violent energy.

The thieves screamed, turned to run. One fell dead. Noren knocked another arrow, sprang after them. He could let no one who knew Elninya lived survive.

He followed them out of the thicket, into the fading daylight, slowly gaining on them. As soon as he could see them clearly, without the trees obstructing his view, he slid to a halt, and shot. In the same moment, the thieves turned.

He knocked and shot another arrow. This time missed. The thieves dashed off to either side. One of them hurled a knife at him, and he had to duck. Another arrow was on the string. This time, he took his time about shooting and did not miss.

The last thief was fast disappearing through the fields in the fading evening lights.

Noren sprinted after him.

As he ran, Noren lamented the fact he had never learned to shoot while moving himself, even if he shot a moving target well enough. He had already lost two arrows that day, and making them right so they flew true took time and effort. The dusk was gathering around him, and he did not try to shoot again. Quickly he grew hot from running, despite the increasing cold. His legs, lungs, and stomach protested.

It had been a long time since he had run down a deer, and now he was chasing a man, not a deer, and it was more urgent. He could not give the man a day, or days, to let others know a dragon lived.

This was not working. He had no guarantee the thief would tire before he did. For both of them, this was a chase that would determine life and death. Only for him it was two lives. For the thief it was one.

Or was it? He felt Elninya in his thoughts, and whether he wanted it or not, she shared with him something only a dragon could know: what one of the thieves thought of always, what kept him going, was hatred of the father who had rejected him, and love for the wife and daughter whom he could barely feed.

Despite himself, Noren wished that he knew more of the thieves' stories than Elninya could gleam, especially since neither of them really understood the workings of the society down here.

Just then, the thief stumbled and fell, in a sort of pit or ditch. Noren showed no mercy. As the thief was rising, Noren knocked an arrow and shot the shadow he could barely see in the darkening light. The shadow fell into the grass or ditch, and without making sure the thief was really dead, Noren turned and made his way back to the shadow blotting out the stars, that was the thicket.

He went to Elninya, stroked her neck and murmured to her for a few moments, then gave her a rabbit. Then he bumbled around in the dark trying to gather wood, and lit a small fire on the other side of the thicket, where he prepared and cooked the rabbits, before laying down with Elninya and pulling the blankets over them. It was chillingly cold.

He slept long and hard, and when he woke it was not pre-dawn, but early morning. He jolted into full awareness at the realization it was so late, then rushed to get the rabbits and share one between himself and Elninya. He was just about to put the other rabbit in the saddlebag when he realized the bag wasn't there!

The thieves must have started running off with it when he had showed up last night. He left the rabbit with Elninya to look for it.

Sure enough he found both saddlebags, and the water-skins, on the edge of the wood with the horse. Poor Evena! She had been saddled up, and the saddlebags and water-skins were hooked to the saddle. Apparently the thieves had just been getting to the bridle; it was left lying in the drenched grass, and the horse was still picketed. Noren picked the bridle up, irreparably damaged, and berated himself for not remembering to check on his horse like he always did.

But it was too late for that. He wiped the bridle as dry as he could, then checked the saddle to make sure it was put on right. It was time to get out of here before a farmer came by.

A few minutes later, he and Elninya were riding down the road again, and Noren found himself wondering about the thief problem.

He suspected no one else ever thought about it. No one else had been changed by a dragon bonded to his soul. No one else *knew* a dragon, who somehow knew everyone with whom she had contact. Not perfectly, not everything, but within a few minutes as well as a friend of years might in the important ways.

ℕ

Twigs snapped. Leaves crunched. Underfoot.

A human form slipped through the trees in the dim pre-dawn light.

A robber. Noren reached for his bow.

Waking, Elninya screamed. *"No!"* she shouted into his mind.

Too late. She had caught him in the act of releasing the string. He could not take it back.

A horrible scream trembled in the air. Racking screams of anger.

Elninya, his dragon, his soul-bonded's, anger poured over him, and Noren wished his arrow had pierced his own arrow. Scalding hot, yet her anger seemed to freeze his soul. It was not hatred, he knew that, knew that nothing was less like hatred, but it was more terrible than any other anger he had ever felt.

This fierce being, capable of this anger at one she loved so much, was much more than 'his darling dragon.' Her thoughts, clearer and more fiery than he had ever felt them before, pounded inside his head. *"Noren! Coward. Murderer. You kill a girl – looking for eggs – because you're afraid to die. It is better to die than to kill the innocent."*

His anger rose to meet hers, though he could tell that she was hurt, not only because of the girl's pain and death – and that must be agony to her, too – but because it was painful for her to be angry with someone so close to her. Maybe as painful as it was for her. She stood in front, her teeth bared, looking fierce and terrible despite her helpless ugliness.

And he actually yelled at her. "Elninya, you know what happens if we are discovered! They'll burn us." He summoned all his imagination, to try to show her how horrible that would be.

Though the effort unnerved him, it did not move Elninya. Strange thoughts and feelings flowed from her, dispersing the horror. She seemed to mock him. *"So? It is fitting for a dragon to die by fire!"*

Whatever she was trying to communicate, whatever she shared about her understanding of death, it was so far from him he could not understand it at all. Her response seemed to be a retort, or rebuking. *"Well, why do you think your life – or mine – matters more than hers? Do you know that she is in agony now?"*

Elninya poured upon him the girl's pain, mental, emotional, and physical, as well as he could. He cringed and fell to his knees sobbing. For the first time trying to hide his thoughts from Elninya, he thought, *I am not ready to die. And I cannot bear to lose you.*

It did not work. Mentally, Elninya flew at him. *"Coward. You are afraid. Afraid of death, and of loneliness."* Something more he did not hear. Maybe that was not what she said, but how he heard it.

But it was true. He could not deny it, and it strung him to that core. In that moment, he knew why he *would not!* die. Never could he make his life, or himself, as he should. What was it that made him value himself and Elninya above everyone else? What had made him think himself brave and kind? Why did he fear their deaths so much?

He was a great coward. He could no longer deny it. But what was he to do? Where was he to go? He had no contentment that could not be taken from him, no matter what. Insecurity bred fear, and fear evil. What could give him security? To be without evil?

Elninya withdrew from him, to give both of them a relief from the pain they were to each other. He collapsed in melancholy thought.

He wondered first at the clarity and forcefulness of Elninya's thoughts. Not a month and a half ago she had been an infant, able only to comprehend what an infant can – love and sweetness and need and satisfaction. Her thoughts were all affectionate and mild, even hazy.

He hated how independent of him she now was, and yet how close. Her ferocity and strength startled him. He could not comprehend how one person, so dear and sweet, so unfathomably close, could be so fierce, capable of such anger, and strong enough to be angry with the one who was so close to her, who felt her anger so keenly, whose pain she also felt.

She might understand him, but he did not understand her – or himself. It was unnerving.

Briefly touched his mind, and the pain of her anger sharpened for a moment. *"I do not understand you."*

That was hardly a comfort.

She withdrew again, but they could still feel one another and the agony that meant. Noren felt that there was no escape. Elninya was pain to him, yet he could not live without her.

"You can."

Noren shook his head. He could not decide what the voice sounded like, or where it came from, or even how loud it was. It must be a figment of his own imagination. He ignored it, and went on thinking.

Suddenly, thoughts formed themselves in his mind, and whether they were his or Elninya's he did not know. *This is why the Dragonriders are hated so. This is the sin of the Dragonriders. Afraid to be killed, they kill anyone who just might reveal them, and are hated the more.*

Noren rose, to make preparations for leaving the place as early as possible. Elninya, sensing what he was doing, touched him again. *"You must tell them."*

It was beginning to get light now, and Noren almost danced and screamed with his own frustration and rage. *Elninya! I can't! And besides, that's like saying, 'Here I am. Please kill me.'*

"They have a right to know." Elninya's voice was quiet and still, as unmovable as the very mountains. He dared not argue with her. She

was stronger than he was, and he could not bear her anger.

Noren hunted through his saddlebag, for the piece of paper the dried fruit had been wrapped in. Though he hated it, he wrote what Elninya told him to, and stuck it on a twig on the edge of the little wood. It read:

"Here I, Noren, a Dragonrider, killed your daughter."

He stared at it, hating it so much, yet not daring to challenge Elninya, then added.

"I'm sorry. I hate that I did it."

The words did not help much. The message bothered him only less than Elninya's anger. He hated it, and again he felt he would rather die. It was the greatest insult to his pride that he could imagine, and the stupidest thing to do, too. Elninya spoke to him, and he realized that, despite her anger, she loved him as much as he could imagine.

Nonetheless, she hurt him again. He could not help but hear her response, though again he did not know if it was really her that he heard, or only what he could make of what she said: *"Good. Your pride must die."*

Once again, she baffled him. She was harsh and unyielding. Yet she felt his pain, even when she did not understand it, and had sympathy for him. He knew she wanted him not to hurt. He even knew she was doing this because she wanted him not to hurt. Because she knew his fear was hurting him and wanted to help him past that.

And, for himself, if he felt he would rather die that pin that message there, certainly he would rather die than have this anger between himself and Elninya.

He went to tack up Evena, and as he was finishing, he asked Elninya *Will you forgive me?*

Her reply only confused him more. *"How could your darling dragon not forgive you? O Noren, my love, I can never forgive you, for I can never hate you, or hold anything against you. But I hate your fear and your action, and I shall forever. And ever I shall work in him for your cleansing, no matter the cost to either of us."*

The last sentence was total nonsense to Noren, and he felt the clarity and fire fading from her thoughts.

Can't you just go back to being a hatchling?

She was in the saddlebag now, and Noren had one foot in Evena's stirrup. He was about to mount her. This time Elninya did not even bother to try to articulate for him. She was completely exhausted, and could hardly keep awake a moment longer. She growled a negative.

10
Caref

After that morning, things between Noren and Elninya were never the same. Neither of them could change what had happened, and Noren got the idea only he wanted to do so. Elninya wished he had not killed the girl, but it was better that he know what he could do, than live in the illusion that he was brave and kind.

She was still his darling, yet even when they cuddled the shadow of what had happened, both Elninya's anger and Noren's shame, came between them, changing their relationship and not for the better. Noren did not know what to do with himself, so he tried to make excuses of different sorts, even if they were only reasons Elninya were no better. But none of the excuses satisfied him, and telling himself why Elninya was not any better tore at him, too.

Elninya sometimes shot his excuses to bits, too, and Noren could not help but hear her. The way they were bonded did not allow either of them to ignore the other if they were determined to be heard. But he withdrew from Elninya as much as he could, trying to keep his thoughts from her so she would be less able to attack his excuses. None of it made him any happier, and she felt dejected and sad too.

At one point, she told him that if he would simply accept his guilt, accept that he had done wrong and want to be different, he could live and love with her like before.

But he could not live with his failure!

𝒩

By noon, Noren had realized that his name was now a danger, in and of itself. He had declared that he was a Dragonrider and murderer, and the first was worse than the latter even if it had stone alone. He would have to come up with another name to go by.

He sensed disapproval from Elninya, even though she did not speak to me. Minutes went by, before he thought at her angrily, *Well then, what* would *you have me to do?*

Elninya's reply upset him even more.

What?! Walk right up to them and say 'Here I am. I'm an honest Dragonrider so I just asked you to kill me, instead of making you work at it'?! Or run away and abandon Silmavalien?

Noren had some difficulty in keeping from shouting out loud, even though Elninya had not gotten angry. She did not shift at all.

He had no idea where Silmavalien was, and it was not *abandonment* not to find her. He had never promised to find her, and it was not obvious that it would be better for her. As for being a Dragonrider, that was not wrong. It was being a murderer.

Noren's mind went through dozens of angry arguments, but though Elninya must have known them all, he did not present them to her. Instead, he said, *You would die with me! You are one of the last dragons, and you certainly should not die, for you did no wrong.*

Something that he could make no sense of passed from her to him. It seemed like pure confusion. He knew she was saying something about death and life and ending and beginning and what matters and what is real. But whatever it was to her, to him it was sheer nonsense, like saying that tree leaves ate fire or that goats were incinerated roots – only even more nonsensical, even less comprehensible. He could not even know that it was false, for it was simply nonsense. It seemed like a contradiction in itself, and he could understand no more.

I think I have a more accurate idea of what death means.

To Noren's absolute surprise, Elninya responded. He did not have an idea of death at all. He had an idea of dying, and an idea of wrongness, mixed up together with an idea of nobility.

Noren told her that the conversation was over. They were getting nowhere. He would be Caref to all but her, for the moment. She accepted his decision – it was his to make – but he could still feel her displeasure, even though he knew she was not trying to make him feel it.

The third morning after the dreadful day, they rode into Kranah.

This city, the central city of Silrah, was not like Delenois. It was surrounded by a high rampart that seemed to be carved out of one stone and towered up above him like the highest cliffs of the mountains. Even higher towers looked down from their heights, and in the center of the city rose a citadel higher still but carved out of the same stone.

From its highest spire flew the flag of the kingdom of Silrah, fluttering in the breeze.

Noren gasped as he saw it spread out in the wind. The winged creature on the flag was a dragon. A crimson dragon with folded wings, perched like a hawk on a branch, and surrounded by a violet crown, a crown the color of the end of the rainbow. Both dragon and crown showed strikingly against the cerulean blue background that must surely represent the sky. Just as bright against the blue showed the frame of the flag: spring green and textured to look like scales.

 He recognized the flag. More than one bard had described it to the people of Treas, even though none of them had ever seen it. But he had never dreamed that the winged creature was a dragon. A dragon on the flag of a kingdom that persecuted dragons, and no one noticed!

From the second highest spire flew a flag bearing a red mountain on an emerald background. The flag of the province of Tali, which included Treas.

Noren took Elninya into the city in the saddlebag. As with Delenois, guards monitored the coming and going of people. When asked, he told them that his name was Caref.

Noren soon learned that it was well that he had done so. The hottest news in the city was of himself. Apparently, a rider had carried the news to Kranah ahead of him. Already everyone was talking about a Dragonrider named Noren, though some people though his name was Norn, and others that it was Ren.

Noren asked another man, who seemed friendly and talkative, about his 'sister', and once they talked about all the Silmavaliens the man knew of, he asked Noren, "Have you heard of Noren?"

Noren tried to express interest, and did his hardest best to look undisturbed. "No. What about him?"

"He's a Dragonrider, Caref. And a powerful one. So powerful in fact that he kills people in front of their families, and announces who he is. He is probably the most powerful of the Dragonriders. And his dragon eats people. Whole families!"

Noren wanted to laugh. Him? Powerful? Not really. And not only was Elninya far too small to eat people, but she would rather die. The whole situation made Noren itch to get out of Kranah. Not only was it disturbing and aggravating, in and of itself, but it made him upset at Elninya – whose fault it was, in this scenario. Not that it was not his fault, too. But he could not bear to think about that. That was another reason the stories bothered him. They reminded him of what he had done, and had no certainty that he could not do again.

Instead of laughing, Noren quickly said, "How horrible."

The man agreed. "Given how the Dragonriders behave, coupled with how powerful they are, and how dreadful the curses of dark magic, it's a good thing we have all those laws about them."

This made Noren's stomach turn. "Perhaps," said he, knowing that he meant the exact opposite, and wishing he could say it.

"Then say it."

And die? No, returned Noren. Meanwhile, the man asked, "Then you think otherwise?"

"I don't know," Noren lied again. *Time to get out of here.* "Anyway, it's time for me to move on."

"Goodbye. Take care."

"You too."

He went on to follow the same tactic he had in Delenois to search for Silmavalien, except now he was asking after his sister. He had little hope of finding her here, for it seemed unlikely that Silmavalien would live in such a fortress-city as this, especially when it was surrounded by farms and fields, and far from any forests or mountains. In fact, how would she even get this far undiscovered if she tried, alone and on foot and probably with a larger dragon?

Nonetheless, for some reason, he looked her for here, even though he really did not want to be here. As he talked to more and more people, he grew more angry with Elninya for what she had made him do, and more uncomfortable in Kranah. The stories told about him everywhere. Everyone was talking about him, and they were already more rumor than fact, as well as there about twenty different versions.

In addition to the one he had already heard, there were a few main variations. In one, a man with arrows walked into a farmhouse and shot a girl who was cooking eggs. He then announced that he was Noren the Dragonrider and flew away on his dragon. In another, Noren had shot the girl while walking through a small wood, and then gone to announce to her parents who he was and what he had done.

But though there were many stories, on one thing everyone agreed: he had announced what he had done and his identity. On another thing, almost everyone agreed: he had killed at least one girl.

There were equally numerous explanations as to why he had done it. His purpose was to intimidate. Any maiden a Witch-Dragonrider killed would be his in the afterlife, and he had 'loved' the girl. The girl was born to become a heroine and demon-hunter, or to give birth to one.

He could not endure listening to the things said about him. He was so ashamed that he had killed the girl, and it was even worse that he and Elninya had reinforced the fear people had of Dragonriders. As the day went on it got harder and harder to control his expression and tone of voice so he would not give himself away. Even suggesting that a Dragonrider might not be a witch, or that a dragon might not be a demon, was an offense punishable by lashes or death.

It was cruel and, had he believed in demons, Noren would have believed this was their work. He itched to challenge the people to think about the dragons on their own, to think for themselves. The flag, with its obvious dragon, was an ever-present reminder, even when for a moment he was not being forced to hear the rumors. Should the people not know that their flag bore a dragon?

Elninya shivered almost constantly, but at least the constant jostling of the saddlebags by the press of people hid her trembling, whenever Evena was standing still so her motion would not hide it. When Noren touched her mind, or her fear touched his, he could not help realizing that her fear was different from his. Her fear was not choice, action, intention. Attitude. And if he were really brave, he would be able to suffer her fear, without fear being his intention.

Before he left Kranah, Noren found a map shop and used the rest of his money to buy a map of the kingdom that he could use to track his search for Silmavalien. He quickly marked it, and then left the shop. For the hundredth time that day what sounded like her name pulled him up straight, but it was only a mother talking to her child named Mavalien.

Noren headed out of the city directly after that. He told the guard he had a friend further down the road to bed him up, and he wanted to get there by dinnertime. The guards told him to be careful about himself. He turned his face and rode on, unable to conceal his laughter. Even before the laughter lines faded from his face, he thought grimly, *Little does he know how truly he spoke.*

That night he stayed in a thicket a way out of the city, and then the next day he rode away north, towards the mountains again.

Elninya was about to get too big to fit in the saddlebag, period, and she could not fly. He thought that he had enough time – or perhaps one should say space – to ride out of the densely populated areas and get into the foothills of the Great Aravin Mountains before Elninya could not be hidden in the saddlebag anymore.

11

The Nightmare and the Bow

It was lovely to see thickly forested hills and mountains again. The hills were still small compared to those among which Treas was nestled, and there were no conifers, only oak trees and a few other deciduous trees. Nonetheless, they were riding in amongst the feet of the mountains, and it was good. Noren dismounted Evena, and let Elninya out of the saddlebag in which she was painfully cramped. They were still on a path, and it was possible they might encounter someone, so he walked on the edge of the path, leading Evena by the reins. Elninya walked on the outside, where she could disappear into the trees if anyone came by.

Noren had never seen or felt her so happy and excited since she had hatched. It was with glee that she tread in grass and oak leaves and scratched herself on bark. She reveled in the freedom which the solitude provided. She felt like she was already soaring through the sky, high above the earth, and it flowed over from her to Noren. He stepped lighter than he had in weeks.

Outcroppings of rock rose up. With every mile they went, it looked and felt more like his home – to which he might never return. But he liked it.

They veered off the path and spent the night against a south-facing boulder that held up a hill much taller than Noren. The next day it rained, and he went hunting. For the first time in many months, he hunted deer, and for the first time ever he spent the night away from Elninya. It was still drizzling when he brought the deer back early the next day, though it cleared up enough for Noren to start cooking the deer after Elninya gorged herself on her portion.

Noren kept the hide of the deer inside the saddlebag that had been Elninya's, hoping to sell it later. While traveling they still kept to the path. Noren wanted to make sure Silmavalien was not in Zyel, a large foothills village he had heard about that might be perfect. He also wanted to see if he could get anything for his deer-hide there, since he would only be able to collect so many.

They camped far from the path, and otherwise Noren did not worry about being found. If he did not want to find the only other Dragonrider he knew of, he would never return to civilization. He could live quite comfortably in the mountains for the rest of his life with

Elninya, and presently that life was far more peaceful than it had been for a very long time. They still needed to get higher into the mountains to be really safe, since all the myths spoke of an evil in the mountains, a demon-god, and the fear of it kept people from climbing from much higher than the foothills, or at least staying there.

But even so, there was little chance of being found here, and they could travel at a leisurely pace. The nights were colder than they were on the plains already, but it was also easier to find better shelter, and Noren was not in a hurry to go higher where they would be even colder, though he thought next winter Elninya would be large enough that it would not be a problem. He doubted the cold would bother a fire-breathing dragon, and she would easily keep him warm even on the coldest night.

One evening the smells of a meal being prepared wafted to them on an evening breeze, and Noren realized they were closer to Zyel than he really wanted to be except to visit. They backtracked a little, until they found a good place to spend the night, and Noren used the lingering dusk to gather wood for a fire. Then he and Elninya huddled close together under an evergreen oak, and watched the beautiful, twinkling stars wheel through the patch of sky visible from where they lay.

All the sky looked to be flecked with stardust, and a wavy band of diffused starlight, with a couple dark spots, crossed the sky. Myriads of stars filled the night, some very bright, others dimmer, and low in the southern sky hung a cluster of stars, neither too dim and bright. A diffused blue light surrounded the spectacle of breath-taking beauty, and Noren aimlessly wondered what the constellation was supposed to represent, since he had forgotten.

N

In the morning, Noren did not go to Zyel, but out hunting. He brought back a deer, and a few days later he went to the town, using the name Caref in case bards had already carried the rumors this far, and sold the deer skins for a fraction of the price they would get in one of the plains cities. Probably, the people would sell the deer skins to one of the bards, or send a merchant down themselves, for far, far more than he had gotten. But it was still good for him. He asked around for Silmavalien, and the people seemed to think he was weird, but the village was small enough he was able to be quite confident she was not there.

It was dark, but light still lingered in the west when he returned to Elninya. The next day, they journeyed further up, into the mountains, leaving the path totally behind. They traveled a few days further, and then Noren decided to try to spend the winter at about that height. Not much further up there would be a lot more snow, and the cold would be more of a nuisance.

𝒩

Noren did not know whether he was paralyzed by fear, or afraid because he was paralyzed. A stench of panic and death filled the air. *Move! Move! Move!* he screamed at his arms and legs. Then, somehow, his thoughts turned to Elninya. Her courage, her strength, her love. Everything that she was, whether he knew and understood it, or neither knew nor understood it, whether he hated it or loved it. Without thinking, he raised his bow, knocked an arrow, and drew it.

A huge, bowed and twisted shadow sprang across the meadow. Noren froze with mysterious panic. His thoughts turned mush. Fear melted his mind, so that he did not know what he was afraid of. He did not even know *that* he was afraid. Fear itself consumed his whole mind, leaving no room for *him*. Just sheer terror, terror beyond comprehension.

A bow twanged, shattering the darkness. He knew it was a bow, but the sound was like no bow he had ever heard. It was more a music that was like bow-stings, rather than a bow-string that was like music. It was beautiful, but even that word, even that thought, felt inadequate and misleading. It was the sound of stars and starlight, and not of anything that is of earth. It was neither masculine nor feminine, neither soft nor hard nor sharp, neither mild nor stinging, neither glassy nor misty, neither sweet nor rough. It was a musical twang.

A streak of light shot through the darkness. It was like a shooting star, except that it was not across the night sky. It was across a forest glade in the evening.

In its light he saw something ugly and terrible. Before he could see more, he had released his bow-string. It twanged too, a boring, vulgar sound against the first, which still rang in the air. In that split second before his arrow pierced the monster and it fell, he saw it.

It was large and lumpy. It had small yellow eyes with an evil gleam in them, fangs, and green skin. Its face was a disgusting mockery of the human face as was its whole form. Its shoulders and arms were much too long for it, and seemed to be twisted, almost as if out of joint. Somehow, even in that terror, Noren recognized it, out of the myths he had not believed: an orc.

Terror filled him again, as more of these nightmare monsters than he could count slipped out of the trees and surrounded him. Their presence seemed to fill the glade, which ought to have been mildly and beautifully filled with evening light, steeping it in an impenetrable blackness deeper than a misty night without the moon. He screamed *"No!"* and his knees bucked. Blackness smothered his mind.

Then the musical twang played in the air again.

Lines of light streaked across his vision, and the repeated musical twang hurt his ears in a way that was almost pleasant.

The orcs screamed and howled, and the cacophony of their voices rubbed his ears raw in a most unpleasant way, like screeching metal. A blackness of terror enveloped him again. An orc stepped on his back, his muscles screamed in protest. Another fell on him. A knife scratched his shoulder, and another his ribcage.

Then came a moment of blessed relief. The blackness and terror were gone, leaving a clarity in his mind which he had always before taken for granted. Only now did he appreciate it, knowing that it could be lost, at least temporarily. His muscles trembled violently, and his back felt bruised. The scratches on his shoulder and side stung and bled, but his shoulder hurt more.

None of it compared to how deeply disturbed he was.

How much or which parts of the myths might be true he could no longer even guess at. It was more complicated than he had ever expected.

Orcs and dragons both were, but orcs and dragons were not in league. Or at least not all of them. He shivered. Monsters of nightmare indeed! And who knew of him and had saved him? Certainly not a mere man. The musical bow with its arrows of light told of someone at least like the gods and goddesses.

Noren opened his eyes and stood. Perhaps twenty orcs lay dead around him, and a few more on the edges of the clearing. Of all the arrows, only his remained. He stooped to pick it up and cleaned it on the grass. Then he hurried to Elninya with the last of the fading light.

He sat down with her in his arms, slowly chewing venison more for the action of chewing than to eat. Question after question raced through his mind. Why were the myths right about orcs and evil in the mountains, and so wrong about dragons and Dragonriders? Why did a people who hated dragons tolerate a dragon on their flag? Was it all a scheme of the Big Demon – maybe his name was Dragnor, Maalok, or Satein, maybe it was not – to keep the human race as slaves? What did he get from it? Were most people just stupid? Who had helped him and why?

He thought of no answers, no explanations. Finally, tired from the fright, he went to sleep, but the sense of his whole world, and even his sense of self, being disturbed haunted his sleep. Life could never be the same after it. Where he thought he was safe, he had found himself in danger just as great, and there was nothing he could do about it. This new sense of helplessness, of being completely at the mercy of someone else, was unendurable, and he did not know whether it made it better or worse that he did not know who that someone else was, or if it even mattered.

However, there was nothing to be done about it. So he tried to go on living life as he had before, as best as he could. He tied deer skins together to make a better top blanket, and tried to find as many ways as possible to enjoy the world with Elninya. When it snowed, he tried to build a snowman and a snowdragon, but since he only remembered seeing one real snow in his life, he did not really know what he was doing. The snowman and dragon did not stick together, and mostly all he got for his efforts were cold, burning hands. But though the snow was cold and Noren wished it would go away, the white landscape was beautiful, glimmering under the frosty stars.

Winter slowly passed and turned to spring, and he and Elninya spent most of their time together, playing or exploring, or just sitting together. She grew as quickly as ever, and before her wings even looked like she might be ready to fly, he could hardly pick her up.

The blue flowers of spring appeared, and Noren started to supplement their diet with bulbs, and that was when he realized Silmavalien might be beyond his reach – except through sheer luck. Her dragon was significantly older than Elninya, and once he or she could fly and hunt, why would they remain in the obvious danger of civilization?

Obvious, because the wilderness was dangerous, too, and he could not forget the nightmare creatures, or his mysterious defenders, if that was what they were. More than once, he was startled or wakened by the musical twang, and at night sometimes he saw the bright streak of the arrows of light.

12
Minth Flies

Every day Airrock flew better and longer than the day before, and in about a week she was staying in the air for a good hour at once. She loved to fly so much that Silmavalien imagined it might not be long before it was hard to get her out of the sky.

Then she hunted her first deer and dropped it at their camp. Silmavalien rushed to her and gave her a hug, and Airrock straightened under her arms with pride and pleasure. She was a good flier, a good hunter, a good dragon! She had brought back food – like Silmavalien!

It really meant a lot. Silmavalien had begun to be afraid that she would be unable to hunt nearly enough for the dragons long before they could hunt for themselves. Now Airrock would be able to help her with that, but she also realized Airrock was going to be flying further and further from now on, and she was not a cautious dragon, even if she remembered the Fire Shadow, so Silmavalien made sure to remind all the dragons about staying away from the abyss or soaring above it.

They were all trying to fly now, though none of them learned as fast as Airrock, even the ones who were older than she was. She often tried to help them, showing them how or telling them what she thought they should do, especially if they asked. Watching it amused Silmavalien, and she was glad the first one to learn to fly had been Airrock, not Coroneth. She might sometimes be pushy where she was not wanted, but she was nothing like the way Coroneth had been, and when Silmavalien pointed out to her that her wings were shaped differently than most of the others and she needed to take that into account, she was graceful about it. Silmavalien knew Coroneth would have argued, and would never have left people alone to try by themselves unless he was forced.

But she was a little about Minth. A month or two passed, and all the others learned to fly except for Jareth and Daurth, who were the youngest. But Minth could not fly, even though his wings looked developed enough to fly, though upon closer consideration she realized they were not yet as big as some of the others'.

One afternoon, the two of them were walking along the cliff edge. It was a pleasantly warm autumn day, and the ground was wet from last night's drizzle. They enjoyed the view and the afternoon sun, which would vanish behind one of the cliff-like ridges all too soon. There was not enough sun here, thought Silmavalien, though it was nice for the albino dragons to be in the shadows of the mountains so often.

Suddenly, pine needles and dirt slid off the rock, carrying Minth with them, over the edge. Next moment, Silmavalien was lying flat, reaching over the edge. "Minth!"

Minth was already twenty feet below her. He had managed to unfurl his wings, and she felt the effort as he struggled to fly. He was falling slower now, but he was still falling.

Silmavalien closed her eyes. Fear no longer flowed through the two of them. This was a challenge. They must learn to soar.

She felt the air under his wings. She felt him strain to lift himself. She felt as clueless as he did. She did not know how to fly.

Minth swept his wings down. Folded them in slightly, raised them, unfolded them again, swept them down. What Airrock made look effortless and natural took intense concentration. Silmavalien stepped in to help, learning from everything he learned, helping him concentrate on what to do, while he fought. It took so much strength, and it was hard for him to focus on getting the motions right. Slowly, he started to rise. Together, they flew. Barely.

At last Silmavalien sat up, away from the cliff-edge. It would not help for her to fall, too. She looked up, and there was Minth, a little above her, hovering over empty space. And he was flying almost on his own. He wobbled a bit, but he was doing it.

The wonder of it swept her away. *They were flying!* This was what they were meant to be! This was what it was to be a dragon! *Up, up!* she urged him, and like a miracle they flew.

Air rushed past, under their shared wings. The earth slowly fell away before. His wings and shoulders burned, but the flight seemed timeless. A moment, and forever.

At last, Minth could fly no longer. He glided wearily down. Almost tore his wing on a pine and barely pulled it in, in time. Struggled to rebalance before landing. Struck the ground with a jolt, and fire bloomed in his joints as the force rippled through them.

Silmavalien dashed to his side. Tenderly she stroked his wing, unfolded and lying limp upon the ground. When he asked, she helped him move it. She felt the burning soreness in his muscles and joints. One of his shoulders was badly strained, as were several wing joints.

When Minth was sufficiently recovered to limp around, the two of them returned to their camp. He did not care for dinner that night, and Silmavalien took several blankets and slept next to him. He spread his better wing over her like a tent. He was now almost as big as she was.

"Minth," Silmavalien whispered out loud. "You aren't a little baby anymore."

No, he was not little. That was strange. Maybe he was not a baby anymore, but he was still a child.

You're pretty big for a child. Soon you'll be bigger than me.

Yea, that was true. Was it not nice?

It would be awful if I had to feed you. You eat so... much. I like your wing, except that it hurts.

She would like his wing even better. And soon it would not hurt...

Yes, you can fly now. That's so cool.

Not really. He could *not* fly now.

Okay. You flew. You know how to fly.

At that a warm glow of satisfaction filled Minth. He flew!

In the morning, he was even more stiff and sore and could hardly move his wings. Even if he could have, the pain in his shoulder was enough to keep him from moving more than he had to. Silmavalien went out to hunt, and Veine kept her company.

The purple-necked dragon flew around or ahead of her, only occasionally landing to walk beside her for a few minutes. Once she landed on the bough of a large sequoia, and Silmavalien had to stop admire the view for a minute. Veine was so beautiful up in the tree like that, and Silmavalien realized there was something bird-like about her, and yet she was not bird-like. Yet somehow she also seemed both like and unlike a cat, and like and unlike a wolf. There was something, Silmavalien thought, about all the dragons – not just Veine – that was like every animal she knew, and yet the dragons were not like any of the animals. In every one of them, it was a little different, but it was there. An inner fire, a soaring freedom, that was like that of the bids, but more deliberate. A wildness that were purposeful and cultivated, without being any less wild. A ferocity that was instead a directness, a darting or diving of every thought, every motion, every emotion, a single-minded fire.

And yet none of the dragons thought in words, or even comprehended words or numbers. Their thoughts were all something like emotion, feeling that had form and shape and color. Something truer than words, or a truth of which words could not know, but which could only be communicated dimly through form and color and song.

S

The next day, though Minth was still sore, he wanted to try to fly again, even though he could hardly walk on his hurt shoulder. But he did not really need his front legs much for taking off, and what really troubled him was a strained hip.

Finally, he got into the air, but his wings were so sore he could fly for a minute or two, before he had to land, which hurt even worse.

Silmavalien wished she could do something about both his pain and his frustration. She could feel that need to fly again throbbing as painfully as his sore joints, and she sat next to him afterwards and sang their bonding song again.

> How I want to fly with you
> In the sweet earth amidst sky
> And fly
> In the starlight too

Powerless on earth we lie
Helpless cry to one above
Whose love
Draws us close and high

A thought from Minth; why had they forgotten the Lord of the Light? When had they thanked him for the peace and home they had been enjoying these last months?

Silmavalien's hands flew to her head. They hadn't since ... she had forgotten.

Minth called the rest of the dragons to them, and they all gathered together to thank the Lord of the Light and to ask him to keep taking care of and protecting them.

S

It was five days before Minth dared to fly again, but both he and Silmavalien were surprised at how much stronger he was already. He flew until his wings burned, climbing and dipping, circling and soaring and gliding. He flew until he did not feel awkward in the air anymore, even though he was hindered by his sore muscles, while the other dragons kept their distance, letting him and Silmavalien figure this out together.

When he finally landed, even his tail ached. But flight was just a thrill, and he reveled in using his new ability to the utmost. He lay flat for a while, satisfied but utterly exhausted, and then his stomach clenched. *Hungry.*

Veine, who had come over after he landed, squawked at him. Something about his stomach and eating.

That was when Silmavalien that dragons did have a sort of vocal language. It had no words, but it involved diverse tones that seemed to be related to each in other in a way like music. There were syllables, too, though she could not pronounce them and she knew they were not words, but more like a different dimension of music, that the dragons used to communicate certain things that did not need the mental touch.

Over the next few weeks after this realization, she also realized why it had taken her so long to notice. Minth's communication was very elementary. He rarely responded to any of the dragons, except with an exclamation of frustration which Silmavalien eventually learned to mimic. It was something like *hwumf-whergle-hwuh-whumf.*

She decided not to worry too much about it, because it was what it was. Minth had never been the healthiest or strongest dragon, and she did not know if the way he had been raised was the reason or not, but he was getting stronger, not sicker. And he enjoyed flying so very much, sometimes alone and sometimes with the other dragons.

Often, she would stand hear the edge of the cliff – though since Minth fell off she tried to keep a little more distance between the edge most of the time – and watch her dragon-friends soaring far below. Once Minth even glided all the way down to the sea. It was the first time any of them had ever seen the sea, and he lay down on the warm sand and shared everything about it that he could with Silmavalien. How it was always rumbling and growling, and foaming at the mouth, and always lunging up and out, to see how far it could get. It was an angry monster, restless in its imprisoning den. The monster of the deep.

It's scary?

Certainly the sea was scary, but it did not bite. Last time it lunged – which it did all the time – his tail got in it. It did not feel like other water. It was almost hot by comparison, and strangely stingy.

Probably because it's angry, she commented.

The flight back up, after rolling in the sand, was much harder than the lovely, refreshing glide down. But it was still a thrill of wonder and delight. He told Silmavalien that the sea air was thick and stifling. It made it harder to breathe, and by extension, to fly.

A few days later, Airrock apparently felt the need to fly up to the snow-capped peaks. Yet long before she got there, the air grew so thin that she struggled to breathe and could climb no higher. Silmavalien reassured her, her flying was already quite remarkable, and after grumbling a bit she settled. She just really wanted to fly up there!

Silmavalien smiled, happy that Airrock was who she was. As much as she loved flying, there did not seem to be anything competitive about her at all.

The next day she and Minth went hunting together.

13

The Demons Stir

The hall of the Nightmare Lord dripped with a horrible light that had turned to darkness. In the center was a throne lit with a horrid fire that surrounded the Nightmare Lord.

A remnant of an ancient dignity, a majesty from long ago, hung about him, the shadow of what he was. A shadow that was truly darkness, for the light of heaven that dwelt in his eyes was becoming a blackness deeper than a starless night. It was not a lack of light, but a corruption of light, and his beauty had become horrible.

A small demon, with bones of shadow about which licked an evil fire, something that might look like a lesser version of the Fire Shadow, stood before the Nightmare Lord. A voice that was like the light, containing hints of a past glory but turned to horror and terror, spoke. "What is it now?"

"Very bad news. Dragons have been sighted in the airs over the Steep Descent."

A shudder passed through the hall, and the darkness of corrupted light shifted subtly. "How many? What age?"

"Five, though more than three have never been seen at once. They appear to be young. One is teal, one is silver, one is white with a purple neck, and two are white."

Five dragons. The last time there had been five dragons alive, let alone five dragons together, was more than a century ago. What had happened that five dragons should be raised together without the nightmare, which was everywhere, finding out?

It must have to do with the ever-active Ellenari.

"What gender are they?"

"The white dragons are certainly male. The teal dragon appears to be a female. The others are unknown."

A female dragon? The last female dragon had died more than fifty years ago, and the curse had been specifically designed to kill female dragons before they could hatch. It had also been designed to make all the dragons defective, and one of the first things it caused was albinism.

How had it become so ineffective that certain eggs were passing through it untouched? How hated the complexities of creation!

"Where in the Steep Descent are they?"

"The north shore, east of the plains of Arosië."

"Do they have riders?"

That was unknown. Ellenari were always about. Avoiding them was hard enough, without trying to go precisely where they did not want one to go.

Forces of greater power must be sent to destroy these young dragons.

𝑺

Silmavalien looked up from under Minth's wing. A terrible figure commanded her attention, which she somehow to be feminine. Tall this lady stood, but she could have been eight feet tall or twenty feet all. She had the appearance of stone, and a green snake wound itself up her body. When it reached her shoulders it split, and its two heads rested on her head, the forked tongue flicking in and out. Her ears were long and tapered, even more so than those of a fox, and her hair looked like a thousand snakes of stone in every color. Her slanted eyebrows were light green, and the light in her eyes was both attractive and frightening. She reminded Silmavalien of Aelaza, and yet there was something totally different about her.

Silmavalien shivered, and forced herself to look away from those eyes....

"Why will you not look into my eyes?" The thought of a voice – or else the voice of a thought – so soft and smooth, yet somehow stony.

Silmavalien spoke out loud. "Who are you?"

The shape was that of a goddess, but she was not sure she liked this goddess. Nor did she know any god or goddesses. Not even the Lord of the Light.

Minth tightened his wing over her, and she felt him cry, *No!*

Even the stone-goddess recoiled at his protest. Fire leapt from her eyes.

Silmavalien grabbed her hunting knife, and scrambled out from under Minth's wing. "Lord of all light!" she cried, holding up the hand that bore the ring of light, with the knife in it. She fancied that she saw a ripple of light pass through the blade, as though it were water. Minth rose to his feet and roared.

The stone-goddess seemed to rush upon them. She was like a dryad turned to stone yet not frozen. Perhaps only a dryad turning into stone. She was her own queen, and would never have another. The dark beauty that was all around her drew Silmavalien, binding her more strongly than before.

"Come. Be like me."

Silmavalien stared, open-mouthed. She could not move. To be a queen? All she wanted and feared passed through her mind. The ring on her hand seemed to burn her. She felt Minth reaching out to her, but was unable to respond.

Then she saw Aelaza between her and the stone-goddess, like a star beneath a mountain, but she did not know how she knew the star was Aelaza. Only the whole thing seemed wrong. The mountain should have been beneath the star, or else the star should have been beneath a greater light. Why did Aelaza not leap up this stone cliff, just like any other?

Why was Aelaza a star, and this thing a mountain of darkness? Why could she not leap up it, this time? Then, like a whisper, came the thought, *She's there for me,* and then, *What am I supposed to do?*

Silmavalien saw Airrock fly in the face of the medusa, only to freeze mid air and crash to the earth.

"When you try to rule you freeze. The only way to be able to fight her is unconditional surrender to the King." Silmavalien did not know if it was a dragon or Aelaza who spoke.

I cannot. I simply can never say, 'I am thine. Do whatever you want with me.'

"What else would you have? 'I reserve the right to affect me to myself?' That is a prison."

I cannot bear what another could do to me. There may be things I cannot accept! Things that must never happen to me or Minth or –

"Can you accept starvation because you reserve the right to feed you to yourself?"

That is different.

"It is not. In the end, if you choose to be your own queen, that is where you will end. Untouched by anything because you won't let anything you can't control past your fear. Alone, you are not sufficient for yourself."

"I can't!" Silmavalien screamed. "I just can't! Aelaza, please!"

Silmavalien, we must do this together.

Minth raised his wings and leapt into the sky. He spoke to Aelaza, and for the first time in their relationship Silmavalien did not understand what he said. She saw images, but could not put them together. Chains. A dragon curled around and covering himself. Closed eyes. Hands with a snake wound through and around them. She could make no sense of any of it, and Aelaza's reply was almost equally incomprehensible.

"He has said that he will act when it is time, wherever the heart will let him. He will break the chains and melt the stone, kill the snake. Will she step out, move, and drop it? Now, I shall tell the demon that this time is not for its victory."

Aelaza stepped forward. A gleaming blade shone in her hand, glittering like a twinkling star. Ripples of light passed over and through it, and Aelaza struck the stone-goddess. Silmavalien did not see it, but the air rang with the sound of that sword striking something like stone. The note hovered, sharp and beautiful. The very air seemed to shiver, and something like a ripple of blue light spread outwards. For a moment the cliffs and the forest rang and echoed with a music beyond the music of the world, but the note fell short, dying out in a way it somehow not have done, as if the victory were not complete. The battle had been won, but the war was still being lost.

Silmavalien glanced around, but Aelaza had already vanished. The Ellena moved as fast as her own thoughts. *What was that about?* she thought, and sank down to the ground in a heap of bewilderment. All she knew was that a demon had showed up. Why was the Steep Descent no longer safe? Was there no safe place in the world?

"O Lord of Light, please banish the demons for me!"

There was no reply, not even the faintest whisper in the depths of her heart.

14

Defeated

Always before Silmavalien had moved in response to danger, and she followed the habit. Perhaps, they were still too close to the Shadow's lair and that was why this had happened. So the first thing that she did that morning was to go with Minth to spot a descent for herself and Daurth to take, since Jareth had learned to fly a few weeks ago, so they were the only two that could not glide down the cliff.

How convenient it would be if they could! They would be able to get so far away, so quickly, if everyone could fly.

There were many strips of green along the cliff face, but none of them looked like they even might go all the way from the top to the bottom. From memory, Minth showed her one far to the west.

Silmavalien spun around. An arrow had just passed right by her ear. She had felt the wind and heard it. But she saw nothing. Panic surged over her, like the fingers of the sea Minth had shown her weeks ago. She tried to fight the presence of the nightmare, as it welled up near the core of her being. But she was not strong enough, and she knew it. Just as she was physically no match for an orc, so she was spiritually no match for one. Her soul was a fortress without walls, and an orc was a legion of soldiers.

A wave of terror assaulted her, and in moments she was on her knees, trembling with terror, paralyzed with her. Her heart felt numb. Anguish, despair, and terror surged through her, like a raging storm unchecked. She was overcome. No longer herself.

Deep inside, Silmavalien knew that it was not over yet. The light that had saved her before could still save her. But she knew also that the Lord of Light might want something that she was unwilling to give. Or was it that he wanted something which she might be unwilling to give. She wanted... she wanted... she knew not what. Someone to be with her. A way out of all pain whatsoever. A world where there would be nothing to fear.

Even so nearly lost, she felt the air rushing past her as Minth shot overhead. A shock of pain. Sharp pain. Burning pain. Searing pain. She and Minth screamed together, the pitch of their voices matching. But this pain was a different pain, so acute that she just wanted to lie still and wait for it to subside.

But that was why it threw the nightmare aside for a moment. Her love for Minth rose again. Rising onto one knee she pulled her bow from its quiver, strung it, knocked an arrow. She never aimed it, only let the string go, and the arrow flew at the blurring form of an orc.

Even as her bow twanged, there was a sound like the twang of light, and with a streak as from an arrow that was light. She felt the nightmare forced to recede, and she knew that had just been Aelaza's bow.

Her vision still darkly clouded, Silmavalien sprang to Minth's side. As he dove to her rescue – in more ways than one – an arrow had flown into his shoulder, and Silmavalien shuddered when she saw it. It had gone in to the fletching, and all the orc arrows she had seen were barbed.

Hoping that Aelaza would hear and come, she yelled, "Aelaza! Please help me! Minth is hurt!"

There was no reply.

She collapsed at Minth's side and put an arm over his shoulder, careful not to cause him more pain where the arrow was embedded, like a splinter, in his flesh. Somehow a gulf had opened between them. She could still sense his thoughts, and feel his emotions as her own, but it was not the same as it had been. She leaned her head against his neck and sobbed with despair. She could not for the life of her remember what to do for an injury such as Minth's. She was totally helpless before the terrors of nightmare. The Lord of Light had forsaken her because of her failures. How much longer would Aelaza – who was certainly his servant – continue to fight for her?

But why was Minth able to act in the presence of the nightmare?

He turned her mind to what had happened only the night before. To the influence of the medusa and the words of Aelaza. He tried to tell her of his question and request to the Ellena and her reply, but still she failed to comprehend. He tried with ever increasing urgency, and, finally, an inkling reached Silmavalien.

Mentally, she shrank away. *I can't. I just can't! I don't know him. And there are things I just can't face. You know what I know. He's powerful and he might me in a sort of way. But he's totally beyond me. I* can't *trust him.*

She did not really understand what Minth said. Something about how someone had to be in control, or at least that they were not, or maybe something about the person who was in control was, or should be, the wisest and the best.

Right now, it was more important to take care of Minth's wound, and Silmavalien pushed these thoughts away to concentrate on that. She told Minth what she was going to do, and then slipped her knife into him, alongside the arrow shaft. He flinched but held still. Then she pressed the arrow against the hilt of the knife and pulled both out together. He trembled with the pain, but somehow still held still, because otherwise it would have been impossible for her. Even so, it took far more force and there was far more tearing than she would have liked.

She and Minth walked back to the camp, and she made a small fire to prepare some herbs. First she washed his wounds with infusions of cleansing herbs, and then she bounded his wound with poultices, using one of her cloaks to tie around his shoulders and chest.

After that, they set out westward, towards Minth's way down. The other dragons kept her company, and several of them walked beside her at a time, but Minth spent most of his time in the air. Flying hurt his shoulder wound, but not as much as walking did, and the wind was less likely to rip the bandage off than tree branches were.

Though the walk ought to have been relaxing, and the dragons tried to help her, Silmavalien couldn't relax. Every fiber of her seemed to tingle, and even the near-constant movement of birds in the trees startled her. Every detail of her surroundings stood out, and it was agonizing to be able to count the needles on a pine tree.

Her tension, in turn, affected the dragons, who responded to it differently. Coroneth grumbled and several times she had to yell at him to get him to get his nose out of what air current Minth should be gliding on. Airrock did not seem affected at all, or maybe she just flew a little harder, but she was also exploring what she could do in the air. But Minth was closest to her, and she knew he felt her tension most, yet somehow it did not come back on her. Somehow, it was not the misery to him that it was to her, even though he was the one who had actually been hurt.

Painfully, it seemed to her that her baby Minth could handle everything, and she could not handle anything.

Minth touched her mind gently, replying that neither of them could handle anything – and neither of them had to do so. There was one who could handle it all for them.

She knew what Minth was getting at, but she also knew the gulf between them was as painful to him as it was to her. It made her want to scream. She had no idea how they would survive. She was not sure how much she wanted to survive. Not with this horrid gulf between her and Minth.

And between her and some of the other dragons, too. A gulf that was mostly her fault. Tiela threw up a barrier to protect herself, as did several others, and Silmavalien could not blame them. It was even better for all of them that they did so, than that they help the fear grow.

But Veine and Songeth seemed to respond similarly to Minth, remaining open to her, and suffering her tension, but without sending it back to her. She was so grateful for them, and she felt she did not deserve them. But she did not wholly like it either. When Songeth sang, his song was so beautiful that it was painful, and she quickly came to hate it. There was something unendurable about it. Something too obvious to be said.

By nightfall, her tension had not left at all. She still felt like a hunted animal, and when she finally did sleep, she woke more than once, feeling like someone was fighting desperately a couple paces away. She could not see or hear anything, but the dragons assured it was not just her imagination. Even Airrock, who seemed not to know what fear was, felt it.

When she slipped back into sleep, her dreams were full of nightmares, always fighting creatures like Aelaza, always, always fighting over her.

Worst of all, she knew she had to choose who won.

15

Nothing Left to Do

Aelaza stood on the rampart of a great castle and watched Silmavalien.

The Lord of All Light had made her to be *his* Aelaza. She had chosen to be *his* Aelaza. She *must* live in his will, and his will alone. Though this was sometimes painful, it was a pain that brought with it no desire to escape. Her entire mode of experience was utterly alien to mortal, time-born creatures, and she did not really understand them much better than they could understand her.

Her creation was beyond the world, outside of time. She might refer to herself as young among the Ellenari, but what she meant by that had nothing to do with how long she had been around, a concept that did not apply to the Ellenari. She developed and grew, but never by leaving behind what she 'had been'.

Her experience was more like a castle. First a single stone is laid. That stone remains. Not changed by what is built upon and around, not remembered, but there, yet the stones that are laid around it give it greater meaning. At the same time, other parts of the castle are also built, and the stones don't follow each other one by one as experiences within time.

Watching Silmavalien struggle – and worse – live in fear, rejecting what she could be, was as great a pain as Aelaza knew. Unhurt herself in any way, it was as if she were being hurt.

"Lord of Light, do your will."

The commitment rang through every stone of her. It was his will she desired to do and be, and she trusted him completely. She knew he knew better than she did, and that it would be impossible for her to know better, however painful the situation with Silmavalien.

She wanted so greatly for Silmavalien to be what she was meant to be, to be free of fear and triumph over the nightmare, and to know her lord. Yet though she knew redemption could be, knew a will could change, she did not understand how. When all is eternally reality, fixed and unchangeable, how can a flaw be *removed?* How can the choice to be in the wrong place ever be undone? Always, one makes that choice, and it is a part of who one is.

More glorious than all the pain was the tingling anticipation of the moment when she could be crowned with the sight of Silmavalien, beautiful and perfect, all the fear and wrong somehow healed. She had yet to be privilege to behold that glory, and she longed to understand redemption better.

But now, the battle for the heart and soul of Silmavalien had become intense, and Aelaza felt that her precious time-born friend was slipping away, further into fear and slavery to the nightmare. Every moment here was a battle, and the nightmare terrors, whether the shades of Ellenari who were trapped in the wrong they had chosen or given form from the fear and hate of time-born creatures – such as Silmavalien herself – were everywhere.

She knew that to kill the dragonspeaker, Silmavalien, was only one of their intentions. The Nightmare Lord wanted demonised dragons and Dragonriders to serve him, and he wanted to destroy the dragons as they were created by the Lord of Light. To spread to others the disease of fear that had broken him was his chief desire, and this was not something she understood any better than she understood redemption.

But it was also something she did not want to understand any better, ever.

She wished she understood why the nightmare terrors were permitted to affect Silmavalien in ways forbidden to her, and all other Ellenari as far as she knew. They could fight alongside Silmavalien, and she understood why they were not to influence her in certain ways.

She must be free to choose and be herself and for herself.

But why was the nightmare allowed to do so? Why was the nightmare allowed that power to destroy?

Nonetheless, she knew and trusted that the Lord of Light used unthinkable things to bring about wonderful good. It was not in memory that she saw Malchoris bursting with fiery joy, so free and glorious in the darkness, so far from every other star, the nearest galaxy a mere pin-prick of light, in that moment when he was lit, as every star is lit.

S

When Silmavalien, she expected to see a host of Ellenari led by Aelaza and locked in interminable battle with legions of orcs, Fire Shadows, medusar, and other demons.

And when she opened her eyes, she saw none of that, but she still just wanted to fall apart and give up. Yet she knew she had to go on, so she got up, ate a little, and shouldered her packs.

About an hour later they reached the descent Minth had told her about. It was as steep as the descent they had used months ago, but this time that was not so dreadful. She no longer had a bunch of clumsy dragons to keep from slipping and falling. Only Daurth could not fly yet, and he was not nearly as clumsy and weak as most of them had been then.

However, with the memory of that descent in her mind, she stopped about twenty paces from the cliff edge to ask for the Lord of Light to make their passage safe and to thank them that they were still alive. Somehow it felt empty and vain. She felt that certain that he did not hear and did not care.

Later in the morning, Silmavalien was trudging down next to Daurth, while all the other dragons, even Minth, soared somewhere out of sight. The cliff bulged out, and only a narrow bridge of rock, perhaps two paces of rock, spanned the bulge and connected the two stripes of land.

She rounded a corner of the ridge-liked bulge and there, just two paces ahead, stood a demon, all too like the Fire Shadow!

Deathlike flames glowed throughout a form of darkness as black as a starless night, and evil eyes like flames of poison looked at her an unspeakable hate that seemed to infect her being. Daurth roared, but she screamed in horror and collapsed against the cliff wall.

She could fight no more. She could not hope for any victory against the nightmare monsters. She had already been utterly defeated, and only the Lord of Light or one of her servants could save – if he wanted.

She released herself to the horror and death she knew awaited her. The cold stillness of despair numbed the razor edge of agony and fear.

The moment froze.

"Will you give yourself into the power of One who will not force you?"

It was a voice Silmavalien knew, and here she was. At the end of life, alone. Her strength gone, who she was lost. She had not nothing left, not even the will to stand. She had just given up to fate, to the nightmare

Now she had to choose. Would she be devoured by the nightmare before her, the terror of a world that hated her, and the shadow of the gods she had once worshiped? Or would she give herself to the Lord of Light?

There was nothing left to do. One moment staring into those eyes full of the hate of hell was enough. No. Faced with this despicable darkness, she knew. Whatever it meant, whatever it cost, the Lord of Light was her only refuge.

The very air, the rock against which she had collapsed in defeat, all rang with victory. It was the same note which the sword of Aelaza had struck on the rock of the medusa and which had fallen short then.

It did not fall short now. The whole forest and mountain rang with it. The sky itself seemed to tremble with it.

Silmavalien clung to the rock, unable to rise, as the earth beneath her trembled with victory. Looking up, she saw that the demon that had so terrified her was gone for the moment. Earth and air sang with joy. And all Silmavalien could do was to cling to the rock. It was over. She had given up.

She had found the One it was beautiful to give up to. She had given herself into his power, and with that trust the nightmare had lost its power over her.

The war had been won.

16

Light!

Silmavalien was happier, and so were all the dragons, especially Minth. In that one instant, everything changed, and the shadow that had fallen on her life and kept out the light of joy was gone.

She rose, steadying herself on the rock. It seemed like the sun had never shone before. On rocks above her perched the dragons, glowing with joy, and standing atop the cliff she thought she could just see Aelaza, shining like a bright and victorious star.

She continued down the cliff, and all the rest of the day, neither she nor any of the dragons felt even the echo of a nightmare creature's presence. Though the mountains soon cast all in shade, since they were so tall the sun only rose above them briefly, everything was bright and clear and peaceful. The air itself seemed radiant, and the myriad needles of the conifer trees sang in the gentle breeze that floated up from the sea far below.

Night fell long before she and Daurth could reach the ledge below, so they sheltered in a small cave that kept the cold of the sky and the wind way from them.

S

Had a voice wakened her?

It was the dark before the dawn, but she could remember nothing but a tingling sensation. Had a star spoken to her? It felt like she imagined the voice of those twinkling but unwinking eyes of light that ever shone out of the darkness might sound.

Inarticulate fear. Disgust that threatened to obliterate her from the inside out. This again?

She tried to push it back, but only felt more terrified. The ring of light tightened on her finger – not painfully, but enough so she noticed.

"Lord of All Light, I can't fight this alone!" she cried.

It was not much, but it was enough. The ring glowed with a soft luminescence that did not light up its surroundings. Even her finger remained pitch black, though the ring seemed made of light, and when she fixed her eyes upon the light, the terror had no power over her, though she still felt the presence of the nightmare.

The dragons were all awake now, and glowing eyes of many colors filled the room. Occasionally Silmavalien glanced up to meet her eyes, but she always returned her gaze to the ring.

Hours passed.

The light of the ring grew and grew until it was so bright she could not gaze at it steadily. Slowly it illuminated its surroundings. First her finger, then her hand, her arm, her whole body, the floor at her feet. Finally, the entire cave was filled with a light of such brilliance and color that it reminded her of the starry ways within the mountains' stone.

She turned to face the cave mouth, the hand that bore the ring uplifted. Before she had a moment to take in the forest as it appeared in the unearthly light, a cloud of arrows flew at her.

Somehow they never reached her. She strung her bow, and knocked an arrow. Crying out to the Lord of Light for she knew not what, she released it to fly into the mob of orcs at the cave entrance.

The twang of the bow-string and the whizz of her arrow took on a new sound that was indescribable as the light of the ring. It flickered in its flight like a rainbow among the stars, and among the orcs it was a white-hot fire, too bright for Silmavalien or any of the dragons to look at.

A few of the orcs stepped out from the white-hot inferno. Dropping her bow, Silmavalien drew her knife. The instant the hilt touched the ring the whole blade shone with the same light that terror could endure. The dragons rushed to her side.

A curved orc blade rang against Tiela's shoulder, but only scratched her brilliant turquoise scales. With a swift jerky movement she bit her attacker in the face and pounced on him. The orcs focused their attention on the dragon, and Silmavalien saw her opening. Her hunting knife flashed and an orc fell.

A moment later the dragons leapt past her and tore apart the orcs that were still focused on Tiela.

Somehow, this time the energy of the battle died away instantly into exhaustion and relief. Silmavalien lay down right there, and in a few minutes she was asleep, with one of Minth's wings spread over her.

When Silmavalien woke, the morning was clear, and the ring no longer shone. Only Daurth and Minth were still in the cave with her. She and Daurth ate, and then they continued down the precipice. But first she hugged Minth, and told him how much she loved him. He gently nuzzled her face in return.

The beauty of the landscape struck her anew when she looked out from the cave. Almost every tree and flower had its indescribable wonder, a beauty or grace she could not explain, as if something from a realm of deeper meaning was breaking through the form and colors. Her eyes was constantly drawn to beauties all around her, and there was so much she felt she could have stared forever in wonder and fascination. Even one twig, one fern, one flower, one patch of bark showing through a vine clinging around the tree's trunk, seemed adequate for infinite wonder. Seemed almost to demand it. She would never be able to fully admire how beautiful they were, if she spent all her life on it.

Yet she knew, almost at once, that this beautiful world was not at peace. In fact it seemed to be more at war than ever. Again and again she heard the musical twang of Ellenarin bows, and saw the streak of light that followed the arrow.

She started to sing a new song, with words that came from nowhere, coming as she needed them and vanishing after she sang them:

...This is just a little bit of love, but it's so much more
Than anything we'd ever come to on our own
It's bigger than anything we can know
But it's what our hearts long for...

Something stepped *out* of the rock, just in front of her. It towered above her and looked as hard and gray and rough as stone, though dingy, threadbare rags hung about it. Foot-and-a-half-long fangs extended from what was not really a face.

She jumped backwards and fell into the cliff wall. Suddenly, this thing reminded her of the medusa. With fumbling fingers she grasped the hilt of her hunting knife and drew it, just as the creature bent down. It was going to grab her!

It grabbed Daurth and tossed him off the trail. She screamed! He could not fly!

She felt the dragons as if their bodies were hers. Minth and Veine dove from above, the other six flying towards them as they could. She felt them pouring into Daurth everything they could think of to help him fly, and then she felt their minds join with her to, helping her to see and think and move faster than she could alone.

Directed by Airrock's thought she struck at the monster's arm, just as it came down from hurling Daurth into the sky. The sound was metal striking stone. Despair washed over her. She had no weapon that would injure this thing.

The arm of stone came down again, and she sank to the ground, pressing herself into the cliff as hard as she could. The knife fell from her hand. Crying out against a terror like the nightmare panic, one word escaped her lips. *"Light!"*

Something like a light that was so brilliant Silmavalien feared it would blind her flashed around them. It seemed to come from another sky, or another world, or another kind of existence. But when she opened her eyes after the flash she knew somehow it was not her surroundings but her eyes that had changed. There seemed to be so much more light everywhere.

Perhaps it came from the place where her bonding song with Minth came from. The place her bonding song with Minth had let her glimpse. With that in her soul, she should not be so afraid of dying, should she?

Looking around, she saw the monster was only a heap of dust. She picked up her knife, blew the dust off, and sheathed it. At once she began picking her way down the trail. Daurth might be gliding well enough now, but she had to go down to him, and she did not yet know how long that would take.

And whether she should be so afraid of death or not, she very much was. Dying was horrible.

17

Lighter

Silmavalien still had not made it to the bottom by nightfall, and Minth and Veine stayed with her. They kept her warm, since she could not find any reasonable shelter, while the rest of the dragons stayed with Daurth, who was so sore he could hardly move.

Silmavalien feared that this was a perfect time for the terrors of the nightmare to try to overwhelm them.

So it was. That night Silmavalien and the dragons with her were wakened by Aelaza's bow, and Silmavalien thought it sounded closer and more desperate than ever before. Opening her eyes she saw the Elena standing a few feet away, shooting her bow faster than Silmavalien had not dreamed possible. But then again, everything about Aelaza was impossible. It even seemed as though a light from a realm beyond the world lit her, so that though she did not glow she alone in that dark world was lit up.

Though Silmavalien remembered that Aelaza had only about five arrows, she never seemed to be out. She moved almost as fast as her arrows of light, and at times she would leap over Silmavalien, and out of sight, though she always remained in that strange light. Then she would reappear right where she had been, maybe a second or two later.

Rising, Silmavalien tried to ask Aelaza if she could help her fight, but the Ellena did not respond. Somehow, Silmavalien knew that she knew, but she lay back down. It was not as if she could see the shadows Aelaza was fighting anyways.

A few minutes later, Aelaza moved even closer to them. In a movement fast as light her bow was in her quiver and her sword was in her hand. Her combat took on a form even more bewildering, as her sword moved faster than the eye could follow, darting against invisible foes in a hundred directions at once. The way she moved around Silmavalien and the dragons was more intricate and amazing than any dance. Something about it lulled Silmavalien to sleep again.

She woke to an overcast morning that looked as if it would turn to rain. Aelaza was sitting just a few feet away. There was something extremely odd about her pose that Silmavalien could not name.

Then the Ellena spoke. "Ellethorn. You would say, Good morning."

At the sound of her voice Silmavalien suddenly realized what was odd. She was the sort of tired where a human can hardly take another step, yet she remained in perfect readiness for whatever would come next. Whatever her experience, Silmavalien could not comprehend it, and perhaps for the first time she realized how alien and inhuman Aelaza was.

Sitting up, Silmavalien said, "I would have helped you, last night."

"Perhaps human beings can will what they cannot, but I do not know, and I'm not sure you know either."

She said it so calmly and plainly that Silmavalien could not feel hurt, but she had to ask, "Why? What?"

"I am not sure that there is a difference between willing and doing. However, be that as may, the battle I must fight you cannot. And the battle you must fight I cannot."

"You mean like that one with the stone giant? I couldn't fight it."

"Of course not. We do not receive your gift – though at times we may taste it. It is most beautiful and glorious."

Silmavalien cocked her head, then asked, "What gift?"

"The gift that the Lord over Light as you say, Shallim-Araldor, bestows upon you. I cannot say more."

There was something about the way Aelaza said it that made Silmavalien she would never get more out of the Ellena by trying. So instead she asked, "What do we do now?

"That is up to you."

Since Aelaza would not give her any more information, she went about her day as if she was not there. She assured Daurth that she was coming as quickly as she could, then ate and continued down the descent. Aelaza stayed close by her, and at first there was calm. The wind was cold and smelled of rain, but there was no sense of the nightmare. Before long it started to drizzle now and then, but Silmavalien was sure it would get heavier.

Then she saw Aelaza take a flying leap to a protrusion some ten feet up the cliff from where she stood. Fearing that the Ellena would leave her, she stared, open-mouthed, while Aelaza ascended perhaps a hundred or so feet in a few seconds. There, small indeed from where Silmavalien watched, she notched an arrow and let it fly. Then another... and another... and another. The effect was like a rain of shooting stars, in rhythm with celestial music. Within moments Aelaza's quiver was empty, and she leapt sideways down the cliff. The towering conifers hid her from Silmavalien's view.

Feeling bewildered and confused, Silmavalien continued down.

The sound of Aelaza's bow resound through the wood and sometimes echoed against the cliffs, but Silmavalien often missed the shooting star-like arrows, and though the sound was beautiful, she knew what it meant.

The battle with the nightmare was not yet over. Why did the nightmare creatures not leave? She decided she would ask Aelaza the next time she got a chance. If Aelaza would give her an answer.

The rain grew heavier and soaked her clothes. Suddenly, she noticed Aelaza was walking beside her. She turned her head to ask her question, only to find she had slipped. A moment later she realized she was slipping into the soaking earth.

"Help!" she screamed.

The Ellena did not answer, but she felt Minth at once. For what it was worth, he banked, turning in his flight to come to her as fast as he could, though he had no idea how he would help with this problem.

Next moment, she was in almost complete darkness. The hole through which she had fallen shone above her, but it did little to cast light on her surroundings.

Then she realized she still had the mint-colored glow-stone from the Riders' Passage. Finding its gleam in her bags was easy enough, and what she saw in its light made her gasp.

She had seen enough dragon eggs that even in the dim blue-green light it was unmistakable. She reached out and touched the taut, cool and smooth leathery surface that contained a life she would not have been believed was possible a year ago.

She rested against the slope of mud she had just come down. Somehow she knew the egg was about to hatch, and it was worthless to try to find her way out until it did.

She reached out, and touched a gold dragon. A tingling glory, like rays of sunshine in the morning, like sunlight glimmering off of water, like clouds flaming with unburning light at dawn, bound their souls together.

"Lighter."

She whispered his name with awe. His vibrant burning eyes locked with hers. She passed her hand over his smooth, hard scales, and then the leathery membrane of his white wings.

"Lighter," she said again, and Minth's joy joined hers.

Sometime later, she shook herself from the doze that she had fallen into. She shouldered her packs and knelt to pick up Lighter. Now to find a way out of here.

She took a step forward – and found herself sliding again.

18

About the Dragon-sword

"Minth," Silmavalien scolded. "You need to pay more attention to staying out of the sun."

All the white dragons had sunburned to various degrees, but Minth's case was the worst. His entire topside was red and the skin was peeling. He was going to be very uncomfortable, and he was going to have to make sure he stayed out of the sun – completely – for several weeks.

"We need to oil you," she said, and his mint eyes whirled slowly, acknowledging her. In his present condition that was going to hurt, but he understood it would only hurt more if he did not let her.

You're going to have to bring your kills to me for a while, she told them all. *I'm running low on fat again.* As they grew larger, the amount of oil required to keep their skins moist was incredible, and the fact was, she needed them to bring more of their kills to her than not, especially if she was going to harvest the oil from the easiest places to get it, and the dragons did not want her to waste time she could be spending with them if they could help it. Only Wydth, Tiela, and Airrock never needed it, though Veine only rarely needed it.

But right now, with himself sunburned so badly, Silmavalien thought Wydth might want to be oiled too, if she had any left after taking care of the others.

She stepped back and decided that would do for Minth's wing for now. It would need a new coat soon, but it might be better with the sunburn to do it more often and lighter anyways. She tilted her head considering. She did not really know, and she did not want to cause him more discomfort than necessary.

She could always finish later. That was his thought, and she smiled. The next dragon lined up, and Silmavalien considered the fact it was a good thing that they were doing almost all the hunting now, and she might have gotten lazy if she did not have to take care of their skins.

She spread oil over Daurth's neck as gently as possible, hoping that if she was going to find any more eggs, she would find them soon. It would be nice for everyone to be able to fly, and she would feel so much safer that way. So much less vulnerable, not just to falling off cliffs, but to being found, too.

The next day they journeyed further west along the ledge. She was in no hurry to go down to the plains below, where there might be humans, who might hunt dragons like the humans on the other side of the mountains would, but she would rather be further from the Shadow.

That evening, she decided to take an inventory of her packs. Lighter lay down next to her while she rummaged through things, and once she had finished her inventory, she pulled out the broken sword Lexamarian had given her. She slid the shards out of the sheath and laid them on the ground at her knees where she carefully fit them together. She ran her fingers over the hilt and crossguard, and then together she and Lighter examined the sword.

Careful, she told him. *You can look, you can smell, but don't touch it. Don't move it.*

He drew his snout back a little, and she bent over the broken sword.

Like the ring, it was beautiful, and the workmanship was unlike anything she had ever seen before. The hilt was gold, with tracings of silver, and the pommel gleamed with gems of a deep red and a brilliant green. The cross-guard glittered with stones that matched those on the hilt, though she knew if she turned it over the stones would be varying shades of blue. Beautiful and unfamiliar letters that looked nothing like the writing she knew ran the length of the blade.

After she and Lighter looked at it for a while, she turned the sword over. On this side, the cross-guard stones were reds and greens that matched the hilt, and the intricate carving on the blade reminded her more strongly than ever of the ring. But Lighter was getting bored, so she did not spend too long looking at it, just enough to determine that the break ran through the image of a dragon with wings raised.

She put the sword back in its sheath, which she now realized was just as intricately detailed, and put the sheath back in her bags, thinking about what Lexamarian had said. Something about this dragon-sword being reforged among the Ellenari and a champion of the Dragonriders taking it up. Then the Shadow that guarded the Riders' Passage would be slain. She wondered if it was a prophecy, or just the ramblings of a dying woman, and decided she would ask Aelaza if she could.

Several days passed in a similar way, with Silmavalien and Lighter leisurely moving west along the ledge and no hint of the nightmare creatures. Then, one morning Aelaza came down the cliff in a flash, and leapt right in front of Silmavalien where she had been having breakfast.

Startled, she jumped to her feet. "Is something wrong?"

Aelaza shook her black hair into a peacock's fan. "The giant is sleeping."

"What's that supposed to mean?"

"Do not think it is over yet," said Aelaza.

"Are you referring to the –"

"– apparent absence of the nightmare." Aelaza cut her off smoothly and calmly. "Yes, I am."

Silmavalien nodded. "I appreciate your warning." Though was that the right thing to say to something like Aelaza – something that might even be one of the gods, the Arrows of Light – when she did not mean it? – "Actually, I'd noticed too. It's such a relief... I wanted to ask you about something."

"Oh." Aelaza did not move.

Silmavalien pulled the sword out of a bag and showed it to Aelaza. "When Lexamarian saved us a long time ago from a bear, she referred to this as a Dragon-sword. She said it was very important and I should take care of it. She also said that it would be reforged by the Ellenari? and borne by a champion of the Dragonriders. I *think* she said that when it is reforged the Shadow in the abyss by the Riders' Passage will be vanquished."

"You met Lexamarian?" Aelaza asked flatly.

Silmavalien did not know how to respond. "Yes."

"What else did she tell you? Where is she now?"

"Not to be scared of the nightmare creatures, and that light hurts them. Information on how to recognize the Riders' Passage, and not to attempt it without an Ellen. Convoluted instructions about the spring of Nerya in the Hall of Dragon Eggs and the vale of Aros Cor on Ellen Island. That's all I can remember right now. She died."

"I believe the Hall of Dragon Eggs is in the Riders' Passage, not far from the lake of Nerya. I'm surprised you haven't been there. I'd thought that was where most of your dragons were from. I don't know how the nightmare creatures would get close enough to the waters of Nerya to kill the eggs. The Aros Cor Valley is in the Greater Aravin Mountains, north of Dragonsong, which is where the third end of the Riders' Passage is. Ellen Island is of great ancestral importance to the dragons, and lies far out into the sea, approximately north-northeast of here. That's for clarification.

"I'm glad you met her. Apparently she tried to give you as much of the most important information as possible. She was supposed to guide and protect the next rider. She lived much longer than most humans do.

"As for the Dragon-sword, keep it. Now is not the time, but it will come. That sword is prophesied about. A Dragon-rider will arise to bear it, but I think you will deliver it."

Hope filled Silmavalien. "Is Noren a Dragon-rider? Where – how – is he?"

"Now is not the time," Aelaza repeated, as firm but also as hard, opaque, and unemotional as a rock. She was even more alien than Silmavalien had realized.

With that, she took a flying leap back to the cliff and was quickly out of sight.

𝓢

The days went on, and turned into weeks. Lighter grew, and was soon walking and wandering about a little. He ate voraciously, and grew faster than any of the other dragons, except perhaps for Wydth. At night Songeth and Silmavalien sang together, and the other dragons listened, or sometimes joined in with their own voices. Every day that it did not pour, they moved a little further west.

The weeks turned into a month, and went on. Still no nightmare creatures attacked. Since Minth hatched, it was the most comfortable her life had ever been. She was content, she did not have too much work to do, and the weather was nice even if she longed for more sun.

But in her heart she knew it could not last forever.

19
Flight

Noren sat with his back to a warm rock, the evening sun streaming across him. He had gone to Zyel less than a week ago and exchanged all his deer skins for coins. Even though he had sold them for a fraction of what he would get if he was the one who made the journey down to the plains cities, he had more coins that he had ever owned or carried before.

Not that coins mattered, when one lived as a lone man in the wilderness. With a dragon. He smiled.

Then the smile faded. The world felt like a war was being waged around him, with so much out to destroy him. He knew the nightmares were never far, though he had had no close encounters with them again. But the light-bow was never silent for long, and he often saw the light-arrows. And all too often, he felt the uneasiness and the fear that meant the nightmare was near.

But now was not the time to dwell on this. Elninya demanded his attention, and he shifted a little to watch her more easily.

She was climbing up a large tumble of boulders again, and she insisted he watch her while she jumped with wings spread. Her excitement pushed his darker thoughts away, as he gave her attempt to learn how to fly his full attention.

She had not gotten far yet, but this time Noren thought her flapping actually did something, and he felt her wonder wash over him.

It was glorious to feel herself born on the air, even if only for a short while. It was exciting and nerve-tingling, miraculous and other-worldly. The last of his glum thoughts vanished in her happiness, and he sat straight.

"Do it again," Noren said out loud. "I think, maybe I saw you rise a little." Just a tad. Just at first. Maybe.

"*Yes!*" She spun round and hopped up the rock formation more exuberantly than ever. Spreading her great white wings she leapt from the topmost boulder. Next moment, down came those wings, and the air shuddered under them. She folded the last joint and brought them up again, then *down*.

Noren had already jumped to his feet and was bouncing on his toes. "Elninya, you did it!" It was not maybe this time. It was for certain.

Just as she started to fall, she had lurched upwards for a moment before continuing her fall.

Elninya roared her pleasure and delight, then ran back up a boulders.

A wave of disappointment passed through dragon and rider together. She half-fell half-glided down, just like she had three tries ago. But she would not give up! She tried again and again, while Noren tried and tried not to say much, but to encouraging. But her wings were sore, and she was tired, and frustration soon won. The last time she glided down she stood among the jumbled rocks at the bottom and let her wings and tail hang.

Noren walked over and stroked her underneath her wing-joints, where she loved it best. "It's okay, Elninya," he said softly. "You worked hard today. You'll catch it. You did great. You just need to rest, so your body and mind can sort things out." He switched to mental communication, and showed her toddlers learning to walk and run, and some of their mishaps, until she laughed.

𝒩

As Noren lay under his covers that night, he thought about how he could look for Silmavalien now. By now, her dragon would certainly be able to fly. Why would she stay in the obvious danger of civilization?

Anyway, she would probably go into the cities for supplies. That would be where he would start.

The next day, he went hunting while Elninya practiced leaping off the rocks. Even with his mind focused on tracking, he was aware of her initial excitement, and then her frustration when no matter how many times she tried, she could not repeat what had happened yesterday. He knew no amount of encouragement to take it easy would work, so he let it be, and after a couple hours of frustration she decided to quit on her own and take a nap.

There was no doubt in his mind that after a few days of this she was going to be quite grumpy until she learned how to fly. He wished he could help her better.

When he got back with the deer the next afternoon, she insisted on trying again for him, though she told him she was sure it was not going to be impressive.

Noren walked up and gave her a tight hug around the neck. She would go ahead and try, if she wanted to. Maybe she would figure it out, but it did not matter if she did today or not. He loved her, and he thought she was beautiful no matter how long it took her to figure out to fly.

She was not sure if she listened, but he followed her to the boulders, and clapped for every attempt she made. And she *did* rise again, more than she had that time a few days ago, but that was not why he clapped. He clapped for *her.*

ℵ

Within another week, Elninya had learned to fly. Noren's favorite thing was to sit back and watch her soar and glide through the air. She shared the thrill of flying with him, and he could not wait for her to be big enough to carry him. She assured him she wanted that too.

Over the next couple weeks, the amount of time Elninya could spend in the air increased rapidly, and she began to help Noren hunt. It was soon clear that she was a much more capable hunter, since she could soar over the mountains and spot a herd with far greater speed and ease than he could. After that, it was a matter of a silent glide and a dive that never failed after her first few tries.

She had practiced, she told him proudly. And she was a dragon! Dragons were all born to hunt!

That, Noren remarked to himself, was a good thing, given how much they needed to eat.

All of that, he soon realized that it was going to take a while before she could spend all day or night in the air comfortably, which is why they needed to be able to continue his search for Silmavalien.

But, to be honest, that was okay. His feelings about her were still in an unfortunate and confused state. Though he still found himself thinking about her all the time, he had mostly avoiding spending much time delving into his feelings. But it was time to change that.

He knew he desperately wanted to be with her and that he wondered if she still thought of him as her betrothed. At the same time, he was still upset with her for fleeing on the eve of their marriage day. He had trusted her with his life, and he felt hurt and resentful that she failed to trust him with hers. He *knew* she would *never* become a witch or collaborate with demons. How had she failed to understand that?

It made him think perhaps they were not meant to be husband and wife. Not that either of them could marry anyone else, since they were both Dragonriders – hated and rejected by all who were not Dragonriders.

And that thought made him angry in a totally different way, and one which disturbed his relationship with Elninya. When his thoughts went there, she could not help remembering what he had done, and how his way of defending himself only contributed to people's hatred of Dragonriders. Except, Noren thought, that had been *his* thought about the results of what *she* had made him do. But he tried to pull that thought back. It would not make things better for either of them to get into a fight with the other, since neither of them was ready to change his or her mind.

Finally, Noren decided they were ready to back to civilization and resume their search for Silmavalien. Elninya did not want to, but she was willing to do it for him, and however confused his feelings were about Silmavalien, they had to try. With him riding Evena, they began the journey down the mountains. Once they got to the lower foothills, around where Zyel was, Elninya took to flying at night and high enough that it was not obvious what she was. Once they reached the plains, Noren took a small road to avoid Kranah, and once again became Caref.

Elninya complained that she was going to find lawful and inconspicuous hunting rather difficult.

20

Go Down

"Go to the plains."

Silmavalien shook her head to dispel the voice. She stood near the edge of the cliff, gazing out over the plains. The wide expanse of green, fading to blue-gray with distance, would still take weeks to reach, if she traveled purposefully. But she saw no reason to do so. She and all ten dragons were happy, content, and relatively safe. She loved this life, and at the moment no evil threatened them. There was no reason to think the plains would be better.

Silmavalien walked away from the cliff and was about to continue her search for herbs, when a dragon touched her mind. Not a problem. A demand. Something he wanted.

She put her hands on her hips, and stared up into the sky, where Coroneth circled in preparation for landing. "You want us to hunt a bear. What sort of an idea is that?" She spoke out loud, though he could not hear her with his ears.

A surprisingly vivid visual picture of nine dragons attacking a bear with an arrow in its shoulder flicked from the dragon's mind to hers. She got the idea. Nine dragons and an experienced huntress could take care of any bear, quite safely.

She continued talking out loud. It was her only way to use or hear human speech, which she found that she needed. After all, even dragons used their own form of vocal communication.

"If you want bear so much, why don't you just go find one? You're so confident, I bet you could take one all on your own. If you don't want to do it alone, convince Tiela to go with you."

She already knew what his response would be.

"Okay. Do you have a bear in mind?"

An image of black bear, foraging. Fifteen miles west.

That's a long trek, Coro! This hunt could take several days. Why don't you and the others just go do it together? Or, we'll do this in three or four days.

No, came Coroneth's response. She was special. She was the dragon-mother. She should do things like this with them. Besides, the bear would soon be done with its current foraging grounds, and he thought it most likely that it would go up the precipice.

Have you already bossed the rest of the dragons into agreeing with this?"

At his next reply, Silmavalien reverted to talking out loud. "This was Veine's idea. Uh-uh. Veine spotted the bear and decided to hunt it. She thought it might be fun to do it with *someone*. This was *your* idea. Did you boss the rest of the dragons into agreeing with you?"

"No? Well, that's an improvement, Coro." She strode over to where the albino dragon had just landed, and scratched him between the shoulders. She had already known he had not tried to boss some of the dragons, since Minth, Daurth, or Tiela would certainly have let her know, but some of the others might not have. Airrock might not even have noticed.

Coroneth leaned into her scratching, but he continued nagging her. Finally she told him to politely ask each of the dragons what they thought, and to remain in the contact to watch how he did. Coroneth was not mean; he did not intend to bully. He was just overbearing and arrogant. He did not take no for an answer, as if he just did not understand the concept, and he tended to give the other dragons the impression that he was smarter and they should go along with his ideas, no matter what their original inclinations were. So it took a special effort on his part to be kind in some situations.

He was learning, Silmavalien as she listened in, though she was sure that when he thought his advice or ideas actually mattered, it would be more difficult for him. First he spoke to Veine, sharing with her his improvement on her idea. *Improvement* might not have been the best choice of concept, but he was learning and it did not bother Veine, so Silmavalien did not interfere.

The purple-necked dragon was ecstatic at the idea. She did not need everyone, she told Coroneth, but it would be *fun!* Silmavalien smiled. She might occasionally miss some of her old friends from Treas, but she had a village of dragons, and their companionship was more than enough for her. This would be very, very good, and the only thing lacking was that she wished Noren and his dragon could be part of it, too. They would have to find them sometime, once Lighter was all grown up.

Minth interrupted that thought. What was this he was hearing? They were going on a group hunt! If he wanted? Of course he wanted!

Silmavalien laughed and sent Minth a mental hug, and then Coroneth, fairly glowing with pride, spoke to Tiela. His mental tone of voice now was both softer and more natural, as if something about Tiela blunted his arrogance, and it did. Perhaps it was just the way she stood up to him and let him see what he was really doing when he was too overbearing, but whatever it was, it worked.

She would not mind, she said, and Silmavalien knew she meant exactly that.

Coroneth twisted his head around to look at Silmavalien, his eyes glowing purple, after that. He did good, didn't he?

She tightened her arm around his neck. *Yes.* She knew he tried. Now like that. Like with Tiela, even with the ones who could not brush off his arrogance.

He nodded, and she felt his almost fierce determination. Then he reached out to Airrock, and she almost chuckled to herself. This Airrock, and she was going to be different. She often was, and she did not disappoint Silmavalien's expectations.

If Coroneth wanted bear, she told him, she would have no problem hunting the bear herself.

Amused, Silmavalien interjected. *Do you mind waiting for the rest of us?*

That made Airrock laugh. No, she could do that. Whatever they wanted.

Next Coroneth finally reached out to Songeth, something Silmavalien had been expecting him to a lot earlier. *Nice,* she said, as Coroneth started emphasizing everyone who had already "agreed" to come. *That's not necessary.*

But Songeth was a bit like Tiela in some ways. He would not mind coming, he said in a tone that reminded Silmavalien of her.

Next, Coroneth reached out to Wydth, and finally Daurth and Jareth, and Silmavalien did not have to intervene again. He asked nicely, perhaps almost too politely, but she understood why he had saved these three for last. None of them wanted to come, and he had probably guessed that. She got the distinct impression that Wydth would rather not, though he might if everyone else did, and that Daurth and Jareth were only a little more interested.

And then Lighter chimed in. Minth had told him what was being planned, he said, and he'd love it so much! Except, he was not sure if he could come?

That was what settled it for Silmavalien. If Lighter wanted to be part of this so much, he would get to be, and she would go with him.

Though he was still very young, he was more active than anyone else except for Tiela and Airrock had been at his age. He would be able to keep up with her well enough for this group hunt.

Finally, Coroneth got to leap into his element and actually exercise his talents. When they prepared the hunt itself, Silmavalien marveled at his skills, and wondered if some of his bossiness came from not having a good place to exercise what he was good at. Even here, she had to check him once or twice, reminding him not to be bossy and to let the other dragons have a say in how they did things. She had to remind him to assume they *could* leave if they wanted or do another way, and that it was okay if they did.

But she had to admit, he was a very good organizer when it came to it. Once he made sure to listen and not demand, he did a very fine job of making sure that everyone – even Lighter – got to have enough of a role in the hunt to find it exciting and satisfying, without putting anyone – even Lighter – into unnecessary danger.

S

The evening after the hunt, Silmavalien stood again, a few feet from the edge of the precipice. Far below her lay the blue-gray sea, with its always-shifting ever-so-subtle variations, and a few faint lines of white rippling across it surface. Most of the dragons had been down there now now, and she knew from them what it would look if she were much closer to it. She knew what it colors were like, gray and sparkling blue like a deeper, darker sky, and sea-green. She could see the white foam of the breakers crashing against the cliff-like ridges that ran out from the mountains in her mind, as well as what some of those places looked like when the sea was higher instead of lower, and the waters broke in chaotic patterns above the tops of the rocks.

She turned a little towards the west, where the plains lay, almost as far below her as the sea and much nearer than they had been several months ago. Shades of slightly varying greens dappled them, but from this height she did not know whether those greens were thick forest or a grassland with no trees. Wisely, none of the dragons had been down there yet.

And if she had come out here a few hours earlier, she would have been able to see where the shadow of the mountains ended, and those various greens glimmered in the sun, before they grew gray and purple with distance.

"Go down to the plains."

What!?

"Go down to the plains."

No, of course not. Lighter could not fly. She would not risk meeting humans with not only herself, but a dragon, earth-bound. Besides, they were comfortable and happy here in the mountains. It was must be only her imagination. She had heard voices of nonsense in her mind before. This was another of those. Or a demon that had laid a trap for her. The Lord of Light took care of her. He did not ask her to do preposterous and dangerous things.

21

A Matter of Horses

Down in the plains towns were everywhere, unlike the scattered villages in the mountains. One warm spring afternoon, a thirsty and uncomfortable Noren rode an Evena who had to be just as thirsty and uncomfortable into another town. He wasted no time taking to the animal watering tough next to the wall in the center of the town and getting her a drink.

"Hey there! What are you doing'?" yelled a burly farmer as he stepped out from behind a horse.

"Watering my horse," Noren replied, calmly. He had discovered that the temperaments of people in the villages varied a lot. Some were more hostile than they seemed, and sometimes someone really did not like strangers. If he ended up being in the middle of a fight between a townsperson who could not stand strangers, and one who was afraid the other man would chase his trade away, it would not go well for him.

But as this man took a few steps forwards, Noren got the idea he was not really hostile. "Well, what are you doin' with our water?"

"What I said I was doing. Do you not have enough to spare for one rider and his horse?" He took a moment to glance down the well, where the water level could not have been more than twenty or so feet down. "Your well looks like it has plenty of water, to me."

"Well, we do have enough water. If you pull your own water, you can have it." The man had been walking towards him the whole while, and now he was acting outright friendly. He held out his hand. "I'm Corin. You?"

Noren took Corin's hand. "Caref."

"You here for something?"

"Actually, I'm looking for a friend of mine, from where I come from. She wanted to settle in this area of the country, but I don't know exactly where."

"What's her name?" asked Corin.

"Silmavalien."

Corin thought for a moment, then shook his head. "Nope, not here." A grin spread over his face. "Though... I do have a horse I want to sell, and you might want to buy."

Noren looked at Evena, still drinking and slurping. He *had* been thinking he might want a different horse. She was faithful, gentle, and willing, but more of a farm horse than a cross country horse. She could use better food, more water, more rest, and less heat. Also, if he got another horse he could return her to Treas. He did not *really* want to be stealing.

"Okay," said Noren, returning his attention to Corin. "Tell me about the horse."

"Why don't you refill the trough? Then we'll go see the horse."

While Noren worked to pull water up, Corin talked. "You could trade yours in – we could use a farm horse – or pay in coins."

Noren paused for a moment to reply. "I'm afraid I can't trade Evena. I'm borrowing her from a friend."

"He's a desert courser stallion," – *Desert courser?* thought Noren. *That's good.* He'd heard of desert coursers in the stories, and the talk he had overheard in the cities and on the roads had confirmed that the legends were based on truth. The desert horses from across the Green Sea kept weight easily, could run nearly forever, and did not mind dry heat – "He's about three years old, and you'll have to get him over being afraid of everything, but if you've heard the stories they're only a little exaggerated." Corin went on, warming to his subject, and then finished. "I breed and sell them. Mostly to the King's Couriers, but not always. I'm known around here" – Corin gestured with his arms – "as Corin the Courserbreeder. It might just become a name for my family." He grinned at the thought.

By now Noren had nearly finished re-filled the water trough. He got a drink for himself and gestured to Corin to lead the way.

"Are those the coursers?"he said, pointed to a log-rail fence, beyond which were maybe ten mares and as many foals, probably between newly-born and two years. Two mares looked like they might be pregnant again, and a little ways from the large tree stood a lone horse that looked like a stallion.

"That's the breeding herd and the foals still too young to ride. They're all tame, and being worked with."

They continued to walk along the fence, and past another fence that divided the enclosure. A little beyond a wide copse of trees stood, and drowsing in their shade were several horses. Corin explained that he grew the trees near the fences and watered the horses there so they would be easy to find and catch.

Then he showed the horses to Noren.

N

Noren held Victor's rope with one hand – that was what he had decided
to name the small golden chestnut stallion – and produced all the coins
he had for Corin. He had no idea what a good price for such a horse
would be – he did not even really know what quality Victor was – but he
had managed to argue Corin down to a price he could give. He would
have to ride him bareback until he could make him a saddle, but for now
he thought he could make Evena's bride fit him, even though his head
was much smaller.

A couple hours later, Noren sat in a copse having dinner with
Elninya and watching the horses. He had not really thought about the
fact that Evena was a mare and Victor was a young stallion until now,
but they were busily making him aware of that fact, as Victor harassed
Evena until a couple smart kicks backed him off, at least for a while.

The next day, Noren rode Victor north, since he was taking
Evena back to Treas now. It took all his attention to manage the horse
bareback, since he was still crazy about the mare, who Noren had to lead
behind him on a line, with the saddlebags attached to her saddle. By
noon, he was so sore that he dedicated that was enough for the day. He
left the horses in a thicket far off the road to graze and work things out
between them and went hunting for rabbit.

Elninya glided in well after dark while he was cooking the rabbit,
and crouched to watch him across the fire and complain about how
hungry she was. Though at least they should reach the foothills in a
couple more days, and then there would be good hunting.

The next day went much the same. Victor was lame on one leg,
probably from provoking Evena until she had kicked him, but that did
not stop him from trotting constantly, when Noren would have been
perfectly happy if he had just walked.

A few days later, Noren was almost sure the horses had bred.
They were both relating in a new way, and if anything Victor was more
manageable, though that could just be that he was spending all day with
Noren and learning to act like a riding horse, instead of a beast who did
what he chose. Noren was getting more comfortable, too, as his muscles
adjusted to riding bareback. But Elninya had left him, flying ahead into
the foothills where she could hunt and fly freely.

He could not begrudge her that, even if he liked her company.
Not only was it actually safer, but she was only coming into civilization

for him. Finally, he reached the mountains himself and left the horses to go hunting.

About a week later, Noren rode up on his old home after nightfall. He was willing to ride after dark since he knew the area well, even after a year's absence. He tied Evena to a tree just outside the village, where someone was sure to find her early in the morning, and left a pile of four deer skins beside the tree.

It would not nearly pay for his use for the horse, or for the bit and bridle he was about to take. Perhaps the addition of the foal would help. It might not be exactly the kind of blood that was valuable to them, but he knew new blood was valuable in and of itself, too. Then he took a portion of a paper bag and wrote a note on it.

I, Noren, return Evena to you. Sorry for the delay. I have been involved in the quest of the white oval, and must continue my search for Silmavalien. I cannot stay to meet you. I wish I could. I hope to see you all once again, especially you, Mom and Dad.

— Noren

Knowing that this last would never happen, he poked the note onto a twig where he hoped it would be seen, but where Evena could not eat it. He left the saddle on a nearby branch, flung all his bags over his shoulder, and returned to where he had left Victor. But he did not sleep until Elninya landed next to him later in the night and put her wing over him.

Noren woke late in the morning and berated himself for being lax. He was far too close to Treas and possible discovery, so he led Victor away as quickly as he could, not bothering to eat. Well into the evening he found a place to picket him and ate heartily. He was not going to return to civilization just yet.

A week and a half later Noren had something half-way between a bareback pad and a saddle. He had found a good flat stick to give form to the saddle so it would sit where it was supposed to and not roll around Victor's belly, and had whittled it with his knife to correct its flaws. Then he had folded a deerskin around it, to give himself something to sit on and to protect Victor from chaffing. It required a breastplate as well as a girth, and the stirrups were simple strips of deer hide that he could stick his feet through. It was not as nice as Evena's had been, but he hoped it would do.

A week later, once he had confirmed it did work, they came down from the mountains again, once again against Elninya's wishes.

Already Noren could tell that Victor, though much smaller, was much better suited for his purposes than Evena. He needed less water, and less food, and he did not get exhausted. He seemed to enjoy traveling, and Noren got the idea that Evena had always been unhappy about being by herself. Noren could tell Victor would rather have another horse around, but he also felt like the desert stallion was happy enough with just his rider and really saw Noren as a companion and friend.

Though that might be because Noren himself was already beginning to love him in a way he had never loved Evena or even imagined that he could. They seemed to understand each other better, too.

22
Decision

Something big snuffling and moving around woke Silmavalien in the middle of the night. She opened her eyes.

A bear had gotten into one of her sacks filled with meat. Without speaking or moving she woke the dragons. *Kill it.*

All around her dragons stirred. Several of them roared. The big dark bear did not seem to like it. He growled self-defensively, then turned and ran.

After a few moments, Silmavalien sat up. She got to her feet, and examined how much damage the bear had done. He had eaten most of her meat – only a dozen mouthfuls were left, and she was not about to eat after a bear – and totally torn apart one of her precious, irreplaceable sacks. From now on, someone would always keep awake to watch. Tiela volunteered to watch the rest of the night, and Silmavalien went back to sleep.

Silmavalien found it more difficult than usual to get up in the morning. Sometime in the evening, while she was trying to patient enough to thoroughly cook the rabbit before eating it, Minth reached out to her. A flick of thought, stronger than it usually took for her to notice him.

Was there something wrong? – Minth's question. Why was she feeling so distant from her dragons, even Minth? She had hardly spoken to any of them all day. – Her realization.

What's wrong? – Minth's thought. Was she unhappy.

Maybe. I don't know. She thought for a moment. *I suppose I feel a little discontent, like something's not quite right.*

Like what? Why? Those thoughts were Lighter's and Veine's.

I don't know.

She did not want to know, and she did not want to think about that fact either. She felt Minth notice that, but then she felt him at a loss as to how to help.

Ask the Lord of Light to show her? – Airrock's thought.

It could not really hurt, now could it? Silmavalien knelt. She slipped the ring of light off her finger, and placed it on her palm. *Lord of Light,* she prayed silently, *we think of our lives and all we have. Please show me why I don't feel content, and what to do about it. Thank you.*

No answer. She sat down. Just a moment later she got up to check if the rabbit was ready yet, for what felt like the ten thousandth time.

S

Silmavalien released the arrow. It sped, quick as the eye could follow, to pierce the wild pheasant.

A cruel, ugly, gargling laugh. Overwhelming terror.

"Lord of All Light!" She was falling, had dropped her bow, somehow just managed to draw her knife.

A heavy weight fell across her. She rolled onto her side as it struck her, plunged her knife into the orc, where it lay for a moment on her thigh. *Help!* she screamed with her mind.

Already nine dragons were racing towards her with everything they had.

The orc rose and Silmavalien, struggling against a terror which threatened to paralyze her, struggled to rise, too. His blade scraped across her lower arm in the struggle, leaving an open gash.

Two dragons dove from the sky and narrowly avoiding impaling or splattering themselves on trees. Airrock dove a length ahead, then Coroneth, and Silmavalien looked up from she knelt. It might have been her imagination, but white fire spurted from Airrock's nostrils and bright yellow from Coroneth's.

The orc was gone.

Silmavalien glanced at her arm. *Get my bags!* Blood spurted from the gash, and ignoring the pain she set about trying to bind her bearskin cloak around her arm, pulling it as tight as she could to slow the bleeding. *I hope I don't bleed to death.*

Minth, supported by the other dragons. She would not. She would not. She would live. Do not fear.

"Oh my lord," she moaned, "why'd you let this happen? I call on you. Why couldn't you have made a blast of light, or sent Aelaza, or something!"

"You –"

It was the voice she recognized, but it faded. She feared to hear. She could not hear. The voice abandoned her.

A couple minutes later, Airrock returned with her bags, and Silmavalien was wrapping fold after fold of cloth around her arm. When she finished she tied a strip of leather around it all to hold it secure.

But she felt weak, shaken, and almost dizzy. She doubted she would have survived without the dragons, but what she felt now reminded her of the shadow that had fallen on her soul in the valleys on the southern side of the Greater Aravin Mountains – so long ago as it now seemed.

"O Lord of All Light, don't let things stay this way," she pleaded, then leaned back against the pile of her belongings and closed her eyes. Around her ten dragons gathered, all watchful and all caring.

She slept.

A couple hours later she woke, still weak, but wanting to sing. Yet she had no idea what she should sing, or even if she could sing.

Sluggishly, she noticed some of the dragons weren't there anymore, and Jareth, Daurth, and Coroneth told they had left to hunt for them all. Beside her, Lighter was snuggled up under her uninjured arm, and he reminded her more than ever of Minth, who was now much too large to be cuddly in this way. She felt close to her dragons again, but deep inside she was desperately afraid it would not last.

The line of fire in her arm burned as hot as ever.

S

The next several days were more or less uneventful. Silmavalien recovered enough to do things. With her uninjured arm, and the occasional help of the dragons, she was able to build a campfire and cook. She could not hunt, so the dragons brought her their own prey to take what she wanted from, and she sensed their kind but gentle amusement at the turn of events. Minth – and the others – were happy to do for her what she had once done for them. They even managed to get water for her.

But her discontent remained, growing a little darker every day.

After about a week, Silmavalien walked to the nearest stream. She untied the leather around her arm, and then unwrapped the blood-soaked cloth, until only what was stuck to her skin remained. Then, she put her arm in the cold water for a few seconds at a time so she would not chill the wound and plied the cloth away.

At last it was done, and she was able to verify that the gash was not infected. But it felt so good to have it open to the air, so she left it unwrapped for the moment, and leaned comfortably against Minth's side.

"Will this ever be over? Will the world ever be safe and

comfortable?"

Minth had no answer for her, only his love.

"Lord of Light, can this, this, this discontentment be over, please? I want to feel purpose and meaning. I want to feel joy and peace. Please!"

Minth listened, watched, felt.

"Go down."

After my arm is healed. I can't right now.

"You know that is only an excuse."

"Okay." *Tomorrow morning.*

"No. Now!"

Silmavalien struggled in her thoughts. It was too extreme, too unreasonable, too stupid. Yet... yet, he had never really let her be lost, and he had done amazing things for her. No, no, this time it was really stupid. What harm could waiting the night hours possibly do?

Finally, she gave in.

Silmavalien quickly re-wrapped her arm, and called the dragons. She gathered her belongings and picked them up, then began walking west.

The disappointment in her heart deepened. Nothing seemed to have changed within her. There was no flood of joy or confidence. No deeper feeling of purpose and desire. No contentment. Nothing.

She did not know why she kept walking. She just did.

23

Command

Three days later Silmavalien was making her way down a narrow strip of green that zig-zagged across a precipice. The sun had risen above the mountains and for the moment there were no clouds, so that it shone down on her, clear and warm and bright.

She turned a corner.

The strip spread out into a wide flat mountain meadow. A line of orcs standing shoulder to shoulder, weapons in their hands, barred her way.

She stopped dead.

"Go back," commanded the largest orc in the center of the line. "Return above, and we will leave you be."

She almost obeyed. But, no. She was to *go down to the plains*. Terror crushed all her thoughts. Should she go back up and find another way down? She was about to turn around and sprint back up the incline.

"Go down."

The command was firm, unshakable like a rock, and it gave her something to hold to in the fear. *I will trust you. You have helped me before. You will help me again.... But how?* How?

"Just go. Never fear. I am with you."

"Lord of Light!" she cried, a prayer for him to act, and for courage for herself. If she was to act without fear ...

Even as she spoke, she took a flying leap down upon the orcs and dove between two of them. A blade slid across her arm near the shoulder, but she just ran with all she was worth. Behind her the dragons roared. She thought she felt a wave of heat, but it could easily have been her own effort.

Then she was falling, sliding, tumbling hopelessly.

She kept hitting lumps in the rock with different parts of her body, but the pain did not matter right now. She tried to grab of something, but only scraped half the skin off her hand. Certainly, she would be smashed to piece when she got to the bottom.

It felt like she fell for hours, but then she felt something slow her tumbling, sliding fall. The precipice curved out into a flat ledge. A few moments later she was still.

She was still, and every inch of her body hurt. Pain exploded in her side with every breath. Every inch of her was bruised, and her arms like they had been scrapped raw.

She could feel a bruise formed on her head. She was lucky not to have been knocked out. She reached out with her right hand – that arm felt scraped, but she did not think it was badly cut – and touched a lump of rock, inches from her head. At once she drew back in pain. It felt like fear coated her hand and arm.

She wiggled a foot and gasped at the slice of agony. *Everything hurt.*

Out of the corner of her eye she saw Veine gliding down, carrying Lighter by the scruff. She felt all the dragons now. None of them were harmed, they assured her. But they were worried for her.

Her sight blurred and went gray. She was going to die soon. She reached out to Minth. *I love you.*

"Lord of Light," she whispered, "why? Please? What about our dragons?"

S

Silmavalien tried to stretch, but stabbing pain stopped her mid-motion.

Memory flooded back. Why was the pain so much less intense than she remembered? She had the oddest feeling that someone had poured healing water, liquid light, over all her wounds, and even down her insides. Why was she even alive? She should have died from the blood loss. *Was* she dead? Was that why she felt better?

No, she was *not* dead. Minth's assurance could not have been clearer, and the other nine chimed in a chorus of agreement. Lighter twitched his golden scaled tail in the edge of her vision.

From the position in which she lay Silmavalien inspected as much of herself and her surroundings as she could. She was wearing one of the gowns she had taken with her from Treas, only it had been cleaned, but she seemed to be in the same position she had fallen in. She was laying on something soft, perhaps some sort of mysterious plant matter. What she could see of her arms and her hand was wrapped with a thin layer of a soft cloth.

Then she saw the ledge and gasped, then winced at the pain. Only a few feet from she lay it dropped right away. She could see a somewhat distant line of tree-tops beyond, and far beyond that the sea and the plains.

Slowly, carefully, and too painfully, Silmavalien raised herself on her right arm, and looked up. She nearly fainted again. It must have taken dozens of miracles to get her down that precipice alive. One *small* section of cliff, narrower than she was long, curved upwards to meet the sheer cliff face so smoothly she could not tell where it changed from being sheer to not-so-sheer. All around it, the rock of the precipice and the ledge she lay on met in an angle like that of the ground and a straight wall.

Had she been just a little off, in either direction, she would have died. Countless rocks, some of them jagged, projected from the cliff face, but a comparatively smooth gully ran through the rocks to the top. Had she not come down through that, she would have been hurled over the precipice, over the ledge, down, down, down, faster, faster, faster.

Her head swam just to think about it.

Again, 'slowly, carefully, and too painfully' Silmavalien raised herself to a sitting position and inspected her own body. The sword-cuts on her left arm were nicely wrapped with the same soft, gauzy white stuff.

Who wrapped me? she wondered. *What is this cloth-stuff? Why did they do it?* Did the dragons know?

But she had hardly thought when she knew that none of them knew any more than she had. Lighter and several others had been with her all afternoon, and they were certain that at least two of them had always been awake, but they had not seen or felt anything.

Silmavalien continued her 'slow, careful, and too painful' inspection of her body. Her ribs were wrapped tightly with a double layer of the same soft material. With her uncut, though badly scraped and therefore wrapped, arm she pulled up the cloth of her gown to inspect her legs. Most of them was lightly wrapped too, while the more severe wounds were more heavily. Her foot was tightly and heavily wrapped. She breathed a sign of relief, which was cut short. *"Ouch!"*

Still, she could move it without the pain she had felt earlier, or rather she could hardly move it at all. The wraps kept it secure, just like the ones wrapped around her ribs made breathing and moving less painful.

She scanned the evening sky, in which stars were beginning to twinkle. The crisp purply color of the evening sky drew her out of pain and into delight. She loved the flaming glow of the sunset, just visible beyond the edges of the Greater Aravin Range, so far, far away. She loved that sliver of a crescent moon.

Moved to an attitude of gratitude, she bowed her head. She could not get at the ring on her finger, because her hand was wrapped, but maybe that did not matter. In awed whispers, she prayed, "O my Lord of All Light, thank you for my life, and my dragons' lives. Thank you for taking care of me and that we're all right. Thank you for the stars. Thank you for the sunset. Thank you for the moon. Thank you for the sky, the air, the mountains."

Glancing around again, she saw the pile of her belongings and next to it, what she had wearing before whoever had taken care of her had done so.

But her bow was not in her quiver, and she needed it. She whispered another prayer. "Lord of All Light, would you please help us find my bow. You know how much I need it. Thank you for hearing and caring about me."

Directly afterwards Silmavalien asked the dragons if they could help find her precious bow, which was probably 'down below' somewhere. They would, they said, and they did not mind, but Airrock did not forget to remind her that she did not need it nearly as much as she thought she did. They could easily bring her food, and they would be happy to do so.

A soft breeze blew, and she shivered a little. "Can you bring me some wood, please?" she said into the air.

Tiela spread her wings and glided down. Airrock and Wydth followed from where they had perched on boulders a bit further up the precipice. More of the dragons followed, but Minth stayed where he was next to Silmavalien, and Veine glided down and landed between her and the ledge.

That way, she would not have to worry about falling off the cliff if she somehow moved in her sleep. And they would keep Lighter safe, too.

Again, 'slowly, carefully, and too painfully' Silmavalien to her bags and took out some wrapped rabbit to eat. Then she pulled her bearskin cloak over herself as a blanket, and Minth put his wing over her like a tent.

A few hours later the dragons had collected a pile of wood, and built it so that it was just like they had seen Silmavalien make it so many times before, but she looked as warm and comfortable as she could be, they did not wake her.

N

The Nightmare Lord stood in his throne and growled. The air thickened with his wrath. "Ten?! Ten fire-breathing dragons? I thought it was five."

"No, my lord," replied the imp. "One is a hatchling gold male. One breathed fire, but six sputtered flame. Given the dragons' behavior she survived running off the cliff."

"She? This is a Dragon-keeper and a female? Who is she?" The Nightmare Lord's voice was like thunder, a horrible thunder but one that had its glory and power because of the echoes still alive in it of what it had once been

"Silmavalien of Treas."

"Silmavalien of Treas! How?! By my calculations, she was one of the last five humans on the world who might be a dragon-keeper. Is this certain?"

"Certain."

"It's ridiculous!" yelled the Nightmare Lord. "How does she walk in the one direction where there's a dragon egg, miles and miles away! Before I destroyed the dragons she'd hatch dozens in weeks! How does she charge through orcs and run off cliffs and live! It's ludicrous." He drew his serrated-blade and swished it back and forth. "And how many female dragons are there?"

Frightened, the creature of fear and hate replied, "Three, my lord. O my lord, do not harm your servant, my lord."

The Nightmare Lord swished his blade to and fro several more times, perilously close to the demon. Then, he drew back. He flung his arm and sword high. "Gargoyles, arise and descend upon Silmavalien of Treas. Abysstreaders, go forth and obliterate. Go!"

A voice spoke, more strong and firm than the foundations of the world. "You may not. Stay."

Even the Nightmare Lord fell to the ground, cowering and covering his ears. Fear was as much his lord as it was any of the nightmare's servants.

24

Things To Be Thankful For

Silmavalien woke to the chittering of birds. Soft light filtered through Minth's almost-transparent white wings, and he was humming. Oh, how she loved the thrum that emanated from his sides. Contentment, like a wide, strong rider flowed through him and then into her.

He raised his wing and folded it back against his side, exposing her to the morning air and light. Veine no longer lay between her and the edge; instead the female dragon soared over a cliff high above, hunting a herd of deer close to the edge. Where Veine had been, there now lay the branch of a grape, bearing many clusters of the large purple-red grapes that were her favorite.

She knew who had brought them. Airrock. *Thank you,* Silmavalien sent to her, though Airrock was not the type of dragon to take thanks.

Without too much pain, she managed to reach the grapes and pull off several clusters. *Thank you, O Lord of Light, for this.* She offered the thought as the fruit popped in her mouth.

Minth nipped off one of the clusters and quickly devoured it, stems and all. His delight flowed over her. *Yumm.* The grapes were good!

Songeth and Tiela flew in from the sea and landed to perch on the cliff above her. They started chattering, and she understood that the dragons had held a council while she slept. They had decided that at least two of them would always be with her, in addition to Lighter. At least until she was fully recovered, that was.

Amazement and gratitude filled Silmavalien. *Thank you all.* Not *that* long ago, though soon it would feel that way, she had been the dragon-mother who cared for and protected them. Now they were the dragon guardians, who cared for and protected her. *Thank you.*

Thank you, Lord of Light. Thank you for these loving and caring dragons. Thank you for this *life.* Then with a new perspective she prayed, *Thank you for giving us an opportunity to learn just how great all these dragons really are, through what happened yesterday.*

Minth swung his head around, and gently kissed her cheek. *Finally!* seemed to be the gist of what he was feeling and telling her.

Oh. You understood long before I did, didn't you? She understood a surprising *no*. He had not. Not *really*, and not *long*. She kissed his nose, and realized she had never really told him how sorry she was for imposing so much fear on him as a hatchling. She kissed him again and told him.

Love flowed through him and from him to her. She returned it. The love uniting them more closely than ever, he turned, spread his wings, and glided down. He was hungry.

Silmavalien watched him descend, smiling. How he was grown from the helpless little thing he had hatched as. Now his shoulders were as high as her elbow, and alone of all the dragons, he had really *breathed fire!* That was the heat she had felt above, though he could not figure out how to repeat the flames just yet. But they looked like a thick molten red substance! He told her all about it, excited about his flames, even though they had come out of a moment of sickening terror and worry. He showed her how his stomach had clenched when she darted forward, how the buckets of fire had poured out of his mouth with every breath, and then sputtered out.

She suggested that maybe he had used up all his 'fire-substance.' And she did not know how long it would take to come back, but he might have to wait for that before he could try again.

Lighter wandered back over from where he had been exploring the ledge under the watchful eye of Airrock. He lay down next to her, making sure to be careful not to let his tail or wings touch her, and told her how soft and nice her bed was.

She invited him to snuggle a little closer to the parts of her that were not too hurt. There really was something about him that was very like Minth, though she could already tell he was not going to look much like him, and he was going to be much bigger, too. Bigger even than Wydth she thought, and whereas Minth's shoulders only came up to her elbows, Wydth was already almost as tall as she was.

She reached over and gently touched the scaleless skin under Lighter's chin and behind his ears, the only parts of him that were soft and smooth enough they did not hurt her scraped and cut fingers.

Soon, she lay back, too injured and weak to do anything, far too rested to fall asleep, and rather bored. Songeth lost no time in letting her know he would do something about this. He called for Veine to come and take his watch with Tiela, then flew off to coordinate a warbler orchestra.

The music was beautiful, but before long Silmavalien found

herself far more tired than she expected and started drifting off.

Hours later, she woke to the gust of wind as Minth landed on the ledge. With a start, she realized he was past due for being groomed and oiled. She probably should have done it a day or two before falling off the cliff, and it definitely needed to be done now. He was not uncomfortable yet, but she could see the skin flaking and the cracks starting in the drier patches.

She pulled a bag to her and started looking for the oil. *Hopefully,* she thought, as she slowly sorted through the chaotic mess, *I can do this without hurting myself too badly.*

Minth stepped a bit further along the ledge and lay down. He would do his best to make this as easy as possible, he told her.

Finally, she got the oil and got to her feet, leaning against Minth to support herself. She was stiff and sore, and wobbly, and she was really glad her foot had been wrapped so well, whoever had done it. Almost every motion hurt, and even just standing with as little weight on it as she could manage, hurt too, though it was not as sharp as some of her other pains. It was at least badly sprained, and probably broken, too.

It took the rest of the afternoon and evening to oil Minth, and she had to take a break to rest half-way through. When she was done, she ate some more grapes and stretched as well as she could without hurting herself. It was very fortunate, she thought, that Wydth did not need oiling, as big as he was. It was a good thing she would not have to oil Veine, Tiela, Airrock, or Lighter either, but that still left four more dragons. She would try to take care of Jareth and Daurth tomorrow, though. At least both of them were still a lot smaller than Minth. She thought Coroneth and Songeth could go a few more days, and she would need more fat oils for them, too.

Can one of you bring me a kill tomorrow? Maybe the fattest one you could find?

They acknowledged her, and then a surge of excitement cut through the acknowledge.

Jareth had found her bow!

S

The next morning Silmavalien went through the things she had been wearing when she fell off the cliff, just to have something to do. The bearskin cloak she had been using as a blanket was badly torn, but she decided she was very grateful she had been wearing it, as it looked like it might have protected her from a lot of things that would have killed her.

She slipped her back into its quiver, and realized she had lost all but five arrows. For a moment she was flailing in a bog of disappointment and anger.

Then came words from she-had-no-idea-where. *Thank you.*

She was alive. And she had her bow, and she still had three of the arrows from Treas, and two others. And as Airrock had reminded her, she did not even need her bow anymore, though she would like to have it.

She took a moment to remember that, then held up the skirt she had been wearing. It was useless now, barely more than strips of cloth still attached at the waist, and most of those strips were so ragged and torn she was not sure she could even use them for anything. She held it in her hands, considering.

She needed to make her own clothes, and hopefully some more durable things. This was only the worst example. Her clothes from Treas has been suitable for a woman's life in the village, from tilling a bed to unhurriedly climbing a tree. None of it was made for hunting in the forest and spend every minute in the wilderness. She supposed she should be grateful her clothes had lasted as long as they had.

Then again, she had no idea where she would be living next. If in a few months she was living in a treeless grassland, her fragile clothing might be just fine, even for hunting, there. But she really had no idea. Her predictable village life had long ago been shattered – if that predictability had not been just an illusion.

At any rate, it was not predictable now.

She let the skirt fall out of her hands, and watched Airrock and Coroneth flying in circles above and below her. The curves that undulated through their bodies, especially visible in their necks and tails, reminded her of the ripples on a lake, constantly moving but always the same. She watched their wings, the way they folded and cupped the air. She wished she could see it better and understand how it worked better, but she could see enough to see that their wings definitely worked a little differently.

She could have watched them for hours without being bored. She wondered when any of them would be big enough and strong enough to carry her.

She especially wondered when Minth would be.

S

Stars twinkled in the sky. Violet-lilac cloud streamers graced the deep blue expanse. Songeth stood on one of the boulders above her, and she could feel his tail twisting around itself. She craned her neck back to look at him.

His eyes, a deep hard purple that matched the sky, locked with hers.

Let's sing.

He opened his mouth, and out flowed a succession of beautiful notes. A shiver of wonder crawled down her spine. Songeth's music pushed the ache in her side to a place where it did not reach her, and she took a deep breath to sing the words that flowed between her and the dragon.

> Stars of wonder
> Twinkling and bright
> All on fire
> High in the sky
> Our light in the night

Evening stars
Ordained to shine
Through the dark
Light from the sky
To brighten the night

Stars and streamers
Reflecting light
Down on earth
Shining up high
To light up the night

Stars of our hope
Bestowing light
Down below
"Fly now up high
"And shine in the night."

The last note floated away, like the fading-purple streamers. The beauty of it lingered inside her and supported her, and she relaxed even further.

Suddenly, consciousness of the pain in her ribs flooded back, and she cringed. Why had she done that? She should have known better.

Minth landed beside her and nuzzled her face very gently. After resting, and deliberately breathing shallowly, she ate several more grape clusters and some rabbit. She told the dragons she wanted the fat in the morning. She was too tired and had already exerted too much that day.

She drank the last of her water, and let the dragons know so they could re-fill it, though it was no hurry. She was not thirty and would not be ready to boil it until the morning.

She kissed Minth on the nose and stroked his cheek lovingly before lying down. "I love you," she whispered. "I'm so thankful for you."

He loved her and was thankful for her, too. Together they thanked the Lord of All Light. Then she lay down as comfortably as possible, and Minth spread his wing over her. Above them, Songeth vocalized a lullaby, and Minth hummed. The rock around her and her own body throbbed with the sound of his contentment.

25

Living on the Cliff—Ledge

Silmavalien spent the day preparing oil for the dragons' skin from deer fat, cooking, and oiling Jareth and Daurth. Yesterday, they had insisted that it was more important for her to rest and heal, and they could go another day, and there was nothing she could do to force the issue.

It was probably a good thing they had done that. Her right foot burned when she stepped on it, and she could hardly use her left arm, either. She could not use most of her fingers, since they had been cut and wrapped as well, and her back too was bruised and sore. It was hard for her to do even the simplest thing, and though several times she wanted to sing, she kept herself from doing so, remembering the agony that had caused last night.

But for some reason, today the thought of singing brought back thoughts of Treas. Autumn nights around a bonfire, the entire village gathered together, and she would sing for all of them. Sometimes, it would be part of a group song, but sometimes she would sing a solo song, or one of her making.

Or it could be a moonlit summer night. Or deep winter, several families tightly gathered around a hearth. Or a bonfire, if it was dry enough for that. She loved all the dragons, and she lived this life she had, but oh, how she missed Treas. It was still, in some way, *home.*

And how she missed Noren. *I hope you're still alive,* she thought, hoping the prayer could reach him in some way. *With that dragon. Will we ever meet again? I'm glad to be blessed with this family of dragons, but how I really wish I could know and love you, too. Have you here, with us.*

Perhaps, she thought, she could ask the Lord of Light to reunite them, and maybe even all of Treas. She wondered why she had not thought of that before, and then added a request that all of Aneri be delivered from the lie. Especially Silrah, since she did not know much about other countries.

And she knew nothing at all about how dragons were regarded in North Aneri, or other continents. That thought led her to review what she *had* been told of them, whether it was true or not, whether even their names were true, since there was very little she could do to keep herself occupied, since she could not even sing. And some of the stories, true or false, were interesting. In Ellenesia, immortal elves were supposed to rule and keep humans in subjection, and far in the south there was a land named Galen, the home of all exotic places. At the farthest point of the world, in the uttermost south, lay Tamrec, from which immortal dragons had flown forth to devour humanity.

Thinking about it, Silmavalien wondered if it was a very different legend, about a very different kind of dragon, than the ones she knew. Some stories had made it seem like the demon dragons of the witch-dragonriders and the dragons of Tamrec were the same, but when she thought about the stories, that did not really make sense. No, she did not know if the dragons of Tamrec were real, but if they were, they were something else, and the legends of Tamrec were almost certainly about something different.

The next morning Silmavalien was so sick and tired of this 'slowly, carefully, and too painfully' thing that it made her want to pull her hair out. Her first prayer was that she would heal quickly, but then she was reminded that she had already been healed quickly. Her injuries would have killed her days ago, if the Lord of Light had not sent some unknown help. All she could reasonably do was give thanks again.

Then she oiled Songeth and sank back down into her bedding, which was amazingly still soft and fresh, to rest. She felt sick, and she did not want to see – or smell – raw meat, so she asked Lighter to take the kill Airrock had brought for him to the other side of the ledge.

She woke early in the morning, to the coldness of dawn's first gray light. She still felt sick, maybe she even felt sicker, but she was bored beyond thought of being unable to do anything. She wished she could toss and turn, but she knew that would be much too painful.

Minth noticed her distress and moved soothingly into her mind, trying to relieve the pain and stress. Mentally, she cuddled against his comforting bulk, and a few minutes later Songeth arrived and joined them on the ledge. He crooned a quieting lullaby, and after what felt like hours of frustrating awareness, while the sky grew slowly light, she dozed again.

She woke again. The morning sun was just barely still far enough north that a few of its red rays still reached her. Minth was hungry again. He no longer ate every day, but she could feel his desire to go hunt. Sleepily, she encouraged him to go. He lifted his wing from over and flew away, and his white wings gleamed reddish in the light. He was beautiful, now. So beautiful.

"Okay, Coro." She spoke out loud just for the sake of it, since Coroneth could not have even heard her through his ears. "I hope you've taken care of your belly already, since it's your turn to be my 'guardian' this morning. I'll work on your grooming and oiling throughout the day, too."

She felt a moment of disappointment. Whatever he was doing, he was irritated to be interrupted. Then pleasure replaced that. He would get to spend the day with her.

You do, she told him, a smile plastered on her face. At least that did not hurt.

Several hours later, Silmavalien woke out of another doze to her stomach growling with hunger. But just the thought of most foods made her want to vomit.

A cluster of grapes smacked her on the face and she opened her eyes to see Coroneth's mouth open in a wide grin above her. She felt his amusement, and it almost made her laugh, before he stepped back and blocked the flow. Laughing definitely would hurt her ribs.

But he might be right that she could eat a few grapes. At least if she was careful to eat them slowly.

That did not do much about the boredom though, but she had an idea. "Would any of you like to go and see what those plains are like?"

Yes! Airrock unfurled her wings from where she perched on the cliff above, and Silmavalien felt the wind in her face. Who wanted to take her place?

Tiela would. Her mental voice sounded groggy with sleep, and she explained Airrock had woken her. But she did not think she was going to go back to sleep right now anyways, and she could always sleep later. She would take Airrock's place so her friend could fly down and have an adventure.

Be careful, Silmavalien reached out to caution Airrock, trying to summon the strength to make her warning stick. *Be careful. You don't know what's down there. We don't know if humans are down there and if they kill dragons.*

She fought to push through Airrock's disdain for that. Humans? How would they catch her? How would they sneak up on her? She would feel them and how could they ever get her in the air?

Arrows, said Silmavalien. *Be careful. It won't hurt you to be careful.*

She wouldn't get hit by arrows, Airrock promised, and

Silmavalien did not know whether to take that as a promise she would be careful, or a promise about her abilities. She was beginning to be afraid this was a very bad idea, but there was nothing she could do to stop Airrock now that she had given her the idea.

And probably she could have done nothing to keep Airrock from getting the idea herself sooner or later. But it might have been better to send someone more cautious first, sometime when Airrock was asleep.

Just then, Tiela landed on the ledge, as close to Coroneth as she could. Their wings brushed as she folded hers, and Silmavalien smiled, but the ache in her heart grew.

She recognized the emotions coursing through Tiela for Coroneth. They were not the same as what she had – did – feel for Noren, but there was no mistaking the similarity. But she tried to keep her hurt inside. She did not want to spoil this for them.

Then Veine joined Airrock, and as they got near to the plains, they shared what they saw with Silmavalien, and it was a welcome distraction. She saw through their eyes the ripple of dirt – like a crumpled sheet, she thought – where the mountain cliffs met the plains. Hills and cliffs ran out from the mountains, much like the rock ridges that ran out in the sea, and where one range of ridges melted into the ground, another smaller row rose up. The hills were covered with wild apricots, plums, peaches, and other trees, some of them kinds Silmavalien recognized, and some of them kinds she had never seen before. Streams wound between the hills on their way to the sea, and beyond the woody hills the dragons saw what looked like grassy plains that turned yellow and dry as they spread to the northwest, away from the mountains and the sea.

The next day, Silmavalien used up the last of her oil again on Minth. She sank down into her bedding and thought. He had been elaborating about how he wanted to breathe fire again, and how good it had felt, but he could not figure out how, so he was asking her for any ideas.

"How about you try to suck in your breath for an abrupt gulp, and right away really clench and pull your stomach in." Almost without thinking about, she was going to demonstrate what she meant with her own body, when a stab of pain reminded her. "And stay away while you do it," she finished in a harsh gasp.

Minth shifted over a few steps, and then out of his open mouth and nostrils streamed a flood of thick, red flame. It quickly evaporated, but Silmavalien still felt the heat where she was. He tried again, right away, and a smaller stream of flame followed.

"We did it!"

Minth tried again, but only sputters came. Then he noticed that his stomach hurt.

"That's okay. You just used that muscle more in the last half minute that you have in your entire life till now... Your fire'll get better and stronger with practice, just like anything else you do. Maybe try a couple times a day, or whatever you're comfortable with."

Airrock flew down from above. She would try next. Graceful and confident as always, she stretched her neck out, pulled her head in, and breathed out a haze of white fire, that spread out and floated up, instead of flowing down like Minth's. It was hotter, too, since it warmed Silmavalien, even though she was much further away.

Airrock sprang into the air and did a back-flip, her wings tightly folded so they would not get in the air. She did it! Someone else got to go next!

Coroneth had an idea, and Silmavalien thought, *When do you not?*

But this time the other dragons followed him exuberantly. Together, he, Tiela, Wydth, Songeth, and Veine spread their wings and leapt from their perches. Moments later, colored fire – red and orange and yellow – filled the skies above Silmavalien.

S

The days went on, ever so slowly. Everything had to be done so 'slowly, carefully, and too painfully," and given this Silmavalien had rather too much to do – cooking, preparing oil, oiling the dragons. It took all her energy, and so much of her time, and far too much pain, and it still left her bored and restless.

However, she was beginning to heal, even if far too slowly for her tastes. She unwrapped her right arm, and found that it was so delicious to feel the air on her still-too-damaged-to-scratch skin. She also found that, though bloodstained, the white gauzy material was still soft, and did not stick either to herself or to itself. That discovered, she decided to 'slowly, carefully, and too painfully' unwrap everything except her ribs and deeper wounds. She re-wrapped her foot after only a short air – she could too easily re-injure it by accidentally flexing it.

Everything else, tender and scabbed as it was, she decided to leave unwrapped overnight, given how good the air felt on it.

The dragons developed their fire-breath. All of them practiced every day, and they learned to breathe the fire for longer and to have more control over it. For a while, Tiela and Coroneth remained mutually infatuated with each other, though several others of the male dragons sometimes tried to get her attention, and occasionally she gave it to them. Then, gradually but quickly, she seemed to lose interest. For a few days, it was back and forth, and sometimes Coroneth or another male dragon would give her attention she did not want, or vie versa.

Then it was over. Silmavalien wondered how soon they would be ready to court and mate, and she worried that maybe she would never be without hatchlings. But, all in all, Tiela's interactions with the males did not remind her of Noren for long, and it soon seemed so different she wondered how she had compared the two even for a moment. Instead, she found that it was rather fun – and funny – to watch.

Though she hoped when they got older the dragons would not fight over this. She would hate to be caught up in that sort of thing. But while all of this was happening, she continued to heal, and they kept growing. One afternoon, shortly after it seemed everyone had forgotten about the differences between male and female, she called to them all. "I'm still sore," she told them, "but I think some of you could carry me, and I think I'm well enough to hang onto you as well as I'll ever be able to do. I won't make you carry anything, but I think I can ride one of you, and the others can grab my bags. Does that sounds like a good idea?"

She took a deep breath, and continued, "We could finally finish obeying the Lord of Light's command for us to go down to the plains. You can take me."

She felt the movement of the dragons' thoughts as they consulted one another. It was evening. Better to do that kind of thing in the morning.

26

Explanations, False and Unknown

Once Noren accumulated enough money to buy Victor a better saddle, he found riding the horse among other people to be a strange experience. When Noren told people that he came from an obscure mountain village, they thought that he was joking. If he persuaded them that he was actually serious, then they asked questions like, "So, how did you get to where you are now?"

He told them that his sister had gone out to look for a different place to live, and possibly a spouse better than anyone she could expect to find in their small, out-of-the-way village. He did not know where she had ended up since then, but they had been close, so he wanted to find her. He was not interested in anything in his village, but he was an accomplished hunter, so he hunted deer and sold their hides, and had bought a horse. He also liked to travel and see things.

When someone asked for her name, and what she was like, Noren told them everything he could that might help them recognize her if they knew her, but which he hoped would not bring attention to anything about her that could point to her being a Dragonrider.

That night, laying in a thicket, Noren wondered if he should tell that story to everyone. Questions would be asked, and it was close enough to the truth, but not too close. It could already be put together from other things he said and did, and it might be better to offer it freely. That might avoid other questions that might raise suspicions, and it would greatly expand his reach in searching for Silmavalien. Yes. He would do that.

He could tell that Elninya felt something negative towards this plan, but it was not clear to him what it was or why. What did she think? What did she feel? Did she think it was wrong? Did she think it would be disastrous?

She could answer none of his questions, and he could get from her only a certainty that Silmavalien lived. Her certainty intrigued him, but he could not understand it, and she could give him no answers to any questions he asked about that, either. He did not know how she could even know Silmavalien, yet in her thoughts there was something of his beloved that he knew could have come from his memories, yet Elninya was certain this was the person that he knew. So certain that, even in his own mind, Noren could not question it.

He decided to go through with his plan of action anyways, and Elninya did not seem hurt by it.

As the days went on, Noren's love for Victor continued to grow. He wondered sometimes if it had to do with the fact that Evena did not belong to him and he had always known he would have to give her back. That might explain why he had never gotten so close to her. But the two horses were also nothing like each other. Even the fact Victor was a stallion might have been part of it, since Noren had always founded he preferred working with Treas' stallions to the mares. But Victor was different from any of them too, and Noren loved the feel of cantering down the road with him. He loved his energy, and that something, that force or power that he displayed in the way he tossed his mane or lifted his head, or just the way he moved, and in his voice!

And he could tell that Victor liked him as much as he liked the horse.

ℵ

The rumors about the evil Dragonrider continued, though they were not as constant a subject of conversation as they had been. Yet by now they had made their way into all the little villages, and people were talking about them there, too, so there was nowhere Noren could get away from it. He hated being reminded of what he had done. Even if he could have believed the excuses that suggested himself to his mind, and been confident the blame did not lie on him but on whoever spread the lie that that dragons were demons and Dragonriders were witches, it would not have satisfied him. *That,* he knew pleased Elninya, and if it could have satisfied, she would not have let him. But he felt that what he had done, and still could do, ought to kill him.

It rendered him fit for torture. It was not an idea of justice or punishment that he felt. It was the stain of his failure on his life, and just as horribly, the stain of it upon the whole world. He felt the irremediable evil of it, the unendurable horror, the anguish of it in his soul.

Finally, he decided to talk to Elninya about it again. Even though he could speak to her across any distance, he feared the conversation would show on his face, and in his tone of voice if he to talk to others, so he waited until he was alone at night, in a rather unpopulated place.

Sitting down on the leaves and wet grass, he asked her, *Why did you make me tell them about it?! I could have written, "I killed your daughter. I'm sorry,"* and left out that *I was a Dragonrider – or my name. It was so stupid to put 'Dragonrider' in there. 'Dragonrider' implies that you shared responsibility for me – if I do something as a Dragonrider I do it with you or by you. You absolutely shared no responsibility! You tried to stop me.*

What I'm saying is, I could have written, "I killed your daughter. I'm sorry," *if I had to write anything at all, and I do not – and never did – see the reason for it. What does it tell them they do not know, that they could possibly need to know, or that might help them – unless I explained that part of the reason this happened is that Dragonriders are considered witches, and not we aren't just afraid for our own lives, but for our dragons whom we love, and that while Dragonriders have committed some horrifying crimes, it is because of this fear, not because Dragonriders are any more evil than other humans, and certainly not because of dragons. Thus, this will not happen if we are no longer hunted and burned alive!*

"*Perhaps I was wrong,*" Elninya answered him, her voice quiet and calm. "*You are probably right that it was a stupid thing to do, and I should not have forced you like that. But it has not done you any harm.*"

I'm embarrassed and upset that I listened to you! It was the most stupid thing for me to do. It was wrong.

"*That hasn't harmed you either. None of it will do you any harm.*"

Noren got to his feet and kicked a root with his boot, mindless of the pain.

"*Noren, I care about you. I love you.*" Her voice was earnest, sincere, and a little sad.

Noren acknowledged her, but he was still upset. "You can't have done – forced me to do – these things out of love for me," he growled under his breath. She heard him, of course, but did not respond.

It's done the whole world harm! he raged to himself. *At least, this whole part of the world. It's only made people more certain that Dragonriders are evil. It's only provided credence to the rumors.*

"*There's an answer to that, Noren. I don't know it, and I certainly cannot tell it to you, but it is. I know it is, and you should know it is, too. And –* " her voice dropped again, even quieter – "*I meant it when I said I should not have forced you. I am sorry for that.*"

You're crazy, Elninya, he said. He loved her, but he meant it. She was all the courage he lacked, and she was crazy, besides. He could feel it. *"It is fitting for a dragon to die by fire."* She had really meant it, and she did all these things because of that. Torture and death were not things she cared about.

𝒩

Sometime after this, a wealthy man of some rank approached Noren to pay him to carry something to another city. While Elninya expressed her displeasure in the back of his mind, Noren consented. *You're a stupid idiot, dragon,* he told her. *This will give me an excuse to go to that place, and look for Silmavalien, without anyone asking me questions. Why do you think* everything *is a bad idea?*

Before long, Noren found himself somewhat regularly engaged in carrying things across Silrah, giving him the opportunity to learn about different places, visit villages, and look for Silmavalien more freely without arousing people's suspicions. But Elninya was very upset about it. She had to hunt in distant, unpopulated areas, while he traveled Silrah. They were often separated, and even though they could communicate freely across any distance, they liked to be together. She wanted to be with him and to sleep with him! Meanwhile, he scolded her. She wanted to meet another dragon, did she not? And there were other benefits to this as well! Without having to hunt in order to eat, he could spend more time looking for Silmavalien. If he found her, he would find her dragon, and Elninya could have a friend. And if her dragon was a male, Elninya could have a mate. He and Silmavalien, and their dragons, could both raise families.

None of his arguments affected her, and their bond meant that her unhappiness made him unhappy too. Yet, he continued. If he quit his new job, that invite questions, and if his explanations was not good enough, it would people suspicious. If people got too suspicious, a serious investigation of him might even lead to discover of what he was, and even so, it was much safer traveling the kingdom as a low-priority courier, who could go wherever he wanted on the job without having to answer questions he did not want to. All that was needed to get himself into even the largest cities was a wave of his pendant.

But he wished he could have Elninya with him, to tell him what she knew about the people he met.

27

Meeting Keya

It was early in the night when Silmavalien woke. Brilliant, gem-like stars shone in the sky above, and the dragons told her Aelaza was leaping down the cliff. Other Ellenari were disappearing above the cliff, going one way or that, but most of them together. She wondered what was happening, but before she had time to wake up fully and become afraid, Aelaza stood before her.

"You and the dragons are to go down to the plain at once," she said.

"Did I do wrong?" Silmavalien asked. "When I thought, this evening, of going down, and the dragons thought it better to wait until morning, should I have pushed it?"

"I do not know," said Aelaza, "and there is no time for me to answer these questions. If you go down at once, you will face no trouble doing so."

"I need to know!"

"Do what you know you must do now, and do not worry or waste time about the past. I'm not human, and I can't help you with this. We will protect you, but you must go at once."

"Okay," said Silmavalien, still distressed. She asked Coroneth to land on the ledge and settled herself on his shoulders. The others grabbed her bags in their mouths or their claws. Tiela grabbed Lighter. With a dizzying lurch, Coroneth dropped from the ledge and spread his wings, stopping their fall, and gaining altitude to glide down to the plains. She gripped him tightly between her legs, and her half-healed wounds burned from the effort.

It was hard for him, too, he told her.

Yes, Coro. I know I'm kind of heavy, but you're only carrying me a short distance, and mostly down!

Still, she followed Coroneth's instructions and sat straighter, even though she hated it. She wanted to lean down and wrap her arms around his neck, to make herself feel more secure. This way, the cold wind blew in her face with a lot of force. But Coroneth told her that it would not help her to wrap her arms around his neck, and it interfered with him. He could not get his wing-beats right with her clutching him and interfering with his neck like that.

There were a lot of dragons flying around and under them, he reminded her. If she did fall off, someone would catch her. He would fly above the others and not get close to the ground until they landed, if that would make her more comfortable.

Then the cold wind turned foul, and they felt a maddening terror. Uncomfortable, tense, and sore as she was, Silmavalien twisted around on Coroneth's shoulders to get a look. She saw two wings moving, blotting out the stars, diving for them. Another glance showed her more of the creatures, farther away or further to the side.

Fear overcame her. Aelaza had lied to her! She had gone down at once and they were having trouble, and they would be destroyed, killed, thrown out of the skies into the ground and the void! She cowered, throwing her arm up and her body forward, over Coroneth's shoulders.

She felt him swerve under her, trying to compensate for what she had done with her weight, and not lose her.

A bow sang, an arrow shot through the air, and she recognized the sound of the bows of the Ellenari – maybe even Aelaza herself. Light filled her mind. She sat straight up, and raised her hand. Lightning gleamed from her ring, and she and Coroneth found themselves in a sphere of light floating in the dark sky, the stars shining far above them. The lightning struck at their pursuers and threw them from the air with a flash of brilliance.

Coroneth, I'm sorry.

He acknowledged her curtly.

In the distance, she still heard the combat of the Ellenari, but they continued downwards, the dragons flying as quickly as the slowest of them could. The faster ones paced themselves not to get ahead of Coroneth or Tiela or Daurth.

The song of the Ellenari's bows faded. New sounds broke in on Silmavalien's ears. They were strangely familiar, and yet new, for she had only heard them through her dragons' ears before. They were the sounds of breakers on the beach. She knew then that they were nearly on the ground. *At last!*

The sound of the breakers faded. Coroneth told her he was about to land. She was so sore, all over, her whole back and torso, too, from sitting on him. She followed his instructions, letting him move her body more than she did as he came into land. He lay down and folded his wings, and only then did she roll down his shoulder and hit the ground.

Silmavalien lay there, sore and bruised yet strangely relieved, as if a musical light vibrated through her. Minth nuzzled her, then made space for the other dragons to nuzzle her, too.

I'm such a far ways from where I lived my whole life. This is nothing like Treas, she thought drowsily.

S

A soft gray light sang beauty through the air. Silmavalien sat up, her sore muscles screaming in protest. She looked around and finally processed her surroundings.

The dragons had landed in a clearing, and in the clearing with was a stone well that looked like it was in good repair. There were people here!

Tiela laughed, but her laughter felt strained, a little forced. The stones looked strange, but how were she, or any of the others, to know that humans did that?

Airrock interrupted the moment. She was flying above a human girl, watching her, she told Silmavalien. She thought the girl was heading towards them. Should they leave?

One human girl? Silmavalien was so tired. *No. We don't need to run away from one human girl,* she decided. *I'd like to meet her – if she doesn't think dragons are demons. She might not. We don't know what this side of the mountains is like.*

They waited. Only Tiela, Minth, and Lighter were in the clearing at the moment, and the others asked if they should come. *No,* she told them. *This is enough of you. You are not helpless hatchlings anymore.*

If they were, twenty of them would be no protection or escape.

A young woman walked into the clearing carrying a water jug. She saw Silmavalien and the dragons and startled. She laid the water jug down, and looked about her. A thousand feelings shone on her face. "Is this real?" she murmured, then said, very shyly, "Hi."

Silmavalien heard her words, but they were not in the language she knew and so she understood only what the dragons did – that she was happy to see another girl, and had feelings strange and positive towards the dragons.

"Hi," said Silmavalien, standing up stiffly. "I'm not from here, but from over the mountains."

The other young woman looked at her strangely. Blue eyes, dark for blue eyes and bright, questioned her. She spoke again, but her words made no sense to Silmavalien. At just that moment, the dragons told her that the other young woman did not understand her words. They spoke different languages!

Silmavalien did not try to answer. She had no idea what to do! She wanted to talk to this woman. It had been so long since she had another human to speak to, and this young woman looked like she might make a friend.

There was a long silence, during which the two women communicated with their eyes. The other picked up her water jug, walked forward, and set it on the edge of the well. She stood next to the well, and pointed to herself. "Keya," she said.

"Keya?" asked Silmavalien.

Keya nodded, beaming. She pointed to herself, then spoke some other words. Then, she opened her hands toward Silmavalien, and spoke a singe word, like a question.

Silmavalien pointed to her own self. "Silmavalien," she said.

It took the two of them several tries to get her name recognizably across.

Keya sat down on the well, and patted the stones beside her. She spoke some more words. Silmavalien guessed what she might be trying to say, and sat down next to her.

Keya evidently approved. Then, she drew herself together, and spoke for a moment. Silmavalien did not get her meaning. Happiness and frustration mingled on Keya's face. She said one of the words again, with emphasis, and the frustration came through in her voice, as if she were saying, *Don't you get it?!*

Tentatively, Silmavalien tried to repeat the word. It was rather a short one. "Quoko?" she said.

"Quoko!" said Keya, and then another word. "Quoko!" It sounded like she was urging Silmavalien to do something.

Silmavalien threw her hands up. "What?" she asked, before she thought about the fact that Keya would not understand the word.

Keya nodded, smiling. She said a different word, then repeated Silmavalien's word.

It took some time, before Silmavalien understood that what Keya wanted was for her to just talk. Upon that realization, she searched for something to talk about, and then decided to just tell her story starting when Minth hatched. Keya watched her and listened to her the entire time, sometimes moving around, an intent look on her face. It was clear to Silmavalien that Keya sometimes gathered something of what she meant. Keya's look would give way to sudden understanding, and sometimes she would interrupt Silmavalien to repeat something she had said – or something that sounded close to it. More often, she would nod, or look at Silmavalien with a rapt look of understanding, and sometimes either of sorrow or of delight.

Watching her, Silmavalien knew that she was often thinking of something in her own life, or at least in her own knowledge, but what it was she could not guess. At one point, one of the dragons told her that Keya was the only girl in her family, and that her family was the only family she knew.

Finally, Keya held up her hand, and interrupted Silmavalien. She spoke, kindly, with interest, words that meant nothing to Silmavalien, then turned from Silmavalien and began to operate the well.

When Keya had filled the jug, she turned to Silmavalien, and spoke a few words. Then, beckoning, she headed back the direction she had come.

Silmavalien stood, indecisive for a moment, the dragons' thoughts running through her own. Keya stopped and looked back at her, and she followed.

28

Song in the Morning

While Silmavalien followed Keya, the other woman kept up a running monologue, of which Silmavalien understood next to nothing.

Keya led her along a path, and to a little hut between three trees. She motioned to Silmavalien to open the door, and it took Silmavalien a minute, fiddling with the handle which was unlike any of the handles in Treas, to figure it out. Keya swung the door wide open, entered, put the jug down, motioned for Silmavalien to follow, left the hut, and went around to the back.

There, on a bench, in the shade of a large tree, sat an older man. He looked at them both, and greeted them. Keya greeted him in return, and explained – so much Silmavalien gathered – that Silmavalien spoke a different language and could not understand theirs, and was a Dragonrider. The look that came over the man's face interested her greatly, and he asked Keya what was clearly a question, though she had no idea what it was about. Keya replied in kind, and Silmavalien gathered that her answer, whatever it was, was some disappointment to the older man, but he still seemed rather happier than otherwise at the explanation, especially after Keya elaborated, with a strange urgency in her voice, on something again incomprehensible to Silmavalien.

Then the older man greeted her warmly.

Feeling very shy, and all the more shy because she understood next to nothing of the conversation she had just watched him have with Keya, who she thought might be his daughter, Silmavalien curtsied and said "Hi," in her own language.

Keya turned to her, and tried hard to explain something to her. Actually, Silmavalien was pretty sure that Keya had two or three main things she was trying to explain, but Silmavalien understood only one of them: the name of the man was Rathenjrath Shilchu.

Trying to be polite, Silmavalien curtsied again, addressing him as Rathenjrath Shilchu, when suddenly he and Keya both laughed. It was the kind of laugh that sounded embarrassed, but she had no idea what could be embarrassing. Had she mangled the name somehow, and called him something inappropriate – or maybe just funny?

Keya then made her understand that she was to call the man only Shilchu. She wanted so much to ask Keya why, but she had no idea how, and she probably would not be able to understand the answer anyways.

But Airrock, who still flew over them, understood, and when she explained Silmavalien started laughing, too. She had called Shilchu 'Grandfather,' while he certainly was *not* her grandfather!

Both Keya and Shilchu looked at her, but she could not explain that she understood now. *How frustrating this is,* she thought, understanding how Keya must have felt when they first met. She tried to stop laughing. It still made her ribs hurt, even though they were much better than they had been a month and a half over.

So, he's not her father. He's her grandfather. Are she and her father oldest children, or is her grandfather older than he looks?

Sore, and exhausted from trying to understand and communicate when she did not share a language, Silmavalien sat down on the soft ground. At once, Airrock dove from the sky. She landed as close to Silmavalien as she dared, and then stood over her, as if standing guard.

She felt the rush of Tiela and Minth's approval.

After a few more awkward minutes, Keya busied herself taking care of preparing various things for a few hours, and Silmavalien followed her around. Before she began a task, Keya pointed to all the various items involved, and named them, and then she explained what she did as she was doing. Silmavalien found it hard to listen to what she was saying, and easier to watch her eyes and her face, and her hands.

When it got kind of hot in the middle of the day – though much less hot than it would usually get in Treas at this time of year – Keya had some conversation with the older man that Silmavalien did not understand any more of than the last time, and then took her a little ways away, into some trees that grew close together and cast a deep shadow, and they sat together, and did little things. Both of them talked, and neither of them understood more than a small portion of what the other said. The dragons asked Silmavalien if they should bring her bags, and she told them they might as well.

In the evening, brothers, most of them apparently younger than Keya, started appearing. All the hubbub in a language she could not understand overstimulated Silmavalien, as people were doing one thing and another all at the same time, talking over each other and asking one before the last could be answer, but still wanting to hear all the answers. That much she could understand, even without the dragons' help, but it ended there, and she wished more than ever that she could understand some of what they were saying, since she was obviously the center of the excitement.

Eventually, Keya seemed to get some sort of satisfactory explanation across to the people – her brothers and father – and took Silmavalien off. It was not long before Silmavalien discovered that what Keya was doing was making sure she had a good place to sleep. They hung a hammock in a tree, close by to the little house, and draped a kind of net over it, and then put soft plants and grasses into it. Keya made sure that the hammock would be comfortable for Silmavalien to climb in and out of, and at one point while they were working Silmavalien noticed other, similar hammocks hanging about. This seemed to be how the family slept in this weather.

After that the men brought out a dinner that was made of meat, a loaf of bread, and fruits Silmavalien had not had in a long time, along with some foods she did not recognize. It was very good, and she especially enjoyed the salt on the meat. While she was eating, several of the dragons settled down, and Minth hovered very close to her. Silmavalien could feel the excitement in the people's voices and knew they were talking about the dragons, but they were respectful and kept their distance.

She leaned back against Minth's shoulder, and thought, *It must be kind of horrid for Keya. Five brothers, a father, and a grandfather. A whole bunch of men, and no woman but herself.*

Keya sat down right next to her, on the other side from Minth. Occasionally, she spoke quietly, naming a fruit or another food, or trying to explain something to Silmavalien. Despite the language barrier, she seemed to enjoy her company above the company of anyone else. Silmavalien thought that maybe there was a great deal that they shared with each other, even without a common language that Keya could not share with her brothers, maybe because they were men.

Finally, dinner was over and people's voices were quieter, as if they were settling down, but she was completely exhausted by it all. Wydth lay under her hammock, and invited her to use him to climb into it more easily. She settled into its gentle, swaying rhythm, and curled up.

It *was* more comfortable than anything she had had in a long time, since the bed on the ledge had dried out and shriveled. In fact, she really enjoyed it, though the dragons complained lightheartedly that they would not all be able to sleep together if she slept in the hammock.

Just as it was getting really dark, Keya appeared, seemingly out of nowhere, waking Silmavalien out of her doze. She was hanging up her hammock so close to Silmavalien's that they would be able to step from one into the other if they wanted. When Keya saw Silmavalien watching her, she cast her a knowing smile.

We're friends already, thought Silmavalien, and dozed off again.

S

Almost at once, Silmavalien and Keya were doing everything together and going everywhere together, even though neither of them understood most of what the other said. Keya was sensitive, and encouraged Silmavalien to do the tasks or parts of them in ways that did not cause her pain, and sometimes showing her easier or alternate ways of doing things. Silmavalien often saw a curiosity which she could hardly begin to satisfy in those blue eyes framed by dark brown hair, near in color to her own.

She had her own questions and curiosities: why was Keya the only woman? Where was the mother – or the grandmother? Why did they appear to have almost no contact with any other humans – despite the occasional contact suggested by the salt, and a few other things Silmavalien had no idea how they would make for themselves?

Before a few days had passed, Silmavalien realized there was something very different about the way Keya regarded the dragons, and the way most of her brothers regarded them. She could not put her finger on it, but she liked Keya's way better, and the dragons had the same experience. They told her one day that some of the boys saw them as exotic, powerful curiosities. As things to be excited about, instead of seeing them as persons even though they could not communicate very well.

Could they still be Dragonriders? asked Silmavalien.

The dragons had no clear answer to her question. She thought some of their thoughts would be, *If a dragon chose them,* if they were put into words. Others were more ambiguous and undefined, suggesting at things Silmavalien could not begin to comprehend.

It was not that the boys were bad or had ill intentions, the dragons clarified. Or even that they were inconsiderate. It was just that the way they wanted to be Dragonriders had nothing to do with knowing what dragons really were.

There were also many things which Silmavalien and Keya could not do together. On Silmavalien's side, this had mostly to do with her dragons. She was a Dragonrider and more, and Keya was not, so that was something they could not share, though she taught Keya how to oil the skins of the dragons who needed it, and Keya gladly helped her do it. It was not long before she figured out how to ask the men to let her have the fat she needed to make the oil. It was easier, she thought, for everyone than asking the dragons, who would rather devour their meals in solitude, now that they were somewhat grown.

She found herself wishing that Keya was a Dragonrider. That way, her friend could know what that amazing bond meant, and share with her what it was like to fly! Since now that the dragons were getting large enough and she was mostly recovered from falling off the cliff, she was learning how to ride them. She and Minth had started flying together, though they kept their flights very short since she was still hard for Minth to carry for long. She could ride Airrock for a lot longer, but she had to convince her sweet and most reckless friend not to show off her comfort and ease in the air, or her acrobatics, while Silmavalien was riding her. Not yet. Certainly not until riding for long times did not make her sore and stiff.

It took a while before Silmavalien noticed how much of a relief it was, that she was gathering and contributing, but not hunting. The men and the dragons did all the hunting that has desired, and she and Keya were never invited to be part of the chores associated with that, except to do what she wanted with the fat.

But, why must it be a life for a life? she still wondered. None of the dragons had an answer, though many had a certain hope of one, a hope that felt as solid and constant as the bedrock but, like the bedrock, mostly hidden from prying eyes.

She did not forget to give thanks to the Lord of Light. It was even easy, and she was genuinely and incredibly grateful. Going down had brought about only good things!

29

Someone Else

Even though she and Keya could barely understand each other, Silmavalien felt her new circumstances to be comfortable and *home-like*. She felt more at home than she had since Minth had hatched. Indeed, she realized after a week or so, she felt more at home than she had since her brother, Varkul, had married Krielasoriel, and brought her into their home. She had not noticed at the time how much that had spoiled the homeliness of their family, but it was clear looking back on it, now.

In a few weeks, she and Keya understood each other fairly well, and daily life got much less frustrated. Keya started translating, telling Silmavalien something one of her family members said, or trying to explain something she saw Silmavalien did not understand, or telling her family something Silmavalien said.

One evening, the two young women were sitting together on some grass, surrounded by the dragons. Somewhat pain-stakingly since they still could hardly speak the same language yet with emotion, Keya explained that she was twenty-two years old, and was passing the age at which most women were married.

Silmavalien, in turn, succeeded in explaining that she was fifteen. That part was easy. Explaining she was engaged to a man named Noren but had to run away was a little harder, but she thought she succeeded.

When she saw the look on Keya's face, and heard the expression in her voice, she realized she had made a mistake. Keya thought people had tried to force her to marry Noren! She tried to explain that it was not like that at all. She *wanted* to marry him. It was because of the dragons that she had had to run away.

Silmavalien did not know how much Keya understood, but she could see that Keya was no longer horrified, or at least no longer the same kind of horrified, and that was enough for now.

Soon after this, they were able to talk much more easily. Silmavalien asked Keya when they went to get salt and who did it. To that, Keya replied, "I see! I have not shown you that, yet. The sea. We get our salt from the sea. Shall we go to the sea tomorrow? I will show you."

"Sure. I'll ride one of the dragons. Maybe more than one."

Keya laughed. "More than one dragon at a time?"

"No!" said Silmavalien. "First one dragon. Then another dragon."

Keya's eyes sparkled, like running water in the sunshine. "Would one of the dragons mind if I rode?"

"I don't think so," said Silmavalien. Then, "Airrock says she'll do it. Wydth would, too." She added, "But I'm not sure how long you'd like to ride. One gets so sore, at least at first."

"Well," said Keya, considering the issue, "how could I tell the dragon I want to go down?"

"The dragon will know," said Silmavalien. She added, "They like you."

"I'm glad," said Keya. "I like them, too."

In the morning they went down to the sea. Silmavalien slid down from Minth's shoulders, and hugged him quickly. The other dragons were already in the water, and he was in a hurry to join them.

"Isn't it beautiful?" asked Keya, shading her eyes with her hands.

"It is," said Silmavalien, "but the waves look powerful, dangerous, and I don't like the smell."

"They are," said Keya, "but you can swim in them, when they're not unhappy, if you're good at swimming. I don't mind the smell. But, now I will show you what those buckets are for, that you asked about. One for you. One for me."

A little while later, Silmavalien stood, looking at two buckets full of sea-water. "Now, how does this make salt? Is there something else we do?"

"I don't know," said Keya. "*We* don't do something else. I don't know if someone else does. What I know is that we do this, and when the water goes away, salt is in the bucket. The water is very salty, and it leaves the salt behind in the bucket, I think."

"I know the water is salty," said Silmavalien. "The dragons taste, and even swallow it, sometimes."

"It will take a while for the water to go away," said Keya. "We leave it here, and come back later."

Soon after this, Silmavalien was usually able to understand what Keya's brothers, or father, or grandfather were saying, even without Keya's explanations or watching her expression. She started to discover why the family lived by themselves. Apparently, there were cities in

North Aneri, and a government, which had demanded to take all the dragon eggs for hoarding. Keya explained they called it safe-keeping. They said they wanted to keep the eggs in a vault where they would be safe. But, this family had dragon eggs, which they would not give up, so they went into the uncivilized south, in the shadow of the Steep Ascent, where only a few people lived.

"The uncivilized south!" Silmavalien said, laughing. "This is north, to me."

"I suppose it would be," said one of Keya's brothers thoughtfully. She did not remember who was named what, though.

Then she asked where the dragon eggs were, and when she looked around she saw a look of some sorrow or deep secret on the faces of most of the others. At last, the oldest man, Shilchu, said, "We only know of one that remains, and where that one is, we do not know."

Thinking about the first conversation she had seen between him and Keya, Silmavalien thought, *Is that why he was unhappy? Because he hoped I had found that egg?* It made sense. She vaguely remembered the sounds of the words he had used, and they fit. Later, she asked Keya about it.

"Yes," said Keya. "I told him you were a dragon-keeper, and that you have come from the other side of the mountains, with dragons. He asked if one of the dragons – the little one, Lighter, in particular – was our egg. Maybe, others were the lost eggs? I told him I didn't think so, and he assumed those eggs had been killed. But, I told him even a dragon-keeper doesn't find *all* dragon eggs!"

S

Silmavalien was going comfortable on the dragons' back, and they grew comfortable carrying her. Minth, and the other white ones, spent most of the day sleeping in the deepest shade they could find, that was big enough to cover their growing bodies, so she rode them mostly at night. She loved flying under the stars, but she knew that many of them wished they could fly freely under the sun, in the full light of day, like Tiela, and to a lesser extent, Airrock could. She often rode Tiela and Airrock during the day, and she kept on having to remind Airrock there could be no acrobatics while she carried Silmavalien. It would be too easy to throw her off bareback, and she had no idea how to make a dragon saddle that would be comfortable for both rider and dragon.

Eventually, one of the dragons suggested she talk about it with the other humans, and she discovered they knew something about what a dragon saddle should look like, but they had no idea how to prepare the leather. So Airrock had to be content with Silmavalien watching her crazy flight maneuvers.

One day, she was telling Keya, and others of her brothers, more about how she had come from the other side of the mountains. She told something of her meetings with the Lord of Light, and about her encounters with the nightmare creatures and the Ellenari. She wondered at the looks on the faces of her listeners – Keya occasionally had to step in to explain what she said – but she thought it might just be the curiosity and excitement that one would expect to come with such a story. She hoped she was doing a good job telling it.

Keya then said, "I think we, too, may know something of this Lord of Light." There was a worried look on her face. "I do not like the arousal of the dark legions."

The men looked at her, and something passed between them.

Keya sat up straight and folded her hands in her lap. "So," she began, "my great-great-grandfather was the rider of a female dragon, who clutched. She had her nest in a place. When the government was trying to collect the dragon eggs – for my great-great-grandfather and his dragon were dead by this time – my great-grandfather went to get them, after we had established this place."

Keya paused, as if thinking about something, or gathering her thoughts. Then she continued. "My great-grandfather came back to us, and told us he had found only one egg, and had put that in a safe place, not far from us. He was grievously wounded, and told us only that he had fought monsters of darkness, and that he had no power against them, but had been aided by one who had the power of light. He told us little more, and spoke very little, and before long he died." Tears shone in her eyes, like drops of rain in sunshine against a clear sky. "Of course," she added, swallowing, "all of this happened before I was born. I never met him."

Keya's one older brother added, "We don't know, but we think maybe the government wanted the dragon eggs so they could all be in one place to be destroyed by the nightmares."

"Of course," said Keya, but Silmavalien knew she did not really believe it, but was just listing possibilities, "it's possible they thought it would be safer to keep them all in a vault and guard the vault – that they wanted to protect them from the nightmares."

"But if Silmavalien and our great-grandfather are correct, then not a hundred men could stand against one nightmare. So, that would only work if there were someone with the power of light to protect the eggs," said another of the brothers.

"They might not know that – or believe it," said the oldest brother.

A conversation about the Lord of Light and the Ellenari followed. Keya's family did not know any more about the Ellenari than Silmavalien did, and she learned only that it was rumored that they had a garden-city hidden high in the Greater Aravin Mountains where no one could reach it without their help. The siblings wondered whether their ancestor had met one of the Ellenari of the very Lord of Light, and then they fell to speculating what the relationship of the Ellenari to the Lord of Light might be. Certainly, the Ellenari had some relationship of allegiance or service to the Lord of Light, but was he their King, the greater and most powerful of them, or perhaps the Father of them all? Or was he something else entirely? How powerful might he be?

Silmavalien said very little, except to occasionally answer questions directed to her, and Keya said nothing at all, but her eyes danced and looked often as if she were viewing things that only she saw.

30

Flying

Noren rode out of Delenois late in the evening, just in time to be out before the closing of the gates. Something very nice about being a courier of sorts was that the guards did not question him, and this time they even recognized himself so they did not even stop him to confirm his job. He rode out with a wave, glad not to be slowed down.

Once he was out of sight from the gates, Noren turned off the road and road up towards the mountains. He left Victor in a clearing to graze, and told him to stay put and not go with anyone else, and climbed up a little further so Elninya could come to him without startling the horse. He would be tired the following day, but he could not pass up on this chance to ride her. She would be very upset, too, if he did pass up on it.

You'll be fine carrying me? he asked her, for the hundredth time that day.

Noren smiled at her firm, confident, and excited, *"Yes!"* She *knew* it would not be a problem.

Before long, he saw her shimmering white length and wings against the rapidly darkening blue-purple of the sky. She landed before him, her happiness flashing forth white beauty.

Noren strode to her, almost bouncing on his toes. He followed her directions and seated himself astride of her shoulders, just forward of her wings, in a little hollow that seemed to be made for him. When he was settled to her satisfaction, she lifted her wings and took off.

"There," she told him. *"That wasn't even hard. You're no heavier than a big buck, and you're rather easier to carry, sitting on my shoulders, than struggling in my claws or teeth."*

I'm glad, said Noren. He felt a little giddy, as she rose rapidly higher, soaring to heights he had not imagined. In a few minutes, she was higher than the topmost spire of Kranah. Yet, the whole experience was somehow familiar and comforting. He had shared flight with her in her memories a thousand times, and he knew what to expect.

They flew for hours. Elninya dipped and soared. Then she brought him up a cliff and landed on the top, where he would never be climb on his own.

My stomach feels queasy, he commented, as she landed.

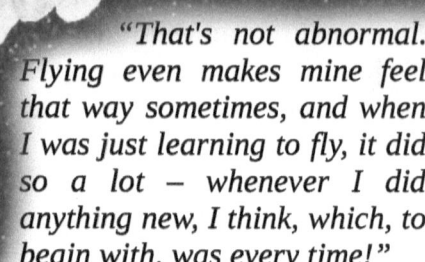

"That's not abnormal. Flying even makes mine feel that way sometimes, and when I was just learning to fly, it did so a lot — whenever I did anything new, I think, which, to begin with, was every time!"

Noren stretched, slid off of her, and walked around a little. He was accustomed to riding Victor, but apparently riding the kind of motion involved in flying was very different from riding a horse's gaits, and he was sore all over. Elninya was shaped differently than Victor, too, so that might have been part of it.

"A little bit of rest doesn't hurt me, either," thought Elninya. Her eyes flashed a bright, glowing green light, as she swung her head to watch her rider pace.

I know that. I can feel it, said Noren, *but I thought you said carrying me would be easy.*

"It is," said Elninya. "There's definitely no fear my strength will give out. But, I usually don't carry a kill very far or very long, or half the other things I've done with you, in the last half-a-night. Also, while it's much easier to carry you on my shoulders than a struggling buck, it is different, so I feel it."

It feels like the greatest thing in the world, thought Noren.

"That it does. Flying is completely different with you. It's real FLYING!"

Noren smiled, and hugged her neck. *It really is,* he said. *I couldn't have imagined it, but it feels like I've been flying ever since I saw you come out of that egg. Sometimes, it's scary, like flying in a storm, and almost being driven into a cliff or the ground. Sometimes, it's like flying into a strong wind, dull, monotonous, hard. But, it seems we're always in the sky, always soaring to something higher, wider, more alive!*

"*It* has *felt like that, since I've hatched – except for the saddlebag. That felt like an uncomfortable return to the egg in which I no longer belonged, when I should have been in the sky.*"

Having paced enough, Noren resettled himself on Elninya's shoulders. His soreness vanished as she took to the air again. Colder airs raced past them, cold enough Noren thought that they might be able to freeze water, even though it was now high summer.

"*When it's day, sometimes I feel like, one day, the blue sky will crack like an egg, and let us into a yet brighter and more spacious world. I don't really see or feel that at night, though,*" Elninya told him as she flew, sharing some of her memories of flying in daylight again.

I can see that, I think, he responded.

Isn't that scary, though? The sun is so bright – we can't look at it, I don't think even you can look at it straight for long. And this world is already so big. The winds are overpowering. Wouldn't a bigger world crush us, or else leave us stranded, and a brighter world would blind us?

An answer, perfectly obvious and glorious, rushed through Elninya's heart and mind, but Noren could not receive it. He was only barely even aware that it was there. He knew nothing of what she saw at all, so little that she could not even try to share with him, but he felt her chuckle underneath him, and *that* was delightful.

Then the eastern sky flushed with dawn. The stars dimmed and slowly vanished, as if making way for some greater light before which they were not fit to shine and in whose presence their light was nothing. Black turned to blue to gray to red. A few clouds seemed all ablaze as if, nearer to the coming sun, fire from its heart reached out to set them flaming, and thus something of its light passed through them to the earth.

It will be a long time before you need the blue sky to crack and release you into a yet-wider, brighter world, again, Elninya, thought Noren. *We can't even begin to think of flying to the sun.*

"*It might not be so long as you think, Noren,*" replied Elninya. "*Maybe, we won't be able to fly to the sun until we hatch a second time.*"

An image formed in Noren's mind of a clear, or mostly-clear shell, that had to be cracked before the light beyond could come through clear and bright and true, and before those within the shell could fly into the wider spaces which had always drawn their eyes and lived in their hearts. He did not know whether the thought was Elninya's, or whether it was the only way his mind could approach her thought.

She soared higher to give him the best view she could of the dawn. Then, she descended quickly, not in a full dive which might have unseated him, but fast enough to make his stomach turn. As she sank, they saw rapidly less of the approaching dawn.

By now, he told her, *I'm sure Silmavalien and her dragon have left the civilized world, and gone into the wilderness. I wouldn't be able to find her, on the little coming-into-town she* might *do, for things like salt or new cloth.*

Elninya agreed with him. She seemed to wait for something from him.

Noren, tired as he was, though the exhilaration of flying with Elninya made him more awake and the union of their minds helped to rouse him, declined to say any more until they landed. When they did, he relaxed for a moment, still on his dragon's shoulders.

I'm sure you, in your flights and travels and hunts, to stay as close to me as you can, while I travel, are ever on the lookout for any signs there might be of another dragon.

He felt her acknowledge him. He also felt unhappiness with where his thoughts were going.

I'm not quite sure how to disengage from my current engagements, and I think I still might have my best shot localizing where Silmavalien might be, in this way. If she'd been somewhere for the last near-year, and vanished a few months ago, and I inquire after her, people might tell me, "Yeah, there was someone like that here a little while ago, but she left about such-and-such a time ago."

Elninya stretched her neck out and voiced a low growl.

Noren dismounted her. He sat on the dry grass. He really did feel tired, and now he had to ride all day.

Yes, yes, I know. I could go to Delenois, and hand my packages back in. Even if I didn't come up with a good reason for it, I would probably have enough time to ride Victor away, and meet up with you. If I had to leave Victor somewhere, he would probably be fine. He's good at making do with whatever grass is around. Maybe, he'd even find a mare to breed and be happy with that. Somebody might get a new foal, and Victor is a good horse, so it would almost certainly be a pleasing foal. Who knows, he might find his way back to Corin, and be added to

Corin's breeding stallions. I think he's good enough.

Noren stood up, and made his way down the incline. He called Victor to him, and the chestnut horse nickered and came trotting to him.

I'll ride you again, some day! Hopefully, it will be soon. You might even be able to pick me up, out of more civilized places, and take me away, and then bring me back, so we can do a lot more of this.

Elninya grumbled in his mind while he tacked the horse up.

31

Blue Eyes, Blue Wings

After that conversation, Silmavalien found herself rebuffing attention from Keya's brothers. Now that they could talk to her, they were interested in her. She explained to them that she was engaged already, to a man she hoped was a Dragonrider, and that she *wanted* to marry him, if they could find each other. It did not help as much as she would have wished, and she tried to stay away from the young men as much as she reasonably could.

A couple days later, Keya and Silmavalien were walking through the woods, enjoying the shade, when Keya asked to stop. The happy burbling of a nearby stream made a peaceful background noise. "I, too, have had experiences with the Lord of the Light," said Keya, quietly and shyly. "I knew you would come, to be my friend and more, but I did not know that you would be you."

Silmavalien nodded. She said nothing, and Keya did not say any more either. At that moment, Lighter, who was just learning to fly, came diving through the tree-tops and landed next to them, breaking the mood.

S

Silmavalien walked through the trees, alone except for Minth and Tiela, who padded beside her. She climbed through some bramble, careful not to hook and tear the clothes Keya's family had given her.

Minth and Tiela spread their wings and soared over the bramble wall.

Carefully picking her way through the branches, Silmavalien stumbled a little. Her hand slid under the leaves, and she recognized the feel of a smooth, leathery surface. Her fingers tingled. She stood aside, and Minth and Tiela started to dig at once, revealing what Silmavalien had found.

A brown dragon egg!

"Hatch for Keya, please," she whispered as she picked up the egg. Tiela nuzzled it with motherly affection, while Silmavalien cradled it in her arms. "One day," she whispered, "maybe you will mate and lay eggs yourself." She felt a kind of quiet thrill go through Tiela.

There was no way Silmavalien could climb through that bramble with the egg, so she climbed onto Tiela's shoulders, and the dragon flew cautiously, since she was not as able to keep her balance while carrying the egg either.

Feeling a sense of fulfillment, Silmavalien turned back towards the home. She felt happy at the thought of how happy she was about to make the whole family, and especially Shilchu! Their egg was found, and she had no reason to think the dragon within was dead, though, sadly, she had known that to happen.

But Tiela assured her that the dragon in this egg was very much alive and healthy, and she did not doubt her.

All the dragons wanted to see the egg!

Don't worry. You will, unless the dragon hatches before you get here, which I hope he or she won't, since I would very much like him or her to bond with Keya.

Nonetheless, holding the egg in her arms, Silmavalien felt uneasy. She kissed the cool, smooth leathery shell. *O Lord of Light, why is there so much evil, so much death and grief? Do you know if it will end or how to end it?*

"Remember that I told you that one day I would reveal myself? I will do so, and your questions will be answered."

I wish you could do that now. I wish I knew what was the fate for all those dragons who died in the egg. I wish I knew the dragons. I wish I knew Dinora. I wish I knew their names. Do you? You told me, then, there was more to life than this, and than this world, but I still don't know what you mean.

"You know that Love must be victorious. Wait."

I wish I didn't have to, thought Silmavalien, not expecting an answer. *I wonder if Keya, or any of the others, think these thoughts and feel these feelings, or things like them.*

Silmavalien wanted to hug Minth, when he told her that he felt this, too. She put the egg down, where Tiela watched it like a mother-dragon, and hugged Minth's neck. She could not hug his whole self anymore, he had grown so much! Even Lighter had grown so much that she could not hug his whole self anymore.

Late in the evening, Silmavalien stepped out of the trees around the path and one of Keya's brothers looked up and saw what she carried. He called the others over, and she was soon surrounded by an excited family of people who were all talking so fast that she could understand perhaps a tenth of what they said, at best.

Keya pressed her way through her excited brothers and touched the egg with a reverent love and tenderness which went to Silmavalien's heart. It was the way she saw a dragon egg. Or the way Tiela saw a dragon egg.

When he came, everyone made way for him, but Shilchu did not touch the egg. But the satisfied happiness on his face warmed her heart. He did not have to say anything for her to know that it was a great comfort to him to know that their dragon egg had not been lost or killed, and when she told him that Tiela had assured her that the dragon within was healthy, he nearly glowed with happiness.

She saw Keya glance at Shilchu, and knew she, too, was happy that he was happy.

While everyone else was still examining the egg, which Silmavalien had put on the ground, Shilchu motioned for her to come aside. "My dear Silmavalien," he said "– whom I think of as a granddaughter, since you are so close with my Keya – I am so glad you have brought this egg to us. I saw my father wounded, ill, and then die, when I was still a boy, to save this egg. I am so glad."

Silmavalien nodded, not knowing what to say. It was clear that he was moved, both by his father's death, even in memory, and by the egg. There was nothing she could say in a moment like this.

S

Three weeks later, Silmavalien, Keya, and Keya's youngest brother were sitting together near when the egg was about to hatch. They had hung it in a hammock, which was always guarded by at least one dragon or human, and Silmavalien decided to take the hammock down from the tree, so it would sit on solid ground where the egg could not fall out, while the dragon hatched.

They could have picked up the egg in their hands and put it on the ground, but Silmavalien and Keya shared a glance, and simultaneously decided that it would not be right to touch either the egg or the dragon until the dragon hatched – or until one or the other of them *felt* like touching.

Silmavalien sat down, but Keya stood, watching the lines appear on the brown egg. Then she motioned to her brother to give the egg a little more space.

"Why?" he asked. "Shouldn't the dragon get to choose me, if he wants? After all, I was here, too, when he wanted to hatch!"

"The dragon will know you, if she wants you," said Keya. "I'm not asking you to go so far, she won't be able to look for you or call to you. Just a little ways away. Get far enough away I know you won't touch unless you should!"

"Will you promise the same?" asked the boy.

"Of course," said Keya.

The boy paused, then looked at Silmavalien. "You?"

"Yes, yes." She waved him away. She did not think Keya knew yet, but she knew the dragon would bond to her.

The egg started to split, and then they saw a perfect blue dragon sitting in the broken egg. Silmavalien gasped when she saw her, and almost felt faint. She was just the same blue as that dragon, dead already, whom she had hatched with the knife, the same day she had hatched Veine, Songeth, Wydth, Coroneth – and the dead Dinora. She looked from the dragon's scales and wings to Keya's eyes – they were just the same color, a blue against which the clearest, brightest sky looked dingy!

Keya waited, her attention rapt, joy on her face, while the dragon first licked herself, and then ate her egg. Only when the dragon had finished licking the goo of her egg off the cloth of the hammock did Keya, as if in a dream, step forward and touch her!

Tanz.

So that was the dragon's name.

At that point, Silmavalien unfolded her legs and stepped away. She grabbed the boy's hand, and led him away, despite his protests. "What?!" he exclaimed. "I don't get to watch?"

"The dragon is bonded to Keya, sure as sure, Nereis," said Silmavalien. "Her name is Tanz, and she and Keya should be left alone. This kind of thing is private."

Some of those words she had just used, she had only learned days ago!

"But I want to see!" protested Nereis. "It's not fair. You've got to see so many dragons hatch, and go through this so many times!"

"Nothing ever happens more than once," said Silmavalien. "The bonding of Keya and Tanz is not like mine and Minth's, or anyone else's. You've got to see more than most. Seeing isn't everything."

"But I want a dragon, and seeing one bond is the next best thing to bonding oneself," protested Nereis.

"I don't know if that's true," said Silmavalien. "But you can ask the Lord of Light if he can make it so you can have a dragon. I don't *know* that he can, but if anyone can, it's he. But he loves the dragons, too. I doubt he'll give you a dragon unless it's best for both you and the dragon. Maybe, it's giving you to the dragon!"

When Silmavalien next saw Keya, her eyes were shining as if they had the sun in them. She remembered that she had first begun to meet the Lord of the Light when she and Minth bonded – in fact, it had been that bonding of souls that had taught her so much about the reality and power of Love. She could not even dimly guess at what Keya's experience – or Tanz's – was.

32
Best Attempts

Noren politely declined the invitation to stay at the inn arranged for him, and told the people that he came from the mountains and the wilderness, and he felt more comfortable out of doors than in. After a bit of small talk about watching the stars, he headed outside.

While Elninya flew in, waiting for the dark to deep enough she would be seen easily, Noren went to the stable where Victor was kept. His horse greeted him with a whinny, and he patted his neck. He spent a few minutes grooming and talking to Victor, then got his grooming materials and went out to meet his dragon in their chosen place.

I'm glad you've been practicing your endurance, so you can fly out to pick me up, fly with me a little, and then be able to fly back out to the wild, Noren thought, almost laughing, as Elninya bragged to him.

It was the first time they had met in physical proximity since they had first flown together. Noren oiled her hide, which took several hours now that she was so large, Elninya told him she would like to fly for a few hours, and then sleep together. She assured Noren that he did not need to worry about this. If anyone approached, she would wake long before they got near and glide away like a white ghost, and it was unlikely that anyone would approach. She would wake well before sunrise, at the first glimmer of dawn, before even the earliest-waking farmers were up.

If they see you glide away like a white ghost, they'll think I'm probably a witch, even if they don't think you might be a dragon! Noren protested.

"*If it happens, and you're concerned about it, get on my back, and we'll fly away for good. We're not likely to find Silmavalien and her dragon in the kingdom, anyway. Your poor horse will be fine. They won't think it's his crime whether his master was a witch or not. – Anyway, you could hide, or run away yourself. Even if someone gets close, and I have to get my shining whiteness, much larger than yourself, away, to remain undiscovered, your body could easily stay hid!*"

Noren chuckled at Elninya's use of the word 'poor.' *You're just teasing me for feeling kind of attached to him?*

"*Not at all, though I don't understand it. But humans use words so funny! Even you use words so funny. That's why I do.*

Elninya was extremely delighted that she was growing bigger, and that she got to sleep with her rider. She was big enough to put her wing over Noren like a big roomy tent! Even in the coldest places she knew, curled snug against her body, and sheltered by her wing, her rider could need little more than a few clothes to stay comfortably warm. And he *was* her *rider* now, her real rider! It made her feel like a real dragon!

I know, Elninya. It kind of stinks for us. The longer we're together – the more *we're together – the more we're able to perceive sights and sounds and smell, or what-you-will, tinged with the senses and soul of the other, even when our bodies are separated by distance, but it's not like it is when we're together.*

Noren was riding her when he thought this, and he felt her impulse to nuzzle him gently. He repressed laughter at the ridiculous thought of how disastrous that would be if she tried to nuzzle him while carrying him in the sky, even though she did not consider doing that. They were used to experiencing such impulses towards each other, and it was really more of a mental and emotional impulse than a physical one, since they were so rarely physically together.

"*End it soon, Noren,*" said Elninya.

I think I will.

Then, they could look for the other Dragonrider and dragon together, really *together.* That would be so nice!

The fact is, Elninya, said Noren, while she was lazily circling down to land, *I'm rather glad you want to sleep with me, instead of just flying with me. I would rather not be so tired as I would be tomorrow if I rode you all night, and did not sleep at all.*

"*I know,*" said Elninya, tenderly. "*But, I hope you do not get sore from riding me as quickly and much as you did, the last time.*"

I don't think I shall, responded Noren.

In the early dawn, when Elninya woke him and inquired after how he felt, Noren knew, at once, that though rather sore, he was not nearly so sore as he had been that first time, two or three weeks ago. At her request, he got on her back, and they flew for a few more minutes together. Then, she landed in the same place. He hugged her and kissed her, and she nuzzled him and blew in his hair, so that she would have blown it into disarray if it had not already been in disarray from sleeping on leaves and dirt and grass. Then, sorrow permeating her thoughts, she flew away, rapidly gaining altitude, so that she would soon be high enough that she would not be taken for a dragon in the growing light of dawn.

Noren watched her go until she was a speck in the sky, so small and distant that he could hardly keep his eyes on it. Then, with a wrenching in his heart, he turned and ran back towards the inn.

Shortly after this, someone offered Noren an opportunity to become a higher-value courier. It was an opportunity to make a lot more money, and fresh horses would be provided from him so he could ride much more quickly from stop to stop. He declined, saying that he loved Victor and did not want to be away from him.

He started to suggest to people, as subtly as he could figure out how, that their ideas about dragons and Dragonriders might be mistaken, even if only a little mistaken. Since he was going to go out into the wild very soon, there was no danger in arousing a few suspicions, as long as they did not develop so quickly that people were sent to arrest him without him expecting it – since, if he was worried, he could always meet up with Elninya and, if possible, ride away on Victor, but if things were already too urgent for that, he could fly away on her.

But his best attempts seemed to go nowhere. He suggested to one person, who he thought might be more receptive than most, "Do you think it might be possible that, once, there was a different kind of dragon and Dragonrider, who were, at least, no worse than ordinary men?"

That person laughed at him, as if he were trying to make a joke.

Several times, he tried to suggest similar things to others, and each time he was met with failure. Sometimes, they laughed, as if they thought he were joking. Sometimes, they laughed *at* him. Sometimes, they looked at him like he was crazy, or maybe worse.

I really wish I had Elninya with me, to help me know and understand what is going on inside of people! he thought, over and over. But this was the best he could do, and the best he could do to make up for what he and Elninya had unwittingly done, even if he *hated* having to make such suggestions. They were such a horrible insult to the real truth, but if he said more, he would be killed, and no one would even have the chance to think about what he said.

"Noren," thought Elninya, her tone both sympathetic and scolding, *"you don't have to do this. You know you could say what you mean, let come what will. Or, you could come away, to me. I would very much like that! Or, I suppose, you could ask me to fly over the place, low enough that I can sense the people with whom you're talking."*

Soon after this, Noren turned in his pendant. "I come from the mountains and the hills," he explained, "and I miss them. I miss lying awake under the stars, chasing after deer, running through bramble and over hills."

"Do you want to sell your horse?" asked the man.

"No. I love Victor, and he keeps well. He'll do well, where I'm going," answered Noren.

He kept also the sword which he had been given and trained to use so that he would more easily be able to defend himself against bandits and be less tempting fare for them anyways.

After that, Noren lost no time going out to Victor. He patted his neck, saddled him up, and rode him out to the nearest wilderness, several days away, where he was met by Elninya.

The next afternoon, he sat down on a tree stump and took out the high-quality map he had, not only of Silrah, but of all Aneri, south of the Aravin Mountains. He knew now that all the kingdoms of Aneri were deadly hostile to the Dragonriders, though their punishments varied to some extent in degree. That was especially notable when it came to the punishments about speaking about Dragonriders. In almost all of them, being a Dragonrider was a crime worthy of death, but the punishments for being sympathetic to Dragonriders ranged from the same deaths they suffered to fines.

But what he was more interested in was what wildernesses might be interesting to Silmavalien. He was pretty sure she would prefer the Aravin Mountains, both because she would have been more likely to be close them, and also because she had grown up there, and knew how to forage there.

However, what if she, too, had encountered the nightmare monsters in those mountains? The myths said that those mountains were haunted by such horrors, so she might look for another place to live, one which she could hope would not be so dreadfully dangerous.

Thinking of this, Noren wondered, too, about the strange defenders, whom he had never seen, but who had the bows that sang like the stars and shot arrows like shooting stars. He would like to know what they were and possibly meet one of them.

Suddenly, Victor nickered, and Noren looked up to see someone who looked like a man standing in front of him.

The man's eyes looked like emerald stones, and a tunic of some shining emerald material hung from his shoulders. At his side he wore a sword, and Noren could not tell whether the metal itself had a greenish sheen, or whether it reflected the green of the man's garments. Over his shoulder was slung a quiver, in which was a beautiful, wonderfully curved bow, and several arrows. His frame was as large as that of the largest man Noren had seen, and hair that was almost white and shone as if the sun lived along its strands, hung from his head. His beard was of the same hair, but his skin was a shade darker than Noren's.

"Who are you?" Noren gasped out, almost too surprised to speak. He rose to bow.

"The name by which I may be known to you, at present, is Hazalel. I am an Ellenar and I have been sent to you, from the Lord of the Light," answered the man. His voice was like the sound of rocks, like rocks falling or rubbing against one another, like wind over rocks or waves upon rocks, and like tree boughs swaying in the wind.

"I have never heard of the Lord of the Light," said Noren. "Who is he?"

"He is the one from whom comes the power that can destroy the nightmare shadows. He is the one who has given you and Elninya the union of souls in love that is yours."

"Is he the one of whom Elninya has often spoken to me, or is that someone else? Is he the one Elninya serves?" asked Noren.

"Those questions are not mine to answer, nor the answers mine to know," said Hazalel. "You wanted to meet me, and so I have come to you, with the only message which I can give you, at this time. I cannot tell you more about the Lord of the Light until you are ready to meet him."

"When and how will I be ready?" asked Noren.

"There is nothing more that I can tell you," said Hazalel. With that, he turned, and, running with a lightness and a strength, and therefore a speed, Noren had never imagined, he vanished into the surrounding foliage. Noren wondered how long he had been close to him. With his speed and skill, he would never be seen – or heard – unless he wished it.

That was hardly the kind of meeting I had wanted! Noren almost growled to himself. *I still don't know what he is. A god? He certainly acts something like a god, but a very subordinate one. Maybe, he is an elf? Elves are allegedly strange beings, with power and life well beyond ours – immortal, even. They might exist, after all, since dragons and demons do, and they might also be very unlike they are said to be, as dragons are very unlike they are said to be. An elf could be thought to be like that, mysterious, and suited to the forest. An elf servant of a god would not be that much of a surprise. Maybe elves are little gods. He said he was an Ellenar, not an elf, but then the continent of the elves is called Ellenesia. Maybe, in their language, an elf is an Ellenar.*

He felt Elninya watching his thoughts, though he could see none of hers, and he wondered if maybe his present thoughts made no more sense to her than her thoughts often made to him.

That evoked a response from her. *"Your thoughts very often make less sense to me than these thoughts do. I do not know what they mean, and often feel that they mean nothing, though I am at least aware of them, and know their form in your mind. Others of your thoughts I do not know at all. I might doubt that they are even thoughts, and, at any rate, I see them not at all, but know only that you perceive yourself to be thinking what you perceive to be something."*

Noren felt offended. *Do you think I'm stupid?!*

"Do you think you're stupid?" responded Elninya. *"Are you stupid?"*

Noren growled. *Why did I want to be with you all the time? You bother me so much!*

"I was with you enough to bother you like this all that time," replied Elninya. Noren knew she was chuckling. She was soaring over a lake, preparing to fish. She had never fished before and was only mildly hungry, but she was excited to try a new way of hunting.

Why did I even bond to you! Why did you bond me!

"You know that answer, and if anyone tried to tell you, it would hurt your knowledge, rather than help it. Maybe that is why the Ellenar can tell you no more."

Noren put his hands over his ears, as if that would help him block out Elninya.

She concentrated on fishing. Noren went back to studying his map.

33

Dying Away into Beauty

Noren soon forgot all about the Lord of the Light, though he remembered the mysterious Hazalel, and sometimes he wished Hazalel would talk to him again. He wanted to learn more about the Ellenari's bows and arrows.

Now that they were alone in the wilderness, Noren and Elninya flew together all the time. She did not press the issues between them, and he never brought them up. Things were between them, for a time, nearly as right and well as they were before his sin, Noren thought. But even this, he thought rarely, and he pushed the thought from his mind as quickly as possible, lest in remembering the shadow should fall on them again. He did not consider that the fact there was something he could not think about with her, something that still mattered to both of them that they could not talk about, meant that their relationship was still damaged, and there was still a shadow between them.

Instead, they stayed busy with other things. They thought about the wind, about the land and how it was formed, about what kinds of plants grew where and why. They watched sunsets, and the stars, and sunrises. They watched flowers open, and they watched leaves unfold. They watched tadpoles swim and transform into frogs or toads. They looked for the eggs, to watch them hatch, and they looked of other creatures, not just tadpoles. They watched streams go by, the ripples of the water as they changed and as they did not change. They watched lakes, and the way their colors and beauty differed from the effects of varying lights and winds. They went swimming together, something that was easy for Elninya from the very beginning, since her long neck made it easy to breathe, her wings outspread made it easy to float, and her sinuous length slid easily though the water. Noren soon learned to swim rather well as well, and they investigated reeds and water-weeds together, watched fishes, and looked at the bottom of lake-beds.

In searching for Silmavalien, his feelings were still conflicted. He dreaded finder her, and so he did not want to put his whole heart and attention into it. He dreaded what he felt thinking about her, dreaded what he would probably feel in her presence. He dreaded trying to tell her how he felt and thought, and he dreaded what she might feel in response, what her response might be. He dreaded, too, the thought that maybe she was no longer interested in him or had found someone else.

One day, several months later, he and Elninya stood on a hill overlooking a lake. Beyond the lake, the sun was setting behind the most beautiful clouds. Bright pink, flaming with orange, variegated with cloudy texture, they composed a beauty beyond thought – a beauty so great that it seemed impossible and unreal for the very reason that it was indeed real. Noren wanted to watch each moment of it, to capture the beauty of each moment, for the ever-changing light revealed new and unique beauty with every heartbeat. At the same time, the lake was also surpassingly beautiful. In the evening light, the water was dark blue, a blue perhaps almost violet. A gentle wind ruffled the waters, so that the light and the water seemed to merge and become one thing, making the water yet more watery than it would have been alone. As much as the sunset and the lake, Noren gazed upon Elninya's perception and thoughts, which so far surpassed his own, he thought.

Elninya pointedly made no comment on whether she thought her perception exceeded Noren's.

The sunset was dying away into beauty upon beauty, ever purpler, bluer, grayer, darker. He did not know whether the thought "dying away into beauty upon beauty" was more his perception or Elninya's, but he knew, at once, that it meant something to her which he did not know and yet, despite the fact that he did not know, could not help hating.

Finally, Elninya said to him, *"You stayed in the civilization of humans so long, not because you thought it was a better way to find Silmavalien, but because you did not really want to find her, and found that a convenient way to pretend you were looking for her, without having to deal with your problems about actually looking for her."*

Noren said nothing, but he knew that Elninya knew that he had no rebuttal to her statement.

"We don't have to look for her, if you don't want."

That will not do any better, said Noren.

Elninya withdrew from him, but her approach of the subject and of his character brought the shadow upon Noren's thoughts. He felt a little angry with her. Could she not have left it alone?!

Nonetheless, her thoughts infected him, or else his thoughts went somewhere where he had never let them go before. It may have had something to do with "dying away into beauty upon beauty."

He realized that his reluctance to see Silmavalien had grown since he had first realized what had really happened and how he felt about that. He saw, too, that it had grown for reasons having entirely to do with himself. He could not, at least he did not think he could, hide what he had done from her, though he could not predict whether Elninya would refrain from telling her, if he chose to try, saying that was his business, or whether she would interfere, and tell Silmavalien's dragon to tell her. Also, Noren did not know if all dragons had Elninya's perception of humans, but Silmavalien's dragon very well might have it, and if so her dragon would pick it up from him and Silmavalien would certainly find out.

All this aside, he did not even know that he would want to hide it from her. It would be wrong, impossible even, to marry her and be intimate with her, and also to hide a thing like that from her. If she were to marry him, she had better know what he was, or had been, and what he could do, or might be able to do.

Other thoughts knocked for entrance on his mind, and he could not deny them. Her betrayal, her deceit, and her lack of trust in him, did not make a wrong half as horrible as his slaughter of that girl. If all that fear of death and of her dragon's death could produce in her was a wrong such as what she had done to him, why, Noren began to think it might be perfectly excusable. It certainly was not nearly comparable to the wrong he had done. He tried to make the excuse that he had done it, had been in such a place that it was possible for him to do it, because of what she had done. But, somehow, the excuse only hurt worse.

Noren quickly became miserable again. To add to his misery, he soon found himself telling himself that he liked the company of his horse, Victor, better than that of his heart-and-soul-bonded friend, Elninya. It was not the liking his horse that was the problem, but the liking of his horse more than his dragon and, quite as important, the reasoning for this liking-more-than. Victor did not know what he had done. In fact, it had happened before Noren ever met Victor. And Victor certainly did not give Noren the impression that he knew, and did not scold Noren or tell Noren what he did not want to hear.

But despite the conflict between him, and the rift between him and Elninya that tormented both of them, and hurt each of them the more because it hurt the other, they continued his search for Silmavalien and her dragon. When they were satisfied with their search of one wilderness area, and the only way to the next was through civilized lands, they would travel in the dark of night, and find the most secluded, sheltered place they could to spend the day. Noren rode Victor, and Elninya flew far above them, but not too far to reach him quickly if she needed to.

The southern climates annoyed Noren and Elninya. Most of them were either hot and humid, and filed with insects that bit and harassed them, or else very hot indeed and dry. Noren had little knowledge of what was safe for him to eat and what was not edible. He had little knowledge, too, of how to move through these thicker, denser forests, or the crumbly rock, the slippery dirt and sand of the dry places. Between that, and the fact he did not know the habits of many of the animals, he found hunting difficult, though fortunately Elninya had little trouble. He decided it would make sense to spend more time looking for Silmavalien in the places that he was more comfortable, since that was probably what she would prefer, too.

Elninya continued to grow rapidly. The height of her shoulders passed that of his head, and she soon carried him with such ease that the only consideration when he was on her back was making sure she did not lose him. His weight could not tire her or hinder her flight in and of itself. When they were flying together, reveling in the feeling as the earth dropped away from under them and the sky opened up around them, in the feel of the wind rushing past them, the warmth of the sun, the coolness of the air, it almost seemed as if there were no problems between them, or even in the entire world.

At least, most of the time. Sometimes, even in the sky, one or the other, and then both, would remember the things that tore them apart and tormented them.

They flew most often at night, because Elninya sunburned very easily. Her size also posed a difficulty. Her skin needed to be oiled somewhat regularly to keep it from cracking and flaking, and if Noren let it go too long, it would actually peel and bleed even if she was careful to avoid sunburning. As she grew, the amount of oil needed to keep her skin healthy, as well as the time Noren had to spend applying it, increased a lot. Even when he could hunt easily for himself, she would find the fattest animals she could and bring her kills back to him. Even just the time preparing the oils was not trivial.

"There has got to be a better way to do this," Noren said out loud. Victor, who was grazing nearby, lifted his head and looked at him. He was another consideration. They could not travel through some of the wildernesses, because it would be impossible for Victor to move through them or find enough food there. Sometimes, he and Elninya would leave the horse in a place with rich grass that he liked, and go for several days somewhere he could not come, but it was not enough to conduct a thorough search. But Noren thought those probably were not the places Silmavalien would choose, either.

"There might be a plant somewhere I could extract the oil from better, if I knew how, or which plant to use. Or a better technique for getting fats and oils out of the meat. Or maybe, if we only knew where or what, there're plants Elninya could rub herself on," Noren continued, looking at Victor. The thing was, he knew of plants one could get oil from, but it had to be an oil that would not irritate Elninya's skin.

The horse nodded, but Noren was sure he had no idea what he was talking about. When Noren did not respond, Victor walked over and nudged him. Probably, he just wanted Noren to pay attention to him, maybe ride or groom him.

34

The Surface

Silmavalien sat with an arm over Lighter's shoulders one morning. The golden dragon stretched his endurance and his young wings to fly with the older dragons, and now he was tired.

In the shadows of the forest, where they were visible only as momentary streaks of white, Daurth and Jareth played, scampering about. Then, suddenly, Jareth pounced.

It could have been a playful pounce. It was not. Silmavalien felt the pain and terror of the rabbit, and she felt Daurth shaking with revulsion. He used to play these kinds of tricks with Jareth, terrorizing the animals when they weren't hungry, but he did not want to any more! But if he did not, then Jareth might find ways to harass him the way he tried to harass Lighter. It wasn't just his wings that could tear, but his whole scaleless body, if someone pushed or spooked him into a tree branch or a poky thicket!

I'm here. Silmavalien sent the silent thought to Daurth, as mild reassurance as it was. She had known about this problem for a while, but she had not realized how big of a deal it was, and apparently neither had the older dragons. Apparently, Lighter himself had not. She knew Jareth was mean, especially to the animals, but not how mean he could be to the dragons.

But she was, by now, the smallest of them all. She could not do anything about it directly. *Daurth. The other dragons will stand up for you. Talk to Airrock and Tiela. If you stay around the other dragons, you should be safe.*

And she would stand up for him?

Yes.

By now, Jareth realized what something was up, and she saw the moment when Daurth straightened, lifting his wings in a gesture of confidence and courage. Jareth saw it, and pulled back.

Daurth lunged forward and bit down on the rabbit, which was far too terrified to flee, and killed it cleanly. Carrying it in his mouth, he stalked away to find a private place to eat it.

She leaned back against Lighter's shoulders, and her thoughts wandered to other problems. Quite apart from these personality problems, Jareth and Daurth seemed little less sickly than Minth, and definitely more sickly than the other dragons. Their growh patterns looked more like Minth's than any of theirs, and their skin was more fragile, and apart from Jareth's cruelties, they did not have as much energy either. She was not worried about them the way she had sometimes worried about Minth, since Minth was not growing sicker, and she did not expect them to, either. Besides, there was nothing she could do.

She had to admit she still worried about Minth sometimes, though. So perhaps the real reason was that they seemed quite a bit healthier than Minth, even if they were not as healthy as the others. But their development seemed retarded in so much the same way, she wondered if maybe Minth did as poorly as he did in some ways because of the constant fear and stress he had suffered during the first months of his life. Had she permanently damaged him by soaking him in the fear she thought was necessary for them to survive?

A lump formed in her throat, and she reached out to him. *I'm sorry.* She couldn't come up with more words, but she knew he understood.

He understood, and he loved her. That was all he had to say, and he *meant* it. Love made all things well, didn't it?

I suppose, she said, still feeling sick at heart. *It should. I wish I knew that it did.*

S

After that, Silmavalien made sure to keep a closer eye on the situation. Jareth's tricks on Lighter and Daurth all but stopped. Perhaps they took a companion to make them work, or perhaps he was aware that the other dragons would not ignore it if Silmavalien asked them not to, and he did not stand a fighting change if *they* played the tricks on him in retaliation. Whatever the reason, the tricks stopped. But he soon went back to tormenting animals, something he did not need the other dragons' help for.

There was clearly something wrong with his empathy, because a creature as empathic as dragons were should not be *able* to be cruel like this, or to enjoy it. But then she thought about the fact it had not unduly bothered Minth or the others when they made mistakes learning how to hunt, and none of them minded killing when they were hungry. Perhaps that was what was wrong with Jareth. He did not have a desire to kill more than he could eat, though, so it might be more complicated than that, but she decided it was worth a try.

She shared her thoughts with the older dragons, and Veine and Coroneth came up with a suggestion: what if they only let Jareth hunt sometimes, and they hunted for him to keep him slightly fat so he would never be at all hungry? It would be a try.

But several weeks later, it seemed to have had no effect. Jareth ate the kills the other dragons brought him, and he did look fatter, but he continued to torment the animals, sometimes to death, and there was not much the others could do about it except to constantly guard him, which did not seem to be in their natures. Most of them did not even want to frighten or beat him up if he scared a rabbit to death underneath their noses, and Silmavalien did not want to encourage Coroneth or Tiela too much. Both of them had a streak of bossiness that could turn them into bullies if they let it.

Finally, she brought the issue to Keya, but though the older girl listened to her sympathetically, Keya did not have any thoughts or advice to give.

S

One late summer day, Silmavalien and Keya sat in a meadow a little ways from the house, cutting and drying fruit to keep over the winter. Dragonflies kept buzzing around them.

Keya pointed out a red-orange one out to Silmavalien. "I like the dragonflies," she said, after Silmavalien saw it. "It's not that I don't like butterflies, too, but the dragonflies are different. They fly more like... more like... more like a dragon, I guess! They fly straighter, they fly in a more, a more rigid pattern. I really can't say it, I think, but... you know, they fly like they could fight. The butterflies don't. I'm still not saying this right."

"I know what you're saying," said Silmavalien. "The dragons are laughing. They say they don't fly like dragonflies."

A little laugh shimmered in Keya's voice. "I didn't say *they* flew like dragonflies. I said dragonflies fly *more like* them than butterflies fly like them."

"Well, Tanz knows what you mean," said Silmavalien.

She looked up to watch the dragonflies. They dove and darted and twisted beautiful, some red-gold, some blue – these had faces of the brightest golden color! – some green and purple.

After a few minutes, Silmavalien looked down again, away from their lovely dance, full of a purpose and directness which she clearly knew to be purpose and directness, just as much as the dance was dance, though she did not know what the purpose was. She did not want to stop watching the dragonflies. She could watch them for years, and never tire of them. Yet, she could not slice the fruit well if all her attention was on the dragonflies.

"I still like the butterflies," she said to Keya.

"So do I," replied Keya. "Just not as I like the dragonflies. But, that's okay. You can like the butterflies best. It doesn't bother me."

You know what Keya means about the dragonflies – or at least what I do? Silmavalien responded to Airrock, laughing a little on 'or at least what I do.' *I thought you might.*

A few minutes later, a bright yellow butterfly fluttered across where she was working, as if rejoicing with the light and day, bewildered by joy and confused with light. The dragonfly seemed able to dart into the wind; the butterfly fluttered upon it, with flowery grace.

She had seen many butterflies before, some of them only in the last year. Orange ones, with intricate black lines on their wings, that she now realized reminded her a little of the artwork on her ring and the sword. Light blue, purple ones. Yellow ones, with lines on their wings almost just like the orange ones. Plain yellow ones, and white, and ones with multi-colored wings, red and black and yellow, with a blue or a green eye. Brown and tan ones.

She had noticed them, noticed the shapes and colors of their wings, enjoyed their beauty. But something about what Keya said, or maybe it was her own growth in these last years from knowing the dragons, made her able to see them in a way she had not before.

Yes, Airrock, there might be a reason why dragonflies are called dragon*flies.*

Songeth's agreement sang through her mind, but Minth only said that he felt like a butterfly, not a *dragon*fly.

She knew what he meant, but she did not know how to comfort him. *I love you. Just the way you are. I don't wish you were different. You are a true dragon. At any rate, you are you!*

And, she added, *I think I like butterflies most, so if that makes you feel better at all...*

It was true. Whatever it was she saw in the butterfly, it was even more indefinable than anything she saw in the dragonfly. Maybe, things were always like that. Maybe, what one saw best, one could say least. Maybe, what one loved or liked best, one could say the least about. Maybe, even what one knew best, one could say or even think the least. She had noticed that the dragons communicated without words, and their communication often went beyond words, touching truths that words were wholly inadequate, or even useless, to convey. And even their communication only hinted at, only suggested, only carried parts of the truth.

So she would not put to words to what she saw and loved in the butterflies, but she wanted Minth to know there was not anything lesser about being more like a butterfly.

She felt him lean into her thoughts, mentally cuddling against her in a way that he had not been able to for a long time, ever since he grew nearly as big as she was. But in their souls, he would always be able to cuddle into her like this, and she would always be able to cuddle into him when she needed to. She was right. He was right. It was good to be a butterfly.

S

Another evening, Songeth called together a choir of birds from the mountains and from the plains, to all add their unique voices to his music. This time, Silmavalien brought Keya with her to hear him sing, and after a few songs he asked her to join him.

> Down the dark'ning halls
> Of frozen night and colder light
> Flies an angel winged
> Of tidings true the messenger.

> Cracks impris'ning ice;
> A burning day and warmer dark
> Dawns in shadow bright
> That brings a death of fairer life.

> A once-frozen life
> Gives way to death as cold as ice –
> Death can break life's death
> Turn living death to dying life.

To die, to rise high –
To touch the grave and touch the skies.
Bright the blackest flame,
A scorching death to higher life!

For the deadest day
Grows alive by dying dark:
Death will evermore
Be release to the regions bright!

From the prison wide
Of coldest ice and colder space
Is the smoth'ring flame
And hotter dark the open door.

The song wrapped her up into it. She could not pull herself free even though she wanted to, and the words sang through her being. A disturbing something drew her, wrapped itself around and sank into her soul, a thought or feeling or something else for which she had no name, and maybe even maybe no previous experience. Deeper far than the Well of Nerya, she felt like it could envelop her in its embrace forever.

How did I even sing that? she thought. But, as Songeth's last notes trailed away into the evening, she gasped as if she had no breath, "Does anyone have any idea what that means? Songeth, do you even know?"

The dragons turned their eyes away, not giving her an answer.

Keya said, "I thought you would know. I did not know it had a meaning. Yes, I did not think of it." Silmavalien turned towards her, and was almost caught in her eyes, which danced like a deep blue vault of sky, as liquid and as dark as a deep lake, shimmering with the sunshine. Hidden glory, light, and joy shot from them like sparks of liquid sunlight, or sprang from them like a fountain slashing out of the ground and flashing in the morning light.

"It bothers me. It upsets me," said Silmavalien. "I do not like it. *Do any of you have any idea what it means?*"

Grudgingly, Songeth responded. He could not answer yes or no or anything else. Even to think in those terms was somehow wrong, and completely missed *it*, whatever it was. Even to think in those terms was to ruin something.

Most of the dragons added their agreement to Songeth, and Silmavalien could not see how their thought-feeling differed from his, though she got the impression that Veine, Airrock, Coroneth, and Wydth thought their thoughts differed very much indeed.

"It doesn't bother me," said Keya. "But maybe that's because I understand it even less than you do."

Several of the dragons took such strong offense at Keya's statement Silmavalien wondered if it showed on her face. *That was the wrong way to think! That was wrong – either way! It was entirely false, and the contrary was entirely false, and any statement or sentiment in between was entirely false. That whole way of thinking was a lie!*

Minth touched her softly, comfortingly, but she shrank from the touch. *He understood.* And it was part of whatever it was he understood or was that had separated them in the past. She thought.

"It makes no sense," she cried, and then added, "or what it means makes no sense. If it made no sense at all, how would I be upset by it? Nonsense is not bothersome like this."

"You see only the edge, only the surface. You are so upset because you do not see the Meaning."

At once, Silmavalien recognized the Voice.

Lord of Light, how? How can I see the Meaning?

"Go through the surface."

How?! How do I do that?

"That is what I will show you, and am showing you, and have been showing you."

How much power do you have? How much control do you have? Are you more powerful than everything else? Are you as powerful as all the gods together, or are you just a god, maybe one of the most powerful, maybe a lesser god? If so, where do you rank? Are you stronger than the strongest demon?

"You know already that I am stronger than the strongest demon. As for your other questions, there is no way for me to answer you yet. You are not ready."

The Voice departed, and Silmavalien knew she would get no more answer right now. If she wanted one. She forcibly did not sigh, did not growl, did not make any other signs to express her frustration and anger. She turned to Keya, and saw that her eyes still shone so brightly that they seemed hard to look at, not unlike the noon-sun, though it was not Silmavalien's eyes, but something else in her, that they overpowered.

She thought how Keya's eyes were almost always shining with something, and it was a something Silmavalien had no understanding of.

That night, Silmavalien remembered how she had thought that Love must be, and must a Who, and must be powerful and triumphant above all else. She had thought she had first thought this after hatching Dinora and the other dead dragons, but now when she thought of it, she thought of bonding with Minth. She had known this Love in bonding with him. And all the songs she had sung – as clearly as the stars shone above her in the unclouded sky, she realized that they were to the Love she met then, and that she had always known this, yet they seemed to be about the Lord of Light, too, or at least connected to him.

He must be closely related to Love: maybe, he *was* Love! What did Minth think?

He could not tell her whether her thought was right or wrong, or even mattered, but he had thought this before, he thought.

It only seemed more obvious to her as she considered it. The songs were to Love, and to the Lord of Light, and in the same way and at the same time. Weren't they? How had she not put the two together, and realized that if the Lord of Light were not Love, then he was closely related to Love?

How had she been so stupid not to notice this?

35

Like Sisters

One day that felt like it would be hotter than usual, Coroneth asked Silmavalien if she and Keya would like to come with them to a lake they had found. Airrock carried Tanz, and Silmavalien found the small blue dragon's displeasure somewhat amusing. Surrounded by so many flying dragons, she desperately wanted to fly, and she did not find being reminded that she was still *much* too young to be any sort of consolation at all.

The lake was a deep and wonderful blue, and almost as soon as the dragons landed, Silmavalien and Keya were playing in the shallows. Tiela kept dousing them with tiny waterfalls that fell from her wings and body as she rolled about and rose out of the water, and soon the other dragons joined her. They seemed to be laughing at how Silmavalien kept shivering and cringing, and Keya laughed, too. But not at her, she thought.

"I've never been here before," said Keya, waving the dragons off so she could talk. "I don't think any of my family know of it. We've lived here for generations. You've not been here a season."

"Dragons fly and can see a lot more than we can!" said Silmavalien. "It's no surprise they found it. It's nice, isn't it?"

"That it is," said Keya. "It is *so* wonderful having a girl-friend."

Tanz squeaked. Keya laughed at her.

"She's pretending to be jealous, isn't she?" asked Silmavalien.

"I wish I had your gift for hearing dragons! But, as I was going to say, the river that flows out of here looks a lot bigger than the few streams that trickle in."

"It might be fed from an underground spring," suggested Silmavalien. "Sometimes, water goes underground for a while, and then the rocks break, to let it back up."

"We'll have to see, then, if we can find where it comes up sometime. There's got to be some signs. The water-currents, maybe, or the temperature of the water. I'm sure underground water is less changed by the temperature of the days than surface water, and water just coming from underground can't have changed temperature much."

"Maybe," said Silmavalien, "but it might be very deep. Too deep for us to get."

"How long can dragons dive for?"

"I don't know. My friends have never dived much."

Keya looked around. She stepped into the very edge of the water, picked Tanz up, and hugged her. "Can you ask one of the dragons to look after Tanz and make sure she doesn't drown?" she asked.

"Umm, what's the need?" said Silmavalien. "There's no reason for us to go anywhere she can't come."

"We're going to go for a swim," said Keya, and then, seeing the look on Silmavalien's face, "Don't you want to?"

"I can't swim," said Silmavalien. "I've never learned."

"What? Was there no water where you grew up? Were girls not allowed to swim?" asked Keya.

"Everyone was allowed to swim. I think a few ones did, as small children. But, there wasn't water for swimming in. The streams weren't much good, most of the year."

"Well, I guess we won't go so far then, that I can't rescue Tanz if she gets herself into water too deep for her. I'll teach you how to swim! It's delicious fun."

S

After that, Silmavalien and Keya visited the lake often. Soon, Silmavalien was able to swim passably. It was an incredibly delightful feeling. When she first felt herself floating on the water without help, it was almost as if she were floating on wonder itself. It could not have been more amazing if she were walking on the water.

When she stepped out of the lake, still overwhelmed by the experience, she found a shady place, screened by trees and bushes so she would have a little privacy to pour her gratitude of the Lord of Light and tell him how much she loved all the wonderful things he had done for her. But there was still so much about him that she did not know, and it made her uneasy. She did not know what her relationship to him or to the rest of the world was, or was supposed to be, and none of the dragons offered her thoughts.

Silmavalien went back into the lake to swim with Keya until they noticed how late it had gotten. They climbed out and sat on the shore, dripping and a little cold, and Silmavalien poured out her thoughts to Keya. In rushing words and interrupted with thoughtful pauses she doubted anyone but herself could understand, she told of her feelings that Love must, by its nature, both be victorious over everything, the highest power, maybe even the only real power, and also be a Someone. A person who could relate.

Keya watched while she spoke, obviously making something of her words even though Silmavalien could not understand how she could be understood at all, so she went on while Keya listened earnestly and quietly, her eyes like a deep well, still, waiting, taking in, reflecting.

Finally, breathlessly, Silmavalien finished with her thought that the Lord of Light might even be this Love, and if not, he was as close to Love as Silmavalien could understand.

Keya said nothing, but Silmavalien saw that, in some measure, she understood her. At least, she understood something. She *knew* something. Her eyes shone with a steady but dazzling light, like the hot summer noons that Silmavalien had known in Treas.

The next day, Silmavalien said to Keya, "This is so wonderful, I am almost overcome by it! Daily, I thank the Lord of Light who brought me to this. Sometimes, I feel so glad and awed I cannot even thank. This life is so wonderful. This is more like home than anything I've ever had – yes, even before my brother took Krielasoriel for his wife. It is peace, and well-being, and safety, and comfort. Yes, there's work to do. Yes, your brothers are pains. But, for all that!"

Keya's eyes shone, and Silmavalien knew that in this they were true sisters. "Yes, Silmavalien. Ever since my mother died, years ago, I have felt like a stranger with no one who understood me. When I met you, I *knew you!* It's hard to describe." She laughed, the sound light with joy and nervousness. "And then Tanz. But, even when I met you, it was like, as you said, more home than anything I'd ever had... at least that I can remember. I... I feel like we're twins!" She started to stammer a bit, but then the last sentence rushed out of her mouth almost too quickly to be heard. She giggled, almost nervously, but it was something else – the simultaneous relief and discomfiting exposure of revealing a very deep feeling.

Silmavalien touched Keya's hand.

S

A few nights later, Silmavalien stopped at the edge of where the hammocks hung and turned away. She was disturbed about Noren, and she needed time and space alone, in the darkness, to think about it. There was something special about the darkness for thinking.

She had no idea where he was, and she was afraid for him, and she wanted so much to him. Since she had received guidance from her ring so often before, she held out her hand to look at it, but the moon was not up yet and a fog had already come off the sea and obscured the stars, keeping her from seeing more than the vague shapes of trees, just enough not to run into anything.

She wanted to see the dragon and the tree and the other details of the picture. Somehow, it felt to her as if they would comfort her, so she went to where her bags were left under the eaves of the house.

Just as her hand closed around the mint-colored glow-stone and she pulled it out, Silmavalien heard footsteps. She froze. Who was coming to her?

The dragons, respecting her need to be alone, were too far away to know.

"Hi," said Keya, cheerily. Then, in a lower voice, "What is going on, Sil?"

"I, I just need to think about something. I... I don't know how to explain it."

"Would you want to tell me about it?" asked Keya.

"Sure," said Silmavalien. She led the way around the house to the far side from where the hammocks hung. She did not know why, but talking to Keya seemed good now.

"Aren't you worried about being out alone in such a dark night?" asked Keya in a whisper.

"No. Several dragons are nearby. They will know if anything comes near."

"Tanz is asleep," said Keya.

"So," said Silmavalien, judging they were far enough away that no one would hear them, "it's about Noren."

"What about Noren?" asked Keya.

Silmavalien walked a little longer in silence. Then, sitting down, she took her ring off her finger and laid in the same hand with the glow-stone. "I'm worried about him. More than that, I think I have lots of feelings I don't understand, and I don't know what to do. My ring has given me guidance from the Lord of Light before, so I want to look at it."

"Tell me about it," said Keya.

Silmavalien started to tell her about the ring, and she interrupted. "You can tell me about that, if you want. You know I'm interested. But I was thinking of Noren and your feelings about him."

In a disjointed fashion, Silmavalien started telling Keya the story of she and Noren had been friends and fallen in love together. She rambled about Noren, telling Keya about everything he told her, trying to give her friend a picture of how he thought. She told Keya about he taught her to shoot and hunt. She told Keya everything she could remember about him, and then always one more thing.

Mostly, Keya listened in silence, but once or twice she asked a question to clarify.

Finally, Silmavalien said, "So I just feel really bad about it. I did even at the time, I think, but I couldn't think of what else to do – that would be safe for me, and, more so, for Minth. Not that I thought of the two things differently. We might as well be one." *We are one, aren't we one?*

"It certainly feels like I and Tanz are one," said Keya. "I'm not exactly sure one what, though. One soul? One heart? One being? One *love?* One...?"

"But, I was to be made one with Noren – in a different way, of course. And he loved me. And I left him. I'm sure he was so worried about me. I bet he is still worried about me. I hope that egg of his hatched, and that he has a dragon friend. I hope the dragon wasn't dead! It would be so horrible if he bonded to a dragon further gone than Minth and not quite so gone as Dinora!" She broke into bitter sobs that shook her whole body.

"I'm sure he's hurt I didn't trust him. If the egg hatched, that is. I'm sure he'd be sure he would have believed me and my dragon, not the old stories," she said, when she could breathe again.

Listening, Keya's heart contracted. Not just for Silmavalien and Noren. She had heard so many stories of that wonderful relationship of man and woman, and she had seen such tenderness and love between her father and mother. Would she ever be able to have a relationship like that?

Or were Tanz and Silmavalien enough? Would it be more wonderful than they were?

"Would he have believed you – trusted you?" she asked.

"I don't know," said Silmavalien. "I know I didn't know. I guess I *think* so. But it would have been such a shock to know dragons were real! I couldn't take the risk."

Keya said nothing.

Crying again, Silmavalien said, "I want to find him. I need to find him. I don't know where to begin."

"He almost certainly didn't cross the mountains?" asked Keya.

"No, I don't know. Airrock couldn't fly over them, not even close, and I doubt he found the Riders' Passage, and we haven't met. The dragons surely would have felt each other."

"Then," suggested Keya, "if you don't know where to look, at least you know somewhere *not* to look. And, so many dragons would find another if that other were in a distance twice as far as the lake is from here."

"I daren't start. I daren't try," said Silmavalien. "The world is so dangerous. There are nightmare creatures, wanting to kill you and steal your soul everywhere. The Lord of the Light sent me here. I daren't go anywhere unless he tells me. Or Aelaza. If she told me, or even another of the Ellenari, I'd take it as from him. The Ellenari protect me for him."

"Then, I will leave you alone, to seek guidance from him," said Keya. Rising, she turned to go, then stopped, came back a few steps, and said, very softly, very tentatively, "Silmavalien, I don't want to hurt you?"

"Yes?" responded Silmavalien.

Keya's voice trembled. "I don't want to hurt you, but I feel I've got to say this. I don't know why I've got to, and some of my brothers would scold me, but the dragons would all encourage me, right? Since I feel I've got to?"

Keya broke off for a moment, then stammered incoherently. Finally, she took another breath, steadied herself, and said, "Silmavalien, would trusting Noren have been more dangerous than what you did do? Just a thought."

"It would have been different. Totally different." The things were incomparable. The word 'risk' or 'danger' in the case of Noren was a completely different word from the danger and risk of what she had done. Noren was a *person*. The other danger was... not the same.

36

Winter on the Plains

Autumn came, winter crept nearer, and the air cooled. It was no longer possible to go swimming in the lake, but this was more than made up for by the fact the dragons no longer had to be careful about sunburning. As the sun spent more and more of its time behind the wall of the Greater Aravin Mountains, Silmavalien could ride any one of her dragons at any time and for however long they wanted. Being able to fly in the day was a great joy.

It was made even more so because the dragons could often fly above the fog. Otherwise, Silmavalien would not have seen clear skies for weeks at a time, since it rained more often than not, and when it was not raining, it was usually misty. But the dawns and evenings were beautiful with a heavenly beauty, and the shrouded sun lit up the mist with glowing, fiery colors, like watery fire. Silmavalien thought the flaming colors did not look as if they would burn her up. They looked more like they would wrap themselves around her if only they could get to her and clothe her with themselves.

Never, in all her life in Treas, had she seen mornings and evenings like these, but for all their wonder, she and the dragons missed the sun. When she talked to Keya, she said she missed the sun, too. But every once in a while the fog lifted, and then the clouds and the light would look more like what she was used to. She welcomed those days like a long-missed friend, and when even more rarely she got to actually see the sun rise or set, it was sheer delight.

She was soon surprised by how warm it was, even though the sun never shone. This side of the Aravin Mountains had been strangely warm, too, but it had been colder than this. But Keya told her the winters were always this.

"I like the mountains – whether this side of the Aravin Mountains, or the other side – so much better," she said.

"I don't know if I would or not," replied Keya. "I've never lived on mountains.

Never even been on mountains for a single day."

Another day, Keya asked Silmavalien where she had got the mint glow-stone, and Silmavalien told her about the Riders' Passage.

"You should call them Earthstars," said Keya. "I would like to get one of my own. Maybe in a different color. I don't very much like mint."

"Well, maybe," said Silmavalien. "If you ever get to take the Riders' Passage. We can't just go there. There's a Fire-Shadow in an abyss that guards the entrance. Also, I was told to go down. I think the Ellenari and the demons might be fighting like mad over there."

"I *was* thinking of going to get one," said Keya, "but I didn't really mean we could."

Another time, when the mist had risen just a little, but still hung about them, and they felt the wetness on their skins, while above them it looked like the sky was falling in tatters of glorious color, as if its fall would be, not the end, but the beginning of a world, Silmavalien said to Keya, "I want to sing you a bit of me and Minth's song. It seems to describe my life, or something about my life, not just getting to know the dragons, but you, too."

"I'm all for it," said Keya. "Sing."

> We will dance together
> In joy like never before
> Now with another and another
> Altogether one forevermore
> In One who draws us more and more

"Yes," said Keya, "I see what you mean. And, I think I also see what you mean, about the songs being at once to Love and to the Lord of All Light."

Yes, thought Silmavalien, responding to Veine. *Maybe the end of one world is the beginning of another. Or, what we call the end of the world is really the beginning of the world, Songeth.*

Keya stood, with a rapt look on her face.

Re-focusing, she looked at Silmavalien. "Do you think," she asked, as if relaying an idea, new to her, and somehow appealing, though Silmavalien could not tell just what sort of appealing from her voice, "that maybe the song you didn't like might have just a little bit of something to do with the idea that what we call the end of the world might really be its beginning, in triumph and beauty?"

"I don't *think* I see that," said Silmavalien, "but there *is* something in the idea." She paused, then said, "I don't know if I see the connection, and I *really* don't want to think about it."

S

All of Keya's family were happy to have Silmavalien and the dragons with them over the wet season. The constant rain washed away all the animal tracks and made the ground slippery to walk on, so it was harder for the humans to hunt, but that did not matter to the dragons. They did not hunt in wind storms, but when the rain was gentle it did not bother them, and they were happy to hunt for their friends. But they sometimes frustrated Keya's family, with their unwillingness to hunt until someone was actually hungry. They would not hunt ahead of time, taking into account the fact that humans had to prepare their food. But while some of Keya's family found this more or less annoying and could not understand why the dragons were like this, Silmavalien would not try very hard to convince them.

It was the way they were, they *were* hunting for everyone, and after everything she had been through since Minth hatched, being a little hungry for a day did not bother her much. Keya did not try to convince the dragons either, even once Tanz learned to fly. Silmavalien was a little surprised by how quickly Tanz learned to fly, but when again she had lots of experienced dragons to help her and she was always trying to fly.

But though the dragons hunted, and the work of the harvest was over, there was still work to do. Keya showed Silmavalien how to keep tools and clothes from molding in the wet, warm winter by hanging them at the right distance from open flames.

Silmavalien began to wonder just how large the dragons would be when they were full-grown, and when that would be. By the end of winter, most of the older dragons stood taller than her head at the shoulders, with Wydth being the largest, though Silmavalien thought Lighter might catch up to him in a few years, since he was just as large for his age. Next came Coroneth, and then Veine and Songeth who were very much the same size. Airrock only barely came up to her head, and

Tiela was only a bit taller though she was much stouter. But Jareth and Minth were right about the same size, just coming up to her chin, while Daurth was still a bit smaller.

Staring up at the misty sky, against which her dragons wheeled in patterns that only they knew and came up with as they flew, Silmavalien wondered if maybe Keya's family knew some of the things she did not. Like when they would be full-grown, or what was wrong with Minth and Daurth, and to a lesser extent Jareth, who seemed the most lethargic of the bunch, and if she could do anything about it.

She got up, trying to flick as much of the water as she could out of her clothes since she had been lying down in the grass, and went to ask Shilchu.

He looked at her, with something in his eyes which she liked, but was not sure she understood. She thought he enjoyed seeing her with the dragons, seeing his daughter with the dragons, and seeing so many dragons growing and flying and playing. She thought he liked her.

She also thought he would very much enjoy sharing his knowledge.

"All right," he began. "Dragons grow for about twelve to seventeen years, but, as you might already be able to guess, or then again might not already be able to guess, most of that growth occurs during the first two years. You already know about when they can breathe fire. What else might you want to know? Oh yes, they can mate as young as two years old, but when they do so, they rarely lay more than three eggs, often less. They carry their eggs for about one-and-a-half to two years, which might seem strange. I've never heard of another creature that can mate when no older than the time they spent in their dam's body." He paused, then asked, "Anything else you can think of, that you want to know? I can't guarantee that I can answer it, but I'll try if I can."

"Umm," said Silmavalien, "most of my dragons seem rather healthy. Even those who have skin problems, Wydth, Songeth, they can do things rather well. Minth, he's slow, he's clumsy, sometimes he feels worse than other times. Daurth is kind of like that, too, only not as bad. I guess Jareth seems rather worse than any of the others, but not like Daurth or Minth. So, I guess, do you know why? Do you know if there's something I could do about it?"

Shilchu gave a great sigh. "No, Sil, I don't," he said. "When my grandfather was alive, there were only a few albino dragons, but more than there had been when he was young, and more than makes sense. Albino deer or wolves, or any other kind of animal I know, aren't very common, and they usually don't seem especially sick, but many of the dragons did. They rapidly declined, more of them sick, more of them albino, but I know little about it, and I don't know that anyone else does. We didn't have any more to do with the dragons, though, after my grandfather and his dragon died. We were kind of out of the way, already, so we did not even hear more than a few rumors, until the officers came to ask anyone if they had dragon eggs and collect them."

He paused, and looked at her tenderly. "I'm sorry, though, about your dragons. I hope they live long, especially Minth."

` "Or I die young?" asked Silmavalien, tears in her eyes at the thought of any of her dragons dying.

He smiled at her.

She smiled back and changed the topic. "The weather here seems good for their skin."

37

A Request of Love

Shilchu did not have much more to say, and Silmavalien scrambled for a way to close the conversation in a way that felt right. Often, in the last few weeks, she had told Keya how nice it was to be here with her, and how wonderful it was that it had now been half year since she had seen or felt the nightmare creatures, so she told Shilchu that as well.

He looked at her happily. "I'm glad you and Keya are friends," he said. "She needed that. And the Lord of the Light is very wonderful, but I do not think any of us know much about him – or about anything, for that matter – yet. But be always grateful to him."

"I try now," she said, and somehow it felt like the conversation was over. She walked away, deep in thought.

The way the conversation about the dragons ended had made her thoughtful. She still knew so little, but the thought of dying made her think of what she had recently thought about the Lord of Light. She knew now that he was Love or, if not, somehow above him, better and stronger than he, was Love, and he was like the Ellenari were to him to that Someone.

But dying? She did not know what death was, except that it was wrong! Love was the most powerful thing, powerful over all. She knew that. If there was one thing she knew, that was it. What then was death? How? How was it to be reconciled with Love? Why did Love allow death? What did Love do with death? Why did Love allow so much pain, so much futility, so much sorrow, so much hate, so much death, in the world?

Silmavalien could not answer her questions, and though she was beginning to feel that the world might be full of hints which, if she could only understand them, would at least suggest the answer, she could not understand the hints, and they upset her so much she could not even think about them most of the time, or realize what they were.

S

Shortly after that, the spring arrived, fresh and beautiful, with the long-missed sunshine. Silmavalien was certain the birds were as happy to see it as she was. They filled the day with their songs that brimmed with a joy so strong it could only be the joy of utter triumph, yet so sweet and innocent that it could have no acquaintance with any battle or strife at all. Their voices filled the air, and as she tried to let their joy fill her mind, she thought there were far more birds here than there had been any other place she had lived. She rejoiced with Songeth, who told her that he learned from the birds just as much as he taught them.

Tiela and the male dragons went into another round of showing interest in each other, and one day Keya saw them teasing each other and asked Silmavalien what it was about. She explained what she knew, and wondered if Keya had asked her because Tanz was still too much of a baby to notice or care.

As she tried to explain, Keya's brows furrowed in an expression of worry, and Silmavalien hastened to explain. "Don't worry," she said. "They can keep to themselves a little, and it's not been bad yet. Of course, they've not yet mated, and Tiela might be old enough. But it's been mostly funny, so far."

She felt like crying. Once again she thought of Noren, and the conversation she had had with Keya about him only made her more confused and conflicted. Keya waited, silently, perhaps sensing she needed something, and finally she blurted out, "What do you think Noren would have done if I had told him?"

Keya looked at her strangely. "I don't know all about him, or what was between you two, but if I understand correctly, and if the relationship between you was anything like how stories talk about it, or how my parents felt about each other, it would have been nothing to him at all to trust you."

"That's what... what I... what I couldn't quite think," Silmavalien said, bursting into tears. After a few moments she added, "Until someone else said it. I couldn't. I couldn't imagine it. I still can't. I mean now, but, then!"

"Noren didn't believe the stories," said Keya gently.

"But he didn't *know* they were *wrong*, either, the way I do now, and if he'd seen the dragon he would have known they were part-right, and he wouldn't have known they were all-wrong, like I did," she protested.

"He knew and loved you," said Keya. "Do you think he *could* have believed you a witch? Do you think he *could* have accepted killing you? – any more than you could Minth?"

"I don't know about *more,*" said Silmavalien. "I certainly am not bonded to him nor him to me as I and Minth are." At that moment, she thought that she felt more miserable than she had ever felt before in her life.

Keya waited for a little while, while she sobbed and mumbled some inarticulate words here and there. Then, after several minutes had passed, she asked, "Silmavalien, if it had been in reverse, if Noren's dragon hatched first, and he had told you, would you have been able to hate and betray him – to think him evil and give him up to death?"

"I don't – I don't – don't – don't – *know!*" said Silmavalien, feeling even more miserable. "If I had, if I could have, I should have been *bad!*" She cried harder, shaking and gasping for air. "And, if I could have then, and all that's changed is that I know more – or rather that I know less – then I still am *bad!*"

Keya did not hear what Silmavalien said, her words were so garbled, and she asked her to repeat herself. While she struggled to speak more clearly, Minth wrapped mental wings around her, lovingly reassuringly her that she wasn't bad.

I know you don't think I'm bad, she replied, distraught. *I know you say that I loved you, that I accepted you, because I wasn't that bad, but really, I couldn't help it.*

So you hatched to me in the first place – I couldn't help it – because I'm okay?

But I did do a bad thing! I didn't trust Noren and I hurt him, and I deceived him, whom I loved and told I loved and promised to marry, because I was kind of bad myself!

Yes, I know I'm thinking in the wrong way. Airrock's, Veine's, and Songeth's thoughts were all crowding her now. *You say cause and effect aren't how I've always thought it – yes, I know you didn't say it that way – and you're probably right. But that doesn't change the last thing I said! I hurt Noren.*

"And who said that all that's changed is that you know more?" Keya's words broke in on the chaos of the dragons' thoughts in her mind. "Never mind that you don't even know you would have done the bad thing."

"But I might be bad, I can't stand it," Silmavalien refused to be comforted. "I don't want to be bad! I was kind of bad, and I might have been worse than I know I was, and I do not want to be bad. So, if I might be bad, I have to have a way of being certainly good, certainly not bad."

"Why don't you ask the Lord of the Light?" suggested Keya.

"Somehow, I think that is a request he would be certain to listen to. Love would certainly listen to and grant that request."

Yes, Minth, I think that is exactly what you were saying. Or something like it. That Love will transform us and make us good.

Was my love for Noren then not true love? Because I had not yet met Love? Somehow, bonding to you and meeting Love were the same. Did it have to be that way?

Yes, returned Silmavalien, laughing a little even through her tears and misery, which might have been Songeth's intention, *that* is the *wrong question to ask – or the wrong way to ask it.*

She straightened and looked at Keya. "I guess I will go and ask the Lord of the Light, or Love, or both, since I don't know they're quite the same, to make sure I'm good, or at least not bad. And then, I shall be more or less happy, since Love is sure to make sure I'm good eventually – as soon as possible? Since, I have no doubt at all that what is best for me is to be good! And, that what's best for everyone else, is for me to be good. Other things, I might not know. That I know as sure as I know that Love is real and victorious. So, I will know for certain that Love will make me good."

"That sounds like an excellent idea," said Keya.

Her mind rang with the jubilant approval of her dragon friends.

So Silmavalien went to a place where there was no one very near. She took off her ring of light, and addressed the Lord of the Light and Love, in turn, with her plea, confident that it would please him or them, she did not know which. She hoped he or them would not be displeased with her uncertainty about who was who. She asked the Lord of the Light to convey her request to Love, if he was not himself Love, for she was certain that Love must be highest. But must Love not also, of his nature, hear all and listen to all, *love* all?

Either way, it did not hurt to ask.

38

Return of the Shadow

The sun shone, a white radiance on the edges of the mountains. The impossibly high peaks shone as if the sun had sent its life-blood, full of burning light, through them, and lived along them just as it lived in the sky, but the cliffs of the Steep Descent were cast in blue shadow.

Silmavalien stood in an open meadow, called by the exuberance and joy burning in her dragons' veins. Keya came and stood beside her, glowing with happiness and excitement, as she watched the dragons circle in the sky, their loops growing increasingly wide. Above them, Tiela and Songeth soared higher and higher, until they were so high she could scarcely see them in the sky. She knew the only her eyes could follow those two tiny dots was because she was bonded to them.

And then they joined, one for a few moments. She had not been wrong in her reassurance to Keya. She was not part of it.

Keya shifted next to her, and she realized her friend was watching her dragon soar and dip with inexpressible longing in her eyes.

"Before long, you will be able to start riding her, now and then, for a little while," Silmavalien said, but Keya did not respond. As the dragons descended, she wondered that it was Songeth Tiela had chosen, and not Wydth. The choice seemed fitting, but at first she had thought it would be Wydth. She wondered if perhaps Songeth, Wydth, Coroneth, and Veine were all siblings.

A few weeks later, she approached Shilchu, to talk to him about her thoughts about Love and the Lord of the Light. Somehow, she did not feel able to have these conversations with anyone in the family except for him and Keya. He did not have much to say, though.

S

It was not long before they were picking the earliest berries and other fruits – earlier than Silmavalien had ever been able to pick them before. She and Keya always went together, but the men often went, too, sometimes with them all in one group, sometimes not. By mid-summer, Keya was riding Tanz, and by autumn, she was learning to breathe fire. Her fire was as blue as herself, and green and violet around the edges.

As Tanz grew bigger and she could do more together,

Silmavalien became aware of brewing conflict. Keya's brothers were jealous, some of them more so than others, and each of them wanted a ferocious fire-breathing beast of his own, one who hunted like nothing in Areaer and whom he could ride. Nereis, who had watched Tanz hatched, only watched her now fly and breathe fire with a glow of longing in his eyes, and though he quarreled with Keya sometimes, Silmavalien felt no darkness in his desire.

But she felt something – whether herself or through her dragons – that bordered on male and hate from several of them, and some of it was focused on her. Once or twice, she overheard them talking. She had too many dragons. Why couldn't they have some of the dragons? There were enough to go around! Each of them could have a dragon, and she could still have multiple dragons!

Then Nereis asked her, "Can you give me one of your dragons? You have so many!"

Two of his older brothers, who were working tools on the other side of the meadow, glowered, and Silmavalien tried to ignore them as she replied to Nereis.

"No, I can't. I don't *have* any dragons. Not that way. You might as well say they have me. It often feels like that."

"Okay," said Nereis. He accepted that easily. "Why don't any of them have me? Do none of them like me?"

"They like you," said Silmavalien. "But I can't answer your question. I don't know how things work. Most things I don't know."

Nereis giggled at that. "I bet you know more than I do!" he said. "And I know a lot!"

She had no idea what to say to that, but she tried to keep a closer eye on the situation, instead of mostly ignoring Keya's brothers as she had been doing, in part to escape their interest in her. She soon noticed that one of Nereis' older brothers was kind to him, though the others scowled at his forwardness in talking about her about the dragons, and he usually hung out with this young man.

But the tension she could feel developing around her was starting to frighten her. "O Lord of All Light," she often prayed, "can you please do something? I don't know what, but can you help these people to get along and love each other like they used to? Why is this happening?" She also talked to the dragons, but none of them could give her any ideas what she could do, and neither could Keya.

This place, that had felt like home, did not feel so peaceful anymore. She felt the shadow again, and though it did not fall on her as it had before, it was still there, oppressive and terrifying, stealing joy. "If I'm disobeying you, for some stupid reason, because I don't want to obey you, and I don't know what your commands are, because I'm sure I won't like to obey them," she told the Lord of the Light, "help me, somehow. Make it so that I can't deceive myself. Whatever. But I don't want to do this again. It's horrible."

One day, when the tension was worse than ever, she and Keya went out with the dragons to be alone. She thought Keya wanted to talk, but when Keya did not say much, she just asked, "Are we going to leave this place?"

"I don't know," said Keya. "I wouldn't know where to go."

"We're Dragonriders. We could go somewhere," said Silmavalien. "The problem would be if we go somewhere the Lord of the Light doesn't want. Then, the nightmare creatures could devour us at their leisure, if he did not protect us."

𝑺

Silmavalien sat bolt upright.

"Wh-what is it?" asked Keya.

For a moment, she did not hear her, caught up in what Veine was showing her. She had come across the brothers who had gone out hunting a few days ago, and they were injured, one of them very badly, so badly she could hardly feel him.

"Your brothers – the hunters – are hurt!" replied Silmavalien, jumping up. "Veine found them."

"Kenaja and Dalchi!" cried Keya. "We'll –"

Tanz, tell her what we're doing, it's faster than if I have to, said Silmavalien, as she called Wydth. He was the biggest and the strongest and, she asked him to bring a few others with him, too. While the dragons came, she and Keya ran to collect the rest of family. She found their father almost at once, and they grabbed some leather straps so they would be able to bind the injured brothers onto the dragons, then she jumped onto Coroneth and Wydth took the father out. Keya and Tanz went with them.

Dalchi was deathly pale when they arrived, and Silmavalien and his father worked as gently but furiously as they could to bind him on Wydth's back. Meanwhile, Keya and Kenaja argued, but Kenaji insisted he would not be bound. Instead, they made something of a harness for him to hold onto, tying the straps around Airrock's neck and chest and over his leg.

By the time they flew back, the other brothers had gotten all sorts of things ready, boiling water and herbs and fresh bandages. They did their best to cleanse and bandage both of the brother's wounds, and Silmavalien could tell that the young man's father and siblings were deathly worried for Dalchi, who was still unconscious and unresponsive, even though they did not say anything. But while they worked on Kenaja's wounds, he told them more or less what had happened. Silmavalien was working too frantically to absorb all the details, but it was more or less what she had expected: the nightmare creatures had once again revealed themselves.

Finally, there was not anything to be done, and everyone except the still-unconscious Dalchi gathered around to eat the night meal. Silmavalien picked at her food, while an unnatural silence replaced the usual rowdiness that occurred whenever more than three of the brothers were in one place at a time. Finally, she broke it. "I do not think that I protect you at all," she said clumsily. "But I may have drawn the nightmare enemy. While I was living alone in the wild, I certainly seemed to. I once thought that moving would always make me safe for a little while from the nightmare creatures, but I know now that it does not. However, if I leave, they might stop coming to you."

"You might not *protect* us exactly," said Kenaja, "but you did find us. Otherwise, I and Dalchi would have died before we were found. If we were found before we died, it would almost certainly have been too late, at least for Dalchi."

His love for his brother shone through his word, and though he did not say it, but she knew he feared that it was already be too late.

"From what you tell us, the Ellenari, or at least one Ellen, helped you," she countered. "Even if that Ellen was Aelaza, I think they will watch you if they have any fear for you. The Lord of All Light certainly wants what is best for all, and you could always ask him to take care of you."

"Would Keya have to go also?" asked her father.

"If Silmavalien goes, I will, too. Sure as sure," said Keya.

Silmavalien looked at her. "You shouldn't, if it's not what the Lord of the Light wants. That's only a way to run into disaster. I don't know, though. I *think* the nightmares hate the dragons. That's the only conclusion I've been able to come to. They may even be behind why the dragons are hated so much and thought to be demons in south Aneri. But I don't know. I know almost nothing."

They talked a little more, as they finished up their meal, and then everyone split to go their own way, except for the father who was going to stay with Dalchi. Shilchu motioned to Silmavalien before she could head towards her hammock. She came towards him, wondering what he had to say.

"You told Keya she shouldn't go with you, unless the Lord of the Light wants her to," he told her, in a little more than a whisper so that others would not hear their conversation. "Otherwise, it's begging for disaster. When you thought of leaving, is it because you think the Lord of the Light wants you to go, or some other reason – like you imagined for yourself it would work best?"

Silmavalien drew herself together and tensed her shoulders. "I definitely haven't heard him tell me to stay. I've asked him to make my way clear. I *think* he wants me to go." She paused, then said, "I can't think of any reason I would want to go. But then, I don't ever know what is coming next. Then, I don't like the way some of the brothers feel about the dragons. The dragons don't like that way, either. We don't think it's good for anyone."

"That might be so," said Shilchu. "I wasn't asking you to explain yourself to me, either. I was just asking you to consider it for yourself."

"Yes," said Silmavalien. She turned and went to her hammock.

39

Flying Through Storms

Silmavalien could not sleep, and several hours later she sat up and swung herself out of the hammock, as softly as she could. She did not want to wake anyone if she could help it.

Silmavalien took her bags and packed everything she owned back into them, along with a little fresh fruit and some of the left-over dried fruit from last year, things she knew no one would miss. In the conversation over the night meal, they had discussed provisions for if she left, and it made sense She had done her share in getting and preparing them.

Finally, she took strips of animal-hide and made them into a sort of rope to tie the bags to Tiela and Lighter. She did not want to burden the dragons with carrying the bags in their claws or their mouth, never mind the fact that was more likely to damage them or their contents, and she did not want to tie anything to the other dragons. But she was not worried about the ropes hurting Tiela or Lighter's scales.

All of that done, she climbed onto Veine, and they flew away into the night. By the stars overhead, she knew it was not quite midnight. But something about the situation reminded her of her flight from Treas with Minth two years ago, even though the preparation for that had been a lot harder. The memory made her nervous and uncomfortable, but she could not think of a better solution. She knew Keya was attached to her. She also knew that she was attached to Keya, and that she might not want to leave Keya for her own reasons. She also did not want Keya to come after her only because she did not want to leave her, and she could think of no other way to prevent that.

As Veine climbed into the air, for a moment she remembered the first time she ever rode a dragon, the night they had flown down from the cliff, but after a moment the memory faded. The stars shone overhead, bright and pure. The night air in her face was sweet and cool and delicious. She often rode at night, so she was used to it. It did not feel more different from another night ride than one night ride always felt from another. The dragons thought nothing of migrating. It was natural to them to move from one place or another.

Then, all at once, she felt the presence of the nightmare. She almost feared she would faint. A cold wind, like warmth fetid with death, blew around her. The stars seemed to flicker in and out, no longer steady in the sky. Panic and hatred flowed through her, tearing her apart, as if she was swimming in a sea of hot death. She hated Aelaza, she hated Aelaza so much for telling her that she would not be troubled if she flew down the cliff at once, and then letting her by troubling by the flying nightmares. Then she hated the Lord of Light, Love himself, for letting Aelaza lie to her – how was it different from lying to her himself?!

These thoughts were not her own. Silmavalien recognized that, or at least that they should not and could be her own, but the panic only further confused her attempts to fight the cries that overwhelmed her. *"I will never forgive! I will never forget! She lied! He betrayed me! I hate! I will never forgive, never forget, never rest!"*

Distantly, she knew that the dragons fought the same struggle, each in their own way. *Love!* she cried out, feeling almost strangled. *Lord of Light!* There was nothing else she could manage. She tried to fight the fear and hate and bitterness, but it was stronger than her. She fought and resisted, and yet more and more of her being was filled by the nightmare enemy!

The light-arrow of an Ellen twanged, singing through the night. She was slipping off of Veine's shoulders! Veine shifted under her, and she did what the dragon told her, threw her weight the other way, and held on as hard as she could.

A gray-winged bird appeared in front of them. Blue and purple light gleamed out from underneath the feathers. Somehow, she recognized it as Aelaza in another form. "That way," Aelaza said, motioning. "Follow me, when I move slow enough for you. Don't worry about it when I move faster than you."

Rain began to fall. Tempestuous and wild winds blew around them. Horrible creatures took form out of the mists and clouds, and neither Silmavalien nor any of the dragons saw more than a part of them at a time. Black and dark-red wings. Fangs dripping with something, whether poison or blood or both or both-in-one Silmavalien did not know. Stony talons. Eyes like a dark green well. Other forms and features peaked out at her, more indistinct or at least more unlike anything real she could use to recognize or remember them.

The presence of fear and bitterness receded only little, as if somehow seeing the nightmares loosened their grasp this time. But it was still all she could do not to give into it and hold onto Veine – though why she wanted to give into it, or thought she wanted to, she could never figure out. It was worse when Aelaza was not in sight, and Minth struggled, too. It was worse for him, because fighting the battle in his mind made it hard to fly.

Aelaza glowed in the midst of storm, and Silmavalien thought that she was the bird of the storm, perhaps its very heart or essence. Somehow, she looked like Silmavalien imagined a storm must look if it took the form of a bird.

She stilled, moving slow enough for their eyes to follow, and showed a few of the dragons a way through the wall of nightmare horrors that seemed almost as thick as the cloud and the rain around them. Then, she darted like a flash of lightning against the nightmares, and for a moment all was bright with the brilliance of lightning. Thunder followed, and Silmavalien's skin tingled, as did the dragons. For a moment, in the tingling, and in the white glare of the lightning, somehow soft and hard at once, they were free! Free from the attack on love, the assault on their very being and ability to love. It was ecstatic peace.

In a moment of freedom and lightning that lingered longer than most, Silmavalien knew that Veine struggled less than she did; perhaps less than anyone else. She felt Jareth, struggling right on the edge of giving in. She cringed away from the indistinct forms of terror and bitterness that dominated him, and reached from him towards her. At what could he possibly be so bitter?

Then the relief of the lightning was over before she could understand him.

Was this happening because she had done wrong in flying away in the darkness. *I've done it again. Forgive me!* she cried out.

The flash of Aelaza's lightning and the power and the storm, and the struggle closed around her soul like a vice again. Would they ever get out? Would this ever end? Where would she be?Were they going back to the house?

Again and again, she knew that it was all her fault, though she did not know how she could have done better. She did not know! She did not know what she should or should not do! Yet, the shadow of guilt oppressed her. It was her fault. *I'm so sorry! I'm so, so, so, so, so, SO SORRY!*

The Voice spoke to her, even in the conflict and darkness. "Love is. You are loved. You are free. Follow Love, and do not fear or worry about failures. Real or not, Love is, and they are over – gone."

Veine lurched and almost spun, fighting the nightmare that was reaching for her, and it was all Silmavalien could do to stay with her motion. The warm of a blast of fire reached out over her, but her eyes were scrunched shut against Veine's neck and she did not see it.

"You might as well do that as much as you want," Silmavalien heard Aelaza tell Veine. "It won't hurt. It can help."

Joy rushed through Veine, and she breathed flames as often as she could. The others dragons followed her example, and if a nightmare came too near to them, they tried to twist and breathe fire back towards it. If they had to pass close to one, there was more fire, and sometimes there was fire for reasons Silmavalien did not understand.

At last, the dragons felt the land drawing near below them. Aelaza appeared again and the clouds opened beneath her. Minth and several others were so exhausted they barely managed to land, even though the wind changed, slowed, calmed, and seemed to help them, putting them down as gently as possible.

Suddenly, the realization rushed through them all. The wind had helped them all along. They had thought they were struggling against it, but if they had not been borne on its wings, they could never have made it through the gaps into the nightmares or out of the paths of their deadly dives. All along, the wind had been fighting for them and against the nightmare evil. It had blown them where they needed to go. Perhaps, the rain, too, had been their protection and help in more ways than they could guess!

Aelaza was already gone before half of them touched the green grassy earth. The presence of the nightmare slowly faded, but Silmavalien still felt the darkened thoughts in Jareth's heart. She worried and feared for him more than ever.

She wondered then if the nightmare creatures had been the cause of some of Keya's brothers evil and unhappy thoughts. Or were they drawn to and helped by those evil thoughts?

It was not a question she could answer. As soon as she could, she took a moment to thank the Lord of the Light and Love for keeping them safe and protecting them. Though she remembered what the Voice had told her, she still felt guilty and a little miserable, and that made it harder for her to pray and give thanks.

Slowly the storm passed. They were all so tired. Silmavalien stood. She staggered a little. Looking around her, she saw the bags laying about. In an indistinct flash, she knew from the lay of them, from the state of their cords, and from the dragons' memories, that they had been lost in the battle and then the storm, and then found by someone else – perhaps Aelaza, perhaps another servant of Love. She saw that what she had almost taken for an extra bag looked like maybe it was actually a dragon, but she was too tired to see well.

She stumbled over to Minth, crawled under his wing. Tired as he was, too, he hummed with contentment and happiness, and from farther away, she could hear Veine humming too, but then she was fast asleep.

It was about mid-morning.

40

The Open Plains

Silmavalien woke to Tanz's touch on her mind. She crawled out from under Minth's wing and looked around her.

Bright blue sky shone through tattered white clouds. The Aravin Mountains were farther away than she had ever seen them. Land full of green grass, almost as flat as flat, spread out as far as the eye could see. No Tanz anywhere!

Tanz was not anywhere near. She and Keya were coming. When they all fell asleep, Tanz could no longer sense them, so they had to wait.

Then you felt what we went through?

Some of it. Tanz did not want to talk on that point.

Why are you coming? Will you have to go through it?

Once again, Tanz would not respond. Keya did not want to talk to Silmavalien through her, either.

Looking around her, feeling the feel of the air on her skin, Silmavalien thought it was late afternoon, a little before evening. But she had never lived on treeless plains, far from mountains, so it was hard to tell from the feel of the air. Not that she was really that far from the mountains! They stood imposing and high, towering up above her. Looking to one side, she saw the sun, hanging in glory, the leading edge of the radiance kissing the wall of the mountains. It could not be rising from behind the mountains; it must be descending to go behind them.

Definitely afternoon.

Silmavalien was still so tired. Only a few of the dragons had even stirred half-awake. They must all be more tired than she was. After all, they had had to fly in that wind. She had only had to cling to Veine. She wondered if the wind had helped with that also, instead of making it harder, like she had thought in the moment.

Silmavalien stooped back down, and lay against Minth's side again. She fell asleep almost as fast as the first time.

The west glowed with the dying fire of the sun when she woke again, this time aware of her hunger almost before she was awake.

Lighter and Airrock were already awake, but Minth only stirred in his sleep at her loving touch. She got some food out of one of the bags, and leaned against Veine, who was just waking up, to eat it. The female dragon nuzzled her with her purple nose, and crooned happily.

When Jareth woke, Silmavalien could feel that he was still upset, but she had no idea what she could say to him. She finished eating, but she did not want to go back to sleep yet. She felt too tired to fly with Airrock, and she wondered how the dragon wasn't tired, but Airrock went flying, while she continued to lean against Veine, and talk to the dragons who were awake. They shared their memories of the events of the night, and they talked about the stars, and about Aelaza, and about the Lord of the Light, and about Love.

Jareth remained sullen and unresponsive, until he interjected to bitterly and condescendingly explain that he did not think Love reigned. There might be no such thing as pure Love. Why had he had to almost starve in the Riders' Passage? Why had last night been such a struggle? Why so many other things? Listening to him rant, Silmavalien realized that, while the wind and the light had helped him too, last night, just as much as they helped everyone else, he did not know it and would not be willing to know it.

But how could a dragon not know Love? She had tried to love him from the first, though she was not very good at loving. But what of Love himself! How could a dragon, a dragon who had bonded, not know him in some way?

She had some sort of sense that Jareth glowered at her after finishing his rant, before tucking his head under his wing almost as if he were embarrassed, and going back to sleep.

By morning, Silmavalien felt sleepy again, but Minth finally woke up. She moved away from Veine to snuggle against him, and though they did not speak, she felt they shared as much, or even more, just by being together in each other's minds.

The early morning air was cold, so she pulled a blanket out of her bags, wrapped herself in it, and lay down on the grass next to his shoulders. As she drifted asleep, she thought this grass was the nicest mattress she had ever had.

When she woke again, the sun had just emerged from behind the mountains for the middle of the day. *I don't like this place,* she thought, looking around. *It's so full of sun and open space, with no heights and no depths and no shade or cover anywhere. You'll have no way to keep from sunburning, either.*

The dragons liked the open plain, they told her. They would not want to live here always, but they liked it. It felt open and free. Yes, she was right about the sun. Some of them already felt it. Some trees would be nice. There were very few, and most of those were far apart. They could not provide enough shade.

Eventually, after some hard thinking – they must all still be exhausted – Silmavalien came up with an idea. The ground was soaking wet from the downpour of two nights ago. The white dragons could dig pits in the mud and roll in them. If they got the dark wet dirt to stick to their pristine white hides, it might do a lot to protect them from the sun.

I know, said Silmavalien, when several of them grumbled. They were already working on her solution but, among others, Coroneth was not happy about it. *You want to be clean, and this will make you yucky and dirty, not all white and pretty. Yes, this won't do at all perfectly at protecting you from the heat and the sun. At least, it will help, until we can think of something better.*

She replied next to a tentative suggestion by Lighter. *I'm not sure how well digging caves would work. Don't you think this mud would collapse very easily?*

Coroneth excitedly announced it might be worth a try. They just would not dig so deep that if the earth collapsed it would bury them deeper than they could dig themselves out.

Silmavalien supposed that made sense.

S

Evening tinged the sky with violet when Airrock first pointed Tanz's shape out to Silmavalien. She stood to watch as Tanz came wearily and heavily down.

Wearing a saddle! Silmavalien how Tanz and Keya had also gotten a saddle. They had not a saddle anymore than she had one. Had the Ellenari given them one, too? How? When? Why?

She supposed the why might be related to the same why for which she had been given a saddle. It might be necessary for them to be able to ride more easily, and to fall off less easily.

Keya dismounted, unhooked the one bag from her saddle, and flung it aside. She started undoing the saddle so quickly she almost looked frantic. Seeing her urgency, Silmavalien approached to help, but then she stood her distance. She had not yet looked at her own saddle, and she had no idea how it worked.

Keya pulled the saddle free of Tanz, and then the blue dragon rolled over and stretched her wings out, nearly – but not – clipping Keya's chin. Keya laid the saddle then, then strode over to where

Silmavalien. Her eyes flashed. "You are really very stupid!" she said.

"I didn't want to go because I felt like it would be nice to go with you, but didn't know the Lord of the Light wanted me to go. I definitely didn't want you to follow me, just because you wanted to be with me, even if you shouldn't," said Silmavalien.

"See?" said Keya, gesturing. "You're stupid. None of what you said even makes sense, except maybe the last part, and your plan for avoiding that was very stupid. It was perfectly easy for me and Tanz to follow you."

"Well, I didn't know that. You have to remember I don't know very much. Did you know that?" asked Silmavalien.

"Of course! Anyone who knows anything about dragons knows they can talk to each other across any distance," said Keya.

"Well, I didn't know that, and I've only been here for a year," said Silmavalien. "No one knows anything about dragons where I come from. I knew they communicate across distance very well. I didn't think..."

"I still think you are stupid," said Keya. On the one hand, she was half-teasing, and Silmavalien did not feel hurt. On the other hand, there was a shadow of sorrow in her eyes and voice.

"If I was willing to go without you, then that wasn't all. I didn't know you should come. I felt like I... should go. Or something," said Silmavalien.

"But I know I should come. At least, I know I am coming. Besides, that's none of your business. It's mine," she said, almost possessively.

"Okay," said Silmavalien.

After a few moments of silence, she spoke again. "So, what happened? Did you have to go through all the nightmares?"

"I don't want to talk about what happened," said Keya. "I can't, yet. Perhaps, I never shall. I daresay there're things that happened to you that you still can't talk about. It was... different, but I won't say how, or from what."

"Okay," said Silmavalien again. Then she talked to Keya about the issue with the sunburn and what she and the dragons had come up with so far.

S

Flying over the plains of Arosië, they soon discovered rich farmlands, towns, and even cities, here and there. At first, they stayed clear of any places where there were obvious signs of other humans, flying over them only at great heights. In the canyon of an old river-bed, the dragons made themselves a den, where they could find shade most of the day.

One day, they talked about the civilization. Silmavalien wanted to know how worried she and the dragons should be about the people learning about them.

"We don't know what it is like, now," explained Keya. "The last time anyone of us went into it, I was a child, maybe six or seven. My father did not stay long, either. He went just to sell some goods, buy some things we could not make, and come back. So, the last time we knew what it was like was generations ago. I don't know how many years."

"And who knows how much it has changed. Come to think of it, I don't know what Silrah was like, that long ago," said Silmavalien.

"So, we shouldn't show them the dragons. Somehow, we should figure out what they are like. I hope they have not become like Silrah. If they have, they have killed the dragon eggs they collected! But, that may have been the evil power's idea, all along. Even so, we should find a safe way to see. Perhaps, talk to some farming family, with the dragons near," said Keya.

Silmavalien jumped in, saying what she was sure Keya was about to say. "Then, if they're hostile to us, and threaten us, we can run away, and the dragons can come, and we can fly away."

"Exactly!" said Keya. "Maybe you're not quite as stupid as I feared."

"Maybe I *am*," said Silmavalien. "It *was* pretty stupid not to trust Noren, not to ask him, wasn't it?"

"Yes, it was," said Keya. "At least, I think it was. I don't know Noren. You did."

"The idea still feels weird to me. Even now, when I think about telling Noren, I feel like, but, if he didn't feel, as I did, what then!"

"Well," said Keya, "it's you who knew him, but if you loved him, he probably wasn't... cruel and unfeeling, like that."

"Well," said Silmavalien, "when I just think about him, and I really think about him, it's unthinkable that he would behave the way I feared."

"Well," said Keya, "it's really not my thing, that. I couldn't know."

41

Flaming Nightmares

A messenger imp of fire and shadow entered the horrible hall of shadow and dark fire, and stopped some distance from the throne.

"It is more bad news?!" The voice of the Nightmare Lord was a thunder filled with the rage and bitter torment of his broken existence.

"Silmavalien of Treas is keeper of ten dragons. With her, is Keya of Arosië and a blue female dragon. They have broken through our barricade, and are together and at large in Arosië. Noren of Treas is in the southern lands of south Aneri, with an albino female dragon."

The Nightmare Lord rose in fury. "What? Why can we not separate them? Why are the Ellenari stronger than our dark and ruthless forces? Make absolutely certain that they and Noren do not come together! Silmavalien must be made to flee from Arosië, but she must not return south. Keep Noren in the south. They must remain apart. And afraid."

Dark fire lashed out from him like horrible lightning, a twisted, corrupted version of the lightning of Aelaza. "Is there any reason to think Noren and Silmavalien know each other are Dragonriders?" he demanded.

"I do not know. He was searching for her, but we do not know what he knew, and he stopped searching about a year ago. We have no reason to think she suspects him of being a Dragonrider."

𝒩

Noren opened his eyes one morning to see Hazalel standing several feet away, watching.

The Ellenar looked at him and saw that he was awake. "Noren," he said, gravely, his voice more rock-like than Noren remembered it, "the nightmare shadows are coming for you. The only power to resist them comes from the Lord of All Light. You must come to him. You need him and what he has for you."

"But who is he?" asked Noren. "How do I come to him? I am quite ready, if I know how, and it is something reasonable."

He felt Elninya watching him with keen attention, nervousness almost, an intense, waiting desire which he could not read, and which was tinged with concern.

"You must be willing to face what you are, to face the truth, and to give yourself up to the Light," said Hazalel. "Until you will face the truth, disaster must befall you."

"What are you talking about?" asked Noren.

"That you can know better than I can."

"Do you know what I've done?" asked Noren.

"The Lord of All Light knows. That matters. You know. That also matters. What I do or do not know does not matter."

"Why?" asked Noren. "Can you just tell me where to find him or how to call him?"

"You cannot recognize him until you are ready to recognize him," said Hazalel. "You must be willing to deal with truth, or you cannot know it."

"What is this Lord of All Light like, then?"

"I could not try to tell you that now," said Hazalel.

"Why can you not tell me anything about him?" asked Noren.

"I have told you, Noren," said Hazalel, "but you do not hear me, it seems. Or else, you pretend not to hear me. Until you can recognize what you have been told, you cannot be told more. There is nothing else for us to say to one another at this moment. Siena norae."

The Ellenar turned and vanished again into the forest.

ℵ

A month or two later, Noren and Elninya started back north, towards the Aravin Mountains. *"I know I couldn't fly to their peaks the last time I tried, but I've flown much more now. I might be able to, now. It's possible that Silmavalien and her dragon found a pass over the mountains, and are on the other side,"* Elninya had told him, over and over again, and Noren had realized both that she was right, and that either way he would give into her. She had given into him plenty.

So, they journeyed north, regardless of the fact that it was autumn and winter was coming near, and slowed down by Victor, but Elninya did not seem unhappy about that, even if she teased Noren sometimes. He thought she actually liked his relationship to the horse.

Why he should even look for Silmavalien, he did not know. Even if it was true that what she had done was not so very bad, she did not trust him, and how could people marry if they did not trust each other in the most basic ways? He certainly did not want to find her, and be around her, and not marry her. Even if what he had done was much worse than what she had done, if she had not done the wrong she had, he would not have done the wrong he had. It did not go the other way around. He had done no wrong that had any part in her wrong.

He knew he was not thinking rightly, but he was upset, and at the moment he wanted to wallow in that. Most of the things the Ellenar had said upset him, and he did not want to think about them or what the Ellenar meant, or even why they upset him so much.

"That is exactly what he did mean," Elninya told him. *"He gave you more than enough to start with. You have plenty to start with. If you want to meet this Lord of the Light, to be free from the power of the nightmare monsters, you must deal with the truth, and with yourself, instead of trying to avoid it, and turning down every opportunity you have. Right now, you could think about this and deal with it, and perhaps meet the Lord of the Light, if you want to. You don't need any more than you have, until you do something with what you have. You know what to do, full well."*

I don't want to hear from you! Don't you know that! You have to know that. You could not tell me these things unless you knew that, growled Noren.

"Very well," said Elninya, sadly, *"but remember this: I – and perhaps the whole world – must suffer for your refusal to face truth."*

Noren growled. *You've done your own making-people-suffer, what with making me write that sign.*

"That is beside the point here. It is done, and I will never force you again. Whether I was wrong or not, it can still help you face your truth. Some things must be dealt with, before others can matter."

Noren growled again. Elninya withdrew. He leaned forward to pat Victor on the neck and tried to compose himself. The poor horse picked up on his tension even when he did not do anything, and Noren did not think Victor understood that what bothered his rider had nothing to do with him, or with any threat in their environment.

𝒩

The sky was overhung with clouds that threatened a cold rain. The wind was chilly, but the clouds were beautiful, dark and white and distant blue. Noren rode Victor through a valley in a range of mountains very small compared to the Great Aravin Mountains. The trees were bare, but the grass was green.

Elninya, flying high in the sky above them, was rejoicing in the wintry beauty, but his own soul felt desolate, and the beauty bothered him, so he tried to ignore it. He had never found such scenes particularly beautiful anyways, though Elninya seemed to find beauty everywhere, and some perverse instinct rose up in him to ignore and deny the beauty she saw.

Then he panicked. Fear was swallowed up in hatred. Overwhelming, intense anger. He was perfectly justified in having killed that girl!

Only a child though she was, if she had seen his dragon, she almost certainly would have reported them and given them over to being burned alive. Elninya hated him. If she had not hated him, she would have understood this. She would not have been mad at him. She would have been grateful to him. Everyone and everything hated him. He hated everyone and everything, too.

For a moment, he felt Elninya's concern. She was worried about him. He felt her love. He knew he loved her.

Then, he knew himself not at all. He did not even think he hated. He did not think of anyone or anything. He did not think of hate at all. He burned with it. There was almost none of himself left apart from the hate to feel hatred. All was hate, inarticulate, tormenting hatred.

Without seeing, he saw creatures whose bones were shadow and whose flesh were flames approach him. Their feet scorched the grass, though it was green and drenched. It smoldered behind them.

Victor reared and wheeled. He sprang into a gallop, but saw the nightmares in every direction. Slammed to a stop. Noren, lost as he was in the hate, fell heavily.

A ball of some burning substance struck him. The pain became more hatred and wrath imprisoning and penetrating his soul.

The bow of light sang. For one moment, he found some freedom. Though in terrible pain, he rose on one knee, and drew the sword he had received as a courier. Struggling to see and think, he struck out at horrors he could only half-take in. His sword passed through them as if they were not there at all. Fear penetrated the agonizing pain, and then overwhelming wrath overtook him. *"NO!"* he screamed, but still the hatred came, and he found himself thinking about how much he hated everyone. Elninya. The girl he had killed. His horse, Victor. Silmavalien. His parents. Hazalel.

Then, he passed into an unconsciousness of hate and pain. There was nothing but hatred and torment. No himself. No Elninya. No external world. No love. Nothing.

N

Noren woke to confusion and pain far worse than he had ever felt before, so that it consumed his mind and body. It mingled with memories of hatred, with external sensations, like the blue of the sky and the touch of the wind, with sheer confusion, and with the bond between himself and Elninya, and the utter bewilderment only added to the horror, so that he was adrift on a sea of torment.

Was there any escape?

42

A City in a Vision

When Silmavalien and Keya tried to talk to a farmer's wife and children, they quickly discovered that they could hardly understand each other. Keya understood the woman and her children's speech fairly well, but they could barely understand her, and Silmavalien could hardly understand them either – though she understood them better than she had understood Keya at first.

But they did not seem to understand her at all.

Keya tried to explain that her friend had come from the south, when Silmavalien felt the presence of the nightmare, and saw it on the face of the mother, and even more in the faces and movement of her children. They, too, were affected, even if they had no idea what was happening.

Silmavalien closed her eyes, clutched the ring on her finger with her other hand, and prayed silently. "Lord of All Light, please let us know what to do. Do not let harm come to this woman and her children through us. Do not let harm come to them at all. I know you love all. If not, then Love loves all, and I address my prayer to Love."

The idea that the Lord of the Light and Love were the same person, the same *who*, was gaining ground with her, but she still was not certain that she was certain.

Kelt felt it too, and tried to bid the woman goodbye. She also seemed in a hurry to part, and then Silmavalien left, walking away. The presence of the nightmare seemed to recede, but they still felt the nearness of evil.

Politely, Keya tried to bid the woman goodbye. She seemed glad to say goodbye also, and to part. As Silmavalien and Keya went away, they felt the presence of the nightmare recede, though they remained aware of the nearness of evil.

A few days later, they tried to talk to another person again, and very much the same thing happened. There were the same difficulties with communication, and the same sense of the nightmare's presence, though the details were a little different. Then, they tried to talk to the first woman again, but it was obvious from the first that she did not want to speak with them or be near them, so they left and went back to their den.

S

Fear. Everything was going to go wrong. Minth, dead. Airrock, dead. The others, dead. Horror. Hate. Her heart pounded. Kill. Destroy. Nothing good. Rage.

She had dropped the arrow she was fletching. This was the nightmare. Not her. Minth lived. They all lived. She knelt to pick the arrow up.

Keya looked at her. Their eyes locked. They should leave. But it was still all she could do to keep the fear and the hate at bay, while she saddled Airrock and attached her bags to the saddle. Keya and Tanz were just ahead of them.

A few wing-beats into the sky, the air filled with orc arrows that seemed to come out of nowhere. Then arrows of light joined the deadly cloud, far faster, following one upon the other. Somehow, none of the orc arrows struck the dragons, and Silmavalien felt certain the arrows of light had been there to shoot any orc arrows which would have hit the dragons out of the air first.

They flew higher, and the nightmare did not seem to follow them. Fortunately, it was now late enough in the year that they did not need the canyon for share, but Keya had remarked to Silmavalien that the nights already seemed as cold as the winters she knew, and the canyon had provided comfortable caves and shelter from the cold winds and the freezing night sky. They decided to fly south, towards the mountains where they would likely be able to find similar shelter.

But Silmavalien felt no sense of rightness or satisfaction in the decision, and several days later she realized that it felt wrong flying back towards the mountains. After Keya went to sleep that night, she stayed up, gazing at her ring and hoping for guidance. Then the image of a city rose up in her mind.

It grew clearer and clearer, and sharper and sharper, and then it was as if she were flying on a dragon and the dragon was diving towards the city, towards a particular building, built of stone. She had never seen a city before, except from far above through a dragon's eyes, and everything got bigger and clearer and closer, she wondered if the picture in her mind looked anything like the reality. But it was so clear and so detailed. She would know those streets and that building again if she saw them.

In the morning, she told Keya about what she had seen, and that she was not going to go to the mountains, but was going to look for the city she had seen. She emphasized that Keya did not have to go with her if she did not want to, but Keya insisted that she would go with Silmavalien, and looked at she was strange for talking about Keya being free to do what she wanted. Of course she was.

They stopped heading south, and on days when the weather and the wind were mild enough, and the dragons were not hunting, they flew, looking for the city Silmavalien had seen. It was several weeks before one of the dragons found one that looked much like what Silmavalien remembered, and a couple days later, Silmavalien and Keya left the dragons a small distance away and entered it on foot, since they still had no idea what the people's attitude towards dragons was around here.

Almost at once, Keya started trying to find people she could talk to, almost as if she already knew her way around in this strange place that was full of stones and too many buildings too close together, and people. So many people that Silmavalien was sure that she had seen more people in just a few minutes than she ever had in her entire life before. She felt clueless, out of place, and uncomfortable, and she tried to listen, but even though she could manage to understand Keya's words in all the babble, she could not understand anything else, even when Keya appeared to.

Then, suddenly, there was a flapping of horrible wings, and a moment later a stench flew over. She almost gagged, and looked around her to see a creature, dark-gray and something like a giant bat, diving at her. Instinctively she reached for her bow, but it was not strung and she had not time to string it. She would never go among people again with her bow unstrung!

Silmavalien dove between two men and ran down the street, trying to twist between people who had no idea how to move out of her way or out of each other's. There was no time to think or say anything, but a flood of images from the dragons told her they were coming as quickly as they could.

But there were so many nightmare creatures in the sky that they had no idea how to get to her! Between the wild twists and darts of her own flight, she caught glimpses of what they were doing, as they formed themselves into something of a fire-breathing ball, and rejoiced in their flames, burning the monsters to ash! It was an exhilarating experience for all of them, but between the exhilaration and the joy, and the worry, and the panic of her own flight, she caught flickers of distress from Minth. He was so useless! His fire was no good. Even Daurth could flame better than he could.

Silmavalien ran down another alley, knife in hand, and dove under an overhang that seemed to slow the winged nightmares. If she had had breath, she would have laughed out loud at him. *I love you, Minth. But where you get your idea of what is useful and what is useless, I don't know.*

She was right. That thought of his was not right. He did not know why he had ever thought such a stupid thing. It was nonsense. He loved her!

She darted back out of the alley, under another, lower eave, and looked across the street. There was the building she had seen in the vision! She took a few moments to catch her breath, gulping down air, and stepped out. She stabbed upwards at a diving creature, and the thing burst apart and sizzled as her knife sliced through it. She didn't look. She ran across the street, straight towards the building.

The great stone door was swinging open. In front of it, armored and uniformed men fought the diving vampire-like nightmares with huge, long swords! She took no more than a glance at them, and darted in through the door behind their backs. One of the winged monsters dove at her, but she stabbed again. Its wing torn and burnt, it fluttered away, and she wasted no time running into the building.

Her ring was glowing again. It should have been dark in all that stone, but it was not, and she recognized the light of the ring. She ran through the passages, forced to a walk sometimes by the twisting turns. There had to be a reason the building was open, and when she saw the drips of greenish-gray blood on the stone, she realized she followed one of the nightmare horrors. She ran faster, only slowing a moment now and again to be sure she still followed the trail.

She remembered hunting the orcs, long ago, on the other side of the Aravin Mountains, and how disastrous that nearly been. Fear threatened to steal away, but she remembered she had not surrendered to the Lord of Light then. Now, she had. That made things different.

And, besides, whatever had almost happened, following the orcs had brought her to Jareth's and Daurth's eggs. She wondered if this creature was also hunting dragon eggs, or if was after the destruction of some other good.

Either way, it must be stopped. "O Lord of the Light, help me! I pray I am doing what you want. If not, show me what you do want," she whispered between breaths.

She really did *not* want any more dragons. But if the eggs hatched for someone else, like Tanz did for Keya, that would be good!

She turned into a room, and there was the horrible nightmare, hovering. She leapt towards it, knife in front of her, no second glances. Her knife pierced the monster, and there was a flash of light and heat. Her hand felt tender, and the creature crumpled into ash underneath her.

She stepped back, and now she took in her surroundings.

The winged nightmare had been biting and clawing at a dragon egg, one of five. She hoped the dragon within was not dead, would not die, was ready to hatch. She laid her hand on the egg. It rocked gently, as if in response.

Suddenly, the nightmare creatures retreated, first from the city, then from the battle with the dragons in the sky. Somehow, Tanz had reached Keya, and all the other dragons were around them. Silmavalien listened to them telling her what they saw, without ever taking her eyes from the egg, which was white but webbed with brown, very much like Veine's egg.

It split, and a curiously colored dragon emerged. He was not a solid color, or even like Veine. Instead, disorganized splotches of white and blue speckled his hide.

Linol!

That was his name, and his joy to have hatched flooded through her. It had gotten so tiresome, being cramped in that egg, confined in a building with nothing int. There had been no light in ages, and hardly even insect to crawl over his egg. Then that nightmare came, and it had been so terrifying. He had almost died of fright and horror alone!

He was so glad she came.

She dropped heavily to her knees and took him in her arms at once. "I love you, Linol," she whispered. "I love you, Linol," she sang, as she rocked him until he felt well enough to be hungry.

He stepped out of her arms and started to gnaw on his egg, and she sat watching him with quiet contentment. Her thoughts wandered to Veine and Songeth and Wydth and Coroneth, and how she had hatched them. She wondered how old their eggs were, compared to these eggs here. Had all these dragons been cramped in their eggs for too long and grown too big, and would they need someone to start the eggs for them? Oh, how she hoped none of them had died of it already!

But, at this moment, she felt no need to open any of the eggs, and it was not something she was going to do without that sense it was *right*.

Then she felt the other dragons' joy join their bonding, rising higher and higher in the sky. Minth's love burst over her in a new wave, and she knew he would take care of Linol with her – as would the others. She even felt Jareth, and she wondered if this time she would not have to protect Linol with him. She hoped he was learning more of Love, but she did not say anything. She just watched Linol eat his egg, and listened to the song.

Then she spread out her hand before her and realized, despite all the heat that had reduced the monster to ashes, she was scarcely burned at all. Her skin felt a little hot and tender, but not at all blistered. She wondered what on earth had happened.

Linol was nearly done eating his egg.

43

Stealing Dragon Eggs

Silmavalien picked Linol up, cradling him against her chest, and started making her way back towards the door. Suddenly, the light of the ring flashed out. She stopped in the darkness and heard sandals on the stone floor, and then she saw the flickering light of a torch.

One of the men she had seen defending the building outside held it, and she realized it was some sort of job of his to guard the city or things or something of that sort. He marched up to her and demanded, "What are you doing in here? What have you been stealing?"

She was not sure if those were the exact words, but that was certainly the meaning of it.

"Nothing!" she said, emphasizing the word. She put Linol down, and held up her empty hands. "I haven't been stealing anything, unless you call rescuing a hatching dragon *stealing.*"

Even if the guard understood nothing else she said, she was pretty sure he understood 'nothing.'

Linol rubbed on her legs and looked up at her piteously. She picked him up again.

The guard spoke some more, and this time she had no idea what he was saying.

"I don't understand," she said. Then, she repeated herself. "I do not understand your words." Tanz reached out to her: her rider was coming to help.

Good. I'm glad Keya is coming.

"Get out of here now."

Silmavalien did not know if she understood the man's words, or if Linol was able to interpret the man's intentions for her, but it did not really matter. He might be big and strong and intimidating, but she was sure she had not been brought here just for Linol. Those eggs, the baby dragons in them, needed better, and she was not going to stand aside and do nothing about.

She shook her head. "No," she said, trying to speak as forcefully and earnestly as she could, hoping the man would understand something. "You've been keeping the eggs badly. Those dragons need to hatch. They need people, so they can hatch. It's bad for them being kept in a stone building with no light and no living creatures around. Linol told me."

The guard stepped forward. Silmavalien stepped backwards. Linol hissed.

Just then, she heard Keya's voice, arguing with someone at the door. She could not hear much of what was said, until Keya raised her voice, loud and clear, "Whatever she's in there for, it's no wrong. She just cares about the dragons. One of them just hatched for her."

The man at the door called something, and the guard who had just been threatening Silmavalien told her to come.

"Not until I get the eggs."

The other guard came in, with Keya, still arguing. But then the guard Keya was talking to turned to the other, and said something Silmavalien understood as, "She's a dragon-keeper. It's impossible to keep them away from the eggs. We'll have to let her have them."

The guard motioned to Silmavalien and Keya to follow them down the hall. The man who Silmavalien had tried to talk to ran ahead and brought back a cloth bag to carry the remaining four dragons. Then they escorted them out of the building and told them to never come back. Silmavalien would not have needed a dragon to understand.

Tiela rumbled softly, and Silmavalien turned around. She and Tanz stood in the street, blocking a whole bunch of people who were gawking at them. Silmavalien could feel her distaste: some of the people liked them and admired her beauty and her sparkling teal scales, but some of the people were unhappy and angry at the dragons. They blamed her for strange wrongs that she could not understand. And then she pointed out one boy of about eleven to Silmavalien: he wanted to talk to her and Keya about something. He was in earnest. He was frightened.

Silmavalien stepped down the steps, and saw Keya motion to the boy. She followed Keya and climbed into the dragon saddle on Tanz behind her friend, cradling Linol in one arm under her cloak, while Keya fastened both their legs into the straps. She held on to Keya with her free arm, feeling unbalanced and awkward on Tanz, who she had never ridden before, with a hatchling under her arm.

"This will be hard for Tanz," said Keya. "Not what she's used to."

"It won't be for long?" asked Silmavalien. "Why is it?"

"No. Not long," said Keya. Then they were in the air and the wind made it hard to talk, but she saw Keya motion to the boy again. The dragons flew low over the city and above the gates, and the boy followed in the throng of people.

Eventually, he sat down in a field and waved to them. Silmavalien still did not understand, but she was too busy holding onto Linol and it seemed only Keya and Tanz knew what they were doing, except that all the dragons knew why they were flying higher now. They wanted to fly high enough people would not be able to see where they landed.

Silmavalien left the eggs and Linol with the older dragons, and then Keya gestured for her to walk with her.

"I don't know what he wants either," she said, as Silmavalien settled into stride beside her. "It must be something urgent, and all the dragons think he is of good-will. We both rode Tanz because the guard took me for the dragon-keeper. I didn't want them to start thinking about anything or re-thinking anything. Any more involvement could bring trouble. Those people are not nice!"

"I know that," said Silmavalien. "Thanks for explaining."

"No trouble. Tanz could tell pretty much what you were thinking. I think you were telling her. If you weren't, you were telling another dragon, and she heard. You wanted to ask me."

"Yes," said Silmavalien.

When they got to the field where the boy had stopped, he got up and came to them, hurrying and crouching a little as if he was afraid for his life. He stopped in front of them and held out his hand, with a rough key laying it.

"I stole this key from the guard," he said. "There's another stone building, just like that one, in another city, where there are other dragon eggs. These people, I think they will burn those dragon eggs, or at least put them out for the monsters to get, if we don't get there, before their riders tell them about what happened."

"Thank you so much," said Keya. Then she turned to Silmavalien and translated, but Silmavalien was already horrified. She had understood that much better, even if she did not follow all the words.

"Can you please take me with you?" the boy begged. "I'll be killed if they find out what I've done, and I don't know how they won't. I couldn't take care. I had to get the key as fast as I could. I wish I could say bye to my family, since I love my mother and father, but I can't go back into the city."

"Yes, yes. I agree with you," said Keya. "It will be no problem for you to come with us. Come."

They turned to walk back towards the dragons, and the boy followed, staying a little behind them. They started planning as they walked. "We'll put my saddle on Tiela. Tanz tells me she says she'd be happy to," said Keya. "You're riding Songeth, today, right? I just don't want Tanz to have to carry any more weight. She's very tired after that."

"I know she's tired and sore," said Silmavalien. "That makes sense. I think the boy can ride with whomever he wants."

"Yes," said Keya. "We should ask him his name." She looked behind her, then said to Silmavalien, "Not right now, I think. He needs time to get over leaving his family behind."

They stopped a little ways from the dragons and waited for the boy to catch up. He stopped in front of them, and it was obvious to Silmavalien he was on the verge of tears. He said something she could not understand, and the dragons told her he was thinking about his family.

"I don't see how..." began Keya, then she seemed to notice Silmavalien looking at her. "He just asked if there's any way we can let his family know."

He started talking again, and Keya repeated what he said.

"I'd go back and tell them myself, but they'd feel even sadder about me being thrown in prison and killed, than about me just disappearing, though they'd be likely to think I was killed all the same."

Keya took a breath, and then turned back to the boy. "I'm thinking," she said, "and if you tell us where your family lives, we might be able to get a piece of paper, write a note to them, drop in on a dragon in the middle of the night, put it through a door or a window, and then leave."

The boy jumped up and down. He spoke far too quickly and excitedly for Silmavalien to follow, and again Keya repeated what he said for Silmavalien.

"That will work, if you know how to write! I'm learning to read a little, and my father can read. Our street is big enough for one of your dragons to land in it. Maybe not the biggest one though."

When she finished the translation, she turned back to the boy again. "That'll be fine," she said. "It doesn't have to be the biggest one.

"Let's let them rest. Tanz needs to rest, and some of the others are hungry and want a meal. We will do that as early as we can tonight, and then fly for the other city with dragon eggs. Do you think we'll be fast enough?" asked Keya.

The boy asked something, and Silmavalien thought he looked much more cheerful now that he knew he was not going to leave his parents without a word.

"I don't know," said Keya. "I've never had a horse or watched one, so I don't know. I would think dragons would be a lot faster. Unless you know, Silmavalien? He asks how much faster a dragon is than a horse."

"I don't know," said Silmavalien. "Dragons fly. That's got to be faster. I don't know. I've seen horses, but I really don't know."

"Then," said Keya, "I will give you the key, and you fly ahead with it, and I will do this. I'm not the dragon-keeper, but if the dragons are willing, I think you should ride Airrock, since she is faster, and I will ride Veine, since she is next fastest, unless maybe Coroneth is as fast, though Tanz will be faster when she's more grown and more fit. Will Airrock be fine carrying both you and him, small as she is, or will it slow her down enough you should take a different one? I think you should take him, since he knows where the city is."

"It doesn't matter," said the boy. "I'll tell her what direction it is. She and the dragon will recognize it from the sky as well as I would."

Silmavalien understood that well enough, but Keya translated again. "Okay," she said. "Tell me where."

The boy started talking, and through Keya he gave her as detailed directions as he knew how to give, or as she knew how to ask for, explaining the roads and the lay of the city. Silmavalien seriously doubted she would recognize things as well as he could, but the boy insisted, and Airrock told Silmavalien she could manage quite nicely with what she had gotten, especially if Silmavalien helped remember.

"I will take Linol, then," said Silmavalien, "and some of the provisions. I don't care to take the other eggs, though!"

She prayed to the Lord of the Light that they would be in time, and that they would be able to safely rescue the eggs.

S

While she and Airrock were flying, Silmavalien learned that the boy's name was Veyan. Since Veine was the one who carried them into the city, she told Silmavalien how it went, step by step, as they brought Veyan to his parents' house, and his parents who were still awake, worrying about him, rushed out the door and excitedly embraced him. They understood what he had to tell him, and then when he bid them farewell, Veyan's parents told him that they hoped one of the eggs would hatch for him. He deserved it, they said, and surely the dragons would know what he had done for them! Veine chuckled a little at that, and Silmavalien smiled.

He tried to tell his younger siblings goodbye too, but they did not understand very well. Then Keya got back on Veine with him and they left as quickly as they could, since they did not want someone to come and investigate the commotion. There was even a dragon standing in the street, for anyone who came close to see, and Veine shimmered in the starlight.

Silmavalien was glad that went well, and a couple days later, an Airrock, who was tired and sore by this time, descended on the city under the light of a half-moon. Silmavalien found her way to the stone building where according to the boy many treasures were kept, and opened it with the key. She took out her mint-colored glow-stone and went in to look for the dragon eggs. It did not take long for her to find them. She put the three eggs into a bag and left the building as quickly as she could, closing and locking it behind her though she was not quite why she locked it. She and Airrock were going to be far away and hard to find by the time anyone discovered they were there. As they flew away, she thanked the Lord of Light heartily, not only that she had been successful, but that it had been so uneventful.

When dawn came, Coroneth had caught up with them, and Silmavalien saddled him and they flew farther. At mid-day, thoroughly exhausted, they settled down again, outside the cultivated area around the city. Lighter and Songeth had caught up by this time, and they decided to keep watch just in case.

Sometime after they re-joined, one of the brown eggs hatched for Veyan. The dragon was a male named Naklath, and he was a beautiful light purple, which, while light and almost pastel, was definitely not pink. Silmavalien and Keya had already decided to try to go back to Keya's family, to see how they were doing and learn how things had gone with them after they left. Silmavalien thought maybe Veyan and Naklath would want to stay with them, and they might even like to keep the dragons eggs as well.

A few nights later, she was looking at the eggs as she often did, as if it was just a wonder to have them, and she found that she had drawn her knife and was running her finger along the blade.

A little fearfully, lest she should be wrong this time, she inserted the point of the knife into the egg, and began to tear it, just like she had done so long ago for Veine and her brothers' eggs.

Soon, a brilliant green dragon, lacking scales, but gorgeously colored, stood before her. Ugly as all hatchlings were, her back was a dark shiny emerald, and her wings were a bright spring green. She pranced forward out of the remains of her egg shell and touched Silmavalien's knee with her nose.

Dance. Her name was Dance, and it fit her beautifully. Silmavalien touched her nose lightly, and then she went back to eating her egg.

Silmavalien hummed a song under her breath for her newest dragon friend. The name did not fit Dance's ugly, hatchling body with its odd proportions yet, but it fit *her* perfectly.

44

Elninya Cooks

Elninya could not help herself from exuberantly sharing her accomplishment for a moment longer. *"I breathed fire! I breathed fire! I breathed fire!"*

Oh.

Wait. How? Where? Why? When? I don't remember. I'm so confused.

"The demons were attacking you. I came as fast as I could. Fire came out of my mouth and nose. It spurted." Elninya shared a picture of the fire: bright, vaporous, and yellow.

"You are confused. You were thinking about how you hated me so much you couldn't live with how much you hated me," said Elninya. Pain coated her exuberance. She obviously found the experience, and the memory, very painful.

Noren's wounds throbbed.

"I thought you were going to die. You were so hurt. Both your body and your mind. Someone took care of you. Victor is fine. He went back to grazing near you shortly after the event, when he couldn't rouse you by nuzzling or gently pawing you. I think he was worried about you, too! Someone took his bridle and saddle off. I know where it is," explained Elninya.

The pain in his body felt like hatred in his mind and soul. He almost preferred the fear to the hatred. How could he hate Elninya? To hate her was worse than death! To hate her *was* death – a death far more horrible and near than the other death.

There *had* to be a way to resist the influence of the nightmare demons. There *had* to be a way not to be overcome, not to be reduced to a mere hatred of all that he loved.

He could not help but get something of Elninya's thoughts, even though she did not speak them. There was a way, but he hated that way. At any rate, he did whatever he could to keep from looking at it.

What on earth, asked Noren, *does how I see death or what I did in the past – I'm sorry I did it and I will never go it again! – have to do with meeting this Lord of the Light and getting the power to resist the nightmare?*

Elninya did not answer him, but Noren understood distinctly that she thought it had everything to do with it, and that this was obvious to her. He was not sure if he got it from her, or from somewhere else, but he too glimpsed a deep sense of the connection between these two things, as if their relationship, the dependence of one on the other, was perfectly natural. But what that relationship was he could not bare to see. Mentally, he put out his hands to block the door and stopped his ears to keep from seeing and hearing it. Once seen and heard, he feared, it could never be unseen, unheard again.

Go away, he growled at Elninya.

Again, he understood clearly, and with the impression that his understanding was in some part his own and not only an echo of Elninya's, that he was inviting the influence of the nightmare and deliberately acting in accordance with it.

But that could not be so. His wish to be left alone by Elninya was nothing like the hatred of the nightmare monsters!

𝒩

Noren grew tired and even more restless because the pain kept him from sleeping. He could hardly move, and eventually, he drifted into a kind of half-sleep that was colored by pain and often interrupted by it. But though the pain itself was sharp and unendurable, it made everything dull.

He realized he was hungry and thirsty. Elninya understood, and he could feel her trying to figure out what she could do for him. Before he woke, someone must have been giving him water and food, somehow. How could she do it?

Vaguely, he was aware of her building up wood for a fire. She nudged the pieces of wood around until it looked the way Noren made it, and then she lit it with her breath. She managed to get the pot he used to boil water, and somehow fill it with water and get it close enough to the fire to boil. Removing it without burning herself was difficult and took some effort and thinking on her part, but she succeeded.

She brought it to him after it cooled. It felt like it took almost more strength than he had to sit up and take it from her to drink, and the pain when he moved was so bad he never wanted to feel it, or be able to feel it, again, but she gently coaxed him through it.

It feels like most of my body is burnt, Noren told her, after drinking and laying back down, panting from the pain.

"Something like that. Its bandaged, though, and I think the

bandages are special. Otherwise, you'd have died by now, I think. So, I wouldn't look," she told him.

He did not want to look.

That done, Elninya considered what he needed next. First water, then food. She went hunting and carried a deer back to the fire, but then she had to figure out how she could cook it. She found a large flat rock, but carrying it back was hard because it was heavy and she could not sink her talons into its hard surfaces. But the pain of breaking her claws on the rock did not matter, she had her rider to take care of, and she brought it back and shoved it close to the fire to heat it. Then she tore the skin off her kill and ripped chunks out of it from the parts she knew Noren liked best. She placed them on the rock and watched it carefully, while nibbling at the deer.

"You wouldn't happen to be willing to eat raw meat?" she asked Noren.

He thought he would be willing to eat raw meat if it was eat raw meat or starve to death, but raw meat could make him sick. He was too lost in the maze of his own pain, weariness, and his avoidance of thinking, and he did not realize what his precious dragon was doing for him.

Elninya figured that she might be able to use her tongue to flip the meat, like Noren always did when he cooked. After all, her own flames did not hurt her tongue when she breathed fire!

It was successful. When she thought the meat was cooked, she took it off the rock. It did not quite look like it did when Noren cooked it, but she hoped it would do. She had no idea what made meat well-cooked or what did not. She was just trying to copy what she had seen. She brought the chunks to Noren, after they cooled enough that she thought they would not hurt him. They certainly did not hurt her skin.

Noren woke again. He did not at first realize how strange it should be to be presented with cooked meat. It was over-cooked on the edges. He looked at it and finally asked, "Where did you get this, Elninya?"

"I cooked it," the dragon said. Her fierce pride in the task she had taken on herself and accomplished for love of her rider shone through her words and colored her attitude with bright, sunset colors.

Her emotions, as much as her words, woke Noren a little farther. "You could not get any out of my bags?"

No, she could not. She was only a dragon, and she did not keep food around for herself. She did not realize that Noren did so, and so she let a raccoon get into the bag and eat the meat.

Noren took the meat from her. It was hard to eat, and raw inside, but he could not deny her accomplishment. Who could have thought she even *could* do this? And he had not even asked it of her. She had thought of it herself.

Elninya assured Noren she would try to do better the next time, so it would be easier for him to eat. It was her first time. She was certain she could get better at this, but he would have to help her. She would need him to tell her what was better. If he could watch her while she did it, and tell her when to flip it, and where to put it, and things like that, she was certain she could do rather well.

Shame and horror washed over Noren and he almost choked on his food. How could he possibly have thought he hated a dragon like this one? How could he have gotten so mad at her, ever? How could he have thought of her the way that he had done ever since that morning when he had done that horrible thing?

Even if she had been very stupid – and he was still certain she had been – she loved him. He could not be angry with her for not knowing all things, being able to think of all things, being smart in all ways. If he could be angry with her about such a thing, it meant there was something evil in him, something nightmarish. After all, he was bonded to her! To be angry with her was pain, and he should have known her, been one with her enough to know her.

Perhaps the nightmare monsters even came out of himself. Or they took from himself the evil with which they overwhelmed him and in which they nearly drowned him.

45

Wings of the Mountains

Keya's family were all alive and well, and there had been no further trouble since she had left. Dalchi was still recovering from his wounds, but he was well on the way to being better, and Kanaja barely had worse than scars. Everyone seemed glad to see Keya and Silmavalien, and Nereis and Veyan made instant friends. Keya's father called for a feast of sorts to celebrate the new hatchlings.

After that, Silmavalien approached Shilchu to talk in private, with just Keya, to talk to him about leaving the dragon eggs with him and his family. He told them he saw no reason why they should not, if everyone else agreed, which he thought they would.

"My grandsons will do cartwheels at the thought they might get to be Dragonriders," he finished.

"There won't be problems if, say, one of them impresses a dragon, and the others don't?" asked Silmavalien.

"There might be," said Shilchu, "but I and my son will take care of that."

"Okay," said Silmavalien. "I'm going to tell you this, and tell to whoever you think is responsible, but make sure it doesn't get to those who don't." She took a deep breath. "Sometimes, dragons are too long in the egg or grow too big for the egg, or something. Then, they can't hatch on their own. When they want to hatch, the person has to help tear the egg open. I've had to do this more than once. If you think one of your grandsons can handle the information, that if he feels he needs to do so, he could carefully open the egg, then tell him, but make sure you don't tell anyone who will use this badly."

"I will keep that in mind," said Shilchu. "Thank you for telling me."

With that, Silmavalien went to Minth and climbed onto him bareback. He spun around and took off. It had been a long time since he had played in the sea and he wanted to visit it with her!

Soon, they were there. She slid down his shoulder, and he waded into the water while she took most of her clothing off so she would not soak it. Then she went in after him and grabbed his tail when he was not looking.

He twisted around so their faces almost touched and croaked

loudly. Her face stretched into a huge smile at the delight in his voice.

A wave surged up around and she let go of his tail. Soon, she discovered that playing in the ocean that Minth had once called angry was nothing like playing in the lake. Even in the shallows, the waves pulled her this way and that with far more strength than she could fight, and they rose up and dunked her underneath them where she could not breathe without warning. She only felt safe because Minth was there, right beside her, and he stayed between her and the deeper water.

They got once she got tired, and then she was shivering cold. It was late in the day and there was no sunlight to warm up in, so Minth lay down on the dry sand above where the ocean reached, and she lay against his belly, where his inner fire would warm her, until she felt warm enough to put her clothes back on and climb onto his back again to fly back.

S

Silmavalien and the dragons stayed with Keya's family, through the winter and into the spring, which the growing Dance loved. She would walk through the grass, looking into all the flowers she could reach and sniffing them. She often asked Silmavalien to walk with her, and through Dance Silmavalien found herself seeing more beauty in the flowers than she thought she ever had before. They struck her again and again, all special and beautiful, even when they were common and she had not really paid attention to them before. She remembered looking at a flower Dance wanted her to see, and marveling at the shade of blue it was, such a special shade of blue, so blue as to be nearly purple, and yet bluer than ever. She had seen that flower, and that blue, before, but yet she had never really seen it until then.

But many of the flowers that Dance showed her were kinds she had never seen before and whose names she did not know. Some of them were plants she had not yet noticed, but sometimes Dance showed her the tiny, delicate flowers of plants she knew of, but whose flowers she had never seen. Dance's love for all the flowers flowed into her. Tiny green ones, which she might have thought un-remarkable, hardly even flowers, but when Dance showed them to her, she felt their beauty and their wonder and did not know

how she could have ever failed to see it. Little purple ones. Big orange
and white ones. So many flowers, all beautiful, the common ones as
beautiful as the most uncommon. Each flower, however common its
kind, unique.

That was how Dance saw them, because she knew them better
than anyone else.

She liked to roll in beds of the flowers, and she would, without
the slightest regret or thought, go one moment from trying to carefully
preserve a flower, to crushing it in her enjoyment of it, and back again.
Sometimes she would show Silmavalien a flower she especially liked,
and then eat it, while others times she would leave it and come back
again and again to look at it and smell it. Silmavalien could never figure
out what the difference was, but Dance noticed no inconsistency, and
Silmavalien thought maybe there was no inconsistency. Or at least, no
inconsistent inconsistency.

She mentioned that thought once to Keya, who often joined her
on her walks with Dance, and was getting to know the flowers, too. It
was only natural, since Dance and Tanz were best friends as well, and
Silmavalien knew Dance shared even more about the flowers with Tanz
than she did with Silmavalien. Keya nodded and reached out to gently
touch a flower, careful not to do it harm, and Silmavalien realized they
behaved in almost the same way Dance did, sometimes delicately
touching the flower, or even not daring to touch it, and yet they were
wearing circlets of interwoven flowers in their hair at that moment.

Maybe the only way to be consistent was to be inconsistent.

Against Dance's vision of the world, and her participation in it,
Jareth's unhappiness stood out more than ever. She wondered why he
could not enjoy the world or see the hand of Love in it. Why there was
nothing that she or Dance or any of the others could do to share their joy
and the beauty they saw with him.

She hated his misery and meanness. Apart from the fact that he
did not try to bully the younger, smaller dragons again, he had been
worse ever since that storm. He was cynical, and he communicated his
bitterness and unhappiness more than ever. He expressed his hatred for
people who hated dragons, and his contempt for people who did not
know things he knew only because he had been born a dragon, even
though no one who hated dragons was anywhere near them, and while
Keya's brothers could be stupid and irritating, they did no harm to him.
He dragged the joy and peace she and the others could have enjoyed

down with his misery.

Silmavalien regularly asked the Lord of Light to help him see Love, trying to put her worries to rest and draw confidence from her certainty that Love wanted the best for Jareth, too. This, the bitterness he was choosing, was certainly not the best.

Sometimes, he noticed her praying and made sure she knew that he noticed, and then she told him about how she had asked Love to make her good, and how she thought that to be able to do evil was to be evil, or at least, it was not to be good, and it was best to be good. It was evil not to be good, because good was good.

But none of it made any impression on him, and even though she was bonded to him, even though she tried to understand him as much as she could without stepping back into the fear and hate that still clawed at her, especially when he ranted about the evils humans did, she could not begin to understand his denial that Love was victorious, his assertion that Love was weak.

Love, simply by being Love, simply by loving, could not be weak or defeated, but must be strong and triumphant! There was nothing more obvious, more foundational, to her, and her bond with Minth, the way that love transformed her, the way she would have rather died with him than give him up to her – to her that was proof enough right there.

S

One bright spring day when Dance and Linol had learned to fly, Silmavalien felt the call in her heart to return to the Steep Descent. She wanted Dance and Linol to get to grow up there, and the other dragons thought it was a good idea, too, Airrock especially. They wanted to fly in mountains again. The plains of Arosië were nice and they might wish to return again, but right now they missed the mountains.

She told Keya and Tanz, who said they would fly out sometimes, and spend some of their time with Silmavalien and some of their time with Keya's family, and then Silmavalien and her friends flew east along the mountains. They kept on the low tiers, close to the sea, until they were well east of the Riders' Passage and the lair of the Fire-Shadow.

Almost immediately, Silmavalien knew this was the right decision, the right place to be right now. She felt her heart soaring with the dragons, whose hearts seemed to soar into the sky as high as the mountains to whose peaks they could not hope to fly. Something about those peaks radiated exuberant, triumphant, steady joy, that yet seemed unstruggling and unassailed – unassailable. They felt that they gained something, that they flew as if on wings, simply by standing – or flying – below the mountains that rose lofty above them. They felt high because the peaks were above them and they could not be above the peaks. Somehow, by being above them, the mountains raised them up to the sky, as if the mountains were wings that raised them higher than they could ever go.

She also learned to enjoy the ocean. Often, the dragons would glide down to the sea, one or another of them carrying her. There, she took off her clothes and put them on a rock above the waves where they would not be damaged by the water, and then went in after the dragons. The sea was wild and fierce, and she would have been terrified of it if she had been alone, but though the dragons were not stronger than the ocean, they were strong enough to rescue her from it, and they invented many games that they could all play together, like snatching her out of the currents.

She learned to swim quite well, and one day she was riding Coroneth when he had an idea. She could tell he did not really want her probing too far into what it was, so she just followed his lead, as he came low down to the waves, but still far enough above them he could fly easily, and slowed his flight, steadying himself with slow, deliberate strokes of his wings.

She got to her hands and knees on his shoulders, and he steadied himself still further. She could feel the effort as he concentrated to get it just right, until she was comfortable enough to stand, her feet spread wide on either side of his shoulder.

Dive!

A wild, furious smile spread across her face, as she caught the final thought from Coroneth. Before she could hesitate she stepped off his shoulders and fell, toes pointed, into the waves.

She went under, and the water closed over her head, but she had done that before. She came up, spluttering a little and spitting out salt-water. A few dragon lengths away from her, Coroneth's head came out of the waves at the same time and he crowed loudly at her.

Yes! It was fun!

Then she noticed Lighter, spinning round and round in the air and trying to grab his tail *while flying,* he was that excited.

You want to do it with me, too?

Yes, no, he didn't know. It was just … hilarious! Fun! He …

She felt Tiela coming up underneath her as she treaded water. The teal dragon came up underneath her, somehow getting her human right over her shoulders, and then came up out of the water and twisted her neck back to look at Silmavalien. Now they'd done that silly diving thing, she would swim with her, right?

Of course. Silmavalien almost laughed, and then she did laugh as she caught the edges of Airrock's thought. The silver dragon rode the winds far above them, flipping all the way over, and then dove. She did not understand all those dragons down below. They were made for the sky, not the sea! Flying was what was best!

Unfortunately, some of her acrobatics were still too much for Silmavalien, even in the saddle.

S

Soon after that, Keya and Tanz came out for the first time. Silmavalien enjoyed having Keya's company, and she tried to tell Keya what she and her dragon friends felt about the mountains, but she mostly stuttered. She just could not put into words, though Songeth sometimes put it into songs. Nonetheless, she got the definite sense that Keya and Tanz felt something similar. Dance obviously enjoyed the physical company of her best friend as well. Silmavalien could tell she really liked getting to fly with Tanz, and showing Tanz all the new flowers here, even though it was funny sometimes, because Tanz was much more into the flying than the flowers.

After about a week, Keya and Tanz went back to their family, but they continued to fly out regularly. Silmavalien certainly enjoyed the mountains more than the plains. It was easy to find inlets between the high cliffs where there was enough shade for Minth to play without worrying about sunburning, even on the summer days when the sun was highest.

But Silmavalien wondered when the nightmare would attack again. It had been a long time she had felt its presence as consistently as she had before meeting Keya, and now she kept expecting to feel that sense of evil, that touch of fear and hate, but it was not there.

She wondered why. Why had the battle been so much less intense for the past year and a half or so? Somehow, it made her uncomfortable. She did not like never knowing when it would begin again or what it would be like.

One day, Silmavalien spread herself out on the rocky top of a hill. She could look one way and see the mountains rising majestically above her, crowned in snow and cloud, or she could look the other way and them drop away in the sky and the sea. She ran her fingers over some grooves in the stone, and for some reason her mind turned to the Dragon-sword. She wondered if maybe the champion of the Dragonriders who would arise to bear it might be Veyan, not Noren. Veyan had already risked himself to rescue dragons, and while she thought the best of Noren, that seemed like a champion of the Dragonriders thing to do and she did not know what Noren had or had not done.

Still, she was not going to give the shards of the sword to Veyan unless the Lord of Light told her to do so. She did not even know if she was supposed to give the shards of the sword to the man, or if the sword was supposed to be re-forged first. At least, that was Lexamarian had seemed to say, but a lot of Lexamarian's instructions had been confused.

Either way, she did not have to think about giving the sword away yet.

Silmavalien rolled over and turned her head towards the mountains. A river gushed from between the rocks, half-way up the cliff above her, and she was struck yet again by the beauty of it. The energy, the seeming purpose, the downward flight and rush and fall of the liquid water! It seemed to bear her soul away almost as the height of the mountains itself did, and she could just glimpse shards of rainbow light flickering in the water.

She hoped that she and Noren would be able to find each other soon. She was seventeen now, and it had been almost four years since the night she had fled Treas. She hoped Noren would forgive her for not trusting him and instead fleeing from him without giving him warning, on the very eve of their marriage. She had meant, or at least thought she meant, what she had said to him, about loving him and wanting him harm.

No, she had meant them. She knew that. But she had also deliberately deceived him. She had hurt him, and that hurt her too, now. *Noren, will you forgive me?* she thought, and hoped the thought would somehow reach him, wherever he was, and he would know she asked for his forgiveness.

46

Hopeless and Helpless

Several days later, Noren could not stand doing nothing anymore. But when he tried to stand, weakness and pain forced him back down. Nonetheless, he kept trying. He could not get very far, but as unthinkable and as unendurable as the pain was, being helpless and doing nothing as he lay in constant pain was almost as pain.

Elninya tried to encourage him to relax and just focus on getting better. *She* was getting much better at cooking, though she had a very hard time paying attention to time. Her thoughts coaxed a laugh out of him, though that was not comfortable either. A dragon cooking! Who would ever have thought!

He wondered if it had ever happened before, or if Elninya was the first dragon in the world to cook.

Far too slowly, he got stronger and his wounds hurt less. When he could sit up easily, he called Victor, and the horse came to him for a while, and stood next to him. Noren rubbed his face gently. The next time Elninya hunted, he asked her to bring the meat to him, so he could cut into thinner slices that would cook better.

However intelligent and capable she was, a dragon simply could not use a knife, and her claws were not the best tools for that sort of precision either.

As he healed, it was if only his body healed. He struggled with hatred every day, almost every hour of every day. He began to wonder whether the hatred came from him and had always been there, or whether it was an effect of the demons' attack. He could sense Elninya was willing to talk to him, but he refused to talk about these things with her.

Only things like cooking, and how to collect rainwater, and how to cover Victor's saddle and bridle to protect them from the rain, and how impressive it was she had learned to cook.

He wished he could actually feel grateful for her, but bitterness and hate swamped those feelings more often than not, and he could not get them to feel genuine.

His body continued to heal, and in a few weeks he was doing all the cooking. Elninya still hunted for him, and she still gathered the wood for the fire and lit it, but he was able to prepare the meat and cook it himself. He was well enough now that Victor did not understand how hurt he still was, and the horse wanted to be ridden. He also just wanted to play. Sometimes, he ran circles around Noren, trying to convince him to play, and sometimes he nudged or bumped him. He intended to be affectionate, but more often than not he hurt Noren. Noren tried to reign in his frustration and explain to the horse that he was hurt, and Victor needed to be careful and gentle, and he could tell the horse tried. But he could also Victor did not understand half of what he said and had trouble telling the difference between what hurt Noren and what did not.

About a month or so after he was injured, Noren decided to take off the bandages so his itching skin could get fresh air. He first realized that they were a thin, gauzy white material, softer than anything he had ever encountered before, and when he unwrapped them he saw they were packed with herbs some of which he knew, but others which he did not recognize. They were dried and shriveled now, but he could still smell a whiff of their fragrance sometimes.

The burns still looked horrible, and anything touching them hurt dreadfully, but the cool air felt delicious on his skin. He laid the herbs aside, draped the bandages over his wounds, and lay down with a single blanket draped on top. Elninya put a wing over him to keep him warm through the night.

In the morning, he re-wrapped himself. It was a long, awkward, and painful process, and it took hours even with Elninya helping as much as she could. She had to be careful not to tear the soft material of the bandages with her teeth or claws, but she learned to wrap the tip of her tail around the bandage so she could pull it into positions Noren could not get it.

He was still far from well, and he wondered how long it would be before he was capable of doing much again. The fear of the demons coming again worried him, but he tried not to think about it too much. After all, he had been so helpless before the demons, he really could not be any more helpless now, and so there was no reason to think or fret about it. If he was to be protected, another must not do it. It made no difference whether he was well or injured.

But that thought made him angry. He wanted to protect and fight for himself. Why must he rely on others – others he did not even know? Relying on Elninya was all right. But being totally and completely helpless before an enemy, so helpless that he not even become either less or more helpless! Helpless, not only to defend his life, but helpless to remain the person he was!

That was not okay!

Elninya touched his mind, and for once he listened to her. He would try not to think in this angry way and to not follow any angry thoughts that came into his mind. But it was far more easily said than done. He *wanted* to be angry, no matter how hard he tried not to be, and he had very little success. If he had any success, the effort only made him grumpier, so that in the end it might not have been success at all.

He could tell Elninya thought something about this, but she did not try to tell to him, and he knew he would not understand it all if she did.

But one day, Noren gathered himself together enough to complain to her. *I can't help it!* he told her. *I can't help it at all. It makes me mad. WHY CAN'T I HELP IT?! I should be able to not be angry.*

Elninya responded to him with a thought that seemed to be saying that what he had just told her was exactly his problem. Something like fighting wind with wind being like fighting hatred with hatred and anger with anger. If you fight wind with wind, you get more wind, chaotic, uncontrollable, unpredictable winds, wild and fierce. Wind was good, though! Wind was so good. Elninya *loved* wind, and her love for wind almost swept him up in it for a few moments. It was more than he had ever realized before, and so much of it was beyond his ability to understand, as almost everything about her seemed to be.

A few days later, she came back to him with another suggestion. Instead of fighting the angry thoughts, when he felt like getting angry, he should think about something else. Turn his mind to something he liked. She gave him examples she thought would help, and Victor featured prominently.

Noren tried to follow her advice, but he could not find anything that did not lead back to those twisted, angry thoughts when he was in a mood where he wanted to hate anything and everything. If he thought about Victor, he got mad at the horse for bumping him too hard, or for having thrown him in the battle with the demons, if battle it could be called. Even if he succeeded in not getting mad at Victor himself, he found himself angry that he could not ride Victor, and it was much the same with anything else he tried. Elninya. Sunshine. Even water.

Somehow, he always found something or someone to feel intensely about, even to hate. To hate so intensely that he found his own hatred unendurable, as if it was burning up his insides. To hate with a hatred so intense he sometimes forgot what he hated, and knew only *that* he hated.

Now, he wondered at his stupidity in ignoring some of the things Elninya had told him. It was clear that he did not hate these things because they were hateful, but that he looked for something to hate because he was full of hatred. But how could he escape it? Nothing he did worked. It only made him feel even angrier that he had no success, that he could not stop hating!

Of course, it would not be better to give up. He knew it would be worse to give into the hatred and indulge it without a fight. Yet, he could do no more than slow the corruption of his soul. He only slow down the rate at which hatred ate up more and more of his being and replaced his humanity with itself. He could not even stop it, let alone win back himself.

He was doomed to utter defeat.

He knew it was not wrong to hate the triumphs of hatred and evil. It would be much worse not to hate it. But it was not enough. It was the best he could do, and it was not enough. It too easily degenerated into the hatred he hated, blaming and hating others for his own failures and defeats, his own hatred.

Why was he so defeated? Why was he so hateful? Was there any hope?

Elninya assured him there was hope. There was victory. But she could not tell him what it was, and not for lack of trying. She could only make him aware of her unshakable certainty, and somehow he gained from hope from her confidence, though it was far from her own certainty. But this hope was enough to offer him some refuge from the hatred, some staying power against its assaults. From it, he gained enough peace not to completely succumb to the hatred that wriggled its way into every thought and feeling, every attempt to love and not to hate, weaving his web into his whole being.

He tried to turn his hope into certainty, thinking if hope helped so much, then certainty would be much better. But no matter how he tried, he could not find anything to anchor certainty. He could only hope that the something that his dragon saw, but that he could not, was true.

In this frame of mind, as he fought this battle within himself, the winter slowly turned into spring. The first trees grew beautiful buds of new fresh green at their tips, and the first flowers opened their lovely petals. His body continued to heal, until he, Elninya, and Victor resumed their journey, at first just walking.

Then the day came when Noren thought his skin was finally healed enough, and he was strong enough, to try to ride Victor again. Victor was so exuberant and happy to be ridden that he would not stop bouncing, rubbing up Noren's still-fragile skin. It was days before he tried again, and by riding Victor for just a handful of minutes at first, and then gradually for longer and longer times, Noren got him better behaved, at the same time he grew stronger himself.

He found that being able to travel and do things eased the tormenting struggle with hatred, putting it as a distance and giving his mind other things to occupy it, but it did not cure him. In a moment, something pleasant, something he was enjoying, could launch him through some memory into a dark labyrinth of hate from which he could not escape.

He was hopelessly and horribly lost. He had not known it was so bad, and perhaps it had not been before the fire demons attacked him.

He tried not to hate Hazalel and the Lord of the Light for having let it happen. He reminded himself over and over that he did not even know if they could have protected him – after all, there was a root of that hatred in himself, which he knew now. It might have happened to him sooner or later, no matter what. The demons might have come out of himself.

And he knew that *someone* had saved him. He would have died without their help. Perhaps, they had done all they could to protect him.

But he knew he was not victorious over the hatred. It was always there, whatever he did, whatever he thought, eating at him, even when he was most aware that it was false, a lie.

After all, why had Hazel warned him? The warning had done no good!

47

In the Shouting Winds

A strange feeling woke Silmavalien from a sound sleep. She lay awake, her eyes closed. She had had a horrible nightmare, and no matter how she tried, she could not remember what it had been.

Then she realized all the dragons were awake, too, with the same feeling they had just had a horrific nightmare but they could not remember theirs anymore than she could.

An oppressive sense of fear and hatred, and other darker things she did not want to know, seemed to fall from the sky, smothering her and ringing her about, as if the mountains above her were evil.

Yet, somehow, she could still think clear, and she knew the mountains were not really evil.

We're going to have to flee, she thought, inviting all the dragons into her thoughts. *Where to? Unless the Lord of Light wants us to stay and fight. We will, if he wants.*

She got up and started to saddle Coroneth, when suddenly she was aware of Aelaza coming across the mountain-forests. The Ellena stopped in front of her and seemed almost to be borne up above the ground by a self-generated wind of fierceness and urgency. "Silmavalien," she said, "we are going to Ellen Island. Get what you need and fly. I will lead you."

She turned back to Coroneth and finished fastening the saddle. "Did I do something wrong? Should I not have come here?"

"I don't know that," said Aelaza, "and I don't know why you would ask me."

Silmavalien quickly tested the straps to be satisfied the saddle was secure, then grabbed her bags, tied them closed, and secured him to the saddle. As she climbed up, Aelaza spoke again.

"Fly north. Straight north, as near as you can, for now."

The other dragons were already in the air. Coroneth tensed his muscles and sprang. His wings unfurled. He lurched up.

As soon as his flight leveled out, Silmavalien spoke to Tanz and told her what was happening, as well as she knew it at any rate.

Then the dragons reached the edge of the tier they had been on. The ground fell away from them and they glided down, then leveled out once they were low enough to hear the waves crashing on the rock. A wind blew down from the mountains and carried them forward, as a mist rose from the sea below.

Then the wind grew turbulent, blowing first one way, then away. Silmavalien clung to her saddle, more grateful for it than ever. Even with it, there were moments she felt as if the wind was going to snatch her off on Coroneth's back. It was so fierce and wild it wanted to blow him over, roll him around, and tear his wings off. Between Airrock and several other of the dragons, Minth struggled horribly, and Silmavalien wished there was something she could do to help him.

If they wind did not calm down and no one came to help them soon, she did not think any of them would survive.

Clouds formed around them, shaped by the wind. They flew through one, and it let them covered in a sheen of wetness. The waves rose up even higher below them, and the roar of their crashing mingled with the roar of the wind. It sounded like the sky and the sea were being churned into each other, and the clouds were the foam of their churning.

Yet, somehow, despite the danger of it, despite the intensity of their struggle in the wind, Silmavalien did not feel afraid, and neither did her dragon friends. Airrock was fundamentally enjoying it, and she felt as if, for this moment, they all understand what Airrock knew and was.

The wind and the waves around them were shouting and roaring in exultant triumph. Or maybe it was only the anticipation of triumph, but at any rate, it was triumphant. She wondered if they were riled up because of a battle being fought on the Steep Descent behind them. Were they trying to participate in it? Were they shouting because they felt so involved in it? Were they cheering on the Ellenari?

Were they even cheering on her?

One thing was clear: though they were dangerous, though they might even kill her and the dragons, these winds were not demonic and they did not serve the nightmare. They might be stupid, but they were not entirely evil, or even mostly evil. Maybe they could not help being dangerous. Maybe the battle of the Ellenari made them do this. Maybe they were helping the Ellenari, and when they helped the Ellenari in the way they must, this happened, and could not be helped. It might be necessary.

She did not know. She knew almost nothing. She realized it with delight. She knew almost nothing, but there was something she did know. At least a little.

Yet she worried for Minth. It was as if the exultation of the winds and the fearlessness of Airrock was not something she could sustain for long. It was still around her, but her and Minth's fear for each other broke through it, and her worry grew on Minth's, and Minth's on hers. It did not help him fly, and she could tell it irritated and distracted Songeth and Daurth and several of the other dragons.

I'm sorry I made you so afraid when you were a baby, she told him again.

Then Aelaza came bursting through the storm behind them. Her feathers shone as if they had the light of the moon within them, and she looked like the queen of the clouds of the storm. Silmavalien thought again how very much unlike a human she was, even though she sometimes looked like one. Taking on a somewhat human form did not mean she was human-like any more than she was like a bird because she took on a birdlike form.

Aelaza reached them and then vanished into the storm clouds, but the wind calmed around them, until they were flying in a patch of quiet winds, though it looked like around them the storm continued to rage. But Silmavalien could feel that the dragons were getting exhausted, especially Minth. He flew clumsily, struggling to stay in the air, struggling to pay attention.

She tried to give him as much of her own as she could.

Then Aelaza appeared in front of her, startling her out of her near-trance. She looked like a human, between her great storm-wings. As before, she seemed to be wearing a sleeveless garment of feathers that came almost to her knees, but the feathers were not a shining black or emerald now. Instead they matched her wings, soft gray with blue or purple light gleaming from under the edges.

Silmavalien stared at her in confusion, for though she knew her for Aelaza, she looked different now. Even her skin and hair were different, her skin a misty white-gray that matched the storm, and her hair a darker storm-gray, and Silmavalien struggled to remember what it was she had heard of that Aelaza looked like now.

Finally, she got it. A harpy! But harpies were supposed to be demons.

Was this a nightmare monster, some evil thing pretending to be Aelaza in order to deceive her and hurt her?

No, she had no reason to think this, to fear this. The stories were made of so many lies. After all, they said dragons were demons, and she knew dragons not demons.

Aelaza's voice broke in on her thoughts. "I'm sorry that this is all I can do for you," she said. "At about dawn, we should be able to reach a rock where you can rest, if you will follow me."

S

When they reached the rock, all the dragons, and even Silmavalien, collapsed in exhaustion. Aelaza was still there when she woke, but she now wore the form Silmavalien had first seen her in. Silmavalien climbed up the rock to stand beside her, and when Aelaza looked at her, she sat down and told her about how she felt when she saw her 'looking like a harpy' in the storm.

"Are there real evil harpies?" she finished.

"Yes," said Aelaza, "the nightmare creatures come in many forms. But I do not think that you are in any danger of mistaking one for me. If there is such a danger, the Lord of All Light, Shallim-Araldor, will prepare you for it, if you listen."

A little later, the dragons started to wake up. Airrock helped Minth and Daurth hunt to restore their strength, while Dance and Linol hunted for themselves, since they were still young and growing faster, and therefore needed to eat often.

They rested a little more, and then when Aelaza indicated it was time to go, Silmavalien saddled Lighter. The Ellena helped her do it more quickly, and then she stood at Lighter's shoulder and looked up at Silmavalien in the saddle.

"I am taking you to Ellen Island now, because it is the only place of refuge which is open to you right now, and also because you will have to come to Ellen again," she said. "When you meet him, you must bring the black dragon here. I may not be able to guide you, and so you must know how to make it to Ellen."

Silmavalien nodded, a little confused, and when Aelaza did not move off, she asked her about why and when, and then she said, "And who is this black dragon? Does he have something to do with an obsidian stone that I found a long time near Treas? It spoke to me, and then it vanished by magic."

"I cannot answer those questions," said Aelaza, in the tone Silmavalien had come to recognize as meaning she could get no more information from the Ellena. "They do not have meaning or answers right now."

Aelaza stepped away, and then Lighter took off. They continued their journey to Ellen Island, with Aelaza leading them from rock to rock and tiny island to tiny island, in a zig-zag path across the sea. Silmavalien ate all the meat she had cooked, and had to cook fish to eat, even though she did not like fish. On one of the small islands where they stopped to rest and recover, Aelaza explained, "There is a shore from which Airrock could fly straight across the sea and make it to Ellen Island. However, I want you to be able to get to Ellen even if Minth is exhausted and the wind does not help you. For this reason, I am showing you the easiest way, though it is much longer."

Finally, Aelaza told them the next island would be Ellen itself. As they drew near, Silmavalien saw that the foliage on Ellen was very different from any foliage she had ever seen before. Something about the way the land itself lay was very different, too. It did not have the sharpness and hardness in the lines of its terrain that she was used to. Instead, it almost seemed to *flow* or else lounge, yet it could be steep and rugged too.

48

Island of the Volcano

When they reached the island, the dragons were too exhausted to do more than land on the beach and crawl under the shade of the trees to rest. But less than two days later, Airrock flew over the entire island, charting it all out, and showed them a strange formation. Somewhere around the center of the island, a little to the northern side, there was a kind of mountain of black stone with some plants growing out the sides of it. It had a hole in the center of it, like a giant bowl in which a strange hot, red substance was boiling up. It had an interesting smell, but she was not sure she liked it.

The rest of the dragons were still tired, and Silmavalien did not make anything of it. Aelaza said this place was a sanctuary and she would trust them, so they put off investigating it. However, a few days later when even Minth was feeling a lot more active, Aelaza came back to them and told them she would introduce them to the guardian of Ellen Island. She took them all up to the edge of the crater, and there on top of the island's bumpy, rock crown stood what could only be another Ellena, but this one was very different from Aelaza.

Her hair was jet black and shone, but as it grew longer it grew duller. Her skin was darker and grayer than Aelaza's skin, and her eyes looked like red-orange jewels. She seemed to be wearing a garment much like Aelaza's, except that instead of being feathers it looked like it was made of red scales, much like Tiela's or Lighter's, that were charred gray here and there. She carried no bow or quiver, but a sword hung at her side, and both the sword and its sheath were made of black metal that did not shine. Red and orange stones decorated the hilt and cross-guard.

She fixed Silmavalien with a gaze that she could not interpret, but she found it unnerving and wanted to shrink away.

Aelaza spoke to her in a language neither Silmavalien nor the dragons understood, and she turned her gaze from Silmavalien and replied in the same language. Then she turned back to address Silmavalien.

"I am called Oaeiae," she said. "I am the guardian of the volcano that lies within this mountain. Into it, the shards of the Dragon-sword must be cast, before it can be re-forged, but the time for that is not yet come. I am pleased to see you and the dragons with you." She addressed each of the dragons by name, and then said, "Great is the work of Shallim-Araldor. We have only to wait. What he says he always brings about. It is wonderful serving him and seeing his masterpieces. Of course, we also are his masterpieces. Everything and everyone who is willing will find himself a masterpiece of Shallim-Araldor."

Silmavalien did not know what to say. But it seemed nothing was necessary, and Aelaza lead her away, before disappearing at the base of the black mountain.

S

The months passed without event. Silmavalien glimpsed Aelaza often, but she did not speak to her. If Silmavalien tried to approach her, the Ellena always moved away.

Dance introduced her to the flowers of Ellen Island, that bloomed all through the non-existent winter, even more temperate than the winter where the Steep Descent overlooked the sea, or where Keya and her family lived. It might as well not have been winter at all, and Silmavalien enjoyed the sunshine, especially on the black sand of the beach. But the sun was always low in the sky, and its light and heat were weak, a mixed blessing, because while she yearned for a stronger sun, the weaker light did not sunburn the white dragons as easily as she knew a stronger light would.

Knowing this was a place of refuge, Silmavalien relaxed as she had not done for a long time. She and the dragons played in the shallows and bays of Ellen Island, where the water was often clear, and in a small, fresh-water lake deeper into the land.

She continued to get to know the dragons better, as they had more time and no fear overshadowing them. They were large, too, now. Though Wydth might have bigger, Coroneth and Lighter were the tallest, and when she stood beside them they *felt* like they could almost have been twice as tall as she was. She enjoyed Lighter's generally relaxed, but sometimes ecstatic sense of fun, which of all the other dragons Daurth seemed to share most. Daurth seemed shy of Coroneth, but Silmavalien delighted in the way Lighter and Coroneth worked together to do fun things, since Coroneth would always crave the opportunity to use his organizational skills and to be the center of other dragons cooperating around his ideas.

Or sometimes, someone else's idea he had adopted.

She delighted equally in Wydth's quieter and more direct nature, and in Songeth's expressiveness. Even when he was not singing, he might have been the most expressive of the dragons, and she thought Linol was most like him in this, though the young splotchy dragon did not sing. But it was clear that Songeth and Linol were best friends, and spent most of their time together. What Silmavalien enjoyed most about their company might have been watching them communicate.

Veine often hung out with them, but in many ways she seemed most like Airrock, but steadier and gentler, whereas Airrock's love was the fiercest of them all. She was as direct as the straight flight of an arrow, and she seemed no more capable of recognizing indirection than attempting it. But she liked to fly far, exploring the winds and embracing them, almost as if she wanted to become a wind herself, or to be one with the wind like Silmavalien and Minth were one.

Meanwhile Veine spent a lot of time helping Tiela, who was making friends with many of the little creatures now that she was grown and hunted larger prey. Jareth was still mean and miserable, and he tried to torment her friends whenever he could. Silmavalien thought the fact they were her friends made him even more interested in tormenting them, and so many of the other dragons helped her to watch over them, including Dance, Minth, and her mate Songeth, who sympathized with her deeply, having his own friends among the birds.

Silmavalien wondered sometimes if that shared interest in befriending the smaller creatures and learning from them, even working with them sometimes, had been a large part of what made them right for each other, even though she sometimes thought of Tiela as more like Coroneth, with her own instinct for organization and a tendency to be bossy at times.

Then came the day when Tiela laid her egg and presented it to Silmavalien. But in the midst of her joy, Silmavalien was disappointed, though Tiela did not seem to care. The egg was white – albino. She had hoped for a brown egg that would hopefully hatch a healthy dragon without any problems.

Not that she loved or valued any of her albino dragons less, but she did not want this one to suffer that.

She was still processing, when Aelaza approached, skimming with unearthly grace over the ground. "It won't be a problem," she said. "It won't matter at all. That egg is to be thrown into the volcano."

Silmavalien clutched the egg close, curling around it, and

screamed, "No! It's a *dragon*. A baby not-yet-hatched dragon. We don't kill a dragon because she's not as healthy as we would have wanted her to be."

After everything, was Aelaza turning out to really be evil? *Lord of Light, Love, help me! LOVE!* There was no way she could fight Aelaza alone.

But the Ellena sighed, then spoke softly, as Silmavalien had never her speak before. "I wasn't suggesting *killing* her. It won't kill her."

"Of course it will kill her!" How could Aelaza possibly think that hot stuff would not burn the egg away and kill the dragon?

But the Ellena continued, her voice still soft and strong. "No, it won't. She's supposed to be a black dragon. When she is thrown into the volcano, she will become an obsidian dragon in an obsidian egg, and she'll be fine when she's taken out at the right time."

That distracted Silmavalien "An obsidian dragon? An obsidian egg? Like the obsidian stone, the obsidian guardian, I found, or met, or whatever, in Treas? Is it like that?"

"I think it is as much like that as anything could be, that I know of," said Aelaza. "I can't really tell you about that, except that it is one of the things Oaeiae is excited for, and which your presence indicates is about to be around us. Are you ready to take the egg with me to Oaeiae and the volcano?"

"*Yes,*" said Tiela.

"Are you absolutely sure it won't hurt the dragon?" asked Silmavalien, at the same time remembering that she knew almost nothing.

"Yes," said Aelaza. "Oaeiae will reassure you as well, if you need it."

"Well, Tiela says yes, and so does Songeth." She knew they loved and cared about their egg as much as she could, and that they might know about things she could not. Cradling the egg against her chest, she followed Aelaza, all the while talking to the baby dragon within.

With Tiela and Songeth walking beside her, she climbed the mountain of the volcano. Standing on its ridge was Oaeiae, and she motioned to Silmavalien to come up and stand beside.

Fearfully, Silmavalien continued climbing up, until she stood over the sloping black-blue rock and looked into the basin, where to her mind there should instead have been a peak. A lava of lava lay before her, red, hot, ever-moving, and sending up a smell that almost made her choke.

"Throw the egg into the center of the lava-lake, as near as you can," said Oaeiae.

Silmavalien did so and stared as the white egg fell, dark against the blinding red.

A small spurt of lava rose up out of the lake.

"Go!" said Aelaza and Oaeiae at once.

Silmavalien climbed onto Songeth's back, and he jumped off the ridge. As he flew away, she looked behind her and saw Aelaza and Oaeiae still standing on the rim of the volcano. Fountains of red lava rose above the rim.

Suddenly, she thought that it was not only terrifying, but also beautiful. Suddenly, she realized something.

Minth, that's what your fire looks like!

Don't you think you have the most amazing fire in the world? — even if it isn't as hot as that stuff?

S

Songeth carried her to a part of the island far from the volcano, and she and all the dragons spent most of their time on the windward side of the volcano, where they did not often smell it. Sometimes, the dragons still soared over it, and showed her what it looked like, now that it had risen up and overflowed its basin. Slow-moving rivers of the molten red substance flowed down its sides and over the island, sometimes reaching all the way to the ocean. They created fires a handful of times, but the regular, heavy rains put the fires out.

It seemed to Silmavalien that all the dragons intensely admired and liked the volcano and its flows in some way that she could not understand, but which felt very important. She did not think they knew what it was either, but she did not know none of them have been shocked or frightened about throwing the egg into the volcano.

Then, one day, she remembered that Aelaza had once told her something about Ellen Island have ancestral importance to the dragons, and she wondered what that meant, though she doubted she would get an answer if she asked.

49

Certainty of Death

Noren stood on a rock, watching as Elninya flew higher and higher into the sky. He had tried to ride her, but had given up. He was struggling to hold on to her, and suffering from the thinness of the air and from the cold, while she was still quite convinced she could fly higher, though she did not know how much.

Now, she passed from his sight, climbing ever higher into the sky. Her wings burned, and the tips of them burned with cold, but the fire in her belly and her labor kept her warm. The mountain slopes and peaks rose high above her, covered in cloud and snow. She did not know how high. She was now among the clouds.

It was all she could do to beat her wings hard enough to continue rising in the thinner air. Her lungs began to hurt. She climbed out of a cloud and saw the white slopes of the mountains rising far above her before vanishing into another layer of clouds!

Even if there was a pass right at the level of the clouds she doubted she could reach it.

Elninya spread her wings and dropped down. When she recovered a little, she flapped and glided down the mountain to where Noren stood waiting for her. She landed heavily, completely exhausted.

He walked to where she stood and put his arms around her neck. After hugging her for a while, he kissed her nose, and sat down next to her.

After perhaps half an hour, he said, "Let's go back south."

After a pause of several minutes – he felt Elninya's exhaustion as if it was his own – Noren continued. "It's rather obvious Silmavalien could not have crossed those mountains. We could try again somewhere else, but somehow I don't think there was a pass that goes all the way through right above that cloud line, and I don't think any dragon could have flown much higher. Perhaps, we should try again, somewhere else, if and when you feel ready for it, and then go south again. We haven't nearly explored all of the south. We and she could have missed each other."

He felt Elninya's exhausted acknowledgement. That sounded like a fine idea.

𝒩

Over the next couple of weeks, they tried again twice, both times
without success. The second time the sky had finally cleared up and only
a few tattered clouds hung around the slopes and peaks. It finally
convinced both Noren and Elninya that there was no feasible way over
the mountains. Elninya could barely support herself on the air, and she
could see that in every direction the mountains rose far above her. There
was no pass, or even anything close to it, which they could take.

They would go south again soon.

𝒩

Noren woke to Elninya fighting, struggling. A net had been cast over
her, and she struggled in vain to escape it. He hardly had time to wake
up, to move, when he felt hands on him.

Breathe fire! he shouted to her, reaching for his sword. He drew
it, and prepared to fight as hard as he could.

Several men jumped on top of him. He held onto his sword and
swung it wildly, but then the men grabbed him from behind and
restrained him, and he lost it. But he knew he had hurt some of them.
How badly he neither knew nor cared.

Her fire did nothing to the net! Absolutely nothing!

Noren was bound and his hands tied behind them. He was
pushed to his feet and made to walk out of the trees.

She was dragged by ropes attached to the net which tightened
around her painful. Noren felt her panic. Her fire did nothing at all to the
net! How? Why? What was it made of? She could not think. She just
kept struggling with all her might, hurting her skin and wings on the net,
breathing fire as much as she could.

The helpless agony of his dragon threatened to smother his own
thoughts.

Victor pranced, flying first one way, then slamming, turning,
flying the other, breaking into a floating trot as if he ran on clouds. The
horse looked terrified.

A boy, maybe ten or eleven, stood at the edges of the trees,
watching. Noren motioned to him with his head. He could not use his
hands. They were tied behind his back.

The boy came forward, weaving his way through the men who
were moving Noren, and watching his dragon with an anxious,

distracted eye. Even bound in the net, apparently helpless, she was terrifying, and her fire, though it did not damage the net, came through it and was deadly. Those who dragged her had to be careful to stay out of its blaze, unless they wished to die.

With wide eyes, the boy stood before Noren. "I give the horse to you. His tack is in the trees. You'll find it. His name is Victor," he said, as quickly as he could

The boy lost no moments. Walking slowly, his eyes all on the horse, he approached the creature, who stopped, stretched out his neck, snorted at him, then ran another way.

Noren was momentarily pleased. If the boy had the patience, he would be able to catch Victor and would do well with him. The horse obviously liked him.

His pleasure in finding a good home and rider for his stallion was short-lived. He and Elninya were going to die. What could he do? There had to be something he could do! He tried to force himself to think clearly and deliberately through his dragon's terror and rage. She could scarcely think any better than she could if she were knocked out, though she was a lot more dangerous. He thought she might be dangerous even to him in this state.

Elninya!

She only dimly acknowledged him.

Elninya! Calm down. What you're doing isn't helping.

Well, what else could she do? She couldn't do nothing! She twisted around, as best as she could, and tried to breathe fire into a different part of the net. Her captors jumped away and back.

Noren looked behind him, and tears rose in his eyes as he saw all the places where the net had cut into her skin and blood was dripping from her.

One of the men kicked him. He tripped and fell. Roughly, they pulled him back up.

Could Hazalel come and rescue him and Elninya from these people? Would whatever rescued him from the demons rescue him from this, too? It was just as certain death!

𝒩

Noren sat on a dirty floor in a dark cell. A little light, barely enough to see his hand by, came in from some grating on the roof. The air was close. His dragon was unconscious. He was alone with himself and his own thoughts. His body ached from the treatment he had received, but at first he barely noticed it. It was the least of his concerns. Even when he began to feel thirsty, it was scarcely more than a distraction.

He and Elninya were both going to die, and there was nothing he could do about it. There was really nothing he could do at all.

He had never been at such close quarters with death, the way he was now. He had thought he was about to die, for brief moments, with battle in his blood, and something he could do, however unlikely he thought it was to work. Now, he sat in a dark cell, while the hours passed, and the cell grew darker, until it was absolutely black, and he knew he would die, but not when he would die, and he had no illusion that anything he could do would change any of it. Yes, he could stomp and yell, if he wanted to do so. He could rage against and hate everyone who had any part in bringing him to this death and, indeed, everything altogether and anything at all.

But there was not a flicker of the thought in his mind that any of it would save his life or put off his death.

50

The Clouds Open

One day, Aelaza came to Silmavalien. "I will lead you back over the sea and to the pass you will take. You are now going to find Noren. He is in great trouble."

Silmavalien almost jumped in the air at that thought. "Really?"

"Yes," said Aelaza. "Now come. Get your things and come."

"Should I leave the shards of the sword here?" asked Silmavalien.

"If you wish," said Aelaza. "Oaeiae will make sure no harm comes to them. But, before I take you, I will take you to see the star Malchoris. Seeing him will help you to know and see the meaning of what will come."

Before Silmavalien could ask more, she suddenly found herself in a place or state unlike anything she had ever experienced. She rested or stood on nothing and a dark emptiness surrounded her, deeper and wider than she had ever thought the sky could be. Before her hung a great globe that seemed to be a sea of white and blue intermingling and burning. Huge arcs of something blue and flame-like leapt from its frothing surface. It radiated terrible heat and just as terrible joy.

There were no stars anywhere around. No matter which way she looked, she could see another orb of fire and joy, nor could she see the twinkling stars she knew. Turning to Aelaza, she asked "So, are stars not really those twinkling, steady lights, cold and joyful and hopeful, that I see filling the night-sky?"

"They are," said Aelaza, "as far as you are concerned. They may tell you as much about the nature of a star as this does. But I will tell you something of the history of this star which you could not otherwise know. The nightmare monsters, the enemy, scattered in an empty place the matter from which Malchoris was to form his light. I helped him gather his matter, for it was not only far from other stars, but too far spread across the sky-fields for him to coalesce on his own. His joy is burning and fierce, bright and strong and steady and undistracted, as is the joy of no star to whom this wrong was not done, of removing it far from all other stars and from the companies of stars that dance together. Now, he dances alone for his creator, him whom we call Shallim-Araldor but who is known to you as Lord of All Light. His dance has a unique joy because of this. He would not trade his privilege to burn alone in undisrupted joy for any other star to dance with."

She looked with a look of fondness and joy which Silmavalien could not understand on Malchoris. Then, she turned back to the human. "I think you and a star might be able to understand each other in ways we Ellenari understand neither you nor a star. A star burns out, something like death, and passes into another world or state, whatever you want to call it, on his journey into the heart of Shallim-Araldor, the Star of stars, from whom he gets all his star-ness. You, too, die. We Ellenari know of nothing in our experience which we can think of as like that. Yet, time and experience for a star is no more like it is for you than it is like time and experience is for us. I will speak no more of this now, except to tell you not to be disturbed if you see what appear to you to be the strangest inconsistencies.

"Meantime, remember Malchoris. I am sure he is glad of seeing you. He is my friend, as are you."

Then she brought Silmavalien back to where she stood on the shore of Ellen.

S

Aelaza gave Silmavalien several large jars of oil for the dragons' skin, and then she led them back over the sea, using a path similar to the one they had used to get here. Mostly, it was straighter. She stretched their endurance, cutting out detours between close islands, and instead flying straight to further ones.

When they reached the Aravin Mountains, she led them mostly west. When Silmavalien asked her what she was doing, she said, "I am going to show you the only pass over the Greater Aravin Mountains which is low enough for even a dragon or an eagle to take."

Once they were in the Aravin Mountains, they were soon met by Keya and Tanz, who said they were coming with them. Aelaza did not comment at all, and Silmavalien could not tell whether she approved, or disapproved, or had no opinion at all. Nonetheless, she was glad of her best friend's company. "I missed you," she told Keya. "I could talk to Tanz, but talking to you through Tanz isn't like talking to you, even though she's bonded to you."

"I missed you, too," said Keya.

"We're going to rescue Noren," said Silmavalien. "At least, I think that's what Aelaza meant."

"Great! I'm so happy for you. And for him, too, especially since he needs rescuing," replied Keya.

A week or so later, Aelaza stood next to Silmavalien and pointed out a valley rising up between the cliffs and ridges of the higher Aravin Mountains. "You will take that to get to the Pass," she said. "I think it will be fairly simple for you, but be careful, since I will not be there to help you."

"Will you be back after we get over the Pass?" asked Silmavalien.

"No."

"How will I find Noren, then?"

"You will," said Aelaza. "It's not mine to lead you to Noren, nor could I. Another will take care of that."

"Another Ellen?"

"I did not say that. Do not assume it. Do what you can," said Aelaza. With that, she turned and leapt away. She was gone almost before Silmavalien could process it.

S

The pass was high and terribly cold. The deep snow crunched and sank under the dragon's feet, and they could not fly because the air was too thin to hold them up and fill their lungs. Even Airrock did not fly, and both Silmavalien and Keya rode dragons, since they suffered even more from the thinness of air. They also sank into the deep snow more.

There was not even anything to capture the eyes or relieve them with beauty. All was stark, unrelieved white, and it was hard to even see distances, making it feel as if every step took forever and their journey into thinner air and more and more cold, pain in their lungs, pain of cold in their limbs, pain of effort in their limbs, would never end.

Then they came over the peak, and it was Songeth who first noticed they were going down now. The dragons stumbled through the snow a little further, and then decided they simply had to rest, curled together for warmth.

A few hours later, Silmavalien insisted they go on. They were not going to recover well in the cold and thin air. Airrock agreed with her, and together they convinced the others. They got up and trudged through the snow until they found a small cliff.

One by one, the dragons dropped off the cliff, too tired to take off, and unfurled their wings, catching the wind. They glided as far as they could, before landing on a snow-covered hill, and Minth stumbled as he came in, barely avoiding hurting himself.

Silmavalien scrambled off of Lighter, almost falling herself though she would not have been hurt in the deep snow, and rushed to him, to make sure he was okay.

Then they slept.

Airrock woke first and went hunting for the young ones, and when she came back the others started to wake up and go to hunt for themselves. They gorged themselves, and two days later they continued their journey down and south, going they had no idea where, looking for Noren.

It was spring now, and on this side of the mountains the sun was hot and warm. Silmavalien made sure to check on Minth's and the other's skin often, to make sure they were not sunburning, and remembering how easily he had sunburned as a baby, she realized that the oil Aelaza had given her did a lot more than save the time of making oil.

It protected their skin from the sun.

She started using it to oil all the white dragons, so they could fly more and make better time, instead of having to fly only at night. Now, they would be able to fly during the mornings and evenings as well, though she was not sure she would trust it to hold if they flew through the middle of the day when it was not cloudy.

In a few days, they were flying over inhabited land and had to be careful that they were not seen. Silmavalien still had no idea where she was going, and when she talked to the dragons they did not have any more idea than she did, but somehow this did not make her as uncomfortable as she would have expected. It still made her uncomfortable, but not as much so as she thought she should feel, though maybe that was because Keya did not seem bothered by it, and her dragons did not seem to care either.

Silmavalien mostly rode the bigger and healthier dragons both because it was easier on them and because they could make better time that way, but one drizzly, overcast day Minth demanded that she ride him again. It had been too long since she rode him for fun, and even if he struggled to keep up with the other dragons unburdened, he wanted her to ride him. She gave in, because she did not want to hurt his feelings.

Maybe a few hours would make him happy, and it would not

matter that much.

Then she felt the presence of another dragon. At the same time a rift opened in the clouds below them.

They dropped down, and there, before them, lay a city.

ℵ

Noren's imprisonment had been long. He did not know how long. The constant proximity of a death he could do nothing about never left him alone, even for a moment. Elninya rarely spoke to him, but he could not help being intimately aware of her feelings about death, however incomprehensible to him they were.

Thoughts about the cruelty and injustice of his situation – and that of countless others before him – occupied his mind only occasionally. Pressing as that issue might be, it was nothing to his immediate issue.

Now he stood under a cloudy sky, tied to a piece of wood outside the city. The grass was green. A little drizzle kissed his face, and his mind scarcely touched the horror and torture of his appointed way to die. It was irrelevant to the larger, more pressing issue: death. Death and life. Somehow during his imprisonment the two had been thoroughly mixed together, until they seemed almost one and the same. The knowledge of one was intimately interwoven with the knowledge of the other.

He had wondered at first why he had not thought long ago about the fact that death would come, sooner or later, to everyone. Why *had* he been so obsessed with preserving his life in this world for as long as possible? Why did it matter so much? Why had it mattered more than other people's lives? These thoughts had knocked on the door of his mind many times before, but he had not let them in.

Why had he ignored them? Why had he done everything he could to push them away?

What was death, anyways?

In the quiet darkness of his cell, which would otherwise have been despair, these thoughts had changed him. He could only sustain the energy of fear and striving, without even being able to do anything with it, for so long, and when it had run out, he had come to learn something which could not exactly be called thinking.

He looked now on the world around him, almost immune to horror: for it was horrible, and so was the crowd of people who had come, to watch him and his dragon die!

The sense of release, of relief, in the feel of the free air, the sight of the green grass, the feel of the rain, and the broadness of the wide sky, even filled with clouds, swallowed up his sense of death, as if *it* were death and death were it, leaving no room for horror.

Understanding no longer interested him. He did not care to know or be able to say why this was. Something of Elninya's thoughts about death, as they had been communicated to him in many ways and at many times, rose in him like the dawn.

Somehow what would have been despair had turned into a quiet something he did not know, and the long closeness with death had made him ready to face that truth. Ready to deal with the question of what was death, really? Ready to face what he was. To change what he was.

The entire view of life and death that had caused him to kill the girl, that had made him unwilling to even considered what Elninya and Hazalel had both told him, that had made him dismiss it as impossible and senseless, vanished. Somewhere, in the dark closeness of the cell, in his changed mind, in the here and now under the sky, the tormenting hatred had fallen away from him, as if it had never been. He no longer hated as he had hated, and no longer did every thought twist into bitterness. He felt no desire to hate those who would kill him, or those who would watch him die and cheer. It did not matter. It did not do anything for him.

He could think about goodness and love it.

He could be happy about the things that were worthy of happiness, about his bond with Elninya, about the boy to whom he'd given Victor.

At the moment when the wood was about to lighted, his eyes were fixed on a rift in the clouds. He stood perfectly still, not even breathing. Something shifted, and a beam of sunlight fell through the clouds. He breathed in deep the air and light of the world.

Suddenly, Noren gasped. Down from the clouds descended thirteen dragons. They hung in the air, forming a tight V-pattern, with one small white dragon at the head. Just on his right hovered a brilliant blue dragon, the color of the sky he had not seen in months, and on his left hovered a silver dragon! Behind them were more white dragons, but some of them gleamed colors too: gold, purple, a gorgeous teal, bright green.

The rider of the foremost white dragon lifted up one hand, and a beam of light streamed out from the rider's upraised hand and fell upon him.

To Be Continued …

In **Return of the Dragonriders Book Three**
DRAGONSWORD

"Luvine stood, frozen in fear. The female Dragonrider stood with her hand inches away from the bottle that contained one of the old witch's most powerful and precious spells. She had to do something!

The witch moved. Noren's sword burst into flame. Whirling darkness and terrors filled the room. Unerringly, the female Dragonrider's hand guided itself to the bottle. She picked it up and crashed it on the ground. Luvine could not believe it, even after all she knew and had seen. How had the female Dragonrider known to do exactly *that?*"

Sign up to be notified about new releases:
https://books2read.com/r/B-A-OUYQ-HMXXB

Follow me on Goodreads:
https://www.goodreads.com/author/show/20243136.Raina_Nightingale

Follow me on BookBub:
https://www.bookbub.com/authors/raina-nightingale

Or, if you like weekly reviews, ramblings of all sorts, and occasional art posts, you can follow my blog:
https://enthralledbylove.com

If you liked DragonWing, *please leave an honest review on your favorite book platforms. It really helps readers and independent authors to find each other. I would deeply grateful and encouraged.*

See you again!

www.ingramcontent.com/pod-product-compliance
Lightning Source LLC
Chambersburg PA
CBHW052038240626

47153CB00006B/2135